JUMPING
THE CRACKS

VICTORIA BLAKE

JUMPING
THE CRACKS

First published in Great Britain in 2007 by Orion Books,
an imprint of The Orion Publishing Group Ltd
Orion House, 5 Upper Saint Martin's Lane
London WC2H 9EA

An Hachette Livre UK Company

1 3 5 7 9 10 8 6 4 2

Copyright © Victoria Blake 2007

A CIP catalogue record for this book
is available from the British Library.

ISBN (Hardback) 978 0 7528 7461 6
ISBN (Export Trade Paperback) 978 0 7528 7462 3 ✔

Typeset by Deltatype Ltd, Birkenhead, Merseyside

Printed in Great Britain at Mackays of Chatham plc,
Chatham, Kent

The Orion Publishing Group's policy is to use papers
that are natural, renewable and recyclable products and
made from wood grown in sustainable forests. The logging
and manufacturing processes are expected to conform to
the environmental regulations of the country of origin.

For Francesca Howard, inspiring artist,
and
Katy Richards, who was there right from the beginning

Acknowledgments

I would like to thank the following: Maureen for reading first drafts; Faith, Keir, Rose and Richard for feedback in the early stages; Teresa Chris for sound advice; the team at Orion including Genevieve Pegg, Gaby Young, Helen Windrath and Jade Chandler; Anne Bowtell for information on coffee machines; Henry Hart for the Oracle of Bees and the Bachelard quotation; Tiziana Dorigo for Isotta. Finally, my thanks to the Pitt Rivers, a unique and inspiring museum, filled with the weird and the wonderful. The Sweetman collection does not exist and neither do Professor Cummings or Justin Gittings but the shrunken heads do and so does the witch in the bottle. May the shrunken heads continue to be displayed for many years to come.

PROLOGUE

Sweat drips off him as he half-runs, half-walks along Holywell; his T-shirt and trousers flap, soaking wet, against his skin. He holds a bag carefully away from his side, not wanting the contents to bang against his body.

The impact throws him to the ground. For a moment he wonders if he's been mugged, but then he sees the man sprawled opposite him whose hands are held ineffectually to his nose and doing nothing to stem the blood splattering through them on to the pavement. Then he smells alcohol and realises that he's collided with a drunk. But where did he spring from on this quiet August night, in this empty Oxford street?

Shit, even worse it's a man he knows. Miles Archer. He looks down at the ground. Archer hasn't spotted him yet. He's stunned, too busy with trying to keep all that blood off his white linen jacket.

'Sorry,' Archer mumbles. 'I didn't ... I was in a hurry ... bit pissed as it happens ...'

To the left is the narrow medieval alley that Archer must have lurched out of. He's about to flee, when Archer staggers to his feet and something rolls away from him across the pavement. He checks his bag; it's empty. Before he can react, Archer's picked it up and is waving it at him.

'Is this yours?'

He's so drunk he hasn't registered yet what he holds in his hand. Now he does.

The shock makes him stagger backwards as if shoved hard by invisible hands. 'Christ!'

I

He grabs it as it falls from Archer's hands, sweeps it into his bag and bolts down the alleyway, past the Turf Tavern under Hertford Bridge, past the Sheldonian and the Radcliffe Camera. Outside St Mary's he stops and looks round to check he hasn't been followed. He pauses, hands on knees, gasping for breath. The spire of St Mary's rears over his head against a star-studded sky.

Hopefully Archer is too drunk to remember the blackened skin and the long black hair, the stitched lips and eyelids. Hopefully he won't remember that he was holding a shrunken head in his hands because that wouldn't make any sense at all. Why in the dog days of August would a shrunken head be rolling across the warm pavement of Holywell? He knows Archer's highly strung, a bit of a loner, not a blabbermouth, not when he's sober anyway. And even if he did say what had happened to him, who would believe him?

Feeling reassured he straightens up and wipes his forehead with the bottom of his T-shirt. The sweat rolls down the furrow of his spine. There isn't a breath of air. The heatwave has scorched the grass round the Camera and is maintaining temperatures of forty degrees even in the middle of the night. No one can sleep. Maybe that's why Archer was staggering around the streets so late – looking for a breeze. Everyone in Oxford is looking for one.

He sets off in the direction of the High. August is a wicked month. Whoever first described it as such was absolutely right. At any rate that's how it's always been for him, a truly wicked month.

CHAPTER ONE

'However much whitewash we put on the walls it's still going to look like a shit-hole.'

Alan Knowles climbed down the ladder and dropped the roller he'd been using on the ceiling into the paint tray. He walked over to the fridge and took out two bottles of beer.

Sam Falconer looked up from where she was painting the skirting-boards, balanced her brush across the top of a pot of white gloss, sat back on her heels and pushed her blonde curls away from her forehead with the back of her hand. Alan was a tall muscular bear of a man with short black hair and several earrings in each ear. He was wearing a torn white T-shirt on which was written in black letters, 'Call me straight and I'll Sue'. For the last couple of hours Sam had been trying to find an ending to the sentence 'Call me Sue and I'll ...', but hadn't managed to come up with anything, not even a hybrid Johnny Cash song.

Alan had come down from London that morning and he'd been sullen ever since he saw the new office. Now that at last he was having a go at her she was relieved. He handed her one of the bottles and sat down beside her.

'When I suggested we open an office in Oxford this wasn't what I had in mind.'

Sam rolled the cold sides of the bottle against her cheeks and then hung her head forwards and placed it against the back of her neck before finally bringing the bottle to her lips.

The tall standing fan she had bought a couple of days ago had developed a headache-inducing rattle and was doing nothing more than stir the hot air like a spoon stirs porridge. The hum of traffic drifted through the open window, rush-hour traffic droning eastwards out of Oxford along the Cowley Road.

Sam smoothed flat a bit of the sheet covering the floor, put her bottle down, got to her feet and walked over to the window and leaned out. She was hoping to be met by a breeze, but all she got was a mouthful of exhaust from a bus accelerating away from the lights. Immediately underneath the window-sill was the lettering that identified the shop below as a bookmaker's.

As she looked down, a very large man wearing a blue cotton jacket stepped out of the bookies' on to the pavement. He stopped and Sam saw his shoulders rise and fall in a vast sigh, hardly an uncommon reaction from people exiting those kinds of premises. He bent down and placed something on the ground. His body was blocking Sam from seeing what it was, but as he straightened up and began to walk away she saw that it was a Chihuahua. She couldn't help but smile and at that moment the dog stopped, looked round at her, and began to bark. Following the dog's gaze the man also looked up at her. The expression on his face was one of utter anguish. Caught in the act of staring down at him, she half-waved but wasn't quite sure why; then, feeling as if she had seen something she shouldn't, she ducked her head back into the room.

'I know you wanted something a bit more upmarket, Alan, but the rents in Oxford are astronomical. This was all I could find to fit our budget. There's only four months left on the lease. We're getting it at a knock-down price, and if it doesn't work out we can get out of here and look for something else.'

'But what kind of impression is this going to give to clients?'

'I don't think that matters. You know that often clients don't want to be seen coming into a private investigator's office. More often than not they make contact on the phone and want to meet somewhere neutral like a bar or a restaurant. What this office looks like isn't really going to matter too much.'

'You've got a beautiful city like Oxford and you were brought up in one of the colleges. Why pick the seediest, grubbiest part of town you can find?'

'When you're brought up in an Oxford college you know that

architecturally speaking your life's going to go downhill very fast. I believe in fully embracing the change.'

'That's absolute bullshit and you know it. It's just a different form of snobbery, Sam. As far as I'm concerned it's a crap business decision and one based on your perverse need to slum it.'

He was right of course and there was no point arguing with him. The edgier aspects of the Cowley Road were undoubtedly balanced out by her return each evening to her parents' house in Park Town. Outside of a college, one of the most prestigious Oxford addresses you could have.

'Like I said, it's cheap, Alan. And you're not going to have to work here, are you? You're going to be rustling up work for us in London, in our more salubrious premises in Putney.'

'We are partners now. You should have talked to me before signing the lease.'

Sam sighed. 'You're right. I'm sorry about that but given the fact that we only signed the partnership agreement a couple of weeks ago, and that for two years I've been used to doing pretty much what I want without consulting anyone, I may take a bit of time getting used to a more consultative approach. Also I'm not that thrilled at the whole idea of having an Oxford office in the first place. It's not that long ago that I couldn't set foot in the place without feeling sick, so you need to cut me a bit of slack about how I operate here. And we were talking about the need to diversify, weren't we? Being here maybe we'll pick up a bit of local business as well as university stuff. I mean, I've got contacts in the colleges, but not for this end of town. Who knows what we might get from being here?'

'If you're not sure about the new arrangements we can always ...'

'Oh shut up, Alan, that's not what I'm saying and you know it. I am absolutely sure about them. We should have become partners ages ago. I'm just saying it'd be miraculous if there weren't a few teething difficulties. It'll take a bit of time for us to sort ourselves out. Anyway, come and look what I've got in this bag.'

Sam swept a sheet off a desk and turned a white plastic bag upside down over it. A lot of large gold letters fell out. Alan ran his hand over them and frowned.

'What are these?'

'Turn round a second.'

'Why?'

'Just do it.'

Alan turned away from her and Sam busied herself with the letters.

'Right,' she said. 'You can look now.'

There on the table she had written, 'Falconer and Knowles, Private Investigators'.

'I'm going to put them up on the window tomorrow.'

A slow smile spread across Alan's face. He patted the letters in silence.

'We don't have to change the name. We can still use "The Gentle Way" if you want.'

'It's a new start, Alan. And anyway in the last year my life has felt like one of those protracted car crashes that closes the motorway for miles in both directions. There's been absolutely nothing gentle about it at all. I've had petrol poured over me and been threatened with being set on fire, I've been beaten up I don't know how many times, I've been shot at and threatened with a knife and hung over Putney Bridge by my ankles, you've been stabbed, and then Mark was kidnapped.'

'How is your brother?'

'He's staying with friends in France over the long vacation.' She patted her face with her fingertips. 'It's the first time my face has been clear of a bruise or a cut for months. Maybe a change of name will bring us better luck; a few nice bread-and-butter cases.' She looked down at the letters. '"Falconer and Knowles" has a nice distinguished ring to it, but you know why I really like this place, Alan?'

'It's scruffy like you?'

Sam smiled. 'The Cowley Road is the take-away centre of Oxford. There are about fourteen different ones within spitting distance.'

'I thought you had some new healthy living scheme going on.'

'I have – it involves one take-away a week and no pasta and pesto.'

'And that's progress?'

Sam nodded. 'More than you could possibly imagine. Come on. Let's go and get some food.'

An hour later the remnants of a Chinese take-away were scattered around them. Sam lay flat on her back with her hands behind her head and her knees up. Alan sat cross-legged opposite her.

'So,' he said, 'shall we run through again what we agreed with the business manager should be the criteria for accepting clients?'

'"A",' Sam intoned in a voice that would have suited Hamlet's father's ghost, 'is for ability to pay. So if they are poor show them the door.'

'Well ...'

'"M",' she continued, 'is for mental state. If they are bonkers, bounce them out of there. If they are loonies, lose them.'

'Sort of. And the others?'

'There was something about goals and legality. Hold on a minute ... can we achieve the client's goal.'

'You're not taking this seriously.'

She turned on her side and propped herself up on her elbow. 'When we came out of the bank I felt as if he'd sucked the life-blood out of me. Everything had been reduced to management speak and accountancy principles. He didn't make me feel as if he had any understanding of how a business like ours actually works. He hadn't listened to us at all.'

'Well, maybe he didn't, but he was giving you an alternative to having your business declared bankrupt. A situation brought about through your complete disregard for the realities of life, i.e. the tax-man, and your refusal to employ an accountant or to open brown envelopes, which ended up with the taxman in your office asking for two years of unfiled accounts, which in turn led to a tax bill of ten thousand pounds that you were unable to pay.'

'You're right,' Sam said. 'All of that is absolutely true. But it wasn't the bank that saved my arse, it was you who had the generosity to put enough money into the business to convince the bank we could still be a going concern.'

'The bank could still have pulled the plug on you.'

'I know, but the thing is you can lay down as many criteria as you

7

like in theory but what do you do if a woman comes into the office and says her child's been snatched by her ex-husband, she's living in a refuge for battered women and hasn't got a bean because the child support agency is a waste of space, and she's worried that the police are not taking her seriously? Do you honestly think that you are going to assess her case on the grounds of her ability to pay?'

'Why not? It's not a sin to operate according to sound business principles. We *are* a business not an extension of the social services.'

'Come off it, Alan, you know you're much more of a softy in those kinds of circumstances than I am. I know we're a business, and God knows I don't want to work for nothing, but you know perfectly well that sometimes the decisions we make are not going to be made purely on someone's ability to pay. Anyway, on the basis of those criteria if I presented myself as a client I wouldn't take me on.'

'Too poor or too mad?'

'Probably both.'

'I'm not averse to us taking on some cases like you've just described and tearing up the bill at the end of the day, but first we have to get the business on a proper financial footing. Once we've done that we can look at those kinds of cases in a different way, but at the moment we're dragging ourselves away from the edge of the abyss.'

'Don't be such a drama queen, Alan.' She walked over to the window. 'Anyway, I've got a good feeling about this place.'

'I've no idea why.'

'I like it here.'

'Why?'

'It's diverse. Tell me where else you could get a tattoo, float in the *eau-de-vie* flotation centre, go and see an art film, buy some old stamps and postcards, acquire a few belly-dancing accessories, hire a bike, and then, to cap it all, buy some ecclesiastical robes ...'

Alan opened his mouth and then shut it as Sam continued.

'All within walking distance of each other. In addition there's Jamaican, Polish, Italian, Indian and Japanese food, and if that's not your thing, there's Uhuru wholefoods. Oh, and let's not forget the party shop.'

'Oh, let's not.'

'Come on, Alan, don't be such a snob. If it doesn't work out we can ditch it at Christmas. Anyway, I like the neighbours.'

'Have you met any of them yet?'

Sam pointed at the floor. 'I've seen a man come out of the bookies'.'

'Who is he?'

She shrugged. 'A fat man, who likes a bet and owns a Chihuahua. What's not to like?'

'You've always had a perverse attraction to misfits.'

'Life's too short to waste it trying to fit in. How's Stephanie getting on by the way?'

Stephanie was Alan's twenty-year-old niece who was renting Sam's London flat while she was in Oxford.

'I think she's OK. I haven't heard much from her to be honest.'

'No news is good news?'

'I hope so.'

'What do you think she's doing to the inside of my flat?'

'She's twenty and it's the first time she's lived away from home.'

'The length of the Fulham Palace Road is hardly away from home.'

'You know what I mean, but whatever she's doing can't be as bad as what you did to it on a daily basis.'

'You mean I behave like a twenty-year-old who's just left home?'

He smiled. 'Her mum's not happy about it.'

'What mum is ever happy about their child leaving home?'

'How do your parents feel about it?'

'What do you mean?'

'Well, you've done the reverse. You've come home, haven't you?'

Sam stared at him and then looked away. 'No, I haven't.'

'But ...'

'No,' she said. 'That's not what this is. It's just a business decision, that's all. And it's temporary.'

'What happens if the business takes off?'

Sam didn't say anything. She pointed at the last spring roll. Alan shook his head and she picked it up.

'I haven't come home, Alan.'

He raised his eyebrows.

'Shut up,' Sam said, biting down savagely.

'I didn't say a word.'

'You didn't have to, your eyebrows said everything.'

CHAPTER TWO

The following morning Sam woke early, at her parents' house in Park Town, north Oxford. She pulled on a pair of shorts and a T-shirt and pushed her feet into her running shoes and let herself quietly out of the house. The heat haze shimmering in the sky augured another sweltering day. She did a few half-hearted stretches of her hamstrings, threw her arms around a bit and then set off jogging slowly along the Banbury Road towards the University Parks. They were a large expanse of grass bordered to the west by Parks Road and to the east by the River Cherwell, in the middle of which sat the university cricket ground and club house. Entering at the corner of Norham Gardens and Parks Road, she set off running south along the perimeter footpath.

She'd woken with the conversation with Alan running through her head. *'You've come home, haven't you? It's just a business decision, that's all.'* Who was she trying to kid? He was right, of course, in some respects she had come home but then why had she got so defensive? The reason was that for Sam home didn't just denote bricks and mortar, it also meant a place where you were accepted, a place of safety. While there was no doubting that Oxford had provided the bricks and mortar, her relationship with her mother and stepfather had never been easy, and for many years Sam had refused to call their house home. The Cowley Road judo club, where she'd first turned up as an emotionally disturbed seven-year-old, had been more of a home to her and for many years the most important person in her life had been Tyler, her coach. There her sense of belonging had been immediate and absolute, and judo had repaid her devotion to it with four World Championship victories and five European Championships.

But she had been retired from competition now for several years and recent revelations had softened her attitude to her mother and stepfather. The last few months they had all been bound together by a powerful common aim – to get her brother well again, and for perhaps the first time in her life she was feeling a strong sense of emotional connection with them.

Not only was she living in their house but now she had set up an office here. The lines had definitely blurred. Could she come back and live here? She didn't think so, not permanently. The cerebral nature of the place would drive her bonkers, but for the moment it was true that she was happier with Oxford and her parents than she'd probably ever been.

She had done one circuit of the park and now started on another. Jogging in all honesty was not really her kind of thing. It was part of a new regime that she had agreed upon with her therapist, Reg, to get her through August. It had been triggered by him taking his annual holiday during that month and Sam saying that it was inconvenient because she always became depressed in August. He had pounced on that statement like a terrier on the neck of a particularly juicy rat.

'You always become depressed in August?'

'Well, yes, doesn't everyone? It's a sort of reverse SAD. Too much sun and the blues descend.'

'What is it about August?'

'I don't know, it's just a horrible month.'

'You realise that the month doesn't have anything to do with it? It has to do with what you're telling yourself about the month.'

'Maybe.'

'So what do you tell yourself?'

'It's a stagnant pool. Nothing comes in and nothing goes out. It's a sort of dead zone. Nothing can advance or develop. God, it's horrible. You just hold on like grim death and then September begins and with it comes hope and new beginnings and everything's all right again.'

'You see that you're talking about yourself?'

'Am I?'

'Put it this way – the stagnant pool is not the month of August.'

Sam stopped on a bridge crossing the River Cherwell and caught her breath. Did she really pay him fifty pounds an hour to say such things to her? She wondered, as she did several times a week, whether she should stop therapy. She had initially got into it to deal with her feelings when her father, Geoffrey Falconer, a man she'd been told had died in Oman in 1975, walked back into her life. She had started it and then stopped it when the issues emerging became too painful to face. But Reg had come to her aid when her brother had been kidnapped and it had been a relief to have the emotional support when she was giving so much to Mark.

Anyway the plan they had put together to get Sam through August had been one of gentle exercise and healthy living, decent food, a bit of physical activity and not too much to drink. Simple in theory. The idea was that she would stick to the plan while Reg was on holiday and that they would assess its effectiveness when he came back.

'Let me emphasise one thing, Sam. With the exercise the stress is on gentle.'

'You don't think I'm capable of gentle exercise?'

'I think you're capable of it. I just don't think it's your natural predisposition. I think that is to test yourself and to push your limits and to grind yourself into the ground. I don't want you doing that.'

'So define gentle exercise?'

'The aim is to stir up some endorphins and enjoy it. You have permission to stop when it hurts.'

So, here she was catching her breath, trying not to feel like a wimp and watching the early morning sunshine glinting on the water flowing under the bridge; a good antidote, she hoped, to thoughts of stagnant pools. A couple of swans were swimming towards her, their dignity diminished somewhat by the two grey, ridiculously fluffy, cygnets following them. One of the cygnets scratched its back with its foot, sending a cloud of down up into the air; it floated for a while and then came to rest lightly on the surface of the river.

Reg was back at the end of the week. She wondered about their first session after his return. What would she say to him? The last month had been … well, dull really. There'd been a few niggles with

Alan but nothing that wouldn't sort itself out as they got used to working together as partners. She'd been dozing away an Oxford August. There wasn't anything to talk to him about, was there?

At that point Sam's thoughts turned suddenly to Rick, her … she hesitated to call him her boyfriend. She didn't like the term anyway and they hadn't been together very long, perhaps lover was more appropriate; at any rate it seemed less proprietary. Sam was too keen on her own freedom to lay claims to anyone else's. Reg was bound to ask her about him.

He'd taken his play up to the Edinburgh Festival and despite promising herself that she wouldn't, she was missing him. At first, looking for and then getting ready the new office had preoccupied her, but now without that distraction she found her thoughts turning to him more and more.

Sam hadn't brought up the issue of commitment or monogamy before Rick went away. She wouldn't have wanted to answer those kinds of questions herself. They'd only been together for a little over six weeks anyway so it was way too soon for conversations of that sort. She assumed he'd want to feel free to do whatever he liked without constraint. But unfortunately or fortunately, depending on her mood, there was no getting away from the fact that she'd had the kind of sex with him that made her stop dead in the street with a large grin spreading across her face whenever she thought about it. Not seeing him, however, was breeding the inevitable doubts and insecurities and one telephone call late at night when he was exhausted and monosyllabic hadn't reassured her. After that they'd agreed not to speak until the festival was over. He was due back in Oxford in the first week in September. It seemed like a long time to wait.

The fact that his Chilean wife Isabel was up there acting in the play with him didn't help matters either. He had always been clear with Sam that the marriage, to use his term, had been a 'visa thing', but before he'd married Isabel he'd had a relationship with her and just before they headed north she had split up with her Serbian boyfriend, so Sam wasn't exactly holding her breath that Rick would still be interested in her when he came back. She was also aware that she had never quite got round to checking with his wife that it was a 'visa thing'. He'll dump me, she thought. The only thing to do is to forget about him, focus on my own life and say that's OK when he comes back.

That was turning out to be easier said than done. A couple of days ago, much to her disgust, she'd found herself browsing in the self-help section of Blackwell's and picking out an astrological book called *Love Signs*. The discovery that Scorpios (her sign) and Pisceans (his) were a very good match had ended up irritating rather than reassuring her.

Sam bent down and picked up two sticks. If this one comes through first he'll want me when he comes back, if this one does he won't, she thought. She threw them into the river then crossed the bridge and waited. In the event neither appeared, and when she leaned over to see what had happened she saw them both caught fast in a bramble which was stretched across the river under the bridge.

Even Winnie the Pooh wasn't coming across with any answers.

Her stepfather Peter was in the kitchen making scrambled eggs on toast when she got back from her run. Sam sat down at the large wooden table and kicked off her shoes. He was a tall elegant man wearing light-green linen trousers and a white open-collared shirt with the sleeves rolled up. He was half-Italian and it showed in the even olive tan of his face and forearms. He was also a mathematician and he brought a mathematician's precision and accuracy to his breakfast-making, which meant his scrambled egg on toast was always delicious.

They had not always had an easy relationship but latterly things had been more relaxed between them. Sam's mother was off looking round nursing homes for an elderly aunt who was finally succumbing to osteoporosis. So, with her brother Mark away in France, for the moment it was just the two of them and they seemed to be rubbing along fine.

Peter carried the two plates over to the table and sat down beside her.

'Mark phoned.'

'Oh, how is he?'

'He seemed ...' He paused. 'Relaxed ...'

'Good.'

'He says he's going to stay out there a bit longer.'

Sam nodded.

'He sent his love.'

She knew it was good for them to be apart. Her difficulties with the Inland Revenue had come about partly because she had been spending all her time in Oxford focused on her brother and had ignored the business. When Mark had found out what had happened he'd been furious and told her to return to London and back to her own life.

She'd been hurt at the time but also known he was right.

'How's the new office going?' Peter asked.

'Almost there. I just need to put up the lettering and I'll be ready for business.'

'August is bound to be bit quiet I'd have thought.'

Sam nodded. 'We're going to give it until Christmas and assess it then.'

'Still doing missing persons?'

'Doing anything and everything that comes in.'

'Diversifying?'

Sam nodded. 'That's the general idea.'

'There might be something I could put your way.'

'What sort of thing?'

'Security work at a museum. I'll let you know if anything comes of it.'

The community hall in Headington was much like any other to be found anywhere in the country with its wooden floors, stacked plastic chairs and a large trampoline tipped on its side leaning against the back wall. Morning sunlight was slanting in through the windows in the roof down on to a few large black rubber gym mats spread out on the floor, and in front of these in some of the plastic chairs sat a group of twenty women whose ages, Sam reckoned, ranged from sixty to eighty.

Sam herself stood next to a wipe-clean white-board holding a black marker in her hand. This was Tyler, her old judo coach's, self-defence class which she had agreed to teach while he was away on holiday. She liked teaching women self-defence. Women should know how to look after themselves and it often didn't take much encouragement for the most shy and retiring of them to turn into ferocious punchers. Across the top of the board she had written the words 'Multiple Attackers'.

'So,' she said. 'What are your thoughts on multiple attackers?'

'Bad news,' said a petite elderly woman with white bouffant hair wearing a pink pastel tracksuit with thick ankle cuffs.

Sam nodded. 'Yes, they are, but what are the kind of things you can do that will help?'

'Keep moving,' said one.

'Try and get something between you and them,' said another.

'Like what?' Sam said.

'A lamppost ... a litter bin ...'

'A bus shelter ...'

'Yes. Excellent ... What else?'

'Try and keep an eye on them.'

'Yes. Has Tyler talked to you about the effects of adrenaline?'

The group nodded.

'So you probably remember that one of the effects can be tunnel vision. Not terribly helpful if you're trying to keep track of more than one person. It's important you remain aware of everything around you. What else is it important to remember?'

'Stay on your feet.'

'Yes. That's very important. Once on the ground you're a much easier target. If you go to ground it's important to try and get up as soon as possible.'

'Any other ideas?'

'Pick out the ringleader and hurt him horribly,' said one of the rather demure white bouffants. 'It'll make the others stop and think a bit before they pile in.'

'Yes,' Sam said. 'That's an excellent idea. Inflict pain on one of them and it is definitely going to give the others something to think about.'

'Can we get on with the practical now? We like that bit the best.' said one of the younger ones.

'Oh, yes,' Sam said.

A tall angular woman with a bob of thick grey hair spoke. 'So if several of them grab you at once, what can you do?'

'Well,' Sam said. 'Basically it's tricky but the only thing you can do really is ...' she paused. 'Well, you know how a cat behaves when you're trying to give it a pill?'

The group stared silently at her.

'Essentially it does everything to avoid that happening. It twists and scratches and bites and wriggles. Well, mine does anyway. It turns itself into a furry tornado that cannot be held.'

'So,' said the demure one. 'Behave like a cat that is being given a pill?'

'Yes,' Sam said. 'Gouge their eyes, twist their noses, tear out any earrings or facial piercings. Ears are good as well. Stamp on their insteps. Do everything you can to inflict as much pain as possible on your attackers. If you hurt them enough they may well let go.'

'Presumably if you hurt them enough you may also make them extremely angry?' said white bouffant.

Sam smiled. 'Yes, there is that risk. Your aim should be to disable them.'

She divided them into pairs and after a demonstration got them to practise scissor chokes.

That afternoon she stood on the pavement outside her office looking up at the window. It had been a nightmare so far and all she'd managed was the lettering of 'Falconer and Knowles'. She was balking at the prospect of sticking the whole of 'Private Investigators' up there, hoping that PIs would suffice.

At that moment the large man she had seen previously came out of the bookmaker's with his Chihuahua in tow.

'I've just moved into the office upstairs,' Sam said, holding out her hand.

'Falconer or Knowles?'

'Falconer ... Sam.'

The man wiped his hand on the side of his trousers and then took Sam's. 'Norman Lester Sweetman,' he said.

Up close he was surprisingly good-looking – warm brown eyes with a good set of laughter lines round them and thick brown wavy hair.

'Would you mind if I asked you something?' she said.

'Ask away.'

She pointed up at the window. 'If I put on the window PIs what would you think it meant?'

'Premium insurance? Prima donnas incorporated? Pristine interiors? Perfect idiots? Predominantly insane? Preposterously inept? Previously indolent. Presently inert. Primarily indiscreet.'

She laughed. 'You're having me on, right?'

He took a large handkerchief out of his pocket and wiped his forehead. 'I am.'

'So ... PI ...?'

'Private investigators?'

'Good.'

'Is that what you are?'

'Yes.'

'Well, welcome to the neighbourhood.'

He began to walk past Sam, the Chihuahua trailing at his heels. The dog too was nicer than she'd expected. He was not a bald rat of a Chihuahua with black and tan markings but had long golden fur with a white bib and white paws. In fact he looked not unlike a baby lion. One thing, however, distinguished him from a lion. His nails had been painted bright pink.

'Interesting dog,' she said.

He stopped. 'The dog is a disaster.'

Sam bent down and the little dog yapped and bared its teeth. 'Oh, I'm sorry.'

'Don't worry. "*Canis timidis vehementus latrat quam mordet*".'

Sam straightened up. That was the trouble with Oxford. Scratch any passer-by and they'd be likely to bleed a complicated equation or a Latin quotation. The whole place was so grossly over-qualified it could be tiresome. Even the plumbers had PhDs.

'And in plain English that would mean what exactly?'

'A timid dog barks more violently than it bites.'

'He doesn't look that timid.'

'He's only just stopped doing that to me.'

'Not yours then?'

He shook his head. 'I am looking after him for a friend of a friend, a cruel joke to play on someone of my dimensions. Needless to say I was not told of the dog's breed before I agreed to do it. I had in mind a more robust animal, a Labrador perhaps, or an Alsatian, a dog with a certain cachet, not a violent dog, you understand, but a dog with a bit of gravitas, perhaps an elderly retired greyhound that might bestow on me a certain elegance that does not come naturally. If I had known it was going to be a Chihuahua with pink nails, I would have politely declined on the basis that I did not want to be made any more a figure of fun than a gentleman my size is already.'

Sam smiled. 'What's his name?'

'Philip, but to me he is simply Pipsqueak.'

By ten o'clock that evening Sam had got the office into a respectable state. There'd been a serviceable desk and chair there already, and from a second-hand furniture shop across the road she'd bought a filing cabinet, another chair and a phone. A phone had been left behind but it was cream coloured and had been covered with what could only be described as a grey crust of dead skin and the mouthpiece smelled. However much she cleaned it she knew she'd never be happy using it. The chair she had bought was a large executive thing made of squishy black leather. She wasn't really into status chairs, especially not ones that made you feel like you ought to have a fluffy white cat on your lap and a tank of piranhas, but it had been by far the most comfortable one they had and because the mechanism that altered the height was broken her feet reached the ground – always a plus.

The window was open, Charlie 'Bird' Parker was blowing his sax and a bottle of beer stood on her desk. It was getting dark outside but she hadn't turned on the lights and was relying on the red, amber and green of the traffic lights to illuminate the pad of paper on her lap. She'd been trying to draft an ad to put in the *Oxford Mail* but neither Bird nor beer seemed to be working any magic. Her thoughts had been turning to Rick and what he might be up to in Edinburgh. Unfortunately the images were graphic and involved his wife. She sighed and looked down at what she had written, 'All your needs will be met' – well, that had all the bounce of a billiard ball.

There was a soft knock on the door. She turned the music down and yelled, 'Come in.'

The door opened and Norman Sweetman came in, holding Pipsqueak in one hand and a white plastic bag in the other. He closed the door behind him and put the dog down. After yapping a couple of times it began to sniff the newly painted skirting-boards.

'Working late?'

Sam's gesture encompassed the beer and the music. 'Can't call this working.' She picked up the beer. 'Would you like one?'

'How kind.'

Sam took a bottle out of the fridge, handed it to him and sat back down. He placed the beer on the desk and went and positioned himself in front of the fan, holding his jacket away from the sides of his body so his torso got the benefit of the breeze. He was wearing blue cotton trousers held up by black braces and a collarless white shirt. His clothes looked as if they'd been made for him because they fitted him exactly.

After carefully examining the chair positioned on the far side of Sam's desk he sat down stretched out his legs and crossed his ankles. Despite the heat, he was wearing suede desert boots and no socks; dark patches of sweat had soaked through the suede. He glanced at the pad of paper lying on her desk and then at her. Sam registered two things simultaneously: first he had the most extraordinarily long eyelashes she'd ever seen on a man, and secondly that he was much younger than she'd initially thought, late thirties she estimated or maybe early forties.

His words broke through her thoughts. 'What are you working on?'

She turned it round and pushed it across the table towards him. He picked it up and read.

'Selling myself isn't exactly my strong point,' Sam said. 'I'll probably get Alan to write it. He's a lot better at all that sort of stuff than me.'

'Alan?'

'The Knowles on the window.'

'Ah. Would you allow me?'

'Be my guest.'

Sam rolled a pencil across the desk towards him. He stopped it from falling on to the floor but instead of picking it up took an ink pen out of his inside pocket and after a short period of contemplation began to write. The traffic lights turned red then amber then green before he handed it back to her. The writing on the page belonged to another era altogether and looked as if a drunken fly had heaved itself out of a bottle of ink and staggered across the page. After squinting at it for a minute or so Sam managed to decipher the following, 'Discreet and confidential resolution of business and personal problems.'

'I like that,' Sam said. 'It sounds soothing. All the ones I'd come up with made us sound like prostitutes.'

He smiled. 'I suppose you should list the things you do.'

'Yes.'

'What are they?'

'Well, the aim is to diversify. We did specialise in missing persons but now we're going to do everything.'

'Such as?'

'Matrimonial, process serving, employee investigations, personal security, investigation of insurance claims ...'

'Computer fraud?'

'Err, no ... we don't have the technical expertise.'

'I would have thought it was a growing field.'

'I think you're right.'

'Personal security. Do you do that yourself or do you use other employees?'

'I can do that myself.'

'So you are skilled in ...?'

'Self-defence. Judo.'

'You personally know how to look after yourself?'

'Yes.'

'Ah,' he smiled and looked relieved. 'On the subject of personal problems I have one myself which I need some assistance with. It's more of a favour, I'm afraid, than business. I have to visit my grandfather in hospital early tomorrow morning and I can't take Pip there. I don't want to tie him up outside because he'll howl the place down. I was wondering if you might have him overnight and then I'll take him off your hands tomorrow morning.'

Pip was now sitting Yoda-like in Norman's lap staring at Sam with his solemn brown eyes.

She frowned. 'I don't think that would be a very good idea. I don't know anything about dogs. I've only ever had cats.'

'They're exactly the same but with half the brains and more generous dispositions.'

'All the same ...'

'I would usually have asked a neighbour but everyone's away on holiday at the moment.'

'What do I feed him?'

'I have food in this bag here and his favourite blanket and written instructions on his food.'

'How far can he walk before he gets tired?'

'He sits down when he's too tired to go on.'

'And then what?'

He shrugged. 'I have found that carrying him is marginally less humiliating than dragging.'

'You'll definitely pick him up in the morning?'

'Of course.'

'OK then, on one condition. I get to take that stuff off his nails.'

'You're welcome to try. You and he will look good together size-wise.'

He heaved himself out of the chair, put Pip down, ran his hand over the little dog's head and laid the lead across the desk. 'I'll see you tomorrow around ten.'

'Is your grandfather all right?'

'He's ninety, he's had one leg amputated already and the other is badly affected by ulcers. He's in hospital for maggot therapy when they ...'

Sam put up her hand. 'Stop – I've heard of it.'

'He also has MRSA.'

'I'm sorry. Are you close to him?'

He had his back to her, his hand on the door. After a few moments he cleared his throat.

'I'm sorry,' Sam said. 'I didn't mean ...'

He pushed open the door but didn't turn round. When he spoke his voice was hoarse. 'He's all I have left.'

The door closed behind him. Sam stared down at Pip who stared back. She berated herself for having asked the last two questions.

There was no need for it. She'd just been making casual conversation and she'd upset him. It wasn't even as if he was a client that she needed to know anything from. Sometimes she was too nosy for her own good, but there was definitely something about Norman Lester Sweetman that interested her. 'A' is for ability to pay, she thought. Well, he hadn't offered any sort of payment but then it was only for a night and he'd written a nice ad for her; a payment of sorts.

She picked up the plastic bag and her feelings of remorse turned instantly to irritation; he'd left her enough dog food for at least a week. She ran to the window and looked down into the street. But the only people she could see were two drunks pushing each other back and forth over a can of spilled Special Brew.

At the bottom of the bag under a Black Watch tartan rug was an envelope addressed to her. She tore it open.

Dear Sam (if I may),

Please forgive me. You realise I'm sure by now that I am not intending to return in the morning. 'Events, dear boy,' as Macmillan said, have conspired against me to make that impossible. But rest assured I will come back for Pip, even if at the moment I'm not able to say exactly when that will be. I knew at once that you were not the sort of woman to exact retribution on a defenceless animal for the mendaciousness of its temporary owner. Please save such feelings for me at a later date.

Pip has certain idiosyncrasies of behaviour – don't we all? But I've found he responds enthusiastically to bribery.

With warmest regards and thanks
Norman

PS Being relatively small of stature I'm sure you need no reminding of the following – a cane non magno saepe tenetur aper. *I have certainly found this to be the case.*

He hadn't even had the decency to give a translation.

Peter was in the garden nursing a glass of wine when Sam got back that night. After a quick Chihuahua explanation she got herself a glass and joined him. They sat for a while in companionable silence, listening to Pip sniffing round the patio. A neighbour was having a party a few doors down and the burble of animated conversation, punctuated with bursts of laughter, floated over on the warm night air.

Peter followed the movement of Pip round the garden. 'He reminds me of a dog I had as a boy in Naples. She was called Isotta.'

Sam was astonished. Peter rarely talked about his childhood. 'You had a Chihuahua?'

'No, she was a mongrel but she looked a bit like him. I found her the summer before my parents sent me to boarding school and begged them to let me keep her. When I got back from school for my first holiday they said they'd given her away. I don't think I allowed myself to love anything as much again until I met your mother and that was over forty years later.'

Sam opened her mouth and then closed it again. Peter hardly ever spoke about his childhood and never in such emotional terms. 'How awful,' she managed eventually.

He shrugged. 'All childhoods have their sorrows.'

Sam sipped her wine and struggled to think of something to say. She'd always judged Peter as being completely emotionally constipated, but now when he had said these things to her she was the one who was unable to respond.

'You know I said I might be able to get you some work?' Peter said, breaking the silence.

'Yes.'

'Well, it's Professor Cummings at the Pitt Rivers. He could do with some advice.'

Like anyone who'd grown up in Oxford, Sam knew the Pitt Rivers well. It was a museum positioned at the back of the Natural History Museum which contained one of the world's greatest ethnographic collections. In 1884 General Pitt Rivers had given his collection to the University of Oxford on the condition that a museum would be built to house it and someone be appointed to lecture in anthropology. Its main claim to fame among the schoolchildren of Oxfordshire was its collection of shrunken heads.

Peter continued, 'The night before last it was broken into. The fire exit was left open. It doesn't appear as if anything was taken, but he's worried it might happen again and I said I'd talk to you and maybe you could do a bit of night security for a couple of weeks.'

'Night security?' Sam said slowly.

'Why would that be a problem?'

Sam swilled her wine slowly round her glass and waved a whining insect away from her ear. Peter was as rational a man as you could come across. He'd quite happily walk under ladders and didn't bother saluting single magpies. She'd never seen him throw salt over his shoulder or worry about picking up a knife he'd dropped. She had always found the fact he didn't believe in God rather reassuring, but the fact he didn't believe in anything, bewildering.

Sam wasn't anything like that. When Mark had been in a coma she'd gone back to jumping the cracks in the pavement, something she hadn't done since she was a child, hopscotching over the uneven flagstones of St Cuthbert's quadrangle on the way back from school. She had made all kinds of bargains with the gods. Like most professional sportsmen and women she had always been highly superstitious. However hard you trained, however good you were, luck always played its part and that's where superstition came in. When she'd been competing everything that she did before a contest was rigidly adhered to. The meal she ate, the music she listened to (usually 'Eye of the Tiger') and the last thing she touched before going out on to the *tatami*, her father's dog-tags. She could not bring herself to admit to Peter that the idea of spending a night in the Pitt Rivers museum held as much appeal as doing the same in the Chamber of Horrors. She knew he would judge her in the same way she judged herself, as a credulous fool but 'A', she reminded herself, was for ability to pay.

'No,' she said eventually, 'no problem at all.'

Automatically her hand went to her pocket. For years when she thought her father was dead she had carried his dog-tags in her pocket and used them as a good luck charm. They were no longer there, but the habit of reaching for them remained.

'I hope you don't mind but I made an appointment for you to meet Cummings, tomorrow morning at midday.'

'No, that's fine,' Sam said, reaching for the bottle and splitting the contents between both their glasses.

Pip had returned from sniffing round the garden and now had his nose stuffed into a terracotta pot filled with red geraniums.

'If you need any help with him?' Peter said.

'Thanks. I might do. I don't think his owner's going to come back for him that soon, so some help will probably come in handy.'

CHAPTER THREE

Sam spent the morning in her office just in case Norman appeared to pick up Pip but she soon realised this was wishful thinking. On the way back for her appointment at the museum she dropped Pip off with her stepfather. Sorting that out would have to wait until later in the day. Now she paused in the entrance to the Natural History Museum looking up at the jaw of a sperm whale towering above her and beyond that to the massive roof supported by its series of cast-iron pillars. It was a monument to Victorian certainty. Nice to feel so confident, Sam thought, and then remembered that the stonemasons, the O'Sheas, had been sacked before the building was completed because they had carved owls and parrots into the entrance way, widely presumed to be a parody of the obstreperous members of Convocation, the university governing body.

Beyond the jaw-bone hung the skeletons of two dinosaurs: the first one was an Iguanodon bernissartensis, a vegetarian, the notice said, but that didn't stop it looking any less ferocious than the Tyrannosaurus rex behind it. Sam stared at the T.rex for a while, taking in the tiny arms and vicious jaws, the gigantic savage feet. Trying to displace her anxiety she began counting its ribs. It didn't work. The Pitt Rivers awaited her attached to the back of this museum and since she was early for her appointment she walked past the shop selling postcards and guidebooks into the area where the exhibits were displayed.

The majority of the artefacts were laid out in free-standing Victorian glass-sided cabinets, edged in ebony and sitting on solid black ebony legs. There wasn't a great deal of space between them and they were stuffed with items which were identified by hand-written labels. Above the main room ran two open galleries holding more exhibits and above those arched a wrought iron and wooden roof. Even with the height of the ceiling and the galleries, on the floor of the museum the overwhelming impression was of a cluttered and oppressive space, and dim lighting contributed to the feeling that when you stepped into this place, you had stepped back into the Victorian era.

A group of children walked past her. She caught the word 'nightmare', from among the burble of their conversation but wasn't sure what it was referring to. In here there were lots of things which could give you those. A teacher passed her. 'We've only become civilised in the last hundred years,' she announced to the children.

Chance would be a fine thing, Sam thought.

She moved slowly between the cabinets trying to argue away her feelings of unease and steering well clear of the ones marked 'Treatment of the Dead' and 'Magic, Ritual, Religion and Belief'. The first time she'd been brought here was shortly after the family arrived in Oxford. She'd been five years old and in a highly disturbed state, following what, at that time, was thought to have been the death of her father. Fear had seized her from the moment she'd set foot in the place and seeing the shrunken skulls had done nothing to calm her down. For the next few nights she had woken up screaming from a series of chilling nightmares, focusing mainly on the small glass bottle which was said to contain a witch.

This was the first time she'd been back since.

She looked up at a huge totem pole; a black wooden carving of a raven's beak protruded several feet out from the main body of the pole. She glanced at her watch and was relieved to see that it was time for her appointment with Professor Cummings.

Professor Cummings was wearing brown corduroys, a tweed jacket and heavy leather-soled shoes. He was obviously one of those Englishmen who did not make decisions on what to wear on the basis of the weather. Whatever the temperature, he looked like a man who would neither shiver nor sweat. He towered over Sam, although at five foot one most people tended to. A shock of thick white hair swept straight back from his forehead, above deep-set piercingly blue eyes. Bending slightly at the waist he held his hand out towards her. She took hold of a dry, warm palm which loosely enclosed her own slightly sweaty one.

'Thank you so much for coming,' he said.

Upstairs in his cluttered office at the top of the Natural History Museum he explained to her what had happened.

'We probably wouldn't have noticed anything if it wasn't for the fact that when Mary came in to open up the museum two days ago the large door which operates as a fire exit was swinging open. It was that which alerted us.'

'Was anything taken?'

'Well, that's the thing. We're not sure. As you know, the cabinets are full of artefacts. Ascertaining quickly that nothing is missing is impossible. We're working our way round the cabinets one by one but it won't be until the end of the week that we'll be sure. A quick check couldn't identify any artefacts having been taken.'

'None of the cabinets were smashed then?'

'No.'

'And no keys have gone missing?'

'No.'

'You've got some work going on at the moment, haven't you?'

'Yes, an extension is being added, the reception is being altered and the upper galleries are closed in order to enable us to build a new stairwell and lift shaft.'

'So you have quite a few workmen about the place.'

'Yes, that's true, there are more people coming and going than usual.'

'Peter mentioned that you wanted someone here at night?'

'Yes, would you be able to do that for the next week or so?'

Sam crossed her legs. 'You think that someone is likely to come back?'

'It would be a precautionary measure.'

'But at the moment you've got nothing to make you think that anyone was trying to steal anything. All you've got is an open door. Presumably it could have just been a security lapse by one of your staff.'

'I concede it could be as simple as that.'

'But you don't think it is?'

'I would feel very reassured if over the next week or so you might keep an eye on the place.'

'Have you informed the police?'

'No, and I'm not going to tell anyone that you are here. If someone is trying to steal from the museum then it is most likely to be an inside job. If the police are involved or people know about you we only end up warning them off. I don't want anyone else to know a thing about you. If someone is stealing from the museum we need to catch them red-handed. If they think we're on to them they'll stop, or leave and go and start doing the same somewhere else.'

'But surely if you've got them checking all the artefacts ...'

'Oh, when I said "we" I meant I.'

'But surely there are too many for you to ...'

'I must stress that you must not under any circumstances talk to any members of staff about what you are doing here. It is a pre-condition of your employment.'

Sam sighed and took a contract out of her bag and handed it to the professor. 'These are our terms and conditions. Would you like to look over them and see if they're OK with you? I may ask a colleague to give me a hand – would that be all right?'

'Is he or she capable?'

'Highly. He's an ex-police officer and my partner. I've worked with him for several years and always found him reliable.'

He nodded. 'I'll look this over and hand it back to you this evening. If there is anything I need to discuss perhaps I could phone you?'

Sam gave him her mobile and office numbers and got to her feet. Cummings did the same.

As they walked out of his office, Sam said, 'Aren't you going to have to tell someone? Who's going to let me in and out? How am I going to explain what I'm doing here?'

'I am usually the last person to leave the building at night and the first to arrive in the morning, so there is no need for anyone else to know you've been here. If you turn up at say eleven o'clock that should be fine and I'll be back in the morning at six.'

'That's long hours to work.'

'I suppose it's never really felt like work to me.'

They walked back down past the dinosaurs and into the entrance of the Natural History Museum. He bowed slightly and extended his hand. Sam took it. 'I'll see you here at eleven then,' she said.

Sam picked up Pip from her father and walked back to her office. The conversation with Cummings had been vague and unsatisfactory. She didn't think he was telling her the whole truth but then clients rarely did that. If someone was stealing then it did sort of make sense not to warn the possible perpetrator that she was going to be there at night. In the end it wasn't really any of her business. People were hardly queuing round the block for her services at the moment, so she might as well just get on with it and make sure she watched her back.

Radcliffe Square was filled with tourists boiling in the sun – a group of Japanese outside St Mary's, Americans walking past Sam towards Hertford Bridge and another group entering the square from the High. Oxford was a strange place at this time of year, full of exhausted tourists up on day trips from London and foreign teenagers who were being taught English in the innumerable language schools of north Oxford.

Although situated many miles from the sea, Oxford was essentially a tidal city. There were three eight-week terms a year, and in on the tide that was the beginning of term came over 18,000 students and out they all went eight weeks later. The character of the town was transformed by this tide, as it cast up on the shores of the city the scruffy bike-riding students who were supposed to be the cream of their generation. Term time could be identified by the massed ranks of bicycles outside the colleges and an increase in activity round the libraries and the lecture halls. Now, in the long summer vacation the colleges were given over to conferences and, despite the tourists and the teenagers, the absence of students made the heart of the town feel hollow.

Back in the office she put in a call to Alan and asked him if he'd be willing to come down and do some nights at the Pitt Rivers. He gave a short and earthy response.

'Are you all right, Alan?'

She heard him sigh. 'Johnny's been let out on parole.'

Johnny was the eldest of Alan's eight brothers and had been in prison for assaulting a police officer. The man had lost an eye in the incident and Johnny had been inside for the last fifteen years.

'Were you expecting it?'

'Course we weren't – he's been turned down all the other times, hasn't he?'

'How's the family?'

'Edgy.'

'How are you?'

'I can't leave London at the moment.'

'Maybe it'd be good for you.'

'There's going to be trouble, Sam.'

'Maybe he's changed.'

'He'll never change. He never has, Sam. People don't. Not people like Johnny anyway.'

Sam put down the phone. She remembered Alan talking about the first time he'd met Johnny. He was five years old and he'd never clapped eyes on him before because his brother had been in prison his whole life. He'd been sitting on the arm of the sofa at his mum's and Johnny had been watching the television. It was then he'd made the mistake of asking him where he'd been. Johnny had swiped him off the side of the sofa without a word. His ears had rung for two days. It had taught him one very big lesson. There were some questions you didn't ask.

Sam stared at Pip who had curled up under her desk. In the absence of any other work her next job was tracing Norman Lester Sweetman and handing him back the dog.

As Sam walked into the smoke-filled bookies' with the dog at her heels, three men glanced at her and then went back to what they were doing. One was playing a slot machine against the wall to Sam's right and the other two were standing with their backs to her, looking up at a bank of televisions, where horse racing, greyhound racing and football was taking place. A race ended and one of them muttered something under his breath, dropped a crumpled betting slip to the floor, and then went back to reading the racing pages of the *Sun*. The smell in here was of sweat and cigarettes, lost hopes and broken dreams.

A ferrety-looking man with greasy black hair was working behind a glass window. As Pip sniffed at an empty packet of crisps and discarded chewing gum wrapper, Sam waited in line to speak to him.

'Hi,' she said when she reached the front of the queue. 'I was looking for some help in tracing a man who I think is a customer of yours.'

He shook his head. 'I don't know where the punters live. I just take their money.'

Sam persevered. 'His name's Norman Sweetman. He's a large man with a Chihuahua. Well, not with a Chihuahua at the moment. At the moment I have the Chihuahua and that is the problem.'

The man shrugged. 'Sure Norman comes in here but I don't know anything about him. I take his money, occasionally give him his winnings, that's as far as it goes.'

'Would any of your colleagues know where he lives or where I might find him?'

He pushed his glasses back up his nose and shook his head.

A man standing behind Sam sighed. 'You going to be all day, love? I need to get this on before two.'

'Sorry,' Sam stood to one side and let him place his bet. 'If he comes in will you tell him I need to see him urgently?' She slid her card under the window and he nodded.

'You the private investigator who's moved in upstairs?'

'Yup.'

Outside the bookies' Sam paused, looking down at Pip. She heard the door open behind her and stepped away to let whoever it was come out.

'You looking for the fat man?'

It was the man who'd been behind her in the queue; he was wearing light-brown trousers that stopped halfway down his calves, trainers and a white T-shirt. He pulled the pair of dark glasses perched on his head down on to the bridge of his nose, shook a cigarette into his hand and lit it.

'Yes, do you know him?'

'You a private investigator?'

She nodded.

'Must be worth something to you then?'

'Depends what information you give me.'

'Where he works.'

'Tenner.'

'Give it then.'

Sam dug in her pocket and handed it over.

'He works in the cinema over there.' He pointed across the street.

'The Penultimate Picture Palace?'

'Ultimate.'

'Sorry?'

'It's Ultimate now, not Penultimate.'

'Oh right, thanks.'

Ten-pound note firmly clenched in his fist, he pushed his way back into the bookies'.

Sam crossed the Cowley Road and after the short walk to Jeune Street found herself looking up at the Ultimate Picture Palace, positioned next to the Elm Tree Pub and opposite the Cowley Methodist church, all establishments which in their own way peddled different forms of escapism. In Sam's day the cinema had been painted all black with a huge pair of white Al Jolson hands adorning the front. These had gone now and instead it was painted cream and grey with its name in red letters. She loved this cinema. When it had first opened it had been known as the PPP and been popular with students because it cost a pound to be a member and then a pound to see a film. Also it had never been that fussed about the age limits on the films, useful for Sam when she was being dragged off to see all kinds of things by Mark, who was eight years older than her.

It was here that she had gone to see *Casablanca* on Valentine's Day with her first boyfriend. It was here that she had been violently sick as she tried to count the number of stuntmen listed in the credits of a late-night showing of *The Blues Brothers*, a film she had gone to after a drunken party in a house Mark was living in as a student. It was here that she had first had rice thrown at the back of her neck before doing a jump to the left and then a jump to the right, before putting her hands on her hips and pulling her knees in tight. Essentially the place was a flea-pit which survived through showing a mixture of current and more idiosyncratic films that appealed to the student population. The idiosyncratic ones could be summed up as arthouse films with lots of sex: *Betty Blue, Blue Velvet. Last Tango in Paris* usually played at least once a year.

Today *Goodnight and Good Luck* was playing and a short queue snaked away from the ticket office.

Sam waited until the last person had been served and then approached the window. 'Could you tell me if Norman is working here today?'

The woman in the booth had short dark hair, elfin features and her lips were covered with bright red lipstick. She was wearing a white vest and had a butterfly tattooed on her upper arm. Her badge stated her name was Helen. 'He's on holiday,' she said and sipped from a can of Pepsi.

'How long for?'

'I think he's due back next week.'

'It's an emergency. I need to get hold of him urgently. Do you know his address or telephone number.'

She rested her chin in her cupped hands and squeezed her cheeks; her nails were sharp pink points under her eyes. A white 'Make Poverty History' elastic band hung from her wrist. 'I don't think we can give out that kind of information. What sort of an emergency is it anyway?'

Sam felt a strong desire to lie and say it involved a death in the family, but then thought better of it. She picked up Pip and sat him on the ledge of the ticket booth; he slobbered on the glass and then licked it.

'This,' she said, 'is the emergency.'

Helen laughed. 'Nice nails.'

'I tried to get it off last night with nail polish remover but he growled each time I picked up his feet.'

'So he dumped the dog on you?'

Sam nodded. 'He told me it was only overnight and he'd pick him up this morning, but there's been no sign of him so far. Have you any idea where he might be?'

Helen shook her head. 'There was an incident here last week and I think he decided it would be for the best if he made himself scarce for a while.'

'What happened?'

'We were showing *Nosferatu*. It's a vampire film with Klaus Kinski.'

'I know it.'

'Well, Norman was in a bit of a state that day. His grandfather's been ill and it's been upsetting him. He mixed up the last two reels.'

Sam considered this for a moment, a smile gradually spreading across her face.

'So what happened was that there was the whole killing the vampire scene, stake through the heart and so on, and then Klaus was up waving his long fingernails and running about on a ship, and right as rain for the last half of the film.'

Sam began to laugh. 'Couldn't you have explained it as a postmodern take on the vampire myth? Didn't someone once play *Psycho* at an incredible slowed-down pace and call it art?'

'Well, maybe but at the end I've never seen an audience look quite so stunned. Norman came down, explained what had happened and apologised. Some people saw the funny side, but unfortunately there was a rather officious man who got pretty pissed off about it. He demanded a refund which he got, but when he said he was going to write a letter of complaint, Norman got stuck into him.'

'How exactly?'

'Well, he started off saying that the man should thank him because the film was a load of rubbish and by mixing up the final reels at least he'd introduced a much-needed element of humour into it.'

Sam laughed.

'Then he said something about the fact that this man had come to see *Last Tango in Paris* about five times last month.'

'Had he?'

'Oh yes, he's a regular and then Norman made some comment about butter that I didn't quite catch ...'

Sam grimaced. 'And then what happened?'

'Well, the man left in a hurry threatening all kinds of things.'

'And Norman?'

'Well, it wasn't really like him to behave in that way. He's got a sort of old-fashioned politeness to him normally. You know he's the kind of man who holds the door open for you so I was surprised. Once he'd calmed down I think he regretted what he'd said. He decided to take a few days off and see how things were once the dust had settled.'

'Do you know where he lives?'

Helen smiled. 'You know he tried me yesterday, tried to get me to take the dog, but he'd done it once too often. Last time I had him, Norman said he only needed him looked after for a day. He came back for him three days later. That's when I painted his nails. It was my protest but Norman didn't turn a hair. I think he quite liked it.'

Sam sighed. 'Please give me his address. I'm not into dogs and I've just opened an office. I can't really look after him properly.'

Pip licked her under the chin.

'Looks like he's quite taken with you.'

'No, he's not really. He's just pretending because he's got an audience.'

'Wait there. I'll go and see if I can find his details.'

Sam and Pip waited in the shadow of the doorway trying to keep out of the direct glare of the sun. A couple of minutes later the woman appeared with a piece of paper in her hand.

Sam glanced at the address and frowned. 'Do you know where this is?'

'I think it's the first road that runs left off the top of Headington Hill when you're heading out of town. Just beyond Headington Hill Hall.'

'Pullen's Lane?'

'Yes, it's somewhere off there.'

'OK, thanks.'

Sam had turned and was beginning to walk away when the woman said, 'Are you a friend of his?'

She stopped and turned round. 'Not really. I moved into an office over the bookies' and got talking to him in the street.'

Helen cleared her throat. 'The thing is he's a very nice man but I think he's got himself into some kind of trouble. He's been distracted recently and short-tempered and usually he's neither. I tried to ask him about it but he wouldn't talk to me. He's very worried about his grandfather.'

'He mentioned he was going into hospital.'

'I think he could do with a friend at the moment, that's all,' she said. 'I sort of hoped you might be it.'

'He dumped the dog on me so I don't feel that friendly towards him. All I really want to do is give him the dog back.'

The woman shrugged. 'Fair enough,' she said and walked back into the darkness of the cinema.

CHAPTER FOUR

It was a short bus ride from the Plain to the top of Headington Hill, and twenty minutes later Sam and Pip were walking down a green and leafy Pullen's Lane. Oxford Brookes University, formerly known to every local of a certain generation as the Oxford Poly, had accommodation for its students down here but it was out of term time and passing the buildings they met no one on foot or on bike. Trees lining the narrow lane and casting deep shadows across the road meant that it was cooler but not cool enough to put off the clouds of midges dancing in the thin shafts of light that pierced the foliage. Here you could almost imagine you were out in the countryside, a relief after the heat and noise of the Cowley Road.

The house was set back off Harberton Mead in a large garden. There was no sign of occupation as Sam walked up the path and rang the doorbell. She rang it again and then walked round to the front where there was a veranda and cupping her hands round her eyes peered through the windows. Two stuffed owls peered back at her, their tufted ears and barley-sugar-coloured eyes giving them a startled expression that matched Sam's own. Along with the owls there were two leather club chairs, a battered matching sofa, and a series of worn red-and-green rugs. Even dear Doris Day would have recognised that the house was distinctly lacking a woman's touch. Against the walls were cabinets not unlike the ones in the Pitt Rivers but Sam couldn't see what was in them due to the angle of the sun hitting the windows.

She turned round and looked at the garden. A lawn ran down from the front of the house to a large cherry tree. Beyond the tree was an area of nettles over which large cabbage white butterflies were dancing. Beyond that was a thick laurel hedge cut into a rectangular shape which acted as a break between the garden and the road. To Sam's left and to the side of the house were the tall canes and netting of a vegetable garden, a greenhouse and a large wooden shed. A couple of wood-pigeons began to call to each other high up in the fir trees at the back of the house.

Other than the birdsong there was no noise here. The garden and house were tucked away from any observation and had a timeless quality. Sam half-expected to see a Victorian gentleman step out on to the veranda and settle down in the wicker chair to read his book. And this matched her impression of Norman – with his weirdly old-fashioned handwriting and method of speech, he felt like a throwback to an entirely different era.

What to do?

She sat down on the top step that led down from the veranda to the lawn and considered her options: wait – although if he was away on holiday then there was hardly any point in doing that; put a note through the door – that probably wouldn't get her very far unless he lived with someone who would take pity on her and tell her where he was. If he lived with his grandfather, which is what she suspected, then he wouldn't be there to pick up the note because he was in hospital. Nevertheless she took out her notebook and scribbled her name and telephone number, explained she had the dog and asked whoever got the note to phone her as soon as possible. Maybe they had a daily woman who would take pity on her.

She felt reluctant to leave. It was a beautiful summer afternoon and the garden had cast its spell over her. She sat for a while, enjoying the martins swooping over her head into the nests under the veranda roof and wondering about Norman Lester Sweetman – both who he was and where he was, and why on earth she'd allowed herself to get into this situation. It was true that business was virtually non-existent and this produced a certain vacuum into which anything could come, including a Chihuahua. But the first time she'd seen him she'd been amused – such a very large man with such a tiny dog – and Alan was right about her attraction to misfits. He'd charmed her, she thought eventually, that was why she'd taken Pip.

But what she didn't have the answer to, was why she'd allowed him to.

Professor Cummings was waiting for Sam when she arrived at the main entrance to the Natural History Museum at eleven o'clock that night. He seemed anxious, dropping his keys, as he pulled the main door to behind them. The main lights had been switched off and in the dark the dinosaurs loomed larger and more threatening.

'Have you discovered if anything is missing yet?' she asked.

He shook his head. 'I've checked about a third of the exhibits. I should be finished by the end of the week.'

'Are you never frightened to be here late at night?' Sam asked as they walked past the gaping jaws of the Tyrannosaurus rex.

'Frightened?' He stopped and frowned. 'Why would I be?'

Scientists, Sam thought, such rationalists.

'Did you never see *Jurassic Park*?'

'Weren't they computer generated? They're just old bones, aren't they?'

It would be exactly the kind of thing Peter would say. She laughed. 'I suppose so.'

Maybe he just didn't have an imagination. Lucky him, because sometimes having one could feel like a bit of a liability. You could use it to frighten yourself rigid.

In the Pitt Rivers he handed her a torch and showed her where the toilets were. 'This is my number if you need me. I'll be back here at six.'

As the sound of his footsteps faded away, Sam looked up at the open galleries and the wooden canoe and sail suspended from the arched roof, then down at the closely packed ebony-and-glass cabinets.

Only six and a half hours to go.

Her hand reached into her pocket, found nothing but a bit of loose change, and came out again. It was time to suppress the superstitious and encourage the rational. At least this was work; this was getting the business back on a sensible footing. This was 'A' for ability to pay and it was no time to get jumpy. She turned on the torch and, trying to avoid looking in the cabinets, she began walking slowly round the museum.

The hours dragged by. Three hours in Sam sat down on one of the chairs in the Pitt Rivers to have some food she'd brought with her. She opened her backpack and took out smoked salmon sandwiches, a Thermos of coffee and two double chocolate chip cookies she'd bought from Ben's Cookies in the covered market. She ate the sandwiches and then opened the Thermos. Peter was half-Italian and although this had never expressed itself in his emotional make-up, it did in his relationship with coffee. He had a plumbed-in, integrated, stainless steel, Miele coffee machine. The only reason Sam knew this somewhat technical description was because it was one Peter repeated with great pride every time he was asked about it. So when he had offered to make her coffee, she had had no hesitation in accepting. Sam peered into the Thermos and smiled. Thank God for coffee, thank God for Peter, praise be Lavazza. She poured some into the lid of the Thermos and inhaled. This should keep her going for the next few hours. The museum creaked and groaned around her. It's old, Sam said to herself, that's all – but it didn't stop her jumping each time she heard something. After the food she felt her spirits revive and although the last three hours dragged she didn't feel too bad when Professor Cummings turned up on the dot of six to relieve her.

He suggested they go to his office so he could hand back the contract.

Sam sat down and rubbed her face. 'Are there ethical issues involved with the display of some of the artefacts you have here?'

Cummings had offered her coffee and to Sam's horror she saw him spooning Nescafé into two cups. 'There are, especially when it comes to the treatment of human remains.'

'The shrunken heads?'

'Not just the heads. We have bones and skin and hair. It is important that all these items are treated with the utmost respect and dignity. We have been at the forefront of drawing up recommendations as to how such items should be exhibited and treated.'

'Do you ever get people objecting to their display?'

'Yes, that has happened. We removed some Maori tattooed heads and we sent back some bones when approached by Australian aboriginals.'

'How are these decisions made?'

'Like everything else in this university, by committee.'

'Do you have any requests outstanding?'

He placed the coffee in front of her and stirred sugar into his own. 'Why are you interested in that?'

'You're worried that someone may be stealing artefacts from the museum. I was just wondering if any particular items were presently under dispute.'

'I don't think that's at all relevant.'

'Do you never think that all the artefacts should go back to the tribes and the countries that they were taken from?'

'I can see the argument but it's a point of view I do not personally share. Many of the items we have are still in existence only because they were brought here – the wooden artefacts, for example, from Polynesia would not have survived if they hadn't been removed from a tropical climate. The museum is an enormous educational resource. Our aim is to teach about other cultures and create links and under-standing between different groups from all over the world.'

'But isn't it true that the bulk of the exhibits could be said to have been looted by Victorian explorers and put on display to prove the superiority of their own society?'

'It's true that the Victorian approach was very different to our own. But that is not an approach that we encourage today. Our aim is to give an insight into other cultures, traditions, it is not to pass judgement on them or to compare our own as being superior to theirs. At the moment, given the worries about global warming, the destruction of the rainforest et cetera, I would think there is more of a tendency to think that Western civilisation is in danger of destroy-ing our world, not enhancing it, and that there is much that we can learn from cultures who live so closely in tune with their natural environment. And incidentally the items were not always looted, as you suggest, they were often part of an exchange of gifts.'

There was a knock on the door and it opened. A man wearing a garish red-and-white short-sleeved shirt, jeans and open-toed sandals came in. He had black curly hair and black-rimmed glasses.

'Oh, I'm sorry, Marcus,' he said. 'I didn't know you were here.' He looked at Sam with open curiosity.

'This is … this is my god-daughter, Samantha. Justin Gittings.'

'Nice to meet you.'

'You're in early,' Cummings said.

'It's the heat. It's playing havoc with my sleeping patterns. Have you got the minutes of last month's meeting? I seem to have lost mine.'

Cummings shuffled through some papers and came up with a stapled sheaf of papers that he handed to the man who then left the room.

'What does he do?' Sam asked, when the door had closed behind him.

'Justin's one of our assistant curators. He's new and filled with enthusiasm.'

I must be getting old, she thought. He'd looked more like a stand-up comedian.

In Park Town Sam fed Pip and took him for a walk. The sky was still bleached of all colour and the humidity was building up in a way that suggested that the weather would have to break sooner rather than later. It was a relief to walk him early when not many people were about, as in that way she avoided the looks of pity mingled with disgust that Sam recognised as being very similar to her own reaction to Chihuahuas. In the past whenever she saw a person with a Chihuahua her immediate thought had been that there must be something psychologically disturbed about them. But the truth was the little dog was beginning to grow on her. Although small, he had a lot of attitude which manifested itself whenever he got near another dog, and the bigger the dog, the more violently he protested. Back home she went to sleep, waking from a disturbed dream to what she thought at first was a shrunken head on the pillow but on closer examination turned out to be Pip, blinking at her.

In the office late that afternoon Alan phoned. No one had seen Johnny yet. It was the calm before the storm. Maybe he'd be able to come down after all. He'd see how things panned out the following day. Sam dozed through the humid afternoon, took Pip for walks and waited for the phone to ring. It didn't. By six o'clock she'd resorted to Bird and beer again, and another long night at the museum beckoned.

She was just about to set off for Park Town when there was a knock on the door. She turned off the music, hid the bottle of beer and remnants of a take-away from the Jamaican Eating House, tucked in her shirt and wiped a napkin across her mouth.

'Come in,' she said.

The woman who came through the door was tall with blonde hair done up in a French pleat at the back of her head. More Kensington than Cowley Road, she was wearing red, open-toed sandals several inches high and a grey linen trouser-suit; a red clutch bag was tucked under her arm. She took off her dark glasses and surveyed the office, her gaze finally coming to rest on Sam.

For a brief uncomfortable moment Sam saw the office through the woman's eyes. Hastily whitewashed-over woodchip wallpaper, blue industrial carpeting and a clapped-out rattling fan would not be this woman's idea of an effective way to present your business. Alan was right. Who was she trying to kid that this was an OK place to see clients?

'Can I help you?'

'I was looking for Norman Sweetman.'

'Oh right. Well, that makes two of us.'

'You don't know where he is?'

'I last saw him two days ago when he deposited a dog with me. He told me he'd be back for him the following day but didn't turn up. What makes you think I'd know where he is?'

'I asked at the bookies' and they said you'd been asking after Norman. I thought you might have found him.'

She had a slight accent; American was Sam's best guess.

'I haven't I'm afraid.'

'If the dog is a nuisance, I would be willing to take him off your hands.'

Sam glanced down at Pip who was curled up behind the desk. 'He's no nuisance.'

'It would be no trouble.'

The woman had walked over to the window which looked down into the back gardens. 'Where is he now?'

'He's here,' Sam replied, pointing at the floor.

'I could take him now?'

Like hell you will, Sam thought.

'And who exactly are you?' Sam asked.

'Look, actually the dog's mine. Norman said he would look after him for me. Now I am here to take him back.'

Sam frowned. The woman must be lying because Pip hadn't responded in any way to her.

'Norman didn't say anything about you picking him up. He gave me enough food for about a week. He can't have been expecting you to do that.'

'I've been abroad. I came back unexpectedly early. Now I want my dog.'

Pip was still curled up nose to tail. This was going to be fun. Sam picked him up and sat him on her desk. He yawned.

'Try taking him,' she suggested.

As the woman moved towards the desk he silently bared his gums. She stopped and twiddled with one of her gold hoop earrings then moved to pick him up. This time he snapped and started to bark and she jerked her hand away.

'He doesn't seem that keen to go with you. Perhaps it would be best if we wait until Norman comes back or alternatively you could get him on the phone and he could explain to me who you are and why I should give Pip to you.'

'You refuse to give him to me?'

Sam held her hands away from the side of her body, palm outwards. 'I don't know why you want him but the dog obviously isn't yours and I'm not doing anything. He's refusing to give himself up.'

The woman sniffed, looked at Pip and then Sam, and flounced from the room. Her perfume remained, mingling with the smells of the take-away.

'Who the hell was that?' Sam muttered. 'Cruella de Vil?'

She went to the window and looking down saw her getting into a black Saab convertible parked outside the bookies'. She scribbled down the registration number as it drove away. Why had the woman lied about the dog being hers and, more to the point, what did she really want with Norman?

'We didn't like her, did we?' Sam said, scratching Pip behind an ear. 'We didn't like her one bit. Anyway, I couldn't hand you over to her – you'd clash with her nail varnish.'

CHAPTER FIVE

Norman Lester Sweetman lifted the latch of the gate which opened on to the path that ran along the back of the garden of the house in Harberton Mead. It was two o'clock in the morning but it was still humid and rumbles of thunder could be heard off in the distance. The house was in darkness and no light spilled from the windows of neighbouring houses; the screech of the little owls that lived in the copse of firs at the back of the house tore suddenly at the silence. The noise didn't alarm Norman for the simple reason that almost every night of his life he had heard it. As a boy he'd perched on the window-sill of his bedroom trying to catch sight of them but had never managed it. Owls were experts at not being seen. Norman envied them; when you were as large as he was, an ability to evade observation seemed a highly desirable skill. He gently pushed open the gate and moved forwards as quietly as he could. Night-spun cobwebs, attached on his left to a bushy privet hedge and on his right to a line of loganberry plants, stretched against his face and he clawed them away. He stopped and listened. His fingers searched the loganberry plants; the succulent berries were a soothing sweetness in his mouth. A car's engine purred in the distance then came closer. He licked his sticky fingers. Headlights broke through the hedge at the bottom of the garden, illuminating the waxy green leaves of the laurel before the car turned into the drive of the house on the opposite side of the road. He waited for the bang of the car door and for the lights to go on in the house before continuing.

Inside his own house he closed the front door and leaned against it, listening. He had been born here and had never lived anywhere else.

He knew every creak and groan, every loose floorboard. Undoubtedly he'd been responsible for loosening a few himself.

On the wall to his left there was the mark where, as a small boy, he'd smeared red wax from an Edam cheese. He remembered softening it and softening it in the palm of his hand until it was as yielding as putty. It had been the morning of his parents' funeral. He remembered his grandfather shouting at him, then taking him in his arms, the smell of cigars on his grandfather's black velvet jacket and the rasp of the stubble on his cheek for ever associated in his mind with love and loss.

It had taken them a while to get used to each other. At first his grandfather had been persuaded that the best thing would be to send him away to school. Much later Norman realised that he had done it for the best of motives, at a loss what to do with a six-year-old boy and thinking that he needed the company of his contemporaries, but at the time all Norman had wanted was his grandfather. He had run away repeatedly until finally his grandfather had asked him what he wanted and Norman had told him that he wanted to stay in the house with him. That was over thirty years ago and it was more or less what he had done ever since. And now the tables were turned; now it was a question of whether his grandfather, his health failing, could remain in this house. It was up to him to make sure that he could. He had to. It was repayment; it was the least that love required. It was what had got him into this whole hell of trouble.

He opened the cupboard under the stairs and took out an old canvas and leather holdall that had once held a set of bowls. He couldn't stay here any more: it was the first place they'd look for him. Maybe they'd been here already. His grandfather was safe in hospital for the time being, so there was no worry that he would be hassled, and Pip was safe with Sam Falconer. He needed to buy himself a bit of time.

He'd done an internet search on her and discovered her record – four times world judo champion and five times European champion. He thought he'd remembered her from features in the local papers at the time she was competing. He'd spun her a tale about the dog, but he didn't think she'd take it out on Pip. With her record she should have no trouble looking after a small dog. Pip would be much safer with her than with him.

His bedroom was at the top of the stairs. He opened drawers and grabbed socks, pants, shirts and a pair of trousers. In the bathroom he put a toothbrush, toothpaste, and shaving things in a wash-bag. From his grandfather's bedroom he picked up a dented silver-backed hairbrush his grandfather used on the thin shreds of hair remaining on his head. He didn't know how long this would last in a hospital, but his grandfather had requested it. He ran a finger through the soft bristles, imagined doing this after his grandfather had died, thought, 'What will I do without him? What will become of me?' Then dropped it in his bag and hurried downstairs. Now there were just the things he needed from the study.

He found the books he was looking for quickly – P.G. Wodehouse, not the old Herbert Jenkins hardbacks, which his grandfather could no longer manage because of the arthritis in his wrists but the lighter, orange-spined Penguins. His grandfather always read Wodehouse when he was in hospital. It was a safe, charmed world to escape into, far removed from the maggots nibbling at the gangrenous mess of his ulcers and the nagging worry that, however fat the maggots became, in the end he would be faced with no other option but a second amputation and all that implied.

In an old wooden filing cabinet he found the photo he needed. He hadn't looked at this for a long time. Not since the day his parents died. Despite the humidity he shivered suddenly. God, it was a shock but he was going to have to get over the fear, he was going to have to get used to looking at this very hard, very carefully. Now was not the time to look away. This was the face that had killed them. The anniversary was approaching. A clap of thunder, closer now, made him jump. He put the photo in his bag and then raised his hand and gently touched his own face as if unsure whether it was still there or not. Another car. He froze, hoping that, like the last one, it would turn into a neighbour's drive or continue past his own but lights slid over the study window, doors slammed and then there were footsteps on the gravel and the murmur of conversation outside. Norman moved quickly into the hall and from there into the living-room. Doors in there gave on to the veranda. Quietly he let himself out of the house. As he reached the gate at the top of the garden he heard the noise of breaking glass. He knew what they were looking for and he knew they wouldn't find it. The only question now was whether he could turn the present situation to his advantage. How much time would he need? How long would he need to keep out of their way? A week, at least? Perhaps a little more. Then there would be an opportunity. He felt the first heavy drops of rain land on his head.

Thank God, at long last the weather was breaking.

Sam, spending her second night at the museum, heard the rain falling on the roof of the Pitt Rivers and felt the same sense of relief as Norman. This night had followed pretty much the same course as the first; three hours in, she sat down and had her sandwiches and coffee. Then for the first time she decided to explore the upper galleries. All she had to do was duck under some yellow tape and watch where she put her feet. It was as she reached the highest gallery, positioned just under the roof, that the storm broke. For half an hour the rain beat down and the thunder boomed overhead. Every now and again the lightning shivered against the semi-circular window just under the arch of the roof. Sam counted the gaps between the lightning and thunder and walked slowly between the display cabinets, hoping that Pip was all right, trying not to look at her watch every five minutes, and trying not to jump when the thunder cracked overhead.

Thunderstorms frightened her. She knew they weren't all noise and no action. Thunderstorms could destroy things. When she was a child and had been living in St Cuthbert's there'd been a vicious storm. She'd been watching it from the spare room, looking into the garden, at the bottom of which was the eighteenth-century library with a stone eagle, the symbol of the college, on top of it. Two forks of lightning had seared through the driving rain on either side of the garden wall, and then there had been a huge crash of thunder and the sky over the library had lit up as if illuminated by flashlights. The stone eagle had exploded into a thousand fragments and Sam, horrified and frightened in equal measure, had seen it make its last flight on to the pavement below. All that remained on the top of the library was its claw still firmly planted on the circular base.

She had burst into tears and run out of the room. Her bedroom window looked on to the library. The last thing she had seen at night before going to bed was the eagle watching over her. In her imaginings, after she had fallen asleep, the eagle stretched and fluttered its wings and then took flight, swooping around the spires and towers of Oxford, skimming the surface of the rivers and circling the tower of St Mary's. It returned before dawn and settled itself back into lapidary confinement. At a time in her life of great insecurity, without quite realising what she was doing, she had infused it with the powers of a guardian angel but now it lay shattered on the ground. Stone, she had thought, could never let you down; it was solid, unyielding and dependable, and entirely unlike human beings who could die and leave you. How wrong could she have been?

The following morning she had followed her mother across the rain-soaked grass to the place where the eagle had fallen and picked up a piece of its wing, small enough to fit into the palm of her hand. She still had it somewhere in her London flat. It had taken the college a couple of years to get the eagle replaced, this time with the precaution of a lightning conductor running down its back. Sam had seen the new one close up before it was winched up the scaffolding tower on to the top of the library. She'd run her fingers lightly over the proud head and curved beak. You're not the one who watched over me, she thought, he shattered, once and for all. In the end, the only reminder of what had happened was the indentation in the paving stone, the point of impact of the fall that on hot summer days Sam would gently rub with her bare foot and persuade herself that she could feel the soft ruffle of feathers, the rhythm and pulse of a beating heart. She realised with a shock that she knew all about investing inanimate objects with spiritual significance; she'd been doing it her whole life.

The whole of this museum was filled with such items.

Now, a crash of thunder directly overhead jolted her back to the present. She wondered if the ghosts of the dead haunted the museum seeking revenge for the removal of sacred artefacts, seeking revenge on the grave robbers.

How would she feel if someone had stolen that piece of eagle wing?

As if they had taken a piece of her soul? As if they'd stolen a most private sacred object?

What would she seek to do about it?

The relief that she felt as the last of the thunder rumbled into the distance was short-lived because it was then that she heard something – footsteps. She looked at her watch – four thirty – too early for Cummings. She turned off her torch and peered over the top of the displays down to the floor of the museum below. A shadow moved beneath the canoe. She blinked. It was dark down there; she could have been mistaken, especially given the images going through her mind. But then she saw it move again. As quietly as possible she made her way back down the stairs. At the foot of the staircase she paused, waiting for a noise to indicate where the person had gone. When none came she set off, moving softly between the cabinets, her heart thumping in her ears.

The man was standing with his back to her. The door to the cabinet was open and he was reaching inside. Sam turned on her torch, walked up behind him and shouted, 'What the hell do you think you're doing?'

He whipped round. A shrunken head swung from his white-gloved hand. Sam stared at the blackened skin, the stitched eyes and lips, the long black hair, and yelled. Her torch crashed to the ground and rolled across the floor. He also yelled but didn't drop the head. It was Justin Gittings; he was soaked to the skin and looked as terrified as Sam felt.

She bent down, scrabbled for her torch and straightened up.

'Jesus Christ,' Gittings said. 'You gave me the fright of my life.'

She shone the torch in his face. 'What on earth are you doing here?'

'What are *you* doing here?' he replied, holding his hand up to block the light from the torch.

The head still hung from his hand. 'Oh my God, couldn't you at least put that down?'

He replaced the head in the cabinet and closed the door and locked it. Then he peeled off the gloves. Water was dripping off him on to the stone floor.

'I got caught in the storm. I'm freezing,' he said. 'I'm going to go and dry off. Do you want to come up to my office and tell me what's going on?'

Sam followed him as he squelched up the stairs to a small office next to Professor Cummings's. He pulled off the short-sleeved cotton shirt he was wearing, towelled his hair and his body dry and put on a blue sweatshirt which was hanging across the back of his chair. Then he sat down, took off his sandals and put the ankle of his left foot on his right knee and began to dry his feet.

Sam hovered in the doorway watching him. 'What were you doing?'

'Well, I've been doing some work on the shrunken heads and after I went home something kept nagging away at me. I couldn't sleep and thought I'd come in and check them again.'

'In the middle of the night?'

He shrugged. 'I knew I wouldn't be able to sleep until I'd done it. I'm not a terribly good sleeper anyway.'

'And?'

'The one I was holding. I'm sure it's a fake. I'll need to check it against photos, but I'm sure one of the heads has been stolen. And what were you doing?'

'Well, I'm not Professor Cummings's god-daughter.'

'That did seem a little unlikely. If he ever presented himself at a font denouncing evil I think there'd be a crackle in the air and the strong smell of sulphur.'

Sam laughed. 'I'm a private investigator. He wanted me to do a bit of night security for a week or so. He was worried after the door was found open.'

'What door?'

'The fire exit. He was worried that someone might be stealing from the museum.'

'He didn't say anything to me about it.'

'He didn't want anyone to know what I was doing.'

He frowned. 'I see ... but he had you working nights?'

'Yes.'

'Curiouser and curiouser,' he muttered.

'What makes you think that the head is a fake?'

'The stitching in the lips is all wrong. It's too neat.'

'How's it done?'

'The stitching?'

'No, the whole thing.'

'The skin is peeled off the skull and the skull and brains are thrown away.'

'So the head isn't actually shrunk?'

'No, if you think about it, it couldn't be because you can't shrink bone.'

'Oh,' Sam said. 'That's disappointing.'

'Then they boil the skin to shrink it, and then stuff the face with sand and stones to put the shape back into it, and then sew up the lips and eyes and the split at the back of the head, and there you are.'

'So neat stitching wasn't their forte?'

'Neat stitching is often a sign of a fake.'

'So what's it made of?'

'Fakes are shrunken heads, it's just that they are heads which have been shrunk to sell into a Western market. They are not original ones, which were the heads of people who had been defeated in battle.'

'So fake heads are whose heads then?'

'Heads of the dead shrunk for commercial reasons.'

'God ...'

'It's a complicated business. If you create a market, people will seek to fulfil its demands.'

'Why did they do it?'

'What – sell them?'

'No, why did they shrink them in the first place?'

'It was part of the culture of the Shuar, Achuar, Huambisa and Aguaruna tribes in the Upper Amazon region between Ecuador and Peru. Men from these tribes were encouraged to take enemy heads as a sign of their courage. But then also the making of a shrunken head was part of a ritual by which the spirit of the victim was pacified and the victim was made part of the killer's group. They believed that there is soul matter concentrated in the head so taking the head increases the totality of soul matter in your tribe and lessens the power of the enemy. There are parallels with modern head-hunting. You could say that if the new god in our society is money and companies are the tribes that make up capitalist society then when one company goes after another's employee it is in order to increase its profitability, its soul matter if you like.'

That all sounded a bit far-fetched to Sam. 'So you think the one in there is one of these fakes?'

'I'm sure it's not the original. What it is exactly I'm not sure.'

'But why go to all the trouble of doing that?'

'If we don't think anything's been stolen there's no crime to report, is there? They can cover their tracks. If the head isn't reported as stolen it's easier to sell. Once it's known, whoever buys it will be in receipt of stolen goods.'

'Is the head a disputed item?'

'Disputed – what do you mean?'

'Cummings told me about the aboriginal bones.'

'Oh, I see. No, not as far as I know. There are some Native American artefacts I believe that the Canadians are enquiring about but nothing else at the moment. Any enquiries are given very careful consideration.'

'Isn't that what the British Museum says every time the Greeks ask for the Elgin Marbles back?'

He smiled. 'I think they just say no.'

'What are you going to do?'

'I'll talk to Cummings and I presume he'll want to go to the police.'

Sam waited until Cummings came in and she and Gittings explained what had happened. Cummings was standing behind his desk with Gittings standing opposite him and Sam was leaning against a filing cabinet.

'I presume we should go to the police,' Gittings said.

Cummings's face was white and drawn, a muscle twitched in his jaw. When he spoke he spat the words out like broken teeth.

'What I don't understand is why you've been creeping around behind my back.'

Sam glanced at Gittings. A second storm was about to break. Gittings had opened his mouth to respond but Cummings was too quick for him.

'You come down here to the museum in the middle of the night and my security people find you with the door to one of the cabinets open and one of the artefacts in your hands. What were you going to do with it? Sell it on eBay? What exactly am I supposed to think, Justin?'

Gittings was blushing furiously. 'Hold on, if we're going to talk about creeping about, what are you doing hiring private security for the museum without telling any of your staff?'

'Well, if I'd told them we wouldn't have caught you red-handed, would we?'

'Let me get this straight. Are you seriously accusing me of stealing?'

Cummings looked down at his desk and began moving pieces of paper around. He was blinking rapidly, the muscle still dancing in his jaw. He cleared his throat and took a breath. A sea change was coming. In this case the calm after the storm.

'Are you going to go to the police?' Gittings' voice was steely.

'We need to be absolutely certain before we go down that route. Once we have brought the police in things will go out of our control and then of course there is the bad publicity to consider.'

'I am absolutely certain. One of the heads in the cabinet is a fake. It is my area of expertise, Marcus, and the most cursory of examinations will confirm it.'

'Right. Yes, of course, if you are certain. You're right. There's no other course. I'm sorry, Justin, I have been under some pressure of a personal nature. Perhaps if you could show me the head in question and then we can go from there.'

Sam followed the two men out of the office. 'Do you still want me working here at night?' she asked Cummings.

'Yes, yes, of course, more than ever if things have been stolen …'

'My colleague, Alan, will be here tonight. I'll update him on what's been going on.'

'Yes, that'll be fine.'

After giving a statement to the police Sam walked back to Park Town puzzling over the night's events. Who would want to steal shrunken heads? Who would go to all that trouble to replace one with a fake? There were surely items in the museum worth much more than the head. Why, when you had a whole museum to steal from, would you choose that? Unless, that is, the heads were just the tip of the iceberg. There was also the fact that Cummings, while being all too willing to accuse Gittings of the theft, had also seemed extremely reluctant to bring in the police. Worries about bad publicity? Maybe. But surely he should be more concerned with finding out the extent of the thefts and who was involved? And what exactly were the personal problems he had referred to?

CHAPTER SIX

Miles Archer took off his glasses, carefully prodded his nose and winced. The swelling was going down but it was still tender to the touch. He was sitting in his favourite seat in the Bodleian and had spent the morning preparing a series of lectures he was due to present next term. The sun had moved round and was striking him on the back of the head. He yawned. It was time for lunch. He left his papers where they were, picked his jacket off the back of his chair and walked out into the Schools Quadrangle.

The midday heat was bouncing off the four walls. It was like an oven, the storm of the previous night having done little to relieve the humidity. For a moment he hesitated, squinting up at where a statue of James I sat on his stone throne, and considered his lunch options: a sandwich in the Botanical Gardens, a pint at the White Horse or a fry-up in George's in the covered market. If he had the pint he wouldn't get much work done, but on the other hand it was the kind of day when sitting in the sun with a pint in your hand seemed the best possible use of your time ... Seeing Neil Pennell, a much-loathed colleague, approaching from the direction of the Sheldonian spurred him into action; he turned sharply on his heels, bolted through the gate into Radcliffe Square, and set off for the covered market.

Although he'd been enjoying writing the lectures the thought of delivering them horrified him. His hands shook and often his voice. He was too shy to be a natural lecturer and did not really have the knack of presenting his ideas in a sufficiently accessible or entertaining manner to enable his students to take much from them. As a consequence the lectures were not particularly well attended.

The most popular lecturers were the extroverts and show-offs, the charismatics and wits who liked an audience and craved adulation. Pennell was one of those. He was, Miles thought, everything he was not, the kind of man who was easy with the young, who could have a drink and a laugh with his students and was a good communicator.

When Pennell died, Miles thought miserably, his obituaries would declare he had been a man of influence, that he had been much loved, an inspiration to his students. What they would not mention was his drink problem and a tendency to get involved with his female students. That would all be tactfully covered over by the use of the word colourful. Miles doubted anyone would bother to write one for him.

He heard Pennell shouting behind him and increased his speed.

The university was insisting that the undergraduates be forced to sign a contract in which they agreed to attend lectures and tutorials. Miles thought that this might swell the attendance of his lectures a bit but personally found the whole idea loathsome. It was a stupid and altogether un-Oxford-like proposal. The great dons of the past – the Bowras, the Jowetts – they would have had none of it. Imagine asking a young Trevor-Roper to sign such a thing. There would have been no end to the vituperation. Treating undergraduates like children was like poking a sharp stick into a . . .

'Miles, for God's sake, didn't you hear me?' A hand landed on his arm as he was about to cross the Turl and he was forced to stop and acknowledge his pursuer.

Neil Pennell stood puffing at his side. Pennell had been given some enormous payout by a television company to write and appear in a history series. The first part had aired to rave reviews last autumn and now he was in the process of finishing it off. Today, for obvious reasons, he wasn't wearing the leather coat he usually sported on television, just a pair of ball-breaking black jeans and a white cotton shirt with one button too many undone. Miles felt nausea stir in his stomach but unfortunately it wasn't the sight of his colleague's portly torso that did it, it was envy – an altogether trickier proposition.

Pennell was one of a small number of his colleagues left in Oxford that summer and he seemed to be bumping into him every other day and every time he did, all he did was complain about how difficult it was to dumb down for television. Miles didn't believe him. He suspected Pennell had taken to dumbing down with all the reluctance a vulture feels for carrion.

'Have you heard about the head?'

'Jenkins?'

'Not *that* head. One of the shrunken heads has been stolen from the Pitt Rivers.'

'What are you talking about?'

'I bumped into Gittings, one of the assistant curators, in Blackwell's ... know his sister a bit. He told me. The police have been called in. You should go and tell them what happened, shouldn't you?'

'Sorry?'

'The other day when you were pissed out of your brains I helped you up to your rooms.'

'Did you?' Miles had no recollection of that at all.

'Come on, Miles. I found you slumped against the college gates covered in blood and I gave you a hand. You were babbling on about heads and Mary Astor and something you had in the fridge.'

Miles blushed the sort of beetroot colour that only truly shy people can muster when they are very embarrassed.

'Don't you remember?'

Miles stared at his shoes and shook his head.

'God, you must have been pissed. Well, I thought it was just a sort of drunken ramble but then I spoke to Gittings and I wondered if something had actually happened to you unless of course you were the one who stole it.' He laughed and hit Miles on the arm with the rolled-up newspaper he was holding in his hand. It hurt but there was no way Miles was going to rub it.

'I bumped into someone and then when I picked myself up the head was on the pavement.'

'Well, presumably that was the thief. Did you get a good look at him?'

Miles shook his head miserably. 'I was blind drunk, blind being the operative word. There was blood pouring down my face ...'

'You should probably go to the police, don't you think?'

Miles sighed. He didn't want the hassle or the humiliation of confessing to the state he'd been in.

'Why don't you go and talk to Peter's daughter, Sam? She's just opened an office on the Cowley Road. There's an ad for it in the *Mail*. Here you can have this. I've finished with it. If you don't want to go to the police, why don't you tell her? She's advising them on security apparently.'

'I suppose I could.'

'Come on, I'll buy you a drink. You look like you could do with one.'

'No, I ...'

But it was too late. Pennell had wrapped a bear-like arm around him and was marching him along the Turl towards the Broad. Resistance was futile. Much to his annoyance, Miles experienced something of the warm glow a bullied child might feel, who has just been taken up by the most popular boy in the class.

'I wanted to ask a favour of you as it happens. You know this television thing that I'm involved with?'

Miles nodded.

'I start filming in October and the thing is I want to lose a bit of weight. You've no idea how fat you are until you see yourself on television. God it was a shock. Vanity's got the better of me, old man. Well, I was thinking a bit of squash might do the trick. You play, don't you? Would you give me a couple of games?'

Miles felt a smile spread across his face. He had a low centre of gravity and quick reflexes. He played regularly throughout the year. Anxiety and a tricky digestive system kept him light on his feet. 'I'd be delighted.'

'Good man.' Pennell slapped him on the back as they crossed the threshold of the White Horse. 'Now I want to pick your brains on medieval history. Never a strong point of mine to be honest; anything pre-Tudor is a bit of a blank. Do you think you could give me a sort of broad brushstroke of the main issues and developments I should be considering? Sort of point me in the right direction?'

He was lying of course, seeking to flatter him. 'I presume you're not going to talk without notes to the camera for half an hour then?'

He laughed. 'I'm no AJP, I can tell you. These days words are not enough.'

'Haven't they given you research assistants?'

'God, no, they're frightfully mean about all that. They'd give me a taxi to John O'Groats but they actually expect me to do all the work myself.'

'Appalling,' Miles said.

As Miles watched Pennell heading for the bar, a cloud of misery descended over him. Pennell was served almost immediately even though the bar was crowded. It would have taken Miles about ten minutes to get the staff to pay him any attention.

Self-loathing mixed with feelings of envy and inadequacy was an uncomfortable brew; the pint couldn't come soon enough.

'I got your address from the *Oxford Mail*.'

Sam looked at Miles Archer slumped in the chair on the other side of her desk. He was a neat, dapper man with short grey hair and thick glasses, attractive in a neurotic kind of way. She quickly ran through everything she knew about him: one of her father's more conversationally challenged colleagues, a medieval historian, an expert in courtly love and hopelessly in love with Mary Astor the St Cuthbert's librarian. Once a year he got very drunk and fell asleep on the doorstep of her flat in Holywell. There were rumours of a great work he'd been writing for the last fifteen years. Supposedly he kept it in the fridge but no one had ever seen it and if he was asked about it he turned bright red and looked as if he was going to have an apoplectic fit. He was liked by his colleagues but known to be highly strung. All attempts to get him together with Mary Astor had foundered on his complete inability to open his mouth in her presence and talk to her.

Sam had a particular affection for him because of something that had happened shortly after Miles had joined the college. She had been walking along one side of the front quad with her mother and Miles was walking towards them. He had suddenly ducked into a doorway and disappeared. They had walked past but Sam had looked back over her shoulder and seen him furtively stick his head out, check they'd gone, and then continue on his way. Sam was familiar with that feeling. There had been times in her life when seeing her mother approaching had made her want to duck into doorways as well.

She smelled alcohol. Well, at least that might loosen his tongue.

'How nice to see you, Miles,' she said.

He was tapping his knee with a rolled-up paper. At least he wouldn't be affected by the state of the office. She could have painted the walls purple with yellow and orange spots and he wouldn't have turned a hair.

'What can I do for you?'

'I was very, very drunk. I didn't think I could possibly have seen it. I thought it was some sort of hallucination. I mean you don't expect to see a shrunken head lying about on the streets of Oxford in August. Well, in any month ...'

'Shrunken head?'

'Yes.'

'Could you perhaps start at the beginning?'

'It was Hardwick's fault.'

'Hardwick?'

'Hardwick, you know, the Senior Common Room butler.'

'Oh, that Hardwick.'

'We were celebrating my new appointment in the traditional manner. I have recently taken charge of the wine cellar.'

'Ah, congratulations.'

'Hardwick had shown me round the cellars and to welcome me to my new position he suggested we open a bottle of claret to see if it was fit for the forthcoming term. I thought possibly it was a little young and he thought it was just right. So when we came to the end of it he suggested that perhaps since we were not quite in agreement we might try another.'

Sam laughed.

'So, I was feeling rather ... pleased with myself and decided to take a walk to clear my head and it was then that it happened. I crashed into someone in Holywell and when I got to my feet it was lying there.'

'The head?'

'Yes.'

'On the pavement?'

'I was very drunk and shocked. He grabbed it and bolted.'

'Definitely a he?'

He frowned and looked down at Pip who was sniffing his shoes. 'I think so.'

'When was this?'

'About a week ago.'

'What made you come to me now?'

'Pennell heard that one of the heads had been stolen; he brought it to my attention. He came across me later that evening in a somewhat ... a state of disarray and I obviously said something about the head which in the morning I forgot I'd said. To be honest before Pennell spoke to me I thought I'd imagined it. I was so drunk when I woke up it was all a bit of a blur. What do you think I should do?'

'You should go to the police.'

'I was blind drunk. They won't believe me. It's not as if I can give a description of the person I saw.'

'They will believe you because it fits with things that have happened.'

'They'll blame me for not coming forward sooner. Can't *you* tell them?'

'I can but I'm afraid they will almost certainly want to speak to you.'

Miles rubbed his face. 'I drank too much in the pub with Pennell at lunch. Have you watched him on television?'

'I have.'

'What do you think?'

Sam paused. She didn't deliberately want to cause Miles pain but ...

'You think he's good, don't you?'

'Yes, I think he's very good. He's humorous, uses colloquial English to good effect and gets to the heart of the story.'

'Don't you think he looks fat?'

Sam smiled. 'Immensely.'

'He's asked me to play squash with him and I'm going to beat the living daylights out of him. I find it impossible to like a man who is so intolerably pleased with himself. Do you know what he said? He said he was going to have to ingratiate himself with his colleagues because he had done a terrible thing in Oxford terms; he had become a success.'

Sam laughed. 'Did he really say that?'

Miles nodded miserably. 'I hate him. I can't help myself. As if being in Oxford in the dog days of August isn't enough to destroy the will of the most optimistic of men. Now I have Pennell to contend with. Wherever I go there he is waiting to pounce.'

'Dog days?' Sam said.

'A time in which malignant influences prevail,' Miles said. 'It has to do with the rising of the dog-star, Sirius, which coincides with the hottest and most unwholesome part of the year.'

'Good,' Sam said, thinking she might lob that bit of information at Reg at their next session to justify her opinions about August.

Miles was rubbing his face. 'I drank too much. Now I'll get no work done this afternoon. Could you perhaps tell the police what happened to me and then if they want me they can come and talk to me?'

'All right,' Sam said. 'I don't mind doing that but they'll probably want to talk to you themselves.' She pulled a pad of paper towards her. 'Let's go through the details again.'

Sam phoned the police, told them what Archer had told her and that afternoon DC Thomas paid her a visit. She was tall and solidly built with shoulder-length curly auburn hair pulled back in a pony-tail. She had pale skin and pale blue eyes. She sat with her notebook open on her knee.

'I'm sorry,' Sam said, 'but I don't think there's really much more I can tell you than I did on the phone. I've already given a statement about doing night security at the Pitt Rivers. You know about Archer. You can get hold of him at St Cuthbert's. Be gentle with him though – he's highly strung.'

'Just a few follow-up questions. I won't take up much of your time.'

Sam sighed. Why was it the police always wanted you to repeat everything ten times over?

'When did you start working at the Pitt Rivers?'

'I've done two nights there.'

'And nothing happened until the night when you came across Justin Gittings?'

Sam rubbed her eyes. The late nights had been making her brain feel muddy. She wanted food and sleep at strange hours and never really felt rested. The stratagem she'd put in place with Reg before he'd gone on holiday had not stood up to her working nights. 'That's right.'

'And that was on Thursday?'

'Yes.'

'Could you go through what happened on that night?'

Sam sighed. 'I was in the upper galleries when I heard a noise down below on the floor of the museum. I went downstairs and found Justin Gittings standing in front of the cabinet for the treatment of the dead holding a shrunken head in his hands. I asked him what he was doing and he told me. I presume he's told you as well.'

'When you challenged him how did he react?'

'Well, he was shocked. The museum has a certain atmosphere at night and there'd just been a big thunderstorm. I'd crept up behind him and shone a torch in his face.'

'How long had you been in the upper galleries when you heard the noise?'

Sam reached for a small bottle of water on her desk and drained it.

'I had some food about three and then went up there after that. So it was probably about four. The storm started when I was up there. When I heard the footsteps I looked at my watch and it was four thirty so I was up there for about half an hour, three-quarters of an hour at the most, I suppose.'

'And the storm was going on all that time?'

'Yes.'

'Was it very loud?'

'Yes, it was. I was directly under the roof and the rain was beating down and the thunder was crashing around.'

'So Justin Gittings could have been down on the floor of the museum for half an hour before you heard him?'

'Yes, he could. I heard him as the storm was dying down. He was soaked through though, so he must have been caught in the storm.'

'Why do you think he didn't wait until morning?'

'He said that he couldn't sleep because something about the shrunken heads had been worrying him and he decided to come in and check them. I thought that was quite a plausible explanation. No one's sleeping at the moment because of the heat. Also sometimes when things are nagging away at you, you know you'll be better off getting up and doing something about it.'

'You're still doing nights there?'

Sam nodded. 'For as long as they want me.'

Thomas took a last look at her notebook and snapped it shut.

Sam sat back in her chair and stretched. 'Is Phil Howard around at the moment?' Phil was her ex-boyfriend and a DS in the Thames Valley police force.

Thomas frowned. 'No, I think he's taken some leave to prepare for his inspector exams.'

'When are they?'

'At the end of the week. You'll let us know if anything else occurs to you or if anything else happens?'

'Yes.'

The policewoman got up and put her notebook in her bag. 'Incidentally the rumour is Phil's got a new girlfriend so maybe it's not just revision he's paying some attention to.'

'That's a relief. The last one was nothing but trouble.'

DC Thomas seemed about to say something then changed her mind, smiled and left the office.

After she'd gone, Sam went and got another bottle of water from the fridge. She'd been hoping to run the registration plate of Cruella de Vil's car past Phil but she obviously wouldn't be able to do that now. A new girlfriend? Well, good for him and good for DC Thomas for not so subtly warning her off. Phil had had some fairly forthright things to say about Rick's likely involvement in Mark's kidnap. It was Rick's cousin Kieran who had taken Mark and because of that Sam hadn't spoken to Phil much recently. But Alan would probably be able to help with the registration number. He had contacts from his time in the Met.

She looked at her watch; Alan was due in about an hour's time. He was going to do a night for her while she went back to London. She had a session with Reg and she'd leave Pip with Peter. She folded her arms on her desk, put her head down on them and was soon fast asleep.

She woke to the noise of Pip barking. She raised her head from her arms and looked ahead of her. The door was open and Pip had Alan pinned to the wall on the landing outside the office. She couldn't help laughing. Alan was over six foot tall and Pip was nine inches high.

'Pip, come here,' she said, and the dog abandoned his bear baiting and trotted to her side.

'What the fuck is that?' Alan said, cautiously entering the room. He was wearing olive-green shorts that stopped at his knees and a tight black T-shirt which emphasised his powerful physique.

Sam yawned, a real jaw-splitter, and rubbed her face. She picked Pip up and put him in her lap. 'Meet Pip.'

'So where's the fat man?'

'A very good question.'

'Honestly, I leave you for a couple of days and you end up with a Chihuahua.'

'I'm looking after him for a bit.'

'You're looking after him for a bit,' Alan repeated and waited. When Sam offered no further information he added. 'I don't like Chihuahuas – they're the lap-dogs of disturbed celebrities.'

'I don't like them either but he's beginning to grow on me.'

'Why?'

'He tried to attack a Dobermann in the park.'

Alan laughed. 'I wonder who he reminds you of?'

'What do you mean?'

'He's small and f . . .'

'Alan, I'm warning you. Don't say that word.'

'What word is that?'

'You know perfectly well the word I mean. I told you I'd fire you if you used it.'

'We're partners now so you can't. Do you mean . . .'

Sam put her hands over her ears and began to hum loudly.

'FEISTY?' Alan shouted.

'Bastard.'

'I wasn't using it to describe you anyway.'

'Yes you were, in a roundabout way.'

He smiled. 'So why have you got him?'

'Norman asked me to look after him for a few days.'

'Norman?'

'Don't start, Alan.'

'I say the name Norman perfectly innocently and you say, "Don't start, Alan." Who's the one doing the starting? Anyway how come you didn't mention him on the phone?'

'He hardly deserved one.'

'Why do I have the impression you're not telling me the whole story?'

'Because you're naturally suspicious, that's why.'

Sam found the piece of paper with the registration number of the car and handed it to Alan. 'Could you check this out for me?'

'Is this for a case?'

Sam blew out her cheeks. 'Not exactly, no.'

He put the piece of paper in his pocket.

Alan took a beer out of the fridge and popped the cap, drank, then leaned against the wall, looking out of the window. Sam eyed him, assessing his mood. Not good, was her conclusion.

'So how are things?' she asked.

Alan turned towards her and shrugged. 'Things are fucked.'

'Has anyone seen Johnny yet?'

'You know Mum's in the care home at Putney Bridge. Well, apparently he paid her a visit and came out with a whole load of bollocks about how if it had been up to him, he'd never have put her in a home. Well, if he was so bothered about that, he should have done something other than sitting on his arse in prison for the last fifteen years.'

'Are your brothers going to give him a job?'

'What – driving cabs or working behind a bar? I can't see Johnny doing anything that doesn't result in lots of money for the minimum of work.'

'How's the family coping?'

'Nothing to cope with … yet … Oh fuck it, Sam, I wish they hadn't let him out. As soon as he's around everything becomes complicated. I get dragged back into the family. I can't help it.'

'Maybe it won't be as bad as you think?'

'He's Steph's dad.'

'Oh, I didn't know that.'

Alan had eight brothers and keeping track of which nephews and nieces went with which brothers and sisters-in-law had always been beyond Sam. What she did know, even though Alan would never have admitted it, was that Stephanie was his favourite.

'Does she know he's out?'

'Of course.'

'How does she feel about it?'

'I don't know. I haven't been able to get hold of her. It couldn't have happened at a worse time for her. She's just got a place to live and a new job and now her father's out, who she hasn't seen since she was five years old. I'm telling you if he fucks about with her, he's going to regret that he ever came out.'

Sam didn't say anything. Alan's background couldn't have been more different from her own. Sometimes she marvelled at how he'd survived his at all. She knew that certain rules applied, certain codes that were completely alien to her. When Alan slid back into the language of working-class machismo, she knew better than to argue or offer advice. She knew enough to wait until he was in a different mood. Otherwise everything she said would be met with the words 'you don't understand'. Everything would come down to class and they would end up staring at each other over an unbridgeable divide which most of the time they both did a pretty good job of ignoring.

She walked over to the window and pulled it shut, then put the lead on Pip. 'Come on. I'll tell you all about what's been happening in the museum while we walk over to Park Town. A shrunken head's been stolen.'

'I don't know, Sam. I leave you for a week and when I come back you're up to your ears in Chihuahuas and shrunken heads.'

'I might be small, Alan, but you'd still need a lot of Chihuahuas and shrunken heads to reach my ears.'

CHAPTER SEVEN

Madeleine Peyroux was singing 'I'm gonna to sit right down and write myself a letter', on the van stereo, as Sam turned off the Headington roundabout on to the A40 heading for London. She wondered what she was going to talk to Reg about. He'd been on holiday for four weeks and in a sense his holiday had also been her holiday and it had been a relief just not to go there.

In the final session they'd had before Reg went away he'd lent her a book of poems. Sam hadn't been that thrilled at the idea. She wasn't that keen on poetry but she'd taken it anyway. In particular he'd directed her to one called 'The Oracle of Bees' by Henry Hart. There was a quotation at the top of the poem by a Guy Bachelard. She didn't know who he was but it had stuck in her mind: 'What is the source of our first suffering? It lies in the fact we hesitate to speak. It was born in the moment we accumulated silent things within us.' Sam hadn't been able to get those words out of her head. She thought about the silent things she hadn't told Reg, the nightmares and flashbacks that had erupted after her first meeting with her father, flashbacks she hadn't yet talked to him about, flashbacks she hadn't revealed to anyone. She should talk to him about that, she really ought to. If therapy was for anything, surely it was for the articulation of those accumulated silent things. She tried to imagine telling him ... '*I was about four I think. I remember the blue of the swimming pool. He was teaching me to swim. He threw me in and I almost drowned. Then he pulled me on to his lap and ...*'

She sighed. The words seemed somehow unspeakable, even in the silence of her own mind. She tried imagining those words coming out of her mouth and couldn't. Even thinking about it made her feel physically sick. And to make matters worse in the recent flashbacks the face had been fading. She was no longer so certain it was her father, but if it wasn't, then ...

He had phoned intermittently to ask her about Mark. Last time he said he was going away for a while. Good riddance, Sam said out loud but she knew in her heart of hearts it wasn't as simple as that. Despite everything his absence tore at her and it always had.

As she came off the Hammersmith flyover, an hour later, she wound down the window and inhaled the welcome smell of polluted big city air. The high rises on either side of her were surrounded by a shimmer of heat haze and exhaust fumes, the traffic slowed. She breathed a big sigh of relief. She loved London – the speed, the diversity, the toughness, even the bloody-mindedness. As a child she'd loved reading the *Evening Standard*s that Peter brought back from his frequent trips to London. She'd looked in the back and imagined herself running away to the big city, renting a flat from the property pages, finding herself a job from the small ads. Living a different life completely, a life where she imagined you could do or be anything you wanted.

Big city anonymity is what she craved. Anonymity wasn't something she was ever going to get in Oxford. She couldn't walk down the High without bumping into someone who had taught her or was a friend of her parents or Mark. London on the other hand was a place where she could be whoever she wanted; she was no longer defined by her family. It was the age-old lure of the big city where the possibilities seemed endless, where you could recreate yourself and get lost in the crowd.

She had a love for London that she could never imagine having for Oxford. Somehow Oxford defied such sentiments. It was too aloof, too damn pleased with itself, too old and perhaps too wise for such sentimentality. To view Oxford in such terms would have been as inappropriate as sticking Harold Macmillan into an episode of *The Waltons*.

She parked in Foskett Road and in the short walk to the front door of the mansion block she lived in, prepared herself for what she might find in her flat. She'd tried to get hold of Stephanie to let her know she was going to be spending the night but had only managed to get Stephanie's voicemail and her own home answerphone. She hoped that Stephanie knew she was coming. It had seemed sensible to have the flat occupied and to have a bit of money coming in towards the rent.

She had handed over her cat, Frank Cooper, to the tender mercies of her next-door neighbour Edie. Usually Edie would have been off on her trips to Spain, tobacco smuggling, but she didn't go in August because it got too hot for her, so she'd been happy to take in Frank. Edie was a natural corrupter of feline souls, which was another way of saying that Frank would be as happy as a pig in shit.

Suddenly Sam had a strong desire to see her cat. She opened Edie's savage beast of a letterbox and whistled through the thick black bristles. Thin envelopes had to be folded at least twice to get pushed through them.

Edie opened the door wearing a black and white striped T-shirt and white cotton trousers.

'All right, babe? You back?'

'Just one night.'

Edie pinched the front of her shirt and flapped it back and forth against her breasts. 'Bloody hot. There's not a breath of wind for love nor money.'

'How's Frank?'

'Oh, he's no trouble.'

They walked into Edie's kitchen. She had a clock on the wall that chimed each hour with a different bird song.

'I'll get him for you.'

She went to an open window that looked out on to the back of the block, picked up a wicker basket and began to lower it. Sam walked over to see what she was doing. As the basket reached the ground she saw Frank Cooper saunter out from under a bush, stretch his front legs, then his back legs and then jump into the basket. Edie began to heave him heavenwards.

'How on earth did you get him to do that?' Sam asked.

'Prawns in the basket, babe. Gets him every time. I can't be doing with bringing him up and down the stairs. My knees can't stand it.'

The basket was now level with the window and Sam heaved it

inside. Frank Cooper, an immensely large marmalade cat, jumped out. Sam leaned down and scratched the top of his head.

'Hey, Frankie, do you remember me?'

Sam nodded.

He brushed his head against her shoe, strolled over to the buffet that Edie had laid out for him, grazed a little and then threw himself down in the shade of the kitchen table. Edie put on the kettle and Sam sat down at the table.

'You know the girl that's living in your flat?'

Sam nodded.

'She's brass, ain't she?'

Sam rolled that expression round her head, trying a bit of mental gymnastics to generate some cockney slang that made sense of it, but all she could come up with was brass monkeys which wasn't much help.

'She's what?'

'A prossie. You know, she's on the game.'

Sam laughed. 'I don't think so, Edie.'

'Well, she's bringing people back there all hours.'

'She's working at a pub so she's not keeping nine to five,' Sam said. 'But she's not a prostitute.'

Edie shook her head. 'She's brass. I'm telling you.'

Sam didn't bother to argue. Once Edie had made up her mind, even if she was stone bonking wrong, shifting her was like trying to prise a limpet from a rock. 'Maybe,' she said.

'No maybes about it, babe,' Edie said, plonking a cup of tea the colour of the Sahara down in front of her. 'I know brass when I see it.'

Half an hour later Sam let herself into her own flat. The first thing that hit her was the smell.

'Hello,' she said cautiously, but it was obvious no one was in.

She walked along the hallway to the kitchen and threw open the windows. The sink looked like it had been deposited from the set of *Withnail and I*. The bin was overflowing on to the floor. Sam took another bag from under the sink threw the top third of the rubbish into that bag, tied up both bags and took them downstairs.

Back in the flat she had a cursory wander through all the rooms; it was impressively messy. She hoped Stephanie hadn't got the message that she was coming because if she had and had done nothing to tidy up she was going to feel decidedly pissed off. Even Sam wouldn't have let the place get into this kind of state but then she wasn't twenty years old. She did a bit more desultory tidying up, gathered up dirty cups, emptied some ashtrays and dumped a load of newspapers in the orange recycling bag that she had shown to Stephanie but which was pristinely empty. Then she left a note saying she'd be back later, closed up the windows and made the short walk to her office in Putney. There was some paperwork that Alan wanted her to check through – a quibble from a client about the size of a bill, some cheques to sign, someone applying for work experience. It was part of a new regime that Alan had put in place to keep on top of things.

She waved at Greg in reception and took the lift to the fifth floor. Alan had made some changes to the office. It was tidier, naturally, but he'd also bought some new filing cabinets and office furniture and hung two prints on the wall – one a large black and white Doisneau print of Paris and the other a Patrick Heron. He'd also moved desks. They'd agreed that he should. So what had been Sam's desk was beautifully tidy and covered by one folder. She sat down, opened it and busied herself with the various items Alan had left her. She was just checking through her time-sheets which related to the quibbled-over bill, and had discovered that she'd actually undercharged the client by quite a considerable amount, when the phone rang. It was Greg.

'Sam, I've got someone here to see you.'

She glanced at her watch. 'Who is he?'

'Says he's a friend of Alan's.'

'OK, send him up.'

'Right.' He sounded unsure. 'You can go up,' she heard him say.

She put down the phone but it rang almost immediately. It was Greg again.

'I don't like the look of him much. Phone me if . . .'

Before she could reply the door opened and Sam put down the phone.

The man standing in front of her was almost as broad as he was tall. He had a shaved head which bore a horseshoe of five o'clock shadow. He was wearing jeans and a white T-shirt and brand new trainers, and although somewhere in his late fifties he had the body of a gym rat, a huge chest and enormous biceps. He looked like a man who lifted weights, heavy weights, every day. A bouncer, Sam thought, someone who needs that kind of musculature for professional purposes. He stared at Sam out of cold, very blue eyes and then looked round the office.

There was something decidedly weird about him. It was coming to the end of a long hot summer but this man looked as if he hadn't seen the sun for years; his skin was grey-white. It was then she realised who he was.

His eyes settled on to hers. 'All right,' he said.

'How can I help you?'

'Where's Alan?'

'He's not here today. Can I help you?'

'I'm looking for Alan.'

'Sorry – and you are?'

'I'm what?'

'Who are you?'

'Well, why didn't you say so? Where is he?'

'He's in Oxford on a job over the next couple of days.'

'When's he back?'

'Who wants to know?'

He turned round as if to leave. Sam stared at the large roll of flesh lying between the top of his neck and the base of his skull. He turned back round. 'Nice office – he's got a nice little set-up here, hasn't he?'

Sam didn't say anything and he continued.

'What's he do?'

'Private investigator.'

'Ever need any muscle?'

Sam shook her head.

'Tell him Johnny came looking for him. Tell him I'll catch up with him later.'

'Why do you want him?'

'Can't a man just want to say hello to his baby brother?'

Sam didn't say anything. That wasn't why he was here.

'Oh yeah, I know. You can tell him thanks for all the visits.'

Sam knew Alan had never visited Johnny in prison.

'And that I'm looking for him.'

After he'd left the office, Sam sat for a few moments looking out of the window. A heat haze hung over the horizon; down below, the river appeared to be barely moving. Over to the left, in front of the boathouses, someone was feeding a large flock of Canada geese. Two young children about eye-level to the birds' beaks were hiding behind adult legs. She chewed on the end of her thumbnail for a few minutes and then picked up the phone.

When she told Alan what had happened there was a sharp intake of breath followed by a loud groan.

'Shit,' he said. 'I'm sorry, Sam.'

'It wasn't a problem, Alan.'

'Look, could you do me a favour?'

'Sure.'

'If you run into Stephanie could you get her to phone me?'

'I haven't seen her yet but if I do I'll tell her to call.'

'Is everything all right at the flat?'

He sounded anxious. Sam didn't have it in her to add to his worries by telling him the depth of the mould growing on the tea bag in the sink. 'Yes, everything's fine. Hopefully I'll catch up with her this evening.'

'Thanks, Sam. Thanks a lot. I'm sorry I wasn't there.'

'Don't worry.'

'I hope he didn't ...'

'It was fine, Alan. Anyway you're not responsible for what your brother does.'

'All the same, I wouldn't wish an encounter with Johnny on my worst enemy.'

'What does he want from you?'

'A piece of the action ... money. Take your pick.'

Sam looked at her watch and began to cross the road. She was always early and had been sitting in the bus shelter waiting for the right time for her session with Reg. She wondered where he'd gone on holiday. Did he go white-water rafting in Colorado? Or was it a Buddhist retreat in Wales? It was impossible not to speculate on the private life of your therapist when the levels of personal disclosure were so one-sided. She rang his doorbell and waited.

It opened and Reg stood there, his tanned round face smiling at her. His feet were bare and he was wearing a pair of navy-blue linen trousers and a pale blue cotton shirt.

'Hi, come in.' He stepped to one side and Sam walked past him into the hall. The walls were painted white and had wooden-framed, black-and-white photographs of different landscapes hanging on them. When she'd first seen them Sam had thought they were by Ansel Adams, but when she'd looked closer she'd realised that they weren't and had assumed they were photos that Reg had taken himself. She walked through the door on the left into his consulting room.

The room ran the width of the house. Over to the left was the office part of the space – a chair, a desk with an angle-poise lamp on it, and a filing cabinet. The desk was a huge thing with a green leather surface, covered in files and it faced into the room. In front of it was a large golden Chinese carpet which acted as a divider between the office function of the room and the consulting area. That area, over to the right, contained two chairs facing each other over a low table, upon which sat a square box of tissues, a jug of water and two glasses. The doors which gave out on to the garden were open today and a slight breeze was moving the curtains back and forth. Out on the patio, bees were buzzing around the lavender and rosemary, and a green hose snaked across the paving stones between the series of large blue ceramic pots containing a profusion of yellow and red begonias.

Sam lowered the small rucksack she had slung over her shoulder to the ground and sat down. Relief flooded her.

Reg had followed her in. 'Would you prefer me to close the doors?'

'No, it's fine.'

'I've been trying to get some air into the house – it was so stuffy when I came back.'

'When did you get back?'

'This morning.'

He sat down opposite her, brown bare feet flat on the floor, and flexed his toes.

Sam looked out of the window at the fat black bees busy on the lavender.

He clicked on a tape recorder which he had taken off his desk and put on the table between them.

'So, how have you been?'

'Well ...'

He waited and then when Sam didn't reply tried again. 'Have the strategies we put in place been working?'

Sam felt a wave of emotion tear itself loose from her stomach and start up her throat. The words she needed to say formulated clearly in her mind. Oh fuck it.

'You left me,' she said and burst into tears.

Reg pushed the box of tissues towards her.

Sam had spent most of the session in a state of inarticulate misery. It was now nearing its end and she was still feeling upset.

'This is why I hate therapy,' she said, blowing her nose loudly. 'This reduction to mush.'

'Talk some more about that.'

'It's humiliating.'

'What is?'

'To feel this vulnerable, this out of control. You have all the power and I'm just like the stuff you're left with after you've used a juicer.'

'How do you feel?'

'I've just told you,' Sam snapped. 'Vulnerable.'

'And what else?'

'Pissed off with the whole thing.'

'The whole thing being?'

'Well, you. I'm fine for six weeks. I'm doing well then you come back from holiday and here I am sitting here reduced to mush in a split second.'

'You blame me for how you're feeling?'

'Yes ... well, no ...' she paused. 'Oh what's the point? You know, before I arrived I was thinking what I would talk to you about and of all the things I could say about how well I'd been doing. You know, presenting my life up for your approval like a cat dropping a dead mouse at the feet of its owner.'

Reg laughed.

'And then I get in here and the first thing I do is burst into tears and accuse you of abandoning me.'

Reg rubbed his hand over his face. 'One year during my first session back with my supervisor after the summer break I'd been telling him how well I thought I'd done while he'd been away. I was telling stories of how well I'd coped and I saw him stifling a yawn. Right at the end of the session he stopped me and said "I'm really delighted things have been going so well for you but here and now, Reg, how are you feeling, because I feel a little disconnected from you."'

'And what did you say?'

'I was furious. The truth is I was furious he'd gone away. I just hated it. Everything I said to him came with the underlying jab of "I don't need you". But you just come straight in and tell it how it is. You don't spend almost a whole session avoiding what you're feeling.'

'It doesn't feel as if I have any choice over the matter.'

Reg remained silent.

'I hate feeling this needy,' Sam said. 'I just hate it.'

'We all have needs. To be human is to have needs.'

'Well, I can't bear it.'

'Because?'

'I'll be exploited, let down ...'

'What else?'

'You'll have power over me.'

'And?'

'You'll abuse it.'

Sam held her breath. There was silence in the room. The only noise was the humming of the bees out in the garden and the tape recorder on the table. Fifty minutes was up.

Reg nodded. 'Well, perhaps we could talk some more about that at the beginning of the next session.'

Sam exhaled. Saved by the bell.

'I'd like to schedule a session for the next couple of days if that's all right with you.'

'A way of paying off your holiday?'

'Sorry?'

'You go away on holiday, all your clients are traumatised by your absence and then you have a whole load of extra sessions.'

'If money's a problem, we can discuss ...'

Sam shook her head. 'Just forget I said that. I'm really sorry ... another session would be a good idea. I'm sorry, Reg.' She dug in her bag for her diary. 'When can you make it?'

Outside her flat, Sam looked up at the open windows. Loud music blared out into the warm evening air. The Arctic Monkeys? Franz Ferdinand? The Kaiser Chiefs? She didn't have a clue. In a different mood she would have quite liked it but she felt vulnerable from the session with Reg and the music jarred. For a split second she considered just getting in the van and driving back to Oxford, but then a wave of exhaustion broke over her and a craving to sleep in her own bed or at any rate on her own sofa.

She rang loudly on her own doorbell to give Stephanie some warning that she was coming in and let herself into the block. The music immediately went off and then the door to her flat opened.

'Hi,' Stephanie said. Sam walked into the front room and Stephanie followed her.

Stephanie slouched with her hands in the back pockets of her trousers. She was about the same height as Sam and blonde, although her hair was straight rather than curly. She was wearing hipster jeans, a wide leather belt with a large buckle and a white vest.

'Sorry about earlier,' she said. 'The place was a tip.'

'I tried to contact you to let you know I'd be in town. I left messages on your mobile and the landline here.'

'I've been having trouble accessing my voicemails and I don't listen to the messages on your answerphone. I'm really sorry about the mess.'

Sam shrugged. She didn't have the neck to tell anyone off for that. Her nose would have grown so long she'd have been able to wrap it five times round her head. 'I'd like to stay the night if that's all right. I'll be fine on the sofa and then I'm going back to Oxford first thing.'

Stephanie nodded.

Sam felt that she ought to engage with Stephanie and maybe talk to her about Johnny, but she felt exhausted from the session with Reg. Anyway, what could she say to her? She was hardly in a position to give her any advice on fathers and it was really none of her business.

'Are you all right?' Stephanie asked.

Sam smiled. 'Thanks. Yes, I'm fine. Do you want some tea?'

She shook her head. 'I'm off to work in a minute.'

'How's the job going?'

Stephanie shrugged. Her hands stuffed into her front pockets this time.

In the kitchen Sam saw that Stephanie had had a major blitz. The science experiment was gone and the stainless steel sink had been scrubbed to within an inch of its life. Everything had been washed up and tidied away. There wasn't even an upside-down cup on the draining board. Sam felt relieved; at least she'd made some effort.

Stephanie had followed her into the kitchen and watched Sam as she put on the kettle and got out some milk from the fridge.

'You won't tell Uncle Alan, will you?'

'Tell him what?'

'You know how tidy he is.'

Sam laughed. 'No, I won't. Anyway you did some sorting out in here, didn't you?'

Stephanie blushed.

Sam patted the kettle. 'Are you sure?'

She shook her head. 'No, I should be going or I'll be late for work.'

'Alan said could you phone him.'

'OK.'

'What time do you get in?'

'Late.'

'I'm going to try and beat the rush-hour and leave early so I probably won't see you in the morning.'

A couple of minutes later and Sam heard the front door slam as Stephanie headed out.

She ordered herself a take-away from Nayaabs down the road and ate it in front of the television. To get over the empty horrors of August's TV schedules she had borrowed the DVDs of the last series of *Six Foot Under* from Alan. She settled down to an evening with the Fisher family, a family whose wide-ranging dysfunction made her feel absolutely at home.

CHAPTER EIGHT

Peter woke to the noise of Pip howling downstairs in the kitchen. He waited to see if Sam was going to respond but then, remembering she wasn't back from London, got up, fed the dog and decided to take him for a walk. He clipped the lead on to Pip's collar and set off taking the same route Sam had taken for her run, along the Banbury Road and into the University Parks. It was cooler today and slightly overcast. He stopped at the entrance to the park and pulled on the green V-necked sweater he'd slung round his shoulders. Pip trotted at his heel, stopping here and there to explore the bushes which grew against the iron railings bordering the western side of the park.

He had had a restless night, his dreams filled with vivid remembrances of his childhood in Naples, and that last long summer before school intervened, before everything was torn away from him. Memories had been swirling round his mind ever since Sam brought Pip home four days ago. It had been a summer surrounded by the warm and loving embrace of his mother's family – his aunts and his grandmother. Images poured in on him now, the colours of their dresses, the suffocating heat and stench of Naples in midsummer, the perpetual traffic jams in the narrow streets, and his dog Isotta running after him, chasing the trailing shoelaces of his black plimsolls in the Neapolitan dust. Two men were jogging towards him and he moved to one side to let them pass. It had been his last summer of freedom, of innocence, of running free. On a whim he bent down and unclipped Pip's lead.

At the time there had been no warning that his life in Italy was going to come to an end; it was only with the benefit of hindsight that one incident stood out. His father had been back on leave for a few days and they'd gone to have lunch with his grandmother. Peter had been sitting on her lap with his eyes closed, his head resting back on her shoulder as she stroked his hair. When he'd opened his eyes, he'd looked straight into his father's face and seen there an expression he recognised as hostile, but only much later understood was one of disgust. That evening he'd listened at the living-room door to his parents' raised voices. His father had used a word he didn't understand, 'molly-coddled', and a month later his Italian childhood had been torn away from him to be replaced by the cold, grey, regimented life of an English boarding school.

But he had never in his wildest imaginings thought that they would give away his dog. One betrayal following so swiftly on the heels of the other, both denied of course by his parents, had been the last straw, and he had never trusted either of them again.

And then all those years later in hospital after a car crash there'd been Jean, her cool, elegant fingers taking his pulse, informing him that he'd broken his leg. It must have been the shock, shaking the emotion loose in him, because he'd started to cry uncontrollably and all he could think about then was the loss of his dog, and the greater surrounding loss of his childhood and that Italian summer, and she had sat by his bed handing him tissues, explaining to him matter-of-factly that sometimes shock worked that way and not to worry.

In Jean he had recognised someone who shared his own reticence, his own veering away from emotion. But, being shy herself, she had not mistaken his shyness for indifference; she had taken the trouble to look beyond that and had obviously liked enough of what she saw, because after a short courtship of three months she had agreed to marry him. And with her had come Mark, aged fifteen, and Sam, aged seven.

The two joggers had done one circuit and were coming round again, breathing heavily this time and sweating more profusely. Peter stopped and looked around him. He'd been lost in thought and presumed that Pip was behind him. He had been just a minute ago, but now he couldn't see him. He walked quickly back the way he had come, calling for him. He passed a man walking his black Labrador.

'Have you seen a Chihuahua?' he asked.

'Oh, he's yours, is he? I just passed him back there,' the man said.

He increased his speed, anxiety growing in him. Why on earth had he let him off the lead? Why had he been so foolish? The dog wasn't even his. All because he'd been filled with some ridiculous sentimental notion that the dog should be able to roam free. But then he saw Pip snuffling under some bushes and his anxiety was replaced with a flood of relief. He felt tears prick his eyes as he bent down and attached the lead to the dog's collar and headed for home.

Had he been a good father? He doubted it. How could he be? The thought had terrified him. He assumed that fatherhood or, more precisely, the birth of your own child must be a transforming event but it wasn't something he'd ever sought. There was nothing in his past to make him think that he would make a good father, let alone a good stepfather. At first he had thought he might get by on a sort of benign indifference but he had quickly been disabused of that notion. Anyway, how could a living stepfather compete with a dead father, a member of the SAS, killed in action? A dead hero was never going to tell you to go to bed or check you'd done your homework. He'd been a better father to Mark than to Sam; that wasn't hard to work out. Mark had followed him into the world of academe and even though his subject, English, had been far removed from his own of mathematics, it still gave them common ground, whereas with Sam there'd been none. She'd been sports mad from the very beginning and then fighting mad and he'd certainly struggled with that. His own experience of sport was of standing, freezing cold, on the edge of the rugby pitch, praying to God the ball didn't come to him, but when it did, running as fast as he could to avoid being tackled. Physical contact sports were his idea of hell and his stepdaughter's idea of heaven.

He remembered the first time he'd met Sam, she'd been peering at him from behind her blonde curly mop of hair like an animal in the jungle, waiting to pounce, waiting to find him wanting. She hadn't had long to wait. His impression had been that she'd hated him, more or less on sight. It was only recently, since the truth had come out about her father, that she had softened towards him. He'd been enjoying her company this summer, she seemed to have mellowed, maybe it was simply the overwhelming relief that her brother had recovered or maybe she was warming to him after all these years. Whatever the case, he'd been grateful to have her company because he'd been missing Jean and until Sam had come along he'd been rattling around the house, unable to think, unable to settle to anything.

As he let himself into the house and unclipped Pip's lead he thought that he should tell her that but then he dismissed it. It would just make them both feel uncomfortable.

That morning Sam had got up early to beat the traffic and had driven back to Oxford. By eight o'clock she was sitting next to Alan on a black leather sofa in the Tick Tock café in the Cowley Road, giving a chocolate croissant and cappuccino her full attention. Alan leaned towards her and whispered, 'Why are we here? The coffee's not the usual strength you require.'

Sam pointed at the wall. It was covered in clocks with different faces. Each clock had the name of a country underneath it. Elvis – Hawaii, Micky Mouse – France, Pink Floyd – Lebanon, Al Pacino in *Scarface* – Paraguay.

'What's that all about?'

'I've absolutely no idea. All I know is that you don't get those in Starbucks. Nor this.' She pointed to a vase covered in sea shells, which contained plastic flowers.

Alan laughed then yawned. 'Bloody boring job. Like watching paint dry,' he said.

'"A" is for ability to pay,' Sam replied.

'Yeah, yeah. I don't understand why Cummings still wants you doing it. They know now that the head has been taken and the police are involved so why bother to pay us to prowl around there at night?'

'I agree. It seems fairly pointless to me as well but why turn down work when it's on offer. Did Cummings say anything to you about how the police investigation was progressing?'

Alan shook his head. 'Cool customer, isn't he? Steph's still not answering my messages.'

'I told her to phone you but she said her voicemail is up the creek. She missed the messages I left for her warning her I was going to be in town.'

'I'll have to go over there when I'm back in London.'

'So, Johnny . . .' Sam began.

'It's such a fucker. Why let him out now when all the previous times he was turned down?'

'On what grounds did they refuse him before?'

'Insufficient remorse.'

They looked at each other in silence. Sam thought that there were a few instances in her life where if it had been a question of parole or not she would have been turned down on the same basis.

'He was never a very good actor,' Alan continued.

'What's he going to do?'

'Go round the family. He's visited Mum. He's come to the office. He'll move round the family checking us out deciding where he can most easily muscle in. He'll be looking for Steph.'

Alan's brothers had their fingers in a number of different pies. Sam knew about some of it, the taxi company and the security business, and had never wanted to know much else. Alan hadn't offered up that sort of information. As an ex-policeman he'd always kept as far away as possible from his brothers' business affairs. Sam used the cab company from time to time but made sure that she always mentioned Alan's name. So far the fares had been cheap and they hadn't sent her any psychos.

'He said he wanted to thank you for all the visits.'

'Fuck him. Why should I have visited him? He never did anything other than hit me.'

Sam shrugged.

'I'm sorry, Sam, but this is really going to do my head in. Johnny's always been nothing but trouble.'

She nodded sympathetically.

Alan got to his feet. 'I should get going. I need to speak to Steph. If he's found out where the office is, he'll be on her trail before too long. I'll drop in on her at your place.'

'Perhaps better to see her at the pub,' Sam said.

'Why?'

'She's only twenty and it's the first time she's lived away from home.'

'Has she turned your flat into a pigsty?'

'Look, Alan, I don't mind. I'm hardly Ms Domestic, am I? Just visit her in the pub. It'll create a lot less hassle for both of you. Given what you want to talk to her about it'd be best if you don't start off the conversation with a row about dirty cups.'

He nodded. 'All right, I will. You could have told her off you know?'

'I know, Alan, but a phrase involving pot and kettle comes to mind.'

He laughed. 'How was she?'

'Quiet.'

They walked out into the street and Sam kissed him on the cheek.

'Good luck,' she said.

'Thanks, I'll need it.'

He had begun to walk away from her when he stopped and patted the pockets of his shorts. He turned round and handed her a piece of paper. 'It's the address you wanted from that car registration.'

'That was quick.'

'It was only a phone call away.'

On the piece of paper was written the name of a company called Omega Exports and an address in London.

'W11?'

'Holland Park.'

'No names?'

'The car was registered to that company at that address. If you want names of individuals we'll need to do a company search.'

Norman sat next to his grandfather's bed, watching him sleep. His grandfather's mouth was open and soft snores punctuated the silence of the room. One hand lay over a paper folded at a partly filled-in crossword, the other was loosely clasped around a pair of glasses. Norman tried to come in at meal times to make sure his grandfather was eating properly but he'd arrived too late this evening, and the remains of his supper lay congealing on his bedside table, the usual stodgy muck that was hardly going to help the bowels of the bedridden. He'd managed about a third of it and left the remains badly hidden under his knife and fork, like a schoolboy hiding his sultana-infested coleslaw from matron.

His grandfather had been an impressive man in his prime, over six foot and well proportioned, but old age and five years in a wheelchair after his first amputation had had their effect. Now the frame of his youth was stooped and he'd lost weight and muscle. Norman looked at his grandfather's arm protruding from the short sleeve of a hospital gown and considered that old age had reduced him to not much more than skin and bone. His face was round and red, the skin covered in the odd crusty patch, the product of too many years spent in the Western desert during the Second World War. One on the edge of his ear looked a bit worrying and Norman made a mental note to ask the nurses about it. His skin was usually checked every six months or so but sometimes patches flared up between appointments. A few wisps of white hair, swept back from his forehead, covered his head.

One thing, fortunately, remained completely unimpaired – his mind.

To Norman that was a rare and beautiful thing indeed.

He knew how lucky he'd been to be raised by such a man, a charming man who never used his intelligence as a weapon, whose manners and modesty made him of enormous influence on the large numbers of students he had taught. Of course the nature of such people is that others can become aware of their somewhat pygmy status but somehow his grandfather had the knack of raising the level of people around him and making learning fun – his *élan*, his brio all contributing to his excellence as a teacher.

He looked into the white plastic bag at his feet and, with the intention of reading it himself, he tried as quietly as possible to remove one of the P.G. Wodehouses he'd brought for his grandfather. But they were right at the bottom under a number of other items and he wasn't quiet enough. His grandfather swallowed, licked his lips and blinked open his eyes. He caught sight of Norman and smiled.

'How long have you been here?'

'Not long – ten minutes or so.'

He put both his hands flat on the bed and tried to push himself into a more upright position, then he put his glasses back on. 'You should have woken me.'

Norman leaned over him and kissed him on the cheek then picked up the bag, put it on the chair and began to empty it. The four, well-thumbed P.G. Wodehouses he put into his grandfather's hands brought forth a grunt of approval. He placed three clean striped nightshirts in the bedside cupboard. They would be better than the anonymous hospital smock his grandfather was wearing at the moment. He took a stalk with a couple of desiccated red grapes still attached to it out of a bowl and threw it in the bin and then replaced it with a large bunch of white grapes. The packet of Fybogel he put on top of the cupboard so that the nurses would see it. Next to that he placed a bottle of Chateau Margaux 1990. He'd removed the cork and then pushed it back in, but not so hard that his grandfather wouldn't be able to pull it out. The nurses might not be so keen on that, but his grandfather was hardly going to stop drinking now, at the age of ninety, and to remove one of the great pleasures of his life would be pettiness in the extreme.

His grandfather had his nose in *Stiff Upper Lip Jeeves* and was laughing. The light caught his glasses and Norman saw that they were filthy, greasy and speckled.

'Pass me your glasses,' he said, 'I'll give them a clean.'

His grandfather handed them over to him, closed one eye, brought the book to within an inch of his nose and continued reading. Norman took a tissue from the box and dipped it in the jug of water; he swabbed both sides and wiped them with a dry tissue. Then he tugged out his shirt from the waistband of his trousers and finished off by rubbing them on the soft cotton. When he had finished he handed them back to his grandfather.

'Much better,' his grandfather said, waggling his head up and down. 'No smears.'

'How are they?' Norman asked, nodding at his grandfather's leg.

'Not very ticklish today. Maybe they've eaten themselves to a standstill.'

Norman smiled. 'It's a good thing you're not squeamish.'

He shrugged. 'If a doctor tells you putting maggots on your ulcer may save your leg and it's the only leg you've got, you do what they tell you.' He stopped and then blurted out, 'I don't know how I'll manage if it doesn't work.'

The sudden silence in the room was broken by the noise of a trolley rattling past.

'What will I do?'

'We will get you a carer and you'll stay at home as usual.'

'But we can't afford it. We can't possible afford it.'

'We'll find the money. You're not to worry about it, Grandpa. It'll be all right.'

The trolley had stopped outside their door and a woman came in to take away the dinner things.

'This is my grandson, Norman,' his grandfather said.

'Hello, dear, your grandfather's told us all about you.'

Norman smiled wanly. 'He's a terrible liar, you know.'

He should be nice to this woman and charm her so that she would in turn be nice to his grandfather, but somehow the energy required for that defeated him. He didn't say any more and was glad when after a bit more small talk with his grandfather, she and her trolley left.

'I don't want to go into a home, Norman.'

'You won't have to.'

'But if I have to have this leg off we won't ...'

'Don't be silly, we'll work something out and it'll be fine. You're not to worry. Do you want me to read to you for a bit?'

His grandfather smiled and handed him the book and soon the two men were lost in the world of Jeeves and Wooster, of Aunt Agatha and Beefy Bingham. Norman read to him until he fell asleep and then went in search of a nurse to find out how his grandfather's treatment was progressing. The short answer was she didn't know but the doctor was going to come and have a look at his leg the following morning and then they'd have a better idea.

As Norman waited for the lift to take him down to the ground floor of the hospital he had the feeling that everything was going into reverse and there was nothing he could do to stop it. When he was a boy his grandfather had read to him before he fell asleep – Dickens, Austen, Scott, P.G. Wodehouse, G.A. Henty, Billy Bunter, stories from the series of *Boy's Own* annuals. His tastes were nothing if not old-fashioned. Now Norman was doing the same for him. The lift came and he got in. It was empty apart from one other man. Norman ignored him, staring down at the floor.

'Don't worry, mate, it may never happen,' the man said.

Norman raised his eyes to the man's face; it was a stupid but well-meaning face. Maybe he found it awkward to stand in such close proximity to someone in silence; maybe his wife had just given birth and he wanted to tell someone about it, maybe he just didn't have a clue.

Norman wasn't in the mood for conversation. 'Isn't that rather a dangerous thing to say in a hospital?' he enquired mildly.

The man opened his mouth to reply but at that moment the lift stopped and much to Norman's relief more people got in.

CHAPTER NINE

That evening Peter and Sam were walking along the Banbury Road on the way to a party given by their old friends, the Eliots. Pip was trotting between them.

'I've been reading a book,' Peter said, 'which claims that the people who live in north Oxford provide the template for all the characters in Tolkein's *The Lord of the Rings*.'

'Oh yes.'

'According to the thesis, I, being an academic, am a wizard.'

Sam laughed. 'I can see why this may be a theory that meets with your approval.'

'North Oxford children are hobbits.'

'Small, precocious and ...' Sam looked down at her sandals, '... with particularly hairy feet?'

Peter smiled. 'The workers in the car industry and the industrialists are orcs.'

'How does that work then? All industry is evil, but the pure life of academic study is good?

'Apparently Tolkein had a loathing for the motor car.'

'What about women?'

'Ah – the most notable female presence is the enormous spider ...'

'Who tries to kill the hobbits ... children ... by smothering them ...'

'Yes, that's right.'

'Sounds like a theory made up by someone who's spent too long in Freudian analysis and hates women.'

'Oxford makes slow progress when it comes to women,' Peter said. 'Unfortunately it always has.'

North Oxford was certainly a weird enough place to be responsible for *The Lord of the Rings*, Sam thought. Originally, when the law had changed and dons had been allowed to marry, it had provided them with family homes. But now the property prices were so high not many young dons could afford to live here unless they'd been the beneficiary of large sums of money that had nothing to do with their academic salaries.

They continued walking in silence and Sam turned her mind to the Eliots. The families had known each other for years, mainly because Sam and Mark had been to school with two of their children, Luke and Mattie. They lived in a large sturdy house on the Banbury Road set in enough grounds to incorporate a swimming pool, tennis court and vast garden. Sam's mother had always had a soft spot for Mr Eliot, a tall, good-looking man who had taught archaeology before inherited money had enabled him to buy his own dig, out near Chedworth.

The Eliots had always travelled, serious travelling as well, the sort you did across deserts in a bone-crunching old Land Rover. Libya, Iraq, China, Russia, South America – the children had been the envy of their contemporaries because they were always being yanked out of school early to go on these journeys. The house was stuffed with objects they'd brought back from their travels, guarded over, after a couple of burglaries, by a pair of badly behaved, under-exercised Rottweilers, who had beds either side of the front door. Sam had warned them about Pip and they had told her they'd lock up the dogs; she didn't want Pip turning into a Rottweiler hors-d'œuvre.

Mrs Eliot was as far removed from Sam's mother as it was possible to be and, as a child, this had been a large part of the attraction of the household. It had been a warmer, more chaotic, more emotional place. She'd felt more relaxed sitting round the Eliots large kitchen table with the wide assortment of misfits they attracted than she had in her own home.

The origins of the Eliots' relationship had once been a much-discussed topic in north Oxford. Rumour had it that Mrs Eliot had been working in a café in St Giles when Mr Eliot was an undergraduate and it had been love at first sight. In those days if you were a scholar and you wanted to get married you had to ask permission from your tutor. Mr Eliot had asked, been refused, and had gone ahead and married her anyway, despite the opposition of his tutor and his parents.

It was pretty obvious to anyone with half a brain cell why that was. Mrs Eliot was a strikingly beautiful woman. She had thick black hair and wide, wide cheekbones. She looked as if she'd been born in Barcelona or Rome or even the High Andes, not the East End of London. In addition she had a very good sense of humour and an enormous amount of charm, and gave the best New Year's Eve parties north Oxford had ever seen. Her two children had inherited the good looks and charm in abundance. It was a heady combination.

Sam had mixed feelings about going. Although the ties between the families had been strong when the children were at school, after she'd moved to London she'd lost contact and eventually they'd all fallen off each other's Christmas card lists. The only information she'd had about the family had come from the times when her mother bumped into Mrs Eliot in the butcher's in Summertown. It was a long time since she'd seen any of them and she wasn't sure if they would have much to say to each other now. Sam was working that night at the Pitt Rivers and she'd dithered about going, but eventually she'd allowed herself to be persuaded, feeling that a bit of human company would do her good after her nights surrounded by the inanimate and the dead.

'It'll be good for networking,' Peter said. 'There may be a few marriages on the rocks and you can hand out your card.'

He'd been teasing her of course and Sam suspected that he didn't want to go to the party by himself. He found Mrs Eliot a bit much. She had the knack of putting her finger right on the emotional button and it always unnerved him.

Now they had reached the house and rung the front door bell. Sam was relieved that the barking she could hear was coming from somewhere fairly distant. The door was opened by Mrs Eliot who kissed Sam and then seized Peter's hands and said, 'You must be missing Jean horribly. I'm a basket-case when Hugh goes away. I absolutely hate it. You must let us cheer you up.'

98

She put her hand through his arm and guided him through the house and out into the garden.

Peter opened his mouth and then shut it again and smiled somewhat ruefully at Sam. Of course, Sam thought. How stupid of me. He hasn't mentioned it but of course he's missing her. They're hardly ever apart.

The majority of the guests were out in the garden enjoying the evening sunshine. Sam felt a hand on her arm and turned round to see Luke standing next to her. They hugged and after a bit of small talk in which they both got the basic information about each other – he worked for his father, had bought a house on Walton Street and was presently single – they walked over to a wooden trestle table heaped with food. Sam picked up a plate and began to fill it.

'So, how have you been?' Luke asked. 'I sort of lost track of you after the judo.'

'I'm a private investigator now. I've just opened an office on the Cowley Road.'

'A private investigator!'

'Yes.'

'How's that?'

'Well …' Sam paused as a number of alternative answers passed through her mind. Interesting – too dull, fun – a downright lie, it passes the time – insipid. 'Well … let's say it's unpredictable.'

'A private investigator,' Luke repeated.

Sam caught sight of her father talking to Mr Eliot and made her excuses. As she joined them Peter said to her, 'We've just been talking about the Pitt Rivers.'

'Right,' Sam said.

'I'd read about it in the papers but not heard anything else,' Mr Eliot said. 'Have they lost anything else other than the shrunken head?'

Sam shook her head. 'Not as far as I know.'

Over Mr Eliot's shoulder Sam saw a man wearing a bright red floral shirt standing by the side of the swimming pool. She walked over to where Justin Gittings was standing staring down into the chlorine blue water.

'Hello,' he said. 'How do you know the Eliots?'

'I was at school with Mattie and my brother was at the same school as Luke. And you?'

'Hugh taught me during my first year in college.'

'I think in Oxford it's not six degrees of separation that applies but half of one.'

He nodded in agreement. 'It's a very small place.'

Sam held out her plate which still contained a number of different food items and he thanked her and took a small quiche.

'Have you discovered any other stolen items?'

He nodded. 'So far we've come across thirty or so. All have been taken and replaced with very well-made replicas. The trouble is we have no idea how long they've been missing. It's making it difficult for the police.'

'Thirty? So there's been systematic stealing going on.'

'Yes.'

'Do the other objects which have been stolen have anything to do with the shrunken head?'

'The only thing that they all have in common is the original donor. They were all given to the museum by Archibald Sweetman.'

'Sweetman?'

'Yes.'

'When were they donated?'

'In 1914 he left a large collection to the museum. His grandson Charles Sweetman was the Professor of Anthropology for many years. He's still alive.'

'Do you know a Norman Sweetman?'

'Norman is the original donor's ...' He paused. 'Well, I suppose he's his great-great-grandson. He's a frequent visitor to the museum. His grandfather brought him in a lot as a child apparently. He has a very good knowledge of the exhibits.'

Sam picked a sausage roll off the plate and offered it again to Justin. 'Have you seen him around at all recently?'

'Norman?'

'Yes.'

He shook his head. 'Not for a month or two. Why, do you know him?'

'Know is not quite the word I'd use. He left me in charge of a Chihuahua under false pretences.'

'Had he disguised it as a Siberian husky or something?'

'No, he told me he was coming back to get it the following day and didn't.'

'Charles Sweetman's in hospital. Apparently he's undergoing mag ...'

'Stop,' Sam said. 'I know what it is.'

'Apparently ...'

'Seriously, stop it,' Sam said.

Justin smiled. 'Norman has a certain charm, I've always found.'

Sam nodded. 'Yes, I discovered that to my cost.'

'He's one of a long line of eccentrics. Archibald Sweetman was a missionary in Prince Rupert in Canada and came back with a huge collection from the Tsimshian tribe. Before that he was in Peru and Ecuador, hence the shrunken heads.'

'If you bump into Norman, could you tell him I'm looking for him and not in a good way?'

'I will.'

'Do you think it's just coincidence that the missing items were all part of the Sweetman donation?'

'I don't know. All we know at the moment is that that's the thing that connects them. Well, that and one other thing.'

'Which is?'

'They are among the most highly regarded artefacts in the museum.'

'Highly regarded?'

'And valued. They're the cream of the collection. The police want to talk to Norman and his grandfather. Apparently the police tried to interview the old boy in hospital but got sent away with a flea in their ear. The consultant said he's too weak to be disturbed. Norman is very well informed about the artefacts in the museum and so is his grandfather. Between them they would know the worth of the items that have disappeared. They may have some ideas about who may have taken them.'

That was one way of putting it, Sam thought.

'How's Cummings handling it?'

'As you'd expect.'

'He was a bit twitchy the other day.'

'He's always been a tricky customer. He's got a problematic wife and it makes life difficult for him.'

'What kind of problem?'

'She's manic-depressive. Every now and again she comes off her medication and then all hell breaks loose. Last time she went down New Bond Street and put twenty-five thousand pounds on to credit cards and then booked herself into one of the most expensive suites at the Ritz. She'd racked up huge debts before he managed to track her down and get her sectioned. Maybe something like that's happened again.'

'Whatever his personal circumstances it was a bit much for him to accuse you of stealing from the museum.'

Gittings shrugged. 'He apologised to me again afterwards. I think it was a heat of the moment thing. Anyway, my brother's manic-depressive and I know how difficult it can be.'

A man joined them and Gittings shook hands with him and Sam took the opportunity to leave. She walked round the edge of the swimming pool. So, Norman Sweetman was the great-great-grandson of Archibald Sweetman and the grandson of a former Professor of Anthropology. She wondered if he had keys to the cabinets, she wondered how it all tied up with a Chihuahua and Cruella de Vil? She remembered what the woman at the Ultimate Picture Palace had said, that he was in some kind of trouble, that he needed a friend.

Luke broke away from a group he was standing with and joined her.

'So,' he said. 'Are you happy?'

'Get to the point, why don't you?'

She stared down into the bottom of the pool and then wished she hadn't. 'In recent times I have found happiness hasn't been a large part of my everyday experience.' She paused. 'God, that sounded horribly pretentious.'

He laughed.

'What about you?'

He smiled but didn't reply. 'How about going to St Giles's Fair next week?'

'St Giles! I'd completely forgotten about it.'

'We thought we'd get a gang of us together and go. You know, for old times' sake.'

'When we were kids it was the hottest date of the year.'

He nodded. 'Definitely, definitely the hottest date.'

'I lost my virginity there. Well, in the Parks not actually at the fair.'

'Didn't everyone? So, will you come? We're meeting on the Monday evening at eight at the Martyrs' Memorial. There'll be some children. You know, sort of as cover.'

Sam laughed. 'That'll be fine. It'll be fun. Although I'm not sure I can cope with the waltzers any more.'

'We can go on the roundabout like sedate old dames.'

Luke took off his sandals, rolled up his trousers, sat down and dangled his feet in the pool. Sam joined him. The sky above them was clear and a deep dark blue, soon it would shade to black and the stars would come out. Torches had been lit around the pool and the reflections from the flames wobbled across the surface of the water.

'Do you know a Norman Sweetman?' Sam asked.

'Sure, he was around when I was a kid. Mum felt sorry for him because his parents were killed in a car crash when he was little. He was pretty weird but Mum ... well, you know what she was like with the halt and the lame.'

'I think I was one of those,' Sam said. 'I thought your mum was great when I was a kid. She was always so ... encouraging ...'

'I didn't mean you,' Luke said.

'Come on,' Sam said. 'I fit the bill at that age.' She paused. 'Still do in some respects.'

'Anyway, Norman was strange. He spoke as if he was living in the nineteenth century. I think it was all the Dickens his grandfather read to him when he was a kid. He got sent down from Oxford, you know.'

'What for?'

'He hacked into the university computer system and sold a whole load of addresses to an insurance company.'

Sam laughed. 'He's good with computers then?'

'You wouldn't think it, would you? But his grandfather had very strong ideas about his education. Made sure he had lessons with some of the best programmers in the university. You know, when most of us were playing Pong, Norman was being taught all kinds of things. His grandfather managed to make sure that he wasn't prosecuted but he couldn't prevent him being thrown out.'

Sam remembered Norman's comment about computer fraud. Well, he obviously knew what he was talking about from first-hand experience. Maybe Norman Lester Sweetman might have his uses. After days of free Chihuahua care he owed her something.

'Why did he do it?' she asked.

'He's a big-time gambler, apparently he needed the money.'

Sam remembered the look of desperation on his face the first time she'd seen him on the pavement outside the bookies'.

It was nearing eleven by the time Sam and Peter left the party and began the short walk home. Pip trotted happily between them. It was a mild night without a breath of wind. Peter was holding Pip's lead and Sam thought how happy he looked with the dog and wondered if her mother could be persuaded to get one. She wasn't quite sure how a dog would fit in to their beautifully manicured garden and their pristine home life, especially the cream sofa. With difficulty, was her best bet, but she decided she would talk to her mother when she came back because she had hardly ever seen Peter so relaxed and she thought it must have something to do with the dog. Probably best not to suggest a Chihuahua and nothing too big either – maybe a West Highland white terrier or long-haired dachshund.

'It was a nice party,' Peter said, breaking the silence.

'It was,' Sam agreed.

'Your mother would have enjoyed it I think.'

'There's never any way of knowing beforehand, is there? Whether a party'll be any good or not?'

'No – if there was it'd save no end of wasted time.'

'Do you know much about Cummings's private life?' Sam asked.

'Tricky wife I think. That's all I know. Not an easy man.'

'What do you mean?'

Peter shrugged. 'Word gets about. He's always been perfectly pleasant to me but I wouldn't want to work for him.'

'What do you know about the Sweetmans?'

'Charles was at St Cuthbert's before I became Provost. Nice old boy. I used to look forward to sitting next to him at college feasts. He had some fairly forceful views on making the college accessible for disabled students.'

'Anything else you could tell me about him?'

Peter shrugged. 'He was universally liked. No one had a bad thing to say about him.'

They'd turned into the road that ran into Park Town. A car was parked by the kerb and as they approached it two men got out of it and blocked their path. They were wearing trainers, jeans and T-shirts, but it wasn't the mundane nature of those sartorial choices that sent a jolt of alarm through Sam – it was the ski-masks.

The man on the left held out his hand. 'Give us the dog and there'll be no trouble.'

Well, it made a change from empty your pockets and hand over your mobile. Peter immediately bent down and picked up Pip and Sam moved in front of them both.

'The dog's not going anywhere,' she said. 'And anyway it's not ours so we're not going to pay out any sort of ransom if you take it.'

'We know that. Give us the dog.'

Behind her she heard Pip's low growl.

Damn, she thought, multiple attackers. In her self-defence classes she always encouraged people to hand over their wallets, money, keys, anything. None of it was worth risking your health for. All those could be replaced. But she'd never dealt with a dog before. For a split second she considered giving them the dog but then she thought about Peter and realised he wouldn't do it.

'Look, love,' the other man said. 'We don't want to hurt you. Just give us the dog.'

'Well, that's good news because I don't want to hurt you either.' Her voice sounded steadier than she felt. She put her hand in her pocket, took out her mobile and held it behind her. She felt Peter take it and then, keeping her hand on him, but with her eyes on the two men in front of her, she began walking backwards, pushing Peter as she went. It was late but if they got back into the Banbury

Road there was more of a chance that someone would see them and these thugs might be put off if they had an audience. Behind her she could hear Peter speaking into the phone.

The man to Sam's left now put his hand into his back pocket and took something out. She registered immediately that it was a can of spray and stepped forwards. Her left hand parried away his right and with the heel of her right hand she punched him straight on the nose. He grunted and staggered backwards, dropped the spray and fell to his knees. Sam applied a wrist-lock that kept him there. Behind her she could feel Peter's hand on her shoulder.

'Come one step nearer and I'll break his wrist,' she shouted at the other man.

She pressed the back of the man's hand down towards his forearm and he groaned again.

The other man paused as if undecided what to do.

Everything was rather nicely under control, Sam thought. The police would be here soon and they'd be OK. At that moment she heard a frenzy of barking behind her and a shout from Peter. Something ran between her legs and then a split second later she was upended. She lost her grip on the man's wrist and she saw Pip hurl himself at the man's face. From the noise he made it was obvious Pip had nipped more than just the ski-mask, but then hot on Pip's tail came Peter.

'No,' Sam shouted, because one thing she didn't want was Peter in the mix. The man who was standing was obviously of the same opinion because he shoved Peter out of the way, sending him flying into a bush, and went to grab the dog. Pip whipped round and snapped his jaw shut over his fingers. The man who Sam had held in a wrist-lock was now on his feet holding his hand to his face. Sam grabbed Pip by the collar and after a short tug of war he let go of the hand, but did not stop a frenzy of yapping.

Peter was picking himself gingerly out of the bush and the two men were standing breathing heavily and holding their various wounds when a police car swung into the road and they were all lit up by the headlights. The two men bolted for their car, gunned the engine and disappeared in a cloud of burning rubber.

Sam turned to Peter. 'Are you all right?'

'I think so. I've lost my glasses. Perhaps you could ...'

But before she could do that two uniformed police officers, a man and a woman, walked up to them and Pip began snarling and snapping at them.

'All right, Rambo. Keep your wig on,' the male officer said. 'Can't you tell we're the good guys?'

The two officers sat at the kitchen table with cups of tea in front of them. Sam and Peter sat opposite them. Pip was curled up on Peter's lap fast asleep, a picture now of canine calm. Peter was looking down at him, running the dog's silky ear between his finger and thumb. They'd given them the details of what had happened and Peter had even managed to come up with the registration number of the car, which was more than Sam had managed in the confusion.

'It's a growing problem at the moment,' DC Townsend, the female officer said. She had a round face and round blue eyes and a blonde fringe. She was younger than her male colleague, his junior in rank and had been doing most of the talking. He was a burly-looking man with a moustache and his name was Hayes. 'A Labrador was pinched out of someone's garden in north Oxford just the other day,' she continued. 'The owner went to answer the phone and when he came back the dog had disappeared. Either people demand a ransom or they sell them in the pub. It's an easy enough thing to do. You could get fifty quid for a pedigree dog. It's easy money.'

'But when I told the man he wasn't our dog he didn't seem that bothered,' Sam said. 'So that would suggest they're not interested in a ransom. Why would we pay out a ransom for a dog that isn't ours?'

'Whose is he?'

'Like I said, I'm looking after him for someone who was looking after him for someone else. So I've no idea.'

'But you made the effort to hold on to him.'

Sam glanced at Peter and wondered what she would have done if left to her own devices. 'Well, I'm supposed to be looking after him. We weren't just going to hand him over.'

'No,' Peter agreed. 'We weren't going to do that.'

'The dog might be micro-chipped. You could take him to the vet and see if that comes up with an owner and contact details. There are also websites where people post pictures of dogs they've lost. It might be worth taking a look at those.'

Sam nodded. 'That's a good suggestion. It may give us some idea what the hell's going on.'

'Maybe the dog's got a rich owner and whoever was trying to steal it knew that, or maybe he's a pedigree.'

'Do people pay big ransoms?'

'We try to discourage it because it just makes matters worse, but the other day someone paid thirty thousand pounds to get a springer spaniel back that was best in show at Crufts.'

'Thirty thousand!'

She shrugged. 'It's understandable. People love their dogs. But if they pay out it creates a market. People are more likely to keep stealing them. There's been a big increase in dog-napping cases this year. It's up about forty per cent.'

'I've just remembered. It's *Legally Blonde*, isn't it?' Hayes said suddenly.

'Excuse me?' Sam said. She was sensitive to comments about blondes, legal or otherwise.

'The film that made them so popular.' Townsend gave him a look. He shrugged and continued. 'It was my girlfriend's choice that night, all right. Feisty little things, aren't they?'

Sam put her head in her hands. The adrenaline had worn off and she suddenly felt exhausted.

'Presumably they were waiting for you, so they know where you live,' Townsend said.

Sam looked up at her. 'Yes, I suppose so.'

'So it would be best to be on your guard. He's small, isn't he, so you don't have to take him out to walk him? You can confine him to the garden. I think that would be a sensible precaution.'

After the police had gone Sam went out and searched the area where they'd been attacked. She soon found the can of pepper spray. When she came back into the house, Peter was still sitting at the table with Pip in his lap.

'I'm sorry,' he said.

Sam walked over to the sink to get a glass of water. 'What for?'

'I don't feel I was much help.'

'Don't be silly. You were fine.'

'I was frightened.'

'So was I.'

'You didn't look it. I felt paralysed.'

'Look,' Sam said. 'It's the kind of situation I train people for and I made a complete hash of it.'

'No, you didn't. I lost control of Pip. He ran between your legs, the lead jammed and I got thrown against your back.'

'Don't worry about it. It all turned out all right.'

He cleared his throat. 'I didn't want to hand him over.'

'No, I knew that.'

'Rather stupid I realise now to put you in danger for a dog.'

'Don't worry about it,' Sam said again.

'I thought I'd have him with me tonight,' he said. 'I don't feel happy about leaving him in the kitchen.'

'Good idea. That is, if you don't mind.'

'No, not at all.'

As Sam watched his back retreating up the stairs she wondered what on earth Peter would do if they managed to track down Pip's owner or if Norman came back and took him. The dog would have to be handed back eventually; she couldn't help feeling it would break his heart.

CHAPTER TEN

Sam had tried phoning Cummings to let him know that she had been held up but got no reply and by the time she set off for the Pitt Rivers it was twelve o'clock. She jogged slowly along the quiet streets; the air had cooled and it was ideal for running. Overhead the stars were burning out of a beautiful late-summer night sky. Working at night was beginning to grow on her. During a heatwave the cool of night-time was a welcome relief. Other than a lone cyclist no one was about as she reached the Natural History Museum. Cummings wasn't waiting at the entrance but when she pushed the door it swung open.

In front of her the dinosaurs hung suspended in the cool night air. Blink and you could almost imagine that they were tiptoeing towards you on those savage clawed feet. Sam raised her hand in greeting, no longer as alarmed by their presence as she had been four days ago.

Everything ends, she thought. If there was any lesson to be drawn from the fate of the dinosaurs it was that everything, however seemingly indestructible, however savage, however terrible, died. Are you happy? Luke had asked her. Anger, anxiety, grief, sadness, the odd burst of euphoria – these were emotions that Sam was much more familiar with than happiness. Happiness had left her a long time ago; she had left it floating at the bottom of a swimming pool when she was four years old. She had an image of it lying there like the skin shed by a water-snake, glittering iridescent in the sun. Would she dive back down there and retrieve it? Deep water terrified her. She had never learned to swim. Again she thought of the poems Reg had given her. Had she become so filled up with the gradual accretion of silent things that she was unable to feel joy?

She went upstairs to see if she could find Cummings. The door to his office was closed but Sam could see that a light was on. She knocked on the door and called his name but when she got no reply, entered the room. A pool of yellow light from an angle-poise lamp illuminated a sea of paper strewn over the desk and when Sam turned on the overhead light she saw that the chaos wasn't confined to the desk. It was as if someone had taken hold of all the paper they could find and hurled it in the air.

She heard a noise and turned on her heels and ran out of the office on to the upper gallery that looked down on to the floor of the museum. At the bottom of the stairs she stopped and listened, but hearing nothing further she made her way into the Pitt Rivers. Glass crunched under her feet and it was immediately apparent why. Someone had smashed the cabinets and as Sam walked further into the museum it became clear that there was barely one that remained intact. The museum floor was covered with splintered glass and wood and disturbed artefacts. Her heart was racing. How could you take such things, rob tombs and tribes of sacred artefacts and think that retribution would not be enacted? Conscious of the violence that had been perpetrated first on Cummings's office and now on these cabinets, Sam moved deeper into the museum, hoping that the violence she had seen hadn't found a human focus, hoping that it wasn't loose in the museum and about to alight on her.

It was then that she saw Gittings.

He had been smashed head first into the cabinet containing the shrunken heads, his eyes stared unseeing down on to the artefacts below, blood dripped on to them from his ruined face. For a split second the famous surrealist image of a knife being drawn across an eyeball flashed into her mind. Something that looked like a thin piece of ivory protruded from his neck, blood dripped from the wound on to a similar artefact next to which was a label identifying it as being an arrow made from human bone. Sam checked Gittings was dead and then felt herself drawn inexorably to the cabinet with the witch in the bottle.

The bottle was smashed to smithereens.

Terror gripped her.

The witch was out of the bottle.

Out of the corner of her eye she saw something move. She froze with the kind of fear that makes you lie rigid in bed after waking from a nightmare. Trying to banish the childlike feelings of horror which had flooded her, she spun round to face it. But she was too slow, now all she could hear were fast running footsteps. She ran out of the Pitt Rivers back into the other museum. She stopped to listen but hearing nothing she walked back past the dinosaurs towards the main doors and looked out.

The moon was up, shining brightly down on to the parched grass lawns at the front of the museum. But there was no one out there. It was just Sam, the empty street and the still Oxford night. Whoever she'd seen was long gone. She was shaking as she fumbled in her pocket for her mobile. She walked back into the museum, ringing 999. She stood with her back to the Tyrannosaurus rex giving the details to the police.

'Where are you now?' the voice said on the end of the phone.

'In the Natural History Museum.'

'Leave the museum immediately. Wait for the police outside.'

'But there's no one here ...'

'It is very important that you do as I say.'

She had just closed her phone and was about to do what she'd been told when she saw a reflection in the glass of the cabinet in front of her. She stared hard at it and the words written on it.

Why are dinosaurs so big?

She didn't know the answer to that. She blinked. Had the dinosaur in the cabinet moved? It was only as the ribs of the gigantic Tyrannosaurus rex struck her on the head that she realised her eyes had not deceived her, the dinosaur behind her was falling on top of her.

As she fell, a jumble of thoughts rushed through her head at the same time. The witch was out of the bottle and the eagle was shattered into a million fragments in the air. Once broken, nothing could be put back together. However deep she swam, happiness would still elude her. However many cracks she jumped over, she would never be safe. She was wrong to have come back here. What had ever made her think that this place could be her home? She must have been mad. Oxford's famous charm and beauty had blinded her one more time. She had been trying to return to a place that had never existed – a happy childhood. It was the last thing she thought as the bones buried her.

She wasn't sure how long she'd been unconscious but the first thing she realised as she came to was that someone was there, looking down at her. She moved and the bones rolled away from her across the floor. The figure was silent, bending down towards her. She scrabbled around her, grabbed the first thing that came to hand and lashed out with it. He swore and jumped backwards, then both of them heard the sirens drawing closer and he faded away into the shadows leaving Sam gasping for breath, looking down at what she was holding, a T.rex tooth, the end now tipped in blood.

'Are you all right, Sam?'
She stared down at the wreckage of bones and then looked up at Phil. Despite the shock of what had happened, she still registered that he was looking good, in a crisp open-necked white shirt and sand-coloured chinos. Although showing signs of tiredness, his face was clear so presumably he was still on the wagon.
'This needs to be bagged,' she said, showing him the dinosaur tooth in her hand. 'It's got blood on it.'
'Whose?'
'The man who pushed the dinosaur on to me.'
Phil grabbed the attention of the nearest SOCO and the tooth was duly bagged and marked.
'What are you doing here anyway?'
'Night security.'
'Watching over the dinosaurs?'
'No, the Pitt Rivers – Cummings asked me to.'
He looked down at the pile of bones. 'Hell of a jigsaw for some-one.'
'Yup,' Sam said and nudged a huge rib with her foot. She was hugging herself, unable to stop shaking. She couldn't get the image of Gittings' smashed and bleeding face out of her mind.

Policemen had swarmed into the museum and now all the usual activities relating to a murder scene were taking place. Cummings, who had been standing over by the entrance to the Pitt Rivers talking to a police officer, now broke away and walked towards them. He looked haggard, stubble covered his cheeks and his face was grey, the rims of his eyes were red.

'Are you all right?' he asked.

'My head's a bit sore, other than that I'm fine. I'm so sorry about Justin.'

He didn't reply but stood staring down at the pile of bones, running his hand up and down the back of his neck.

'Who on earth would want to do that?' he said, finally. 'To Justin of all people. It doesn't make any sense at all.'

'It made sense to someone,' Sam said. 'The destruction made perfect sense to someone.'

A police officer came over and took Cummings to one side. Sam looked at Phil and felt the surge of affection she always felt for him.

'How did the exams go?'

'I'm not holding my breath.'

'I'm sure you did fine.'

'So you've set up an office here?'

She nodded.

'Are you moving back to Oxford then?'

She wondered which answer he wanted to hear and she thought of his new girlfriend. 'No, nothing like that – we're just trying out an office until Christmas. It's the end of a lease. We've hardly had any work come in so I'll probably be back in London in the New Year.'

When she looked at him she thought she saw relief in his eyes.

Sam told the police everything she knew several times, including the conversation she'd had with Gittings at the Eliots', and then went back to Park Town to try to get some sleep. Although she hadn't been able to confirm it with Cummings, she assumed the job at the Pitt Rivers was over because now there would be two police investigations taking place: one for the thefts and the other for murder. Apart from anything, the museum would be closed as it was now the site of a murder and no one would be allowed into it for a while. She was, to all intents and purposes, redundant. Sleep, not surprisingly, deserted her and early the next morning she got up and drove into London.

The address that Alan had given her was in Holland Park and so that was where Sam found herself at seven that morning, parked up in Queensdale Road. It was a broad tree-lined street with large white-painted Victorian villas on either side and Sam in her grubby blue Renault van wished she had a ladder strapped to the top; you could park anywhere with a ladder on your roof and no one would question it. But just sitting here in her Renault in a street lined with Saab convertibles, Mercedes and Mazda sports cars wasn't ideal. She wedged herself into a suitable position so that the door of the house was directly in her eyeline and waited.

It was a relief to be back in London, but she could not shake the images of the last twenty-four hours from her mind. It was as if they were on a film spool that just kept looping round and round: Justin Gittings at the party, the men in ski-masks, the paper chaos of Cummings's office, the glass crunching under her feet, the blood splattered mess of Gittings' face smashed into the glass cabinet and, finally, the broken bottle and the witch. She rubbed her head, which was still sore from where the dinosaur had hit her, and thought how lucky she was to have got away with nothing more than a bruised head and to have avoided the storm of violence that had been unleashed in the museum.

She tried to get her thoughts into some kind of order – Pip, Cruella de Vil, Norman Sweetman and the Pitt Rivers. She closed her eyes. Last night was the first time a link between Norman and the Pitt Rivers had been established. Only the Sweetman artefacts had been stolen and Gittings had said they were among the most valuable in the museum. But where the hell *was* Norman? However frail and ill the police would have to interview Norman's grandfather now. And why had two thugs tried to snatch Pip? No one was paying her to sit outside this house in the intense heat, but if she was going to have to protect the dog she wanted to know what the hell was going on. Maybe this woman would lead her to Norman. She'd had to come up to London anyway because she had therapy that afternoon and Alan was having a birthday party in the evening. She doubted her bank manager would be impressed by this unpaid activity, but it was a way of passing the time until then. The sun beat down on the van and she struggled to keep awake.

By midday no one had gone in or out of the house and she felt like a boiled prawn. She'd run out of water and was beginning to dehydrate. The only advantage of that being that she didn't have to pee in the bucket she had in the back of the van. Oh, the joys of surveillance work, she thought, and was reminded why, whenever possible, she gave these kinds of jobs to Alan.

She decided to call it quits and climbed out of her van to cool off. She tugged her sweat-soaked shorts and her shirt away from her body and fanned her face with the peak of her cap. It was very quiet here. The kinds of people who lived in these houses were all probably off in their properties in the south of France and St Barts.

It was then that the door to the house opened. Sam dropped to the ground pretending to do up her shoelaces and peered round the bonnet of her van.

The woman with the blonde French pleat came out on to the doorstep. Someone, who she was talking to inside the house, joined her. He was a large man with brown wavy hair and he wasn't wearing any socks. He took hold of Cruella's arm and at that moment an Ocado van stopped in the middle of the road. The driver looked down at Sam and asked her for directions to a road she didn't know. By the time he had driven on, Norman was halfway down the street and the door of the house had slammed shut.

Sam tucked her hair under her cap and put on her dark glasses. It was an unfortunate thing, but something that she had learned to her cost, that if you had blonde curly hair people tended to notice you; keeping a discreet distance, she set off after him. She could have stayed where she was and waited for Cruella to make her exit but her curiosity had been aroused and she was fed up with sitting in the van, so it was Norman who got her attention. If he got a taxi, of course, she was stuffed but if he was in financial trouble the last thing he would be doing was getting in a black cab, whose prices these days could bring tears to the eyes of even the relatively well-lined of pocket. She was right about the taxi because he made his way to Holland Park Underground and down on to the platform of the Central line. It was lunchtime now and fortunately the platform was busy. Sam positioned herself behind him and when the train arrived, waited for him to get on, and then followed him.

If it had been hot outside it was ten times hotter down here. Sam sat there feeling a bit of fool in her dark glasses and hat as the sweat trickled down the side of her face. Norman got off at Notting Hill Gate as she had expected. If he was going back to Oxford he would be heading for the District and Circle line and Paddington, but it was on the walk between the Central and the District lines that Sam lost him. She didn't notice what had happened until she was down on the platform waiting for the next District line train and realised he wasn't there. She ran back the way she had come, trying to work out what had transpired, then got on the escalator which would take her out of the station, wondering if that was what he had done. It was as she came through the ticket barrier that she saw him, standing in front of a newsagent's, with a smile on his face.

Sam groaned, took off her dark glasses and shook her curls free of the hat.

'How exciting,' he said, 'my own personal stalker. Is it love or lust which has put you in such hot pursuit of me?'

Sam ran a finger along her hairline and flicked away the sweat. 'What the hell is a fucking *aper*?'

'A boar.'

'To write a Latin quotation down without giving the translation in this day and age demonstrates at the very least exceptional bad manners and at the very worst appalling arrogance.'

He smiled. 'I am justly chastised. Look, do you fancy a beer?'

They found a nearby pub and took their drinks outside. Sam was drinking a pint of orange juice and lemonade, a surefire way to re-hydrate, and Norman had a pint of beer. He opened his mouth and poured approximately three-quarters of the pint down his throat.

'Do you want to tell me what's going on?' Sam said.

'In what sense exactly?'

'In the following sense. You dump a Chihuahua on me, claiming you will be back to pick him up and how long has it been now – five days? Then that blonde turns up demanding it back. I refuse to hand over the dog, then yesterday evening two thugs attack me and my stepfather when we're walking home with Pip, insist we give them the dog ...'

'What ...?'

Sam held up her hand to stop him. 'Then this morning I see you and the blonde on the doorstep of a house in Holland Park. Do you want me to go on?'

'Is Pip all right?'

'Yes, and so am I and my stepfather.'

'Of course, you both as well. What happened?'

Sam sighed. 'Two thugs wearing ski-masks demanded the dog. We held them off and when the police turned up they scarpered.'

Norman ran a finger around the top of his empty glass. Sam's pint stood almost full in front of her.

'Back in a minute,' he said, and picked up his glass and disappeared into the pub.

Sam sighed and looked around her. The British didn't do hot weather very well. The Italians, French and Spanish all managed to look relaxed and stylish in the heat, but the British just ended up looking like boiled hams. A man was sitting on the bench next to theirs wearing a white vest and shorts, the skin of his neck and shoulders looking as if it had just come off a barbecue. She felt like going up to him and screaming 'melanoma' in his pink ear but reminded herself that it was none of her business and instead took another swig of her drink.

Norman returned with his pint and sat down. He took off his jacket and, folding it carefully, placed it on the bench beside him. His braces stretched as he brushed his hair away from his forehead. 'I owe you an apology,' he said. 'I'm sorry I wasn't honest with you from the start.'

Sam raised her eyebrows waiting for what he was going to say next.

He took out a packet of cigarette papers and a pouch of tobacco and started a roll-up. Sam had always liked the ritual of this, much more interesting than just shaking one out of a packet and reaching for a lighter. She watched his fingers patting the tobacco into the right shape, his tongue wetting the paper. He had nice lips, she thought, a sensual mouth, and then she found herself speculating about his love life.

'I'm afraid I needed to leave Pip in a secure situation and felt that if he had stayed with me that would not have been the case. I had hoped to be in a position to take him back at this point but things have not turned out as I had hoped. Incidentally, might I ask where he is now?'

'He's with my stepfather, Peter, who has strict instructions not to walk him outside the house.'

'Good.'

'So, who's the blonde?'

'Yes, I'm sorry about her. I wanted to make sure that Pip was secure with you. So I sent her along to try you out.'

'For Heaven's sake, Norman, why didn't you just tell me you needed the dog looked after from the beginning? Why the bloody subterfuge?'

He stuck out his tongue and removed a piece of tobacco with his finger. 'I'm afraid I was not in a position to recompense you for your labours and we had barely met.'

'So you tricked me and relied on my good nature?'

'I can see why you might put that interpretation on my actions.'

'So Cruella de Vil is who exactly?'

'Cruella?'

'The blonde.'

'Oh,' he laughed. 'An old college friend of mine who's an actress – bit parts in *Emmerdale* and *The Bill*. She's got a neat sideline in ice maidens. She's always fancied herself as one of those *femme fatales* in film noir so I told her now was her opportunity.'

'Couldn't she have loaned you some money?'

He rubbed the side of his nose. 'I think she got wise to the fool-hardiness of such behaviour about one month after we met.'

'And what did you find out from her bit of play-acting?'

'That Pip was in very good hands. You weren't just going to hand him over to whoever turned up, that he was safe with you.'

'What if I had?'

'She would have brought the dog to me and I would have made other arrangements.'

'So what's the big deal with this dog?'

'Well …'

'Whose is it?'

He drained his second pint.

'And what on earth are you doing with it?'

Norman cleared his throat. 'Would you be willing to hold on to him for a while longer?'

'Not if you don't answer my questions I won't.'

He lifted his glass. 'I'll just get myself another and then I'll explain … can I …?' He gestured at her glass.

'No, I'm fine.'

He got up and walked back into the pub.

She sipped her drink and people-watched. A mother, her swollen belly pushing against a buggy, walked past, her child fast asleep, head lolling to one side. A young man barely above a boy himself loped at her side. Sam wondered idly whether her biological clock would ever start to tick. Something had stirred when she started going out with Rick but maybe that was because he'd said he wanted children and so she'd thought about it. She suspected it never would; she suspected that those particular batteries had never been inserted in the first place. She barely managed to look after herself, let alone … she looked at her watch. Norman's pint was taking a long time to pour. She got up and went into the pub. It was quite empty inside and Norman was nowhere to be seen. She walked over to the bar. 'Have you seen a large man in here?'

The barman frowned. 'Sorry, love?'

'The fat man. He was wearing braces. Where's he gone?'

'Oh – he asked if there was an exit out the back, said there was someone he had to get away from. Woman trouble apparently. He went out that way.'

'Shit.'

She followed the barman's directions. The fire exit opened on to a narrow alleyway filled with industrial metal bins on wheels. Norman was nowhere to be seen. She looked at her watch. It was fifteen minutes since he'd walked into the pub. There was no way she'd catch up with him now. 'Fuck it,' she said and kicked one of the bins and then wished she hadn't because it released a miasma of rotting food.

It was as she turned round to go back into the pub that she saw a piece of paper which had been folded and stuck into the bracket that surrounded a light attached to the wall by the back door. She opened it and read the mad ink-soaked fly writing, '*Ira furor brevis est.*' Underneath was the translation – 'Anger is a brief madness.' She scrunched up the note, lobbed it into one of the reeking bins and, shaking her head, walked back into the pub. Suddenly she remembered his jacket. She ran back out to where they'd been sitting, but the jacket was gone. He had told her nothing. She still didn't know why the thugs had tried to seize Pip and she had had no time to ask him about his connection to the Pitt Rivers and the missing artefacts, or about his grandfather. Also if the woman was a bit-part actress, as he said, why was she driving around in a Saab convertible registered to a company called Omega Exports and living in a house in Holland Park?

CHAPTER ELEVEN

She walked back to Holland Park to pick up the van. The heat was unrelenting and she felt exhausted. It was only last night that she'd foiled an attempted Chihuahua-nap, discovered a dead body and had a Tyrannosaurus rex pushed on top of her.

As she was getting into the van, the door to the house opened and the woman came out and got into her car. Although it was hot enough to have the roof down she didn't lower it, perhaps worried by the damage it might inflict on her perfect French pleat.

Sam suddenly wondered if everything Norman had said to her had been a lie. He was plausible and charming, but not a truthful word had passed his lips since she'd first met him. She'd had enough of following people for today, so she waited until the Saab had turned out of the street and then picked a box out of the back of the van and ran up the steps to the house and rang the bell. It was an easy enough way to find out if anyone was at home. If someone came to the door you made up a name and asked them if they were that person, and when they said they weren't, you apologised and said you had the wrong number. If no one answered, you knew the property was empty. This time no one answered, so Sam crossed the street and threw the box back in the van.

Hot days were good for breaking into people's homes. The temptation to leave a window open when you went out was just too great. A tall wooden gate blocked off access to the back of the house; she'd need a ladder. She looked up and down the road. A lot of the houses were being worked on, their white paintwork being touched up while the owners were away. She ambled down the road to where a couple of men in white overalls were sitting taking a break.

'Could I borrow your ladder?' Sam said. 'I just locked myself out of the house. I live at …' She gestured down the road. 'There's a window open at the back.'

The older man squinted at her and said something to his colleague in a foreign language that Sam suspected was Polish.

'Come on,' Sam said. 'Do I look like a burglar?'

He shrugged and indicated where the ladder was, leaning up against the side of the house.

'Thanks.' Sam collapsed it and carried it over to the gate. Once on top of the gate she pulled the ladder up after her and climbed down the other side.

The garden she found herself in was one of those new-fangled designs much loved by TV gardeners, which consisted of wooden decking, slate, pebbles, spiky grasses and twisted metal. At the end of the garden was a pool of some sort. It was a garden for people who didn't.

She looked up at the back of the house and immediately found what she was looking for, a window open on the first floor. She put the ladder up against the back of the house, climbed up it and through the window. She dropped down on to the landing, and after a moment standing still and listening, she went down the stairs to the ground floor and quietly opened the living-room door.

A whole cowhide was stretched out on the wooden floor. Better on the poor cow, Sam thought. Abstract paintings hung on the walls and two huge white sofas were lined up in a right angle round the fireplace. In front of them was a wooden table covered with magazines and bearing a Murano glass vase filled with lilies. Sam knew she had a tendency to confuse clutter and mess with character and personality, but even so this house and garden, although undoubtedly stylish, seemed lacking in basic human warmth.

She moved swiftly over to a laptop resting on a glass-topped desk, opened it and pressed the power button. While it was doing its thing she leafed through a pile of papers next to it. A newspaper cutting from *The Times* caught her eye.

*

One of the finest collections of Native American art is expected to be put up for auction at Christie's in New York on 1st October. Christie's has described several of the items as masterpieces. The items are the property of Julia Sweetman, the great-granddaughter of the Rev. Archibald Sweetman, who travelled to Metlakatla in October 1863, a Christian settlement of Tsimshian Indian converts near Prince Rupert. There he bought more than eighty artefacts from a British naval officer, Rupert Wainwright. It was customary for Native American converts to renounce their old beliefs by giving their sacred possessions to missionaries.

When Archibald Sweetman died, the artefacts were split between different sides of the family. The majority of the artefacts were donated to the Pitt Rivers Museum in Oxford but other items, generally believed to be the cream of the collection, were given to Julia Sweetman's grandfather, Jonathan. These items included elaborately decorated slave killer clubs, apparently used to bludgeon to death human sacrifices, which are tipped to fetch as much as £800,000. A clan hat in the shape of a crouching frog is expected to sell for up to £300,000.

Christie's have hinted that a North West Coast shaman's mask of even greater rarity may also be auctioned. This mask has not been seen since it went missing in mysterious circumstances in 1976. If it comes up for sale it will increase the value of the sale as a whole substantially and is likely to fetch more than £1,000,000.

The sale is expected to provoke fierce opposition from Native Americans, who say that such collections should be handed back to their communities. In response to this Julia Sweetman has said that she has tried to find a museum in Canada prepared to take the artefacts but has been thwarted by bureaucracy.

Why would an actress be interested in that? And, more to the point, how could an actress possibly afford a house like this? The laptop did its four-note welcome and the desktop came into view. She's some sort of fence, Sam thought. Was Norman stealing artefacts from the Pitt Rivers and using her to sell them on? But if that was the case what did she want with the dog? She was just about to see what she could discover on the computer when she heard the noise of a key in the front door. It was too late to close the computer down. She pocketed the article, closed the laptop and just had time to scramble into the embrace of a warmly lined cream curtain before two people came into the room, talking to each other – a man and a woman.

Footsteps approached where Sam was hiding and the woman said, 'I thought you said you'd turned off the computer.'

The man replied, 'I did.'

'You can't have. It's still on – look.'

'Well, it wasn't me. I definitely turned it off.'

Sam heard the woman sigh then the four-note Windows sign-off that denoted the computer was shutting down.

The doorbell rang. 'Are you expecting anyone?' the man said.

'No,' she replied.

'Well, who's this then?'

'Open the door and you might find out.'

Then Sam heard footsteps walking swiftly across the wooden floor. She peered out from behind the curtain into an empty room and tiptoed to the door. In the hall she heard voices becoming increasingly irritable; the workmen were looking for their ladder.

'I don't know what you're talking about,' she heard the man say. 'We haven't got your ladder.'

'What's going on?' This time the woman's voice came from higher up the house.

'Do you know anything about a ladder? I don't know what they're talking about?'

Sam peered out on to the stairs and crept up them to the landing. She pulled herself through the window and climbed back down into the garden. Closing up the ladder would make too much noise so she left it where it was, walked round to the gate and waited.

When she heard the irate voices of the Polish painters walking away down the street, she placed a bin against the gate and pulled herself up. She was facing back into the garden with the top of the gate against her stomach, when she felt a hand on the back of her shirt and felt herself tumbling over backwards into space. Years of judo training stood her in good stead as she brought both her arms down hard on the ground to break her fall. Unfortunately the concrete path she fell on was not as forgiving as the average *tatami* and as she scrambled to her feet both forearms were throbbing with pain.

The man in front of her had a shaved bullet-head and no neck. His head rested on his shoulders like a wrecking-ball on a slab of concrete and his arms were splayed at his side, hanging slightly away from his torso, in a way that denoted substantial muscle mass.

His hand shot out and locked round Sam's throat and the back of her head smashed against the wall. She choked, the blood pumping in her ears, and began to count. She'd been strangled enough times in her career to know that if she didn't do something quickly she'd pass out.

One ... she had ten seconds ... *two* ... before the oxygen levels in her brain ... *three* ... would drop down so far ... *four* ... as to make her unconscious ... *five* ... if she hadn't done anything by then ... *six* ... she'd be unconscious and then ... *seven* ... if he kept the pressure on she'd be ... *eight* ... dead ...

Black dots began dancing in front of her eyes. Adrenaline was speeding up her thought processes. Go for his eyes. Chop him across the throat – very dangerous, could kill him. She clawed at his hands and took enough pressure off her throat to gargle out. 'How's your mother?'

He frowned and moved backwards slightly. 'What about my mother?'

'How is she?' she croaked. 'I haven't seen her in a while.'

He relinquished his grip on her throat and took a step backwards. It was hardly as baffling as Gene Hackman's 'picking your feet in Poughkeepsie' but it seemed to be working.

Sam doubled over, coughing.

'What are you saying about ...?'

She took as deep a breath as she was capable of with a bruised throat and sprinted for her van. Behind her she heard him swear, then running footsteps. She jumped into her van and started the engine. Something slammed against the door and his hands closed on the door handle. Sam pressed the lock down and then leaned across to do the same to the passenger door.

She was shaking so much that she shot the van into reverse by mistake. She got it into first and it jumped forwards. She could see him running along behind, reaching for the back doors. Sam had an image of him climbing in and those meaty hands settling round her throat for a second time, and didn't fancy her chances. Timing was everything. She was travelling quite fast now and approaching a T-junction. She slammed on the brakes and heard a satisfying thump as he smashed into the back. As she accelerated away she saw him picking himself off the tarmac, staring after her.

Not a happy bunny, she thought, no, not happy at all.

CHAPTER TWELVE

Another session at Reg's, with the bees buzzing over the rosemary, his tanned toes wriggling on the wooden floor and the early evening sun slanting in through the patio doors. He clicked on the tape recorder.

'I wanted to pick up where we left off last time.'

Sam stared at him blankly. What with everything that had happened in the last twenty-four hours she was having difficulty focusing.

'If you remember, you were talking about what would happen to you if you were vulnerable ...'

'Yes ...'

'That you would be exploited and ...' he paused, 'unsafe.'

'Yes, I'm sorry I was rude.'

'That's all right, but the point is if you attack people when you feel vulnerable then it's very hard for them to know how they can best help you.'

'Well, they can't, can they?'

'Talk more about that.'

'Other people can't do anything. In the end you're on your own and you can't count on anyone. You can't rely on anyone to save you.'

'And if you do?'

'They'll let you down.'

'Like me going on holiday?'

She blushed. 'Sort of ... I mean ... I don't really think you shouldn't go on holiday. I know you need to recharge your batteries ...'

'You said "to save you".'

'Did I? I don't remember.'

'Yes, just now you said, "You can't rely on anyone to save you."'

'Oh.'

'Can you remember earlier episodes in your life in which you had those same feelings, those same thoughts?'

A bee had flown in from the garden and settled on the glass of water sitting on the table between her and Reg. It curled its body over the lip of the glass and dipped its antennae on to the surface of the water.

'Look,' Sam said. 'The only place that my life ever made any sense was on a judo mat and there it's you and your opponent – one on one. There is no one else there. All my life I've had these incredibly strong feelings and it was the one place I could take them and it all made sense. It was the one place I could take every piece of me. It was where I experienced my self most intensely and at the same time could completely lose myself.'

'Talk more about that.'

'OK, for example, when I became World Champion for the first time. I won with an *ippon*. It was, looking back, the most perfect throw of my career. It had everything. I knew I'd done it because I was looking down at my opponent and the crowd was going wild, but at the same time I felt this compete absence of self, like someone else had done it, like it had nothing to do with me at all. So there were these two extremes side by side – the fact that I'd performed better than I'd ever performed and then this feeling almost as if I hadn't been present.'

'How did it make you feel?'

The bee had launched itself off the glass of water and flown back out through the windows.

Sam shrugged. 'I'd won. I was supposed to be happy. I'd been working towards that ever since I first set foot on a judo mat.'

'And?'

She shook her head. 'After an initial euphoria I felt nothing, numb.'

'Did you talk to anyone about it?'

'Tyler knew something was wrong. I'd trained with him since I was seven and he knew me better than anyone.'

'What did he say?'

'He said stop trying to work it out.'

'And did that help?'

'Not immediately, no, but eventually I let go of having to know.'

'Having to know what?'

'Having to know what had happened to me, having to know why I was feeling that way.'

There was silence in the room.

'You let go of having to know what had happened to you and why you were feeling that way,' Reg repeated.

'Yes. I'm sorry, I know this probably doesn't make any sense.'

'If you were to use an image of how you felt at that time, how would you describe it?'

'I don't know ... like I'd been skinned and left on a desert island and the vultures could smell my blood and were circling ...'

Sam looked at the floor. Down there at the bottom of the pool she'd wanted to die.

The silence in the room grew. Sam didn't say anything and neither did Reg. Outside in the garden the bees continued to buzz over the herbs and two blackbirds called shrilly to each other from different sides of the garden. He knows, Sam thought, and he's waiting for me to say it. I'm talking about judo but what I'm feeling now is located in a different time altogether. I'm waiting for me to say it. Dive down there, she thought, retrieve what you lost and bring it back to the surface.

Reg shifted in his chair. 'Have you heard of the story of Prometheus?'

'Was he the one who was tied to a rock and left there for the birds to peck at his liver?'

'Yes. He defied the gods by stealing fire from them and giving it to mankind.'

'Is that supposed to help in some way, Reg?'

He laughed. 'Sometimes it's comforting to know that people have been battling with those sorts of feelings throughout the ages.'

'I don't believe in God or gods.' Then she remembered that the witch was out of the bottle. 'This is going to sound a bit mad,' she continued.

Reg nodded.

'In the case I'm working on someone was murdered and in the process this bottle's been smashed. It was in a museum of anthropological artefacts and the bottle was described as having a witch in it. When I was a child I had nightmares about this bottle, about this very thing, the witch being let loose, and when I looked at it I had this feeling of complete horror.'

Reg looked baffled.

'Do you understand what I'm saying?'

'You're saying that a childhood nightmare has come true and you're very frightened.'

'Yes,' Sam said. 'I suppose that's it – uneasy anyway.'

'So you believe in a witch but not in a god.'

'Evil,' Sam said. 'I have no problem believing in that – none whatsoever.'

'And goodness?'

'I don't see much of that when I look around me. Do you?'

'What about Rick? Before he went away you were talking about him as a force for good in your life.'

'I knew you'd get around to him eventually.'

'How are you doing with Rick being away?'

'Fine. I've sort of given up on him. He'll be sleeping with his wife by now and when he comes back it'll all be over.'

'You sound very certain of that.'

She shrugged. 'You would be if you'd seen his wife.'

Reg was frowning. 'Is that what you want?'

She sighed. 'I don't know what I want. He wants to have six children and I know I don't want that.'

'Isn't that jumping the gun a bit – you've only just met him.'

'Yes, but if he wants that and I don't, what's the point in even beginning ...'

'It seems to me you're looking for excuses for it to end.'

'Maybe I am, maybe you're right. Maybe that's exactly what I'm doing.'

At the end of the session Reg walked Sam to the door and held it open for her.

'We're going deeper,' he said. 'I can feel it. Do you feel that way?'

Her eyes slid on to his and then again almost immediately. She adjusted her backpack and stepped through the door. 'Yes,' she said. 'I can feel it.'

She drove to Richmond Park and found herself a wooden bench looking out over Barnes and Kingston. The houses rolled away into a horizon, shimmering in a slightly dirty pollution-filled haze. The session with Reg seemed to have sprawled everywhere like a dropped bowl of spaghetti. Going deeper? She was frustrated with herself and her lack of courage. She thought again of the accumulation of silent things. Next time she would talk to him about it, however frightened she felt, however sick. She would just do it and then they could go from there. Being in the park had helped to change her mood. By the time she walked back to the van she had made up her mind and wasn't giving herself such a hard time.

At eleven o'clock that night Sam and Alan were standing out on the balcony of Alan's flat getting some air. From the twenty-sixth floor of this high-rise there was a good view of the lights of London sprawled out in front of them. She held the ice-cold side of her bottle of beer against her cheek and luxuriated in the view. The Scissor Sisters' 'Filthy/Gorgeous' was thumping from the room behind her. The evening had started at the Doves, a pub near Hammersmith Bridge, and then moved back to his place. Now an eclectic group of people were flinging themselves around to the music. Someone was frying bacon and Sam could feel her stomach growling in anticipation. She had been updating him on what had been happening over the last twenty-four hours, but in a drunken somewhat haphazard manner.

'So, what's with the Chihuahua?' he said. 'Is it stuffed with cocaine or something?'

Sam laughed. 'Hardly. If you were going to do that you'd choose a dog with a longer intestinal tract, wouldn't you? And anyway I've been looking after him for the last five days. I think I would have noticed if there was something the matter with him like that.'

Alan shook his head. 'Chihuahuas, shrunken heads, and now a Tyrannosaurus rex, a murder and an attempted dog-nap. Not things you'd necessarily expect to mention in the same sentence. I presume the security work at the museum is over now.'

'I need to talk to Cummings but I'd think so, yes.'

'You going to bill him?'

She nodded again.

'Any work come in from the ad?'

'No.'

'What are you going to do about the dog?'

'Hold on to him until Norman comes back for him.'

'You think this Norman bloke's involved with the thefts?'

'He's got money problems and he's got connections.'

'He'd need someone in the museum helping him, wouldn't he?'

'I'd think so.'

'Could he have been using Gittings and then killed him when he thought the game was up in order to protect himself?'

Sam shook her head. 'Norman's no killer. I'm sure of that.'

'Who's the woman who tried to take Pip?'

'My best bet is some kind of fence.'

'Maybe his cousin.'

'Perhaps, but then why's she trying to snatch the Chihuahua? It's not even his, is it?'

'Perhaps, it is his and she wants him to do something he's not willing to do.'

'Like what?'

'I've absolutely no idea.'

'What did Reg have to say about it all?'

'I wasn't talking to him about that.'

'So what were you talking about?'

She shook the bottle gently from side to side. 'I think it was something to do with defying the gods.'

'And what happens if you do?'

'Oh, you end up having your liver picked at by birds.'

'Or having a Tyrannosaurus rex fall on your head?'

Sam laughed. 'Perhaps.'

'You don't think you have a tendency to over-think things which therapy encourages?'

She laughed. 'Unfortunately Reg is more interested in feelings than thoughts.' She brought the bottle to her lips and drank.

'Well, look at it this way, in fifty or sixty years you'll probably be dead.'

'Is that your way of cheering me up?'

He smiled. Behind them someone had jacked up the volume. 'Oi,' Alan shouted and made the thumbs-down sign, but getting no response he walked back into his front room and soon the music quietened.

When Alan came back a few minutes later he was carrying two bacon butties. He handed her one and then went back into the flat. Sam bit into it, catching the tomato ketchup that oozed out of the sides with her tongue. As the food hit her stomach, she felt her sugar levels rising and her mind turning over all that had happened during the last twenty-four hours.

She took the article she had found in the flat out of her pocket and read through it again. It was a mistake to have taken it. The man who had attacked her had caught her climbing out of his garden and he would have discovered the ladder leaning against the back of the house. It wouldn't take much of an imagination for him to realise that she had gained access to the house, especially if he thought back to the fact that the computer had been on and this article was missing. She should have left it there, and then she wouldn't have drawn attention to the fact that she had been over by the computer because if they thought she had been looking around in their computer they might come to the conclusion that she knew a lot more about them than she actually did.

Hearing voices raised behind her, she turned round to see Alan and Johnny standing in the middle of the room. There was approximately one inch between their respective noses. The group of people who had been dancing had stopped and were standing in a rough circle around them.

Sam had had enough violence for one day and knew Alan was perfectly capable of looking after himself, and she didn't think that getting between two of the burly Knowles brothers would bring her any joy, but all the same she crossed the room to where Alan was standing.

His face was completely white. A few other instances when he'd gone that colour flashed into Sam's mind. What followed had never been good. She touched his arm to let him know that she was there, but he didn't acknowledge her presence and his eyes didn't budge from his brother's face.

'Just one brother paying another a visit,' Johnny said. 'Won't you give a man a beer?'

Alan stalked over to a table, grabbed a can and thrust it at his brother. 'You want a beer? Well, there it is. Now get out.'

Johnny pulled the ring and then in one quick motion jerked the can at Alan, sending a spurt of beer into his face. Alan's hand came up to his eyes and then he locked his arms round his brother and the two of them fell to the floor in an ugly rolling embrace. A table covered in cans, bottles and ashtrays tipped over and everyone stepped back. Sam stared down at them as they grunted and clawed at each other undecided what to do. Her instinct was to stay out of it. This wasn't her fight, after all, and she knew getting involved wouldn't earn her Alan's thanks, but Johnny was now on top of Alan, one hand digging into his face.

Stephanie suddenly grabbed Sam's arm. 'Aren't you goin' to do nuthin'?'

Sam sighed. Shit. She wasn't feeling in the best of shape. Both her forearms were bruised from her fall from the gate and she'd drunk enough to know her reflexes wouldn't be up to much. Alan wouldn't like it, but what the hell. She jumped on to Johnny's back and throttled him, turning her arm so that the bone was against his windpipe, and began to count.

At five seconds Johnny let go of Alan and began reaching behind him to get a grip on her. She let go, pushed him away and stood well back with her hands held out in a pacifying gesture. Alan was standing now, glaring at her.

'Keep the fuck out of this.'

Sam shrugged. It was what she'd expected.

Johnny got to his feet with his hand holding his throat. The can of beer was at his feet. He kicked it savagely and it rolled across the floor, spewing beer. Then after a few more moments eyeballing he strutted from the room. Sam picked up the can and placed it on the mantelpiece.

Stephanie came up to Alan. 'Are you all right?'

'Course I am.'

'Why'd he have to come? Why d'he have to spoil it all?'

Alan put his arm round her. 'He doesn't know how not to, darling. He never did but he can't spoil what we don't let him.' He strode over to the sound system and clattered through a few CDs and the Kaiser Chiefs' 'I Predict a Riot', was soon booming round the flat.

God, I hope not, Sam thought. But if it wasn't a riot that was coming down the line, something else definitely was. She could feel it. The witch was out of the bottle and getting up to all kinds of mischief. She looked at Alan and Stephanie dancing together. He was determined that his party should not be ruined by what had happened but the anger he felt was evident in the way he was moving. Usually Alan was a great dancer, fluid and easy in his body, but he was going through the motions out there and wherever his mind was, it certainly wasn't on the beat of the music.

It was three o'clock and the party was staggering to a close.

Stephanie came up to Sam. 'Are you coming back to the flat?'

'I think I'll stay here tonight and help Alan tidy up. There are some things I need to talk to him about. You're OK to get back by yourself?'

'Course I am.'

Stephanie walked over and hugged Alan goodbye and then left with a young man with the good looks of a Thierry Henry.

Watching them leave together, Sam was glad she'd made the decision to stay at Alan's.

He was picking up bottles in the front room and putting them into an orange recycling sack. Sam joined him, emptying the dregs of beer from open, unfinished bottles and cans. They worked in silence. At least there was some colour back in his face now but the skin still seemed stretched tight round his jaw. They stacked plates and glasses in his dishwasher and cleared up spills on the floor. The unopened beer they put back in the fridge, the full ashtrays were emptied and soaked.

Half an hour later they were finished. Alan picked up a packet of fags that had been left in the kitchen and shook it; it rattled. He hesitated, then said, 'What the hell. Do you want one?'

Sam nodded. 'Why not?' With a certain amount of alcohol in her system a cigarette always seemed like the best idea in the world.

They moved out on to the balcony again. Now the sky was lightening and the stars were on the retreat in the face of the upcoming dawn. Sam lit up and inhaled luxuriantly. She looked up at the stars and then over at the pale line of the horizon. There was a romance to this urban vista that she had never experienced in Oxford. This is better, she thought, better than anything you can see from the top of St Mary's. Down below them a police siren wailed. It was a beautiful time of day. On the rare occasion she was awake to witness it, she always wondered why she didn't do this more often, although the answer was pretty obvious. She preferred snoring in her own bed.

Alan stared out at the horizon, eyes narrowed in the cigarette smoke. Sam moved closer to him so their arms were touching and nudged him gently. He looked sideways at her, sighed and shook his head. 'Wrestling with dinosaurs and big bad Johnny – where's it all going to end?'

Sam shrugged. 'All in a day's work.'

'You looked like a flea on the back of a bucking bronco.'

'I *felt* like a flea on the back of a bucking bronco.'

Above them the big 'W' of Cassiopeia was fading into the dawn.

'Fuck him,' Alan said savagely and flicked his fag-end out into the darkness. They watched its burning tip tumble through the air like a sky-diving firefly.

'The sooner he's back inside the better for all of us.'

'You don't mean that.'

He sighed and didn't reply immediately.

'Johnny doesn't know how not to destroy the things around him. Like Stephanie. I've worked so bloody hard with her, going to see her teachers when she was being bullied about her dad being in prison, keeping her grounded, getting her the job.'

'The trouble is, Alan, he is her father,' Sam said.

'Not in any way that means anything, he isn't. I've been more of a father than he's ever been, than he ever will be.'

'It's natural he's going to want to see her.'

'Come on, Sam. You didn't feel that way about your father, did you?'

'No, that's true, I didn't.'

'And seeing him didn't resolve anything, did it?

'It made some things clearer, Alan, and others more obscure.'

'I don't suppose you're going to tell me what those were?'

She smiled.

'Would you talk to her?'

'About what?'

'You were in a similar position, weren't you? Your father was away all through your childhood and then came back into your life.'

'I don't think that would do any good. I haven't got any nice easy solutions to offer.'

'I'm not asking you to present her with a solution. Just talk to her about your experience. It'll help.'

'I don't see how it could.'

'Please, Sam, as a favour to me.'

'OK, OK, but I've got no happy ending to give her.'

'Just talk to her. You must know a bit of what she's going through. You staying?'

She nodded.

'I'll get you some bedding.'

Sam stayed out on the balcony finishing her cigarette. What could she say to Stephanie? Keep away from him. Don't expect anything from him. Don't let him mess with your head. Don't think of him as a father. Think of him as a stranger – a dangerous one. Whatever you do, don't think of him as a friend. Don't confuse him with someone who cares about you. She sighed. How could she say all that to her? She'd have to think of something more positive, but God knows what that might be.

CHAPTER THIRTEEN

Sam surfaced to the sound of a phone ringing and then plunged back to sleep, finally waking properly at midday. Alan, barefoot and sarong-wrapped, put a cup of tea down on the table, level with her head and sat down to drink his own. Sam slowly sat upright and scrubbed at her eyes.

'Oh God,' she said and yawned.

'It lives.'

'If this is living remind me to try dying really soon.' She scrabbled in her bag and put on her dark glasses. Her head hurt inside from the alcohol and outside from the dinosaur bones, her forearms throbbed and she felt like she could sleep for a thousand years. She dropped her arms on to her knees and winced, both forearms were red and tender to the touch, so was her throat.

Alan padded out of the room and came back a few moments later holding a tube in his hand which he threw at Sam. 'Arnica – good for bruising.'

'Thanks.' She undid the cap and began rubbing it on her arms and throat; it felt immediately cool and soothing.

Later Alan cooked up some brunch for them and they spent the afternoon reading the papers, snoozing and rehydrating. At five they left the flat and walked to Hammersmith Bridge, crossed it and began walking along the riverside footpath that led past the Harrods depository. The footpath was busy with cyclists, walkers, runners, small children and dogs. Sam and Alan strolled, in so far as strolling was possible, amidst all the activity and tried to enjoy the river without being knocked into it.

It took them about half an hour to reach Putney Bridge and from there it was a short distance to Sam's flat.

'Can she cook?' Sam said as they passed the Larrik pub and rounded the corner into the New Kings Road.

'I'd say about as well as you can.'

At the car-wash four or five men in blue-grey overalls were working on a sports car. A man in a striped shirt, with his hands on his hips, watched them. It was a strange bit of road – no new business seemed to last long here. She noticed Café Africa had closed. The only successful long-stayer had been Pro Feet which was now itself on the move elsewhere.

'Shall we suggest a take-away,' Sam said. 'Won't it be easier for everyone?'

'Let's see what she's come up with. If she's made an effort we can't refuse it.'

After a short walk past the grotty concreted-over front gardens of a scrubby terrace of houses they reached Sam's flat. She rang the bell but when there was no reply let them into the hallway. Frank was sprawled outside Edie's front door and flipped his tail back and forth in welcome. It was cool here in the stairwell and he looked in no hurry to go anywhere.

Sam let them into the flat.

'Steph,' Alan shouted, but there was no reply.

'Maybe she's nipped out for something from the shop,' Sam said.

She checked the front room and then pushed open the door to her bedroom. It was dark in here but Sam could just about make out Stephanie lying on the bed with her face turned away from her.

She took a step into the room. 'Ste …' she began. Then she looked down at her feet; her trainers were sticking to something on the wooden floor. She bent down and touched it with her fingers and brought her fingertips up under her nose. At first she thought it might be a cup of tea but the consistency was too viscous and it didn't smell of tea, it smelled metallic. Then she looked more closely round the room. Whatever she had on her fingertips was all over the place. Shaking, her hand reached for the light.

Blood was everywhere. It dripped from the walls and stuck to the soles of her shoes, there were even splashes on the ceiling. It soaked the white duvet cover and the sheets on the bed.

'Is she in there?' Alan said behind her.

Sam turned round and pushed him away from the door into the hall. He staggered backwards.

'Hey,' he said. 'Watch it.'

Stephanie was his favourite niece. Sam placed her hand on his chest.

'Don't go in there, Alan.'

'Come on, it can't be that bad. I've seen messy rooms before.'

'It's not mess …'

She took her hand off his chest. He looked down at the stain her fingers had left on his T-shirt. He pulled his shirt up and away from his body and stared at it. 'What the hell's that?'

'She's dead.'

'What are you talking about?'

'Stephanie – we have to call the police.'

'Stephanie? What are you talking about?'

He moved towards her.

'Don't, Alan …'

But he pushed Sam firmly to one side and walked into the room. Sam picked up the phone, dialled 999, reported what had happened, and then followed Alan into the room. The sun had come out and was shining against the blinds. The blood had gone everywhere; it had run down the blinds and pooled on the floor, it had turned the white sheets and duvet on the bed a terrible, terrible red. It was hard to believe that there was a drop of blood left in the body draped across the bed. She'd heard about this before – arterial spurt – a clean scientific word, but she'd never seen it. She hoped she'd never see it again. Blood-bath would have been a more suitable description.

Alan stood by the side of the bed staring down at his niece. He was staring at her with a terrible intensity, as if all his energy was going into trying to bring her back to life.

'Alan?' her voice was more brittle than she intended.

It was as if her voice jolted him out of his trance because he moved swiftly to the bed and placed his fingers against Stephanie's neck or what was left of it. Old police training, Sam suspected, taking over because it was obvious that Stephanie was dead. The obscene wound running across her throat was evidence of that. Her throat had been cut so savagely that her neck was barely attached to her shoulders.

Not a riot, Sam thought, but this. This was what she'd been feeling. This was what she'd been feeling ever since she saw that bottle smashed into pieces at the Pitt Rivers – not a riot, another death.

CHAPTER FOURTEEN

Sam sat in the passenger seat of an unmarked police car outside the house in Holland Park. It was night-time. DI Paxton, a wiry man with cropped salt-and-pepper hair, wearing jeans, trainers and a white T-shirt, sat next to her.

'You're sure this is the one?' he said. 'They look like the kind who'd sue if we got it wrong.'

She nodded and watched as he got out of the car and was followed across the road by the occupants of the white van that had drawn up behind them. After the bell was rung and a fair bit of shouting, the door was swiftly knocked off its hinges and they all piled inside. Lights were going on up and down the street and soon she saw several people leaning out of their windows watching what was going on. A police raid was probably hardly the norm for this neck of the woods.

Sam had spent most of the last thirty-six hours in the company of Paxton and had come to the conclusion that if you had to have someone crawling over every inch of your life, he wasn't too bad a man to do it. The fact he'd been a contemporary of Phil's at Hendon had helped.

She leaned her head back and closed her eyes. Since she had discovered Stephanie's body it was almost the first time that she had been left on her own. She was numb with shock and exhaustion and images of Alan staring down at his niece kept flashing into her brain. One of the lines of investigation that the police were pursuing was that whoever had killed Stephanie had not intended to kill her at all; their target had been Sam.

She hadn't wanted to believe it. First, because if it was true then she was responsible for what had happened to Stephanie and she couldn't bear to think that. Secondly, because presumably once the killers discovered that they had been unsuccessful, she would still be a target and given the way Stephanie had died that was also pretty horrible to think about.

The police were working on the premise that whoever killed Stephanie must have been waiting for her on the stairs when she came in, had dragged her into the flat and killed her in the bedroom. Saturday nights in the block could be very noisy, depending on the age and proclivities of the occupants of the various rented flats. Loud noise and a lot of coming and going was par for the course, as was late-night ringing of everyone's bells by people who didn't have keys to the outside door but did have keys to the flats. According to the police theory, the killer had waited until they saw a short blonde woman enter the block and then assuming that it was Sam, because she was opening the door to her flat, they had killed her.

The first time they suggested that to her she had protested, but then she had a vivid image of the man with the wrecking-ball head getting up off the tarmac and staring after her and she had told the police about what had taken place earlier in the day, and what had happened with the computer. The police had also insisted on her giving them details of all her cases which had involved people who might have a reason to want to hurt her. When she'd protested that the most likely ones – John O'Connor and Andrew Hughes – were still in prison and due to stay there for a long time, the police had told her that made no difference, hits could be organised from inside prison as easily as outside.

Sam opened her eyes and saw Paxton crossing back across the street towards the car. He leaned down and spoke through the window.

'No one's there.'

'Maybe you'll find some prints.'

'We're not holding our breath.'

'Do you mind if I come in and have a look around?'

She followed him back into the house. A forensic team was dusting doorknobs and door-jambs with grey powder. The main room was exactly the same other than the fact that the laptop and the flowers were missing. She wandered out into the metal, stone and wooden garden. The lights had come on round the pool and she walked down to it, past the ranks of spiky plants. Water lilies floated on the surface of the pond and in its depths fat orange fish skulked back and forth. A piece of paper attracted her attention. She leaned forwards and pulled it out. It had brown marks along its irregular edge that looked like scorch marks. Sam smoothed the paper flat on a paving stone near one of the lights and bent over it, trying to decipher what was on it.

It was a photocopy of the top part of a sheet of newspaper, an old one – *The Oxford Times*, dated December 1976, but the page itself was missing. What she had in her hands was the banner and nothing else. Sam wrote down the date and then handed it over to Paxton.

The police car dropped Sam outside her mansion block. Sam had phoned Alan and told him she'd speak to Edie and then to Floyd, the young man Stephanie had left the party with. Alan had been tied up with the police and now was with his family. She'd agreed to go over to his place later. She told the policeman in the hall who she was and that she needed to talk to her next-door neighbour about the cat, and then opened Edie's letterbox and whistled. As she waited, she glanced at her own front door. Yellow police tape stating 'Do Not Cross' in black lettering had been stretched across it. She had no inclination to. She wondered if she'd ever want to go in there again.

A few moments later Edie opened the door and peered out.

'He still there?' she said, gesturing down the stairwell at the policeman.

'Yes.'

She grabbed Sam's arm and pulled her into the flat. 'When they going to bugger off? I can't be doing with them parked on the doorstep all day long. It's not good for my nerves.'

'I don't know, Edie.'

It was cool in Edie's flat because it didn't get the afternoon sun but Edie herself did not look cool, she was red-faced and sweating and extremely pissed off. They went into the kitchen and Sam sat down at the table.

'Want some squash?'

Sam peered at an ancient bottle of Orangina. 'Just water thanks, Edie.'

Edie got her a glass and put it on the table. 'Can't see the point of that,' she said. 'All it's good for is brushing your teeth.'

'You need to drink a lot of water in this heat.'

'I've got one bloody daughter. I don't need another.'

Sam sighed. Edie obviously wasn't in the mood to be helpful. 'Have the police interviewed you?'

'Silly sods.'

Sam took that as a yes.

'Do you mind if I ask you a few questions?'

'Bloody questions, on and on … and in this heat when my teeth are melting out of my head …'

'Did you hear anything the night Stephanie was murdered?'

'Frankie needs more cat food and cat litter,' Edie said. 'I can't be struggling around with those heavy bags in the heat. Not at my age and on my pension … it's all too much.'

Sam sighed, she had an account with the pet shop down the road and an agreement that they'd deliver to Edie's once a week. Edie didn't have to pay a penny. She opened her bag and took out her wallet, considered what would do the trick, removed a twenty-pound note and placed it on the table between them. Edie's hand slid across the table and covered it.

'Now then, what was you asking?'

'That night, did you hear anything?'

'Course I did, they were having a party upstairs. All I did was hear things the whole bloody night long. Crashing and banging and thump, thump, drag, drag. The mother came down as well in the afternoon, said it was her kid's eighteenth, said sorry there'd be a bit of noise. If she thought that was a bit of noise, I'm bloody Mother Teresa.'

Sam laughed.

'Arctic Monkeys crashing down on my head all night long. "Bet you look good on the dance floor". Bet they didn't. How can you dance to stuff like that?'

'How do you know about the Arctic Monkeys?' Sam asked.

'I'm old, not senile,' Edie snapped. 'Same way as you do I expect. I read about them and saw them on TV.'

'So there was lots of noise, lots of people coming and going?'

'They'd been leaning on the doorbell half the night and I'd been ignoring it but then at three, after most of them had gone, someone just kept ringing and ringing. Wouldn't let up, so I got up and buzzed them in. I couldn't stand any more bloody noise.'

'Did you open the door and see who it was?'

She shook her head. 'I didn't want to look at them, did I? I wanted to get them off my bloody bell.'

It was unlike Edie, Sam thought, usually she wouldn't even let the meter readers in, but then if she'd been up half the night, she could understand why she might do it. Maybe she had let the killer in, but then again he might have been in already. It would have been easy enough to come in with the party-goers and then wait in the basement. From there he would have had a view of the front door and would have been able to see everyone who came into the block.

'Did you tell this to the police?'

'What, and get some kid barely out of nappies wanting to lay the blame on me for what happened? I wasn't going to tell them anything. She's dead, isn't she? Anything I say isn't going to bring her back.'

Sam sipped her water.

'You know before, Edie, when you said Stephanie was brass.'

'Well, she was, wasn't she?'

'What made you think it?'

Edie folded her arms. 'She was having sex with lots of different men. That's what.'

'What did you see?'

'I didn't see it. I heard it when I was taking the rubbish out. I do it in the evening when it's cooler.'

Sam smiled. The reason why Edie left it to night-time to put out her rubbish had nothing to do with the heat; it was so that she could see if there was anything she could pilfer.

'I was on the pavement outside your flat and I heard them. The windows were open, weren't they? They were chopping it off like foxes.'

'Did you see the man?'

'I saw lots of men going in and out.'

'Lots?'

'More than one.'

'They could have been friends, Edie. She was working in a pub. Maybe they were colleagues she was bringing back from work.'

Edie did not look impressed with Sam's suggestion. 'I know what I know,' she said, 'whether you chose to believe me or not, and one of them was a right nasty piece of work.'

'What did he look like?'

'Didn't see him. Heard him shouting up at her flat.'

'When was this?'

'Saturday afternoon.'

'Did she let him in?'

Edie shrugged. 'All that bloody noise.'

'What time was it?'

'2.15.'

'How can you be so certain?'

'I was watching the racing.'

A loud howl wafted in through the kitchen window. Sam leaned out and lowered the basket, Frank jumped in and she hauled him into the kitchen. He slouched over to a shady part of the kitchen by the fridge and threw himself on his back with all his paws in the air. She'd never seen him walk into a kitchen and not head straight for food.

'Is he all right?' she asked.

'Suffering in the heat, like the rest of us, isn't he,' Edie said. 'All I can eat is jelly and custard.'

Sam nodded at the policeman and let herself out of the block. On the other side of the road was a short terrace of houses that faced a car showroom and the bridge which carried the District line towards Wimbledon in one direction and Earls Court in the other. She ran across the road, walking up a path between front gardens packed with tomato plants and rang the doorbell of the first house. An elderly man, wearing baggy shorts and a vest, eventually came to the door.

'Sorry to bother you,' Sam said. 'But does Floyd live here?'

He shook his head and pointed with his thumb to the right. 'Thanks.'

'But you won't find him there, he works for them,' he said, nodding at the car showroom. 'He'll be in one of the garages under the bridge.'

Sam thanked him and set off along the curved road that ran from the New Kings Road to Munster Road. The businesses that had their premises under the District line were mainly garages but there was also a sandwich-making place, a bicycle repair shop and a shop selling Vespas, a method of transport Sam had always hankered after.

The first few garages drew a blank. In the third one a man in green overalls was standing with his back to her, working with an acetylene torch on the undercarriage of a car suspended above him on a hydraulic lift. Sam waited until he had switched off the torch and taken off his goggles and then addressed him by name and he turned round. Her brief impression of him at Alan's party had been that he was very good-looking and seeing him now with the sweat pouring off his face did nothing to dispel that first opinion.

She saw a look of alarm run across his face as he registered who she was.

'It's all right,' she said. 'I just want to ask you a few questions.'

'The police have only just stopped asking me. I don't have anything else to say.'

'Look, you know I'm friends with Alan Knowles. If you talk to me I can tell him and his brothers what you've said. If it's not me it's going to be one of Stephanie's uncles. Which do you prefer?'

'It had nothing to do with me.'

'I didn't think it did but I just want to hear from you what happened.'

He eased himself out of the upper part of the overalls, leaving the arms hanging down around his waist like an extra pair of legs, grabbed a grubby towel off a hook on the wall and wiped his face.

'I'll wait for you out here,' Sam said.

She left the oppressive heat of the garage and crouched down in the shade cast by the wall which bordered the road. Floyd took off his T-shirt and poured some water over his torso, then he took off the rest of his overalls. Underneath he was wearing a pair of khaki shorts, sodden with sweat. He dried himself off and joined Sam, trying to shake some air into the legs of his shorts. She offered him a cigarette from the packet she'd taken from Alan's and lit his and then her own.

'How did you know her?'

'Her cousin was at school with my brother. We all hung out together ever since we were kids.'

'Were you going out with her?'

'Going out? What era you come from?'

'Having a relationship?'

'I told you we been friends from when we was kids.'

'Were you sleeping with her?'

'You want to tell me why that's any of your fucking business?'

'You don't think that's what the Knowles brothers will want to know?'

'All I know about those brothers is they got three brain cells between the lot of them.'

Sam smiled. 'Do you know if she was seeing anybody else?'

He exhaled a cloud of smoke. 'Steph was one free spirit and that suited me just fine.'

'Was she seeing anyone who wasn't so relaxed about it?'

'Everyone knew the score with Steph. She never pretended it was anything other than the way it was. She didn't want no one thinking they owned her.'

'Could you give me the names and addresses of her other boyfriends?'

'Hope you got a long, long piece of paper.'

'Could you tell me exactly what happened when you came back after Alan's party?'

'I can't say I wasn't hoping for some, you understand, but when we got to her place she said she wasn't into it. Her head was someplace else since her father came back on the scene.'

'You mean the fight at Alan's?'

'There was that but also he'd visited her at the pub and that had freaked her out.'

Sam frowned. 'When was this?'

'The day before the party he turned up, sat at the bar, ordered a drink and got talking to her. She was real upset and the manager asked him to leave. He said he had as much right to sit there and have his drink as anyone else, had as much right to come and talk to his daughter. In the end she took him outside and asked what he wanted with her. He said money or a job. She gave him some money but there weren't no job, she'd only just started there herself. Then he left. She was well pissed off at him.'

'After the party did you go into the flat with her?'

He shook his head. 'I left her on the doorstep and went back home. I was cool with it. She didn't want to do it – end of story.'

'Anyone see you come in?'

'My mum was up watching something on the TV. Lucky for me.'

'Yes,' Sam said. 'Very lucky for you.'

She took a notebook out of her bag and handed it to him. 'Could you give me those names now and details where I might find them?'

'I done this with the police already.' He ground out his cigarette butt on the wall behind him and took the notebook and pen Sam handed him. A few minutes later he handed it back to her.

She leafed through the list. 'This all of them?'

'All I know of.'

'Thanks. If you think of anything else will you let me know?' She handed him her card.

'You'll keep her uncles off my back?'

She nodded. 'I'll try but it might be a good idea to go away for a bit.'

He shook his head. 'Boss is on holiday. I can't do that.'

She'd phoned to make sure he was here; it had been a short mono-syllabic conversation. Now she paused, looking up at the tower block rising up against the night sky. It wasn't long ago that she and Alan had been out on his balcony looking at the lights of London spread out beneath them and she had been thinking a whole load of nonsense about the romance of the big city. The city didn't seem like such a wonderful place to be now. What on earth was she going to say to him? A gust of warm wind blew a can of Coke along the path that led to the main doors and Sam slowly followed it and buzzed to gain access. Her stomach twisted and turned in the ride up in the lift. By the time she was standing outside Alan's flat she was feeling sick. She ran her hand over her face and pressed the bell.

He opened the door and stood to one side to let her in. On the way up she'd been preparing herself for some of his family to be here but the flat was empty. They went into the front room.

'Do you want something?' he said.

He seemed preternaturally calm and Sam was unnerved by it. 'Tea. Thanks.'

He went into the kitchen and Sam followed him. She didn't know if the police had told him that they thought the killer had been intending to kill her. In the couple of short conversations they'd had they hadn't covered that.

'They took me over to the house in Holland Park.'

He was pouring water into the teapot but stopped, hand suspended in mid-air. 'Why?'

'I don't know what they said to you, Alan, but they seem to think there's a good chance that whoever killed Stephanie wasn't after her at all. They saw a small blonde woman letting herself into my flat and drew the obvious conclusion that it was me.'

'What did you tell them you were doing in the house?'

'I told them the truth, Alan, and decided that that could fall as it may. Steph's death is more important than my little bit of trespassing. And anyway they're dusting for fingerprints and they're bound to find mine.'

Alan put down the kettle. 'Well they haven't said anything about you to me. All they've been going on about is the family business. Could there be a vendetta against the family? And then of course there's Johnny. No one's seen him. He's not at his parole hostel. They keep asking me where he hangs out and I keep telling them I don't know. He's only just out of prison. He probably doesn't know where he hangs out yet.'

'Do you think he had anything to do with it?'

He shook his head. 'Look, I'm the first one to put my hands up and say he's a violent bastard. I hate him and always have but there's no way he killed Stephanie. I mean why would he do that? He's only just got out of prison. She's his daughter for God's sake. I know he was pissed off at the party and we fought but that was nothing. It's just a bit of facing off between brothers. For Johnny, that was a bit of play-fighting.'

'Play-fighting? It didn't look that way to me.'

'If he'd meant it, Sam, he would have torn out my earring or bitten my nose. I'm telling you – that was nothing.'

'Then where is he?'

'I don't know but it's only been thirty-six hours. He'll turn up before too long.'

'When I spoke to Floyd he said Johnny had turned up at the pub Steph was working at and made a bit of a nuisance of himself.'

'She didn't say anything about that to me.'

'Maybe she didn't want to cause a row.'

'What sort of nuisance?'

'Ordered himself a drink, sat at the bar, refused to leave. He asked her if she could get him a job and when she gave him some money he left.'

'When was this?'

'The day before your party. Floyd said she was upset about it.' Alan handed her a cup and Sam continued. 'Edie said that there was a man who sounds like Johnny who came round on Saturday afternoon and was trying to get in and was shouting for Steph.'

'There's absolutely no way Johnny's involved in this and I've told the police that again and again.'

'So you think they could be right about the target being me?'

'I can see why they're pursuing that line of investigation. After all, you're in a more dangerous line of work, aren't you?'

'What about your other brothers?'

'This isn't about them either.'

'How can you be so sure?'

'Because it's too heavy. Murder's too extreme. If people are looking for revenge they'd do it against property – torch one of their offices or clubs, rough up one of the cabbies. They're not going to go straight to murder because they know there'd be severe consequences.'

'I'm so sorry, Alan.'

'For what? Being a private investigator, being kind enough to let Stephanie stay in your flat for some poxy amount of rent?'

Sam studied the surface of her tea. 'As things have turned out, yes, for both those things.'

They had moved back into the living-room and sat down on the sofa. Alan leaned his head back and closed his eyes. Sam sat sipping her tea in silence. Downstairs the steady beat of the bass thumped up through the floor. Alan groaned and sat forwards. 'Right,' he said. 'Where do we start? If whoever did this is after you there's no guarantee they're going to stop trying to kill you, so we better get on with trying to figure out what the hell's going on. What's our next move?'

'I've been thinking about that and it all comes back to Norman. We have to find him.'

'Why him?'

'Because he's the link. First he drops off a Chihuahua with me, then Cruella de Vil comes visiting, then I discover that the items being stolen in the museum are all from the Sweetman collection and that his grandfather was Professor of Anthropology and Norman had the run of the museum when he was a boy. One thing that has been a constant is that Norman has lied and lied to me. Another is that now people have started dying – first Justin in the Pitt Rivers and now Stephanie.'

'Have you had the dog checked to see if it's been micro-chipped?'

'The police suggested that after the attempted dog-nap but I sort of got overtaken by events.'

'OK, so you need to do that and we need to find Norman. Any ideas?'

'His grandfather's in hospital. That's what he said when he dumped the dog on me.'

'Another lie?'

'No. Helen, the woman who worked with him at the cinema, confirmed that something was going on with him and also at the party I was at Gittings told me that Professor Sweetman was in hospital. He's not in a very good state apparently so I think the best way to track down Norman is to camp outside his grandfather's room and wait for him to turn up. Maybe I'll be able to have a quick chat with the old boy.'

'OK, well that seems clear. You go back to Oxford and get on with taking the Chihuahua to the vet and seeing if you can trace Norman through his grandfather. I'll see what I can find out about the company that the car's registered to. A company search should come up with some names.'

'There's another thing,' Sam said. 'Floyd gave me a list of names of people who were ...' she paused '... friendly with Stephanie. It might be worth checking them out.'

'Friendly?'

Sam didn't say anything. She dug in her bag and handed him her notebook.

Alan opened the book and looked at the list. 'It's a long list.'

'I told Floyd you'd keep your brothers off his back.'

He sighed. 'I can't guarantee that, Sam.'

'He hasn't got anything to do with it. I believed him when he said he dropped her off and went home and I presume the police do too.'

Alan was stretching his arms above his head.

'When I was at the party in north Oxford,' Sam said. 'Luke told me that Norman's parents were killed in a car crash when he was little. Perhaps that would be worth looking into.'

'What do you think that's got to do with what's going on?'

'I've no idea, to be honest. Maybe nothing ...'

'I have to try and get some sleep,' he said.

Sam nodded. 'Do you mind if I doss down on your sofa. I'll go back to Oxford in the morning.'

He gestured at the sofa. 'Help yourself.'

He left the room and came back with two sheets, and a pair of pyjamas. 'These are way too big, but they're all I've got.'

'How are your other brothers handling it?'

'They want everything sorted as quickly as possible. The police are crawling all over them asking questions. They want the police off their backs and the only way that happens is if they find who killed Steph. There's a family conference later tonight.'

'Do you want me to come?'

'Family only, Sam. You know what they're like about outsiders.'

She nodded.

As he turned to go, she said, 'I'm really sorry about Steph, Alan.'
'I know you are ...'

Alan left the room and Sam shook the sheet out on the sofa. She walked out on to the balcony. The view didn't seem so appealing this time. She looked at the streams of traffic flowing in and out of the city, red tail-lights heading over to her right and the white lights of the oncoming cars flowing to her left. Somewhere out there was the person who had killed Stephanie and had perhaps meant to kill her. No, tonight the city didn't seem like such a great place to be. It seemed a brutal place filled with random violence, a place where you could be dancing one night and dead the next. She shivered – cutting someone's throat was a very intimate way to kill someone. Physically it required you to be right up close, to be covered in their blood, to be drenched with it, to participate in the death. There were other ways to kill people that were much less intimate.

A vision of Stephanie lying on her bed, eyes open, mouth agape, came back to her. It would be a while before the police would let her back into the flat but she was in no hurry for that. She wondered if she'd ever be happy about living there again. She turned away from the view and walked back into the flat, got into Alan's pyjamas and lay down on the sofa. After what had happened Oxford didn't seem such a bad place to be going to after all. She was exhausted and despite everything that had been going on, sleep claimed her immediately.

Alan leaned against the bar and looked across the dance floor to where his brothers had congregated in a loose grouping; five heart attacks waiting to happen. It was usually a situation he found himself in only once a year on Christmas Eve when the whole clan met to exchange presents. But on those occasions Alan usually had their wives and girlfriends and children to talk to. It was as if his brothers thought that if they got too close to him his gayness might rub off on them. He didn't care; it was a useful buffer and it was the way the family handled his sexuality – to place him in the same category as women and children – and it was fine by Alan, he had more of a laugh with them than with his burly, bluff brothers. But tonight there were no women and children for him to talk to and so he was leaning on the bar waiting for things to get under way. This was business. Stephanie had been murdered and they were here to decide what to do about it.

He looked around him. The last punters were slowly leaving. There was no sadder place to be than a nightclub when the lights had just been put on full glare. The Ritzy Club, situated in a grotty basement on King's Street, couldn't have been less so if it tried. Half an hour ago when the music had been thumping and the lights were dimmed you could imagine it was all right, but now with the overhead lighting on, and empty of people and the sound of music, there was no disguising what a shit-hole it was. His brothers owned it, had done for years. Bert had won it in a game of cards, so the story went. Alan wasn't quite so sure but it wasn't something you asked questions about, and if you weren't asking them at age fifteen, when Bert had first got the place, you certainly weren't going to be asking them when you were older. He shifted his weight and felt the soles of his trainers stick on the beer-splattered floor.

The last time he'd been down here he'd been eighteen years old, trying to get some money together to see him through college. It was the first time he'd seen someone glassed. He hadn't liked the place much then either and it didn't look any different twenty years on. The banquettes were the same tawdry red velvet but this time covered in a number of masking tape Elastoplasts to stop the stuffing oozing out of them. He turned round and looked behind the bar. One of his nephews, Bert's eldest, about the age he'd been when working here, had just opened an industrial dishwasher and disappeared in a cloud of steam.

'Jimmy, could you get me a whisky?'

The boy took a glass from behind the bar and carried a bottle over and placed it next to the glass.

'Where's your dad?'

'There was trouble at the taxi office. He phoned half an hour ago to say he'd be here quick as he could.'

As he spoke he gestured with his head. 'Here he is.'

Bert's burly frame appeared at the bottom of the stairs. He walked over to where Alan was standing and lightly punched his arm. 'All right, Al?'

Alan nodded. Bert, he could handle. Bert was all right. Bert wasn't a fucking nutter like some of the others. Bert looked across at his other brothers. 'No Johnny?'

Alan shook his head. 'What held you up?'

'Some twat knifed one of the cabbies. Had to get him sewn up.'

All in a day's work for Bert.

'You can go,' Bert said to his son. 'And him.' He nodded at the other man behind the bar. 'Do the rest in the morning.'

'I want to stay.'

'You deaf or something?' and he jerked his thumb in the direction of the door.

Jimmy sighed, threw a cloth down on the bar, had a word with the other man and they both moved towards the exit.

Alan watched Bert walk over and join the others. He thought he'd left all this family stuff behind him, thought he could keep it all nicely located on one day of the year. 'All right, Al,' was the most that any of them said to him, as he handed over cards and presents for their families. They knew nothing about his life. He was gay and an ex-policeman and that made him a double outsider. But here he was twenty years on in this same shit-hole, smelling of stale cigarettes and spilled beer, about to sit down with his brothers, about to try and make them see sense. And this time Johnny was in the mix. And Stephanie had been killed. It couldn't get any worse.

The trouble was this time he was struggling to make himself see sense. Vengeance – he felt the desire for it in himself as strongly as he'd ever felt anything. One part of him couldn't believe Steph was dead, the other part that knew full well was demanding action, crying out to do something, to let off steam, to get the bastard who'd done it. That part didn't want to see sense either, that part wanted to throw itself into the arms of his crazy brothers and embrace every bit of their violence and ignorance, everything he despised.

Bert had turned round and was gesturing to him. 'You coming or what?'

He drained his whisky, pushed himself away from the bar and walked slowly towards them. Yes, he was coming.

They fell silent as he reached them. After all, he was the one who'd been speaking to the police. He was the ex-policeman. He knew more than they did.

He cleared his throat. 'The police think whoever killed Steph might have been trying to kill Sam. She's about the same build as Steph and blonde, and Steph was staying in her flat.'

His brothers stared at him.

'If they think that, why are they crawling so far up our arses?' Bert said.

Alan shrugged. 'They've got two lines of investigation.'

'So she wasn't even killed for herself?'

Alan shrugged. 'It's one of the lines of investigation the police are pursuing. Floyd was the last person to see her alive. He was at my party and saw her to the door, said goodbye on the doorstep and then went home. He lives across the road in the houses opposite Harrington Cars.'

'He need a visit?'

'No,' Alan said. 'He doesn't. The police have checked him out and so has Sam. His mum was waiting up for him and she says he came in when he said.'

'Yeah, but you think what Mum used to say about us.'

'When Stephanie was killed there was a lot of blood,' Alan continued, 'and they couldn't find any trace of blood on any of his clothes, including the ones he wore to the party. It's not him.'

He looked round the group. None of them held his eye except Bert. There was silence in the room. He hadn't gone into the details of how she died and none of his brothers had asked him. A lot of blood. It was the most information that they'd had and it had them looking at their shoes and reaching for their pints.

'What about boyfriends?' Bert asked.

'Her mum don't think she's got any,' Peter said.

'Well, she wouldn't. She'd think she was a good Catholic girl.'

'Sam got a list from Floyd. I'm going to check it out. Has anyone seen Johnny?'

Silence.

'The police want to talk to him.'

'He's goin' to be easier to frame than Whistler's mother,' Bert said.

'They need to talk to him to rule him out.'

'Rule him out ...' The sarcasm in his brother's voice was obvious.

'It doesn't mean they think he killed her. They need to know where he went after he left my party. The longer he stays away the more the police will suspect him. He's got to tell the police what he's been doing since he left the party. If he turns up you should tell him to hand himself in.'

His brothers considered him in silence.

'He's a crazy fucker,' Bert said.

'Mad as a cut snake,' Pete added.

'So, this Sam's to blame, is that what you're saying?' Harry said.

'No, I'm not saying that. She's not to blame. She lent Steph the flat and she looked like her, but she's not responsible for what happened. She didn't know Steph was at risk. If she had, she would have told Steph, but we don't know for sure that they were after her. It's just one line the police are investigating.'

'Who'd want to kill 'er?'

'Sam?'

'Yup.'

'It's a case we're working on.'

'What about?'

Alan didn't want to get into this with his brothers. 'She's going to be following up that side of things in Oxford.'

'If they tried to kill 'er . . .'

'She's a tough little sod,' Bert said. 'She can handle herself, can't she, Al?'

Alan nodded, thought of Sam asleep on his sofa and hoped Bert was right.

CHAPTER FIFTEEN

Early the following morning Sam caught the X90 bus back to Oxford. The police still had her van and were trying to lift prints from it. She got off in Headington and went straight to the community centre. Even though she felt she needed to get on with finding Norman, it had been too late to cancel the class, and at least it would allow her to focus on something else other than the murder and mayhem that had been dogging her for the last couple of weeks. She put out the chairs and by the time the women began to arrive, she was standing by the board on which was written, 'Pension day'.

When they were all seated she said, 'How many of you go to the post office to pick up your pension?'

Three-quarters of the women in the group put up their hands.

'The trouble with pension day is that it's a day when any potential attackers will know where you'll be and that you'll have money on you, so what are some of the kinds of things you can do to minimise the risk?'

'Take someone with you,' said white bouffant.

'Yes,' Sam said, writing that up on the board. 'I know that for some of you that won't be an option, but you are much more likely to be attacked if you are by yourself. Someone else, however frail, will at least be another pair of eyes and a potential witness. What else?'

'Vary the time of day you go to get it.'

'Yes,' Sam said. 'That's very important. Don't always go at the same time of day. If your attacker's been observing you he might be thrown out by you not going at what he thinks is your usual time.'

'Take a dog,' said a thin angular woman with rimless glasses. 'If you don't have one, borrow one.'

Sam frowned. 'I suppose so, yes, but it would have to be a dog you were happy to handle. You don't want to be dragged down the road by a Rottweiler or something but if it was a small dog – why not? Attackers don't like dogs, it complicates matters for them. How many of you have mobiles?'

About half the hands went up.

'Well the rest of you should definitely get them.'

There was a groan from some of the group.

Sam held up her hand. 'I don't care what your objections are and, to be honest, I probably share a lot of them, but if you are willing to put the time aside to do this course, you should be willing to buy a phone. They're not that pricy. You can get a pay as you go for about thirty pounds and then put ten pounds on it. If you have one you can call for help; if you haven't, you're going to be reliant on someone else. It's an easy way to take responsibility for your own safety.'

'My son keeps going on at me ...'

'Well, listen to him, he's right about this. And when you have one make sure you're familiar enough with it to use it and remember to carry it. Don't just put it in a drawer and drive your family mad by failing to recharge it.'

'Are there any advantages to being old women?' said the woman who looked like the oldest in the class. 'All these things you're going through just make me think we make good victims.'

'One big advantage is that you have the wisdom of your years.'

This brought forth a gale of laughter from the group.

'If only that were true,' white bouffant said.

'No, listen,' Sam said. 'The truth is you're much less likely to engage in dangerous behaviour than younger people.'

'Vera went bungee jumping,' one of them said.

Sam laughed. 'What I mean is you're not likely to be blind drunk on a Saturday night in the centre of town. You're not likely to be picking a fight with a bouncer at a club door. Another thing you can do is carry a stick – no one is going to ask you why you were carrying it if you hit an attacker over the head with it. In fact it's a good idea to carry a stick whether you need it or not.'

'But we are a vulnerable group?'

'Yes, but with a few sensible precautions you can minimise the risks. Also if you are attacked, people are much more likely to come to your assistance than if, say, you were a young man. If people see two men fighting, it's difficult for them to work out who the good guy is, whereas with you it's going to be fairly obvious that you haven't initiated any violence. Well, I hope that's the case.'

Sam demonstrated palm-heel punches and got the women to practise.

'Can't you teach us to punch properly?' one woman said, as Sam moved between the groups. 'Tyler never will.'

'Palm-heel strikes are what we teach younger and older women because the bones in their knuckles are more susceptible to breaking if they use a clenched-fist punch. That's all. You can still hit someone hard with the palm but you risk less damage to your hand.'

'Shame,' the woman said.

Sam took the woman's hand in hers. 'Look, you should never tuck your thumb under the other fingers,' she said. 'You'll most likely break it if you hit someone. It should be tucked in down the side here and when you strike you should aim to make contact with the top two knuckles but palm-heel strikes, if executed correctly, can be just as concussive.'

'OK, thanks.'

She left the woman staring happily down at her clenched fist.

At the end of the session, white bouffant approached Sam. 'We were wondering what happened to your head?' She gestured to the bruise on Sam's forehead.

'Oh, that.' She prodded it gently. 'I'm afraid a dinosaur fell on it.'

'Well, there's really no need to be so sarcastic. If you didn't want to tell me, you just had to say.'

And before Sam could explain she had walked out of the hall.

Back at Park Town Sam found Peter sitting out in the garden with Pip asleep in his lap. He was wearing a straw hat and dark glasses and filling in a samurai sudoku with the sort of deftness that left her gawping.

How much should she tell him? This was the question she had

been wrestling with on the bus journey back into town. Somewhat to her own surprise she had come to the conclusion that she should tell him everything. It wasn't her usual approach to her parents – thirty per cent was about the usual amount she divulged. Anything more led to long tedious discussions that she sought to avoid. But in these circumstances she was expecting him to look after Pip, who was being pursued by some pretty unpleasant people, and she was going to need him to do that while she looked for Norman. She had to tell him because she wanted to make sure that if Peter got into the same sort of situation as before, and she wasn't there, that he would give up the dog. If he knew that two people had been murdered then she hoped he would be more likely to realise how much danger he was in.

After she had filled him in, he took off his glasses, folded them and placed them on the metal mosaic-topped table at his side. As they landed on the table, Pip opened one eye and then went back to sleep.

'The police think that someone killed Alan's niece because they thought it was you and that you had seen something on that laptop that they didn't want you to?'

Sam nodded. 'It's one of the lines of investigation they are pursuing.'

'Are you in danger now?'

'I don't know, but the thing is, Peter, if you're in the situation we were in the other night and I'm not there, I don't want you hanging on to Pip at any cost.'

Peter ran his head over Pip's head.

Sam continued. 'It's just not worth it.'

'You mean Pip's not worth me getting hurt over?'

'No.'

'It's an interesting ethical dilemma, isn't it? When people throw themselves into rivers to rescue their dogs they are presumably not thinking that their dog's life is worth anything less than their own.'

'Yes, but often they die and then everyone says what a waste it is.'

'But who is to say that my life is worth more than this bee here hovering over the geraniums?'

Dear God, Peter was turning positively Zen on her. Next he'd be

164

picketing with the animal rights protestors outside the new laboratories that were being built.

'Well, I am for one and anyway Mum would never forgive me if you got hurt over a Chihuahua.'

He smiled. 'How about a St Bernard?'

'Peter ...'

He held out his hand. 'Your mother ... on this occasion would definitely be of your opinion.'

'You could be really badly hurt.'

'Sam, when have you ever seen me behave in any rash sort of manner?'

'Well, there's always a first time.'

'Perhaps you could give me some self-defence tips?'

'If you're confronted by those thugs wanting the dog there is only one tip I'm willing to give you. Hand the dog over and get as much distance between you and them as possible. Don't get into an argument with them, don't try and negotiate.'

'Nothing else?'

'No, there's nothing else I'm willing to tell you. That's it.'

'Well, in my experience it is always a good idea to follow expert advice. I'd better do what I'm told then.'

He put his glasses back on and returned to his sudoku. Sam looked at him filling in square after square and felt far from reassured. He was a stubborn man who didn't show his emotions at all easily, but in the last few days he had shown more emotion round Pip than she had ever seen before. It was obvious he had become extremely attached to the dog.

'Peter,' she said.

He looked up from the sudoku.

'I personally feel your life is worth a great deal more than a bee's and a great deal more than Pip's.'

A bee veered off the plants and flew straight at Sam's head, making her duck.

Peter smiled. 'I think he disagrees with you.'

'I'll check the whole of him over in case the chip's migrated,' the vet said.

Sam winced. 'Do they often do that?'

'Hardly ever, but it's just in case. Usually if they've got one it's here.' He ran his finger between Pip's shoulder-blades. 'It's about the size of a grain of rice.'

The vet was old school, wearing a spotted bow-tie. He ran a hand-held scanner all over Pip, which didn't take long given the size of him, and looked at the display panel and shook his head. 'I'm afraid not. I'll check him for tattoos just in case.' A couple of minutes later he again shook his head.

'No name-tag attached to the collar?'

'He wasn't handed over to me with one.'

Pip had been well behaved up till now but when the vet raised the dog's lips to look at his teeth and gums he emitted a warning growl which the vet ignored. 'You know this is a very nice animal, very nice indeed. I wouldn't be at all surprised if he was a pedigree. He's a really fantastic little dog. You could show him.'

For a moment Sam had an image of herself prancing round a ring with Pip on a lead; she immediately banished it from her mind. It was too camp even for her fervent imaginings.

'One thing you have to remember with Chihuahuas is that they need to be exercised. Some people think they don't have to be be-cause they're so small and they carry them everywhere. I can't tell you the number of overweight Chihuahuas I see.'

'What's Pip like?'

'Well, he's slightly chubby.'

Sam stood disconsolately outside the vet's with Pip by her side. No micro-chip, no tattoo, just a chubby Chihuahua that was becoming an increasing liability.

Walking back to Park Town, Sam considered her next course of action. She needed to find out which hospital Norman's grandfather was in and see if she could talk to him. If that didn't work she could follow the clues given by the dog-nappers' car. There was always the possibility that having been unsuccessful herself, Cruella had hired some local thugs to pick up the dog, and if Sam could talk to them they might give her some useful information.

Sam looked down at Pip, panting in the heat, and wondered what the hell was so special about him to justify all this aggravation and subterfuge. Who would ever have thought that such a little dog could be the source of so much trouble?

She took Pip back to Park Town and then walked to her office. It was stifling. She threw open the window which faced the Cowley Road and then walked over to the other one that looked out on to the back of the terrace and opened that too. The through draught picked up the papers on her desk and tossed them up into the air and across the room. She picked them up and anchored them to the desk with a heavy glass ashtray which the previous occupant had left behind. She took a bottle of water from the fridge, opened it and drank and then, perched on the side of her desk, played back her answerphone messages. The first was from the woman at the cinema and the second from the man who worked in the bookies', both asking her to get in contact with them. Maybe Norman had returned to his old neighbourhood.

She lit a cigarette and leaned out of the back window. Immediately below her was a short drop on to the roof of the back extension of the bookies', from there it was about a twelve-foot drop to a concrete backyard, which was filled with the usual detritus: a green office chair missing one wheel; a couple of black bin-bags; a pile of cardboard boxes which had been flattened, taped together and leaned against the wall. There was also a lifesize cardboard cut-out of Michael Owen giving the odds for the teams appearing in the 2006 World Cup. Next to the broken chair there was an empty cup sitting on a newspaper which lay open at the racing pages. Beyond the concrete was a scrubby lawn which ran for fifteen metres or so before ending in a high brick wall. On the far side of it a tall copper beech tree swayed back and forth in the wind, this late in the summer its leaves were no longer copper but black.

A broken-down fence separated the back garden of the bookies' from the garden next door. A woman with long purple and black hair extensions wearing matching purple and black wafty clothes was leaning against the wall in the shade, smoking. Her goth make-up and clothing denoted that she was Helga, the tattooist. Business was obviously slow in the Cowley Road tattoo parlour.

Sam breathed in the sweet smell of the woman's spliff and

wondered if that enhanced or detracted from her tattooing skills. She stubbed out her own cigarette on the brickwork to the side of the window and turned back into the room. It was then that the door flew open and the man with the wrecking-ball head charged into the room. She took one look at the muscles bunching in his neck and his arms splaying at his sides and did the only thing she could think of – she twisted round and threw herself head first out of the window, hitting the roof below in a forward diving-roll. Jumping to her feet and looking behind her she saw him beginning to squeeze himself through the window after her. She walked to the edge of the roof, steadied herself and jumped. The drop wasn't that far but it was on to concrete and so as a precaution she rolled over as she landed and then was up and running towards the gap in the fence.

She thought it unlikely that she'd be able to get access to the street through the bookies' – the amount of money they handled meant that the cashiers must be locked in, but a tattoo parlour would surely not need that sort of security. She tripped through the fencing and landed at the feet of Helga, who had the sort of high priestess quality of a woman who was well used to people falling at her feet.

She exhaled, engulfing Sam in a cloud of sweet-smelling smoke and said, 'Who the fuck are you?'

A thud behind Sam announced that the man had decided to follow her route to ground level and was close behind her.

Sam scrambled to her feet. 'Bad man,' she gasped. 'Sorry, need access to road ...' And she bolted past the high priestess into the back of the parlour. There was a small kitchen, a room containing pictures of tattoos all over the walls and a massage bed, and then she was in the front of the shop. She ran round the counter and grabbed the handle of the door giving access to the street. It was then that she saw the sign hanging from the door saying 'Open' which unfortunately meant only one thing – that the sign facing any customer trying to come in said 'Closed'.

She was trapped.

She whipped round in time to see her pursuer appear behind the counter. The area between the door and the counter was tiny; there was absolutely no room to manoeuvre. She wasn't going to be able to throw him. Neither of them spoke. She could hardly ask him how his mother was again. Sun was streaming into the shop-front and the sound of their heavy breathing filled the room. The tunnel vision she'd talked to the class about descended on her. Here was the oncoming train. He began to edge his way round the counter. She could smell him now, only a couple of feet away. She saw the material of his trousers over his right knee was soaked black with blood.

Then, Helga appeared behind him. She waved the needle she was carrying in each hand in the air like a matador and, surprisingly quietly for a woman wearing black platform boots, crept round behind him. Their eyes locked over his right shoulder and as Sam aimed a kick at his damaged knee, Helga plunged the needles deep into his arse. He jack-knifed forwards over his knee and then backwards and it was enough distraction for Sam to shove past him and sprint after Helga back into the garden. Helga locked the back door and then grabbed Sam's hand and dragged her through into the next garden.

'I've phoned the police,' she whispered.

There was a loud crashing noise from the shop.

Sam winced. 'Sorry,' she said. 'I'll pay for any damage.'

They waited but the man did not appear. Helga took the remains of her spliff out from the depths of her wafty clothes and looked at it longingly.

'If the police are coming ...' Sam said, feeling miserably straight. She offered her a cigarette from her crushed packet and Helga took it and straightened it. Sam took a lighter from her pocket and, holding it steady with both hands, lit Helga's and then her own.

'What does he want with you?' Helga asked.

'Well ... I guess he wants to kill me.'

They waited where they were until they heard the police car draw up outside and then walked back into the tattoo parlour. The shop door was hanging off its hinges. Fracture lines ran like the rays of a huge sun from around the door-handle where he'd kicked the lock out. A uniformed policeman was picking his way gingerly across the broken glass.

Helga was already on the phone talking to someone about getting the door fixed.

'I'll pay for it,' Sam said again, as Helga came off the line.

She shrugged. 'I know a man. It happens quite often. People are drunk on a Saturday night. They see a glass door, they kick it in. He replaces the door, I add to his dragon.'

'So what happened here?' the uniformed officer said. 'Dissatisfied customer? Needle slip, did it?'

Helga stared at him. 'You are looking for a man with two needles in his arse.'

'Well, that's a useful description.'

'One mean mother-fucker,' she continued.

'With a smashed-up right knee,' Sam said.

At that moment an older uniformed policeman with a bald head and a substantial tattoo on his right forearm crunched into the shop. 'Helga,' he said. 'Are you all right?'

Helga took the cigarette out of her mouth and wafted round the counter. Her lips locked on to his in the kind of kiss that made Sam think that the pair of them should get naked and pretty damn soon. She looked at them, then looked away, then looked at them again and smiled. The other officer looked down at his shoes, rubbing the back of his neck with his hand.

When Helga had finished, she stood back a little and walloped him across the face.

The younger man moved to restrain her but the older one waved him away.

'Fuck you do that for?' he said, rubbing his cheek.

'Where have you been, you randy little sod?'

She took hold of his hand and pulled it towards her, straightening his forearm. 'You see this,' she said to Sam, pointing at the tattoo. 'This is shoddy work. He let some young tart work on him. He shows himself no self-respect. You shouldn't let just anyone touch your body. True quality always shows. Now he has this for the rest of his life and everyone will know he is a cheapskate who has no self-respect.'

The bald policeman was rubbing his cheek. 'I could have you for assaulting a police officer.'

She pouted. 'Darling, you know you can *have* me anytime ... and anyway if I had meant business I would have hit you with the other hand.' She rippled up and down the series of heavy skull and cross-bones silver rings, which weighed down every finger of her left hand.

He blushed and muttered something to his younger colleague who frowned and leaned forwards as if he hadn't caught what he said.

'Go wait by the car,' he yelled and the younger man left the shop.

'Right,' he said, taking a large handkerchief from his pocket and wiping his face and head. 'So what happened here?'

CHAPTER SIXTEEN

The first thing that Sam did after she had finished talking to the police was phone Peter and tell him that it would be a good idea if he left the house in Park Town and went and lived in St Cuthbert's for a while. He had been the head of the college and he still retained some rooms there. If the man who had attacked her had been involved in hiring the thugs who had waited for them outside the house, then he would know where they lived and until he was caught Sam thought it would be a good idea if both Peter and Pip kept a low profile. These days the security in Oxford colleges was much better than when she had been a small child.

He'd not been that happy about it, but when Sam described to him what had just happened to her and gave him more details of the way Stephanie had died he'd stopped arguing. With any luck, she said, the police would pick up the man soon and then everything could return to normal.

Next she phoned Mrs Eliot and asked if there was a chance that she could stay with them. As it happened they were between lodgers. A new PhD student from America was due in a couple of weeks' time, but for the moment the self-contained flat at the top of the house was empty and she was welcome to it.

Then she phoned Alan and told him what had happened. There was a short silence after Sam had finished and then Alan said, 'So it looks as if they were after you?'

'Yes.'

'It was definitely the same man who grabbed you in Holland Park?'

'Yes.'

She didn't know what to say to him. She heard him clear his throat.

'Alan?'

'Mmm?'

'How did it go with your brothers?'

'I don't know, Sam. It went, that's all.'

'Is there any sign of Johnny?'

'No, not yet.'

'Do you think he knows?'

'I've no idea. We'll find out soon enough.'

'What do you think he's going to do?'

She heard him sigh. 'I haven't got a clue, Sam.'

'He's going to be very upset, isn't he?'

'How'd you reckon that? Oh yeah, you're a private investigator.'

They both remained silent for a while after that.

Then Alan said, 'Something's been worrying me. If this same man was responsible for Stephanie's murder, he found out where you lived very quickly. I mean I understand he'd know where to find you in Oxford. It's a smaller place and he'd know where your office was from the woman who visited you there. If they were involved with the attempted dog-nap they'd also know where you live in Park Town, but what I don't understand is how he found you so quickly in London? If, that is, it was him.'

'He would have seen the registration number of my van.'

'Yes, but to find your address from that he'd have to have access to the DVLA in Cardiff.'

'We can do that.'

'Yes, but only because I pull a few old strings and am an ex-policeman.'

'So, what are you saying? This guy's a policeman?'

'I don't know what I'm saying. I just think if he found you that quickly he might be.'

'Well, that's a happy thought.'

'Also if it was him and he came after you again in Oxford, how did he know to do that? I mean he'd have thought you were dead, wouldn't he? That he'd killed you.'

'Maybe he was just coming to have a snoop around my office and when he found I was there thought he'd better try and kill me again.'

'Maybe.'

'Or he might have read a report in the paper that named Stephanie.'

'But there hasn't been one.'

'Shit.'

'I'm going to make some enquiries and see what I can come up with.'

'OK, let me know …'

But Alan had put the phone down.

She stared into the middle distance. Just what she needed – some psycho, ex-cop on her case. But what did he have to do with everything? What did he have to do with the thefts of the artefacts and Gittings's death?

After getting the door put back on her office, she visited the bookies' to see what ferret-face had to say for himself.

As she reached the front of the queue he leaned forwards and whispered, 'I can't talk to you here. I asked you to phone me.'

Sam shrugged. 'Sorry.'

He glanced at his watch. 'Come back at seven when I'm closing up.'

She began to leave.

'Have you seen Norman?' he hissed.

'In London a couple of days ago – he gave me the slip.'

'Thank God. Come back at seven.'

Sam paused on the pavement outside the bookies'. She had half an hour to kill. She walked along the Cowley Road to the Ultimate Picture Palace and presented herself at the window. Helen was there as before.

'Oh hi, I wasn't sure if you got my message or not.'

'I was away and then I had a few difficulties.'

'Is that what those police cars were doing over by your office?'

'It might have been.'

'If you wait there, I'll join you.'

As she emerged from the cinema, she pulled her dark glasses down from where they rested on top of her head to her nose.

'So what is it?' Sam asked.

'It's Norman. You were looking for him weren't you?'

'Yup.'

'Well, I think he might be sleeping in the cinema at night.'

'What makes you think that?'

'Well, he has a thing for Green and Black's organic chocolate and I keep finding wrappers in the projection room and it smells of smoke and we're not allowed to smoke anywhere in the cinema and he's still got his keys. It would be easy enough to do.'

'Why are you telling me?'

'Well, like I said to you before. I'm worried about him. If he's dossing in the cinema that's not good, is it?'

'Has he still got his job?'

'I think so. The boss is a bit of an old hippy and apparently the man I told you about has complained before so he didn't mind. When I told him what happened with *Nosferatu,* he just laughed.'

'But you haven't actually seen Norman, have you?'

'No, but maybe he'll be here tonight. If you watch the cinema you might see him coming in.'

'When does your last film end?'

'Tonight it's eleven thirty. We'll be closed up by twelve. I can leave you my spare set of keys if you like.'

Sam looked at the reflective surface of Helen's dark glasses and wondered why she was being so helpful. Was she being set up? If she waited late at night outside the cinema, if she let herself in, who would be waiting for her? Helen held out the keys and Sam looked down at the 'Make Poverty History' band hanging from her wrist, and took them. Surely she couldn't be all bad if she was wearing one of those? Then she dismissed that thought as hopelessly naïve.

'When do you need these back?'

She shrugged. 'Whenever – I had an extra set cut because I was always losing mine.'

Helen pushed her dark glasses back on to the top of her head and Sam got to look into her eyes. They seemed innocent enough. Maybe she was just being helpful but if she was so worried about Norman, why didn't she wait at the cinema for him herself? Why didn't she help him herself? Why get Sam involved at all?

Helen disappeared back into the cinema. Sam looked at her watch. Seven o'clock. She crossed back over the road and reached the bookies' just as ferret-face was ushering his last punter out of the shop. He let Sam in and locked up the door behind them. Sam followed him across the scraggy floor, littered with betting slips and little red pens, and out into the back of the shop.

'I need to cash up,' he said, and Sam followed him into a stuffy, windowless room containing a safe. He sat at a desk and began to count the money out of a black plastic till tray. Sam leaned against the wall, watching him. Thin greasy black hair was scraped across his head from a side-parting, and the fingers of his right hand were yellow from nicotine. He was having trouble counting the cash and kept dropping coppers on to the floor. Sam bent down and picked up a couple of two-pence pieces and put them on the table.

'You said you'd seen him,' he said.

'Yes, a couple of days ago in London but he gave me the slip.'

'What does he think he's playing at?'

This was pretty much Sam's thinking but she didn't know why ferret-face felt the same way.

'What's your interest in him?' she asked.

'He owes me money.'

'You didn't lend him any, did you?'

He tucked in the top of a plastic money bag containing five-pence pieces and threw it savagely into the safe. 'Where the fuck is he?' he snarled.

'Why the hell did you do that? He's completely unscrupulous about money. You can't trust a word he says. You must know what a bad gambling problem he has.'

'Most people I have contact with have those.'

He'd been scribbling numbers down on a pad of paper and now he tore a piece of paper off the pad and walked over to a fax machine, presented the paper to the machine and dialled a number. He watched as the machine fed the paper through.

'Every month head office sends someone over to check our accounts. They go through everything, count everything ... unless I can get hold of Norman I'm going to be five thousand pounds short when they turn up tomorrow morning.'

176

'You gave Norman five thousand pounds? You must be off your head.'

'He said he only needed it overnight, that he'd give it back to me the following day and he'd give me five hundred pounds interest.'

'From my experience of him he has absolutely no scruples whatsoever. He dumped a Chihuahua on me.'

Ferret-face rounded on her. 'A Chihuahua – what's the problem with a sodding Chihuahua? It's even got a small appetite … this is my job, this is five thousand pounds.'

'OK, OK what happened the next day?'

'Absolutely nothing. I haven't seen or heard from him since it happened and tomorrow the management will come in and then that's me stuffed.'

He opened a plastic folder, placed the piece of paper he'd run through the fax in it, closed it up and put the folder in the safe. Then he closed the safe and spun the dial.

'I'm sorry I can't help you,' Sam said, 'but I'm looking for him too and I've no idea where he is.' She pushed herself away from the wall.

'There is something you could do for me.'

Sam folded her arms. 'Why is it I don't have a good feeling about what is about to come out of your mouth?'

'Tighter,' he said. 'Ouch, not that tight. Do you want my hands to drop off?'

Sam sighed and looked down at ferret-face firmly trussed at her feet. The safe was open now.

'What time will your colleagues be in?'

'Jim usually gets in at eight.'

'OK, let's run through it again.'

'I was closing up as usual when someone appeared with a gun in his hand. He forced me to open the safe and then took all the cash. Then he tied me up and left through the back door.'

'Will you be all right?'

He nodded.

'OK, gag me.'

Sam tore the tea-towel she'd taken from the kitchen area in two and tied it round his mouth. Then she let herself out through the rear door and worked her way through the back gardens, until she reached the end of the terrace and jumped over a wall into the street.

She leaned against the wall and rubbed her face with her hand. Why had she agreed to do it? Well, he'd begged her was one reason, he'd told her he had a six-month-old baby girl, he'd told her he'd never get a job again, he'd told her he'd end up in prison and that his girlfriend wouldn't be able to cope with the baby on her own because she had post-natal depression and the child would be taken into care. He'd gone on and on and then he'd cried … and after that he'd said it would kill his mother to see him in prison, that she was ninety-three and in ill health and he was her only son and the social services weren't up to much and they'd put her in a home and … Sam had said, 'Will you shut up?' and then she'd said 'yes'.

It was probably all lies, but it was the crying which settled it for Sam. She'd do anything to stop it even if it meant colluding in robbery with someone as obviously unreliable as ferret-face. But she wasn't a complete fool. She'd insisted that he write a statement confirming what he was getting her to do and sign it and date it. She had that in her pocket as a safeguard.

One thing worried Sam. Had anyone seen him letting her into the shop as he was closing up, because if they had and ferret-face accused her of being the robber, she didn't really have a leg to stand on. He said that he would tell the police she was asking about the job in the window and that the robber had approached him after she had left.

For a moment Sam considered staking out the cinema but she had a couple of hours to go and she wasn't really convinced that Norman would turn up. Maybe she'd try it tomorrow, but for now she'd had enough.

As she let herself into the Eliots' house she was greeted by the wet thrusting noses of their two Rottweilers. The hall was dark and smelled of dog, and in the living-room to the left the light of a television flickered.

Mrs Eliot was stretched out on the sofa. 'Come and watch with me for a bit,' she said, and Sam joined her.

For a while they watched the screen in companionable silence, a repeat of *The Rockford Files*. Mrs Eliot had always been a keen fan of American cop shows: *Kojak, Harry O, Starsky and Hutch, Petrocelli.* Sam had watched all of them with her at some time or other.

As the credits rolled, Mrs Eliot turned to Sam and said, 'Shall we have tea now or ...'

Sam smiled. Mrs Eliot had always had an extraordinary capacity for tea. She could enrol the most tea-hating individual into having a cuppa. Sam's parents drank it relatively rarely but in the Eliots' household the pot seldom cooled, and even though as a child she hadn't particularly liked it, she'd always drunk it here.

'I'll make it,' she said.

In the kitchen everything was where she remembered it. While she was boiling the kettle Luke came into the kitchen. He was wearing white chinos, a bright red polo shirt and Birkenstocks. He leaned against the fridge.

'Mum got you at it already?'

Sam smiled and stirred the pot. There'd been a time in her life when she'd had a huge crush on Luke. He was older than her, charming, good-looking and very funny. To have the affection for him without the embarrassment that came with adolescent attraction was a relief.

'Do you want some?' she asked.

'Thanks.'

She handed him a cup.

As he took it he said, 'You know we were talking about Norman at the party? He owes me quite a lot of money.'

'Not you as well? You're going to have to join a very long queue, I'm afraid. I haven't come across anyone who knows him who isn't owed money.'

Luke grimaced and looked down at the surface of his tea. 'He ran a book at school. You could bet on anything with him. What colour tie the head would wear at assembly. How long it would take for certain teachers to lose their tempers. How many would get into Oxford and Cambridge. I can't visualise him at school without a notebook and a pen behind his ear and money changing hands. He'd get his grandfather to write him a sick note which always covered the exact week of Cheltenham.'

'Any idea where he might be?' Sam asked.

'Wasn't he working at the cinema?'

Sam nodded. 'But he hasn't been there for a while. I better take this through to your mother.'

Luke followed Sam back into the living-room. A repeat of *Judge John Deed* was on the television. Sam sat down next to Mrs Eliot and Luke stood cradling his mug, watching the screen.

'Luke told me you're involved with Norman Sweetman in some way. Is that true?' Mrs Eliot asked.

'Trying to find him, rather than involved. I'm looking after a Chihuahua for him and he keeps disappearing, and when he's not disappearing, he's irritating me with Latin quotations.'

'You need to be careful of Norman,' Mrs Eliot said.

'I am. Well, I don't believe a word that comes out of his mouth, if that's what you mean.'

'It's not exactly what I mean, no.'

On the screen Martin Shaw was seducing another witness. The light from the television flickered against Mrs Eliot's face. With her black hair swept up in a bun and her bright red lipstick, all she needed to complete the look was a crystal ball.

'He told me once that he was responsible for his parents' deaths.'

'But how could he be? He was only a little boy when they were killed. Surely it was just survivor's guilt.'

'Perhaps, but he was very upset when he told me. You know, it wasn't a whimsical thing. I felt he genuinely believed it.'

'What exactly did he say?'

'That it had been his fault.'

'No other details?'

'No.'

'Surely just a melodramatic seeking attention?'

'Maybe, but I think you should be very careful in your dealings with Norman. His grandfather's in hospital, isn't he? They're very close. God knows what his grandfather's death might trigger in Norman.'

Luke perched himself on the arm of the sofa. 'Don't forget, Sam, Mum never let anything as boring as the truth get in the way of a good story.'

Sam laughed.

'Luke!' Mrs Eliot protested.

'Well, come on, Mum, Norman might be a bit of a dodgy eccentric but you're making him out to be some kind of psychopath.' He nodded at the screen. 'She watches too much crime on the TV.'

Later, after Mrs Eliot had gone off to bed, Sam and Luke sat out in the garden with the Rottweilers sprawled, panting, at their feet. It was midnight but there wasn't a breath of wind. Luke stretched his legs out in front of him and the wicker chair he was sitting in creaked.

'Have you got a bike I could borrow while I'm here?' Sam asked. 'The police have got hold of my van in London.'

'Sure. There's usually a couple in the shed. The locks and keys are in the baskets.'

'Thanks.'

'Fancy some skinny-dipping?'

Sam looked at him. The skinny bit was OK, but the dipping?

Luke laughed. 'Have you still not learned to swim?'

She shook her head.

'Don't they have adult classes where you can learn?'

'I haven't got round to it.'

'Well, I'm going to anyway. You can stay in the shallow end.'

She followed him to the pool, watched him strip off and slide under the water. Still clothed she felt like a voyeur; somehow it seemed like bad manners not to join him. She took off her clothes and slid under the water, resting her elbows against the railing and splashing her feet in front of her. Luke was swimming on the bottom of the pool, his lean tanned body a black shadow in the underwater lights. She remembered he'd always been like a fish in the water. He surfaced next to her and smoothed his hair back.

'You should let me teach you one day.'

'Maybe,' Sam said uncertainly. 'Maybe I will.'

She felt his body nudge against hers, saw his smile. An accident? An invitation? Whatever the intention, she couldn't handle it. She moved away from him towards where the steps led up and out of the pool, but she was shy now to get out of the pool under his gaze. She turned and faced him, keeping her body under the water on the other side of the pool. I must talk to Reg about this, she thought. I have to. I have to talk about it and then I have to learn to swim. It's ridiculous. Luke dived again and swam away from her. She quickly climbed out of the pool and put on a large navy terry cloth dressing-gown draped over the back of a sun-lounger. The chlorine was catching in her throat, making her choke. She picked up her clothes and walked to the end of the pool. He'd surfaced now.

'I'm going to bed,' she said.

'You still on for St Giles?'

'Yes, definitely. When is it again?'

'Four days' time.'

'I'll be there.'

The flat she was staying in was under the roof and stiflingly hot. She threw open the windows, took off the dressing-gown and lay down on the bed. It was too hot to sleep in any clothes. She lay there looking up through the skylight at the stars.

At first there are just the words repeated over and over. 'If you tell anyone they won't believe you. They'll know you're lying. If you tell you'll die. You mustn't tell ever. It's just our secret, our little secret. If you tell, you'll die.' Then there's a face but without features as if a stocking has been pulled over the face. It's like a shop-window dummy, devoid of character. 'Don't tell. Don't ever, ever tell. They won't believe you and they'll know it's all your fault. All of it. That you're a bad girl. You don't want them to think that do you? Do you?' His hand is on her throat now, squeezing, she can't breathe properly but when he lets go the first thing she smells is chlorine and steam coming off the swimming pool. Even though his hand is no longer there she can't stop coughing . . .

She woke gasping for breath, looked at her watch – three o'clock. For a few minutes she didn't move, waiting for the fear to settle down, waiting to come back to her actual surroundings. In her previous nightmares the figure had never spoken, just stood there, masked, silent. Then she picked up her phone and dialled. He wouldn't be there but she could leave a message. She listened to his answerphone message and took a breath. 'Reg, it's Sam. Next time we meet I want you to ask me why I never learned to swim. That's what I want to talk about next time. I want to talk about it now. I have done for a long time but I've felt too ... I haven't been able to before.'

She closed up the phone and lay back on the bed. The words ran through her head. 'If you tell, you'll die.' Time to test that one out, Sam thought. Time to tell. The fear she had felt when she first woke up had now switched to anger. She wasn't going to be able to sleep. She pulled on her shorts, a T-shirt and some running shoes and let herself out of the house. She took one of the bikes out of the shed and set off into town. Warm air flowed around her.

At the foot of Headington Hill she got off the bike and locked it up, stood, hands on hips, looking upwards. Reg's words came back to her. '*With the exercise the stress is on gentle. You have permission to stop when it hurts ... the aim is to stir up some endorphins and enjoy it.*' Well, her aim now was to get a hold of the anger she was feeling. There was no gym to hand, no punch-bag. She did some stretches and then started running up the hill. It was a brutal unforgiving hill, she knew from having done this when she was in training. She got up on to her toes and dug in. She wouldn't stop until she reached the top. She'd do it until her muscles were locked solid with the build-up of lactic acid, until she had run herself to a standstill. And as she ran the words she had dreamed swirled round her head in an unforgiving mantra, '*If you tell, you'll die. If you tell, you'll die.*'

CHAPTER SEVENTEEN

Sam hadn't bothered going back to sleep. After she'd finished running she'd gone back to the Eliots' and had a long shower. Her
legs were aching from the work-out she'd given them but she didn't
care. The words from the nightmare were no longer rolling round
her mind; she may have driven her body into the ground but she felt
much calmer.

She'd arranged to meet Phil for breakfast in the covered market.
It was the quickest way to get an update on the investigation taking
place at the Pitt Rivers. The market was positioned between the High
and Market Street and contained fruit and veg stalls, a butcher's, a
fishmonger's, a delicatessen, a florist, a pet shop, a multitude of different cafés, shoe shops, jewellery shops and most importantly, as far
as Sam was concerned, Ben's Cookies. When she arrived, the only
part of the market showing any activity were the fruit and veg stalls
taking in deliveries from the lorries parked in Market Street and the
café which opened up at the same time as the lorries arrived. Phil was
already seated at one of the café's red Formica tables. Sam ordered at
the counter and joined him.

'What's the matter with you?' he said. 'You're walking all weird.'

'Hill runs,' Sam said.

'You nutter – what are you doing those for?'

'It's a long and boring story.'

'I'm really sorry about what happened to Alan's niece.'

Sam nodded. 'I feel guilty as hell about it.'

'Not your fault.'

'If he was trying to kill me, I think it is really.'

'Rubbish. You didn't kill her, Sam.'

Sam's food arrived at the same time as her appetite deserted her. She still had the flat to sort out and she couldn't bear to think about it. Phil wasn't having any such problem with his breakfast.

'How's Alan handling it?'

'He's trying to keep his brothers under control.'

'Is he succeeding?'

'I doubt it.'

'I spoke to the bloke in charge of the case, DI Paxton. They haven't traced Johnny yet.'

'It wasn't him.'

'You seem very certain. Apparently they argued at the pub she was working at. He was making a nuisance of himself. Then he came to Alan's party and they fought.'

'So, it doesn't mean he killed his daughter. I mean, what's the motivation?'

'Come on, Sam, when did Johnny Knowles ever need motivation for violence? He's been violent all his life and he still is.'

'I don't think he did it and I think if they're going down that route it's a mistake. Her throat was cut, Phil. Do you see a father doing that to his daughter?'

'He gouged a man's eye out, Sam, with his bare hands.'

Sam picked up her knife and fork and then put them back down again.

'So you think this man who attacked you in your office killed Stephanie?'

'I had a run-in with him on that day and gave him reason to believe I'd found out things he might not want me to know.'

Phil had finished eating, pushed his plate to one side and pulled his tea towards him. 'Since you've arrived in Oxford you've brought with you your own mini crime wave. Theft, murder, dog-napping, attempted murder ... what do you know about the theft from the bookies'?'

'What, the bookies' underneath me?'

'Five thousand pounds was stolen and the man was tied up. His colleagues found him this morning when they came to open up.'

Sam arranged her features into a picture of innocence. 'I don't know anything about that. What did the autopsy on Gittings come back with?'

'When his face smashed through the cabinet he severed an artery. Cause of death was catastrophic blood loss.'

'Does Cummings have an alibi?'

'He said he was unable to go to the museum that night because of domestic difficulties and he called Gittings and asked him to let you into the museum.'

'Surely if that was the case Gittings would have said something to me at the party. I talked to him for quite some time. Wouldn't he have said, "See you later"?'

'Cummings said it was a very last-minute thing. He could have phoned him after you'd left the party. There are calls between his and Gittings' phones that fit what he said.'

'So his domestic difficulties are his alibi? Does his family back him up?'

'His wife does.'

'What about the thefts?'

'As far as thefts from museums are concerned, ninety per cent of the time it ends up being an inside job ... so we're concentrating on the staff and also people like researchers, who may have come in for relatively short periods of time, but had access to the artefacts. We've been going through the employment records for the last few years and we'll be interviewing everyone we can track down. Visitors to the museum just don't have the opportunity to steal things.'

'What about the Sweetman connection?'

'We finally got access to old man Sweetman in hospital. Apparently he's undergoing mag ...'

'Stop! I know what he's being treated for.'

Phil smiled. 'He was a bit dithery, apparently, worried about losing his other leg. I don't think they got much sense out of him.'

'Perhaps a convenient burst of temporary senility overcame him.'

'Perhaps.'

'What about his grandson, Norman?'

'We don't know where he is. We've been trying to trace him but the old boy was no help. He said he was worried because he hasn't seen him for the last couple of days and he says it's not like him not to be in contact. He was visiting him every evening up until a couple of days ago.'

'He's lying,' Sam said. 'Your boys are hardly going to pressurise an old man when he's lying in bed worrying about having his leg amputated, are they? I can't believe that Norman isn't in touch with him because he'd know how much his grandfather would worry.'

'You might be right, but, as you say, if Professor Sweetman doesn't want to co-operate we can hardly force him.'

'Is Cummings under suspicion?'

'Yes, as much as any one else is who's worked there over the last few years. Actually, probably more than some, because he's been there the longest so he's had more opportunity than some of the others.'

'And how many of the artefacts have been stolen?'

'They're still trawling through them all ... more keep coming to light every day.'

'So they're finding replicas?'

'Yes – very good ones. It's very difficult to tell the difference some-times. That's why it's taking so long to work out what's missing.'

'So somewhere there's the person who's been making the copies. Presumably that would take quite a lot of expertise and technical skill?'

'Yes, but we've had no luck tracing who that might be. It's tak-ing us a long time to track all the people who have worked at the museum over the last few years. They've had lots of foreign research fellows because of the nature of the exhibits. They're in universities and museums all over the world.'

'Do you think Gittings was involved in the thefts?'

'Well, we did find certain items from the museum at Gittings' flat.'

'What do you mean – museum artefacts?'

'Yes, and Cummings says he didn't know anything about it.'

'Maybe Cummings and Gittings were working together. If Gittings threatened to blow the whistle or wanted to stop, or was blackmailing him, then maybe things got out of hand ...'

'Or Gittings was on to Cummings and Cummings killed him and placed the artefacts in his flat in order to frame him.'

Sam had a picture of Justin Gittings's face smashed through the glass cabinet, the arrow plunged into his neck, his eyes open and unseeing, staring down at the exhibits. She pushed her untouched breakfast towards Phil.

'Here,' she said. 'I've lost my appetite.'

He pulled it towards him. 'You're not still working at the museum I presume?'

'No, Gittings's murder put an end to that. The whole thing became a little more serious than anything that could be sorted out by a bit of night security, but I'm seeing Cummings later this morning to deliver my bill. What hospital is Sweetman in?'

'The Radcliffe.'

'I think I'll pay him a visit, see what I can dig up.'

Phil sighed. 'What for?'

'Someone's trying to kill me, Phil, and someone killed Stephanie. The case has become personal. I'm not just going to sit around and do nothing.' She stood up. 'If you pick him up will you let me know? It'd make me feel a bit more relaxed. I've told Peter to stay in St Cuthbert's with the dog until it's safe.'

They walked out into Market Street.

'Incidentally, are you going out with DC Thomas?'

'Remind me why that's any of your business?'

She looked at him and smiled. 'Call it a historical proprietary interest.'

'Not good enough I'm afraid.'

'You're no fun.'

As she watched him walking towards Cornmarket her phone rang and she checked to see who was calling. It was Reg. She took the call.

'Are you all right, Sam? You sounded upset.'

'Could I make an appointment to see you sooner than the one we've got scheduled?'

'Yes, of course.'

She made the new appointment and hung up.

Cummings's office looked tidier than the last time Sam had seen it, rather alarmingly so. His desk was almost completely clear of paperwork; files and manuscripts were piled on top of each other against the walls. You could see more of the floor but Cummings, slumped in his chair, did not seem happy with the newly established order.

'The police,' he said, gesturing at the room.

'It all looks very orderly.'

'Exactly – looks. But is it? No, it's a complete disaster and I can't find a thing. All my layers have been tidied away. It'll take me days to get back to normal.'

He seemed depressed, Sam thought, not particularly surprising given that a large number of his exhibits had been stolen, a colleague had been murdered and he had a trashed dinosaur in his foyer.

'The tooth,' he said. 'When are we going to get it back? I mean how long do the police have to hold on to it? Surely they must be finished with it by now?'

'I'm afraid you're going to have to ask them about that.'

'I have been,' he shouted. 'At length, almost every day and they keep fobbing me off with ridiculous responses.'

'I'm sorry, but it was what there was to hand. I thought I was going to be attacked.'

'I want the dinosaur back up. It's an important part of the museum. It's a symbol that everything is back to normal and that it's business as usual. It leaves an enormous hole … we can't have a toothless dinosaur it would be …' he tore at the hair growing over his ears '… a complete and utter tragedy.'

After a moment's silence, Sam said, 'It must have been a tremendously stressful time for you.'

He put his hands flat on the surface of his desk and stared down at them as if they were the most fascinating thing he had ever seen in his life, as if the veins burrowing under the skin were the keys to the meaning of life.

'Poor Justin,' he said abruptly. 'That, of course, is the tragedy.' He looked up at her as if seeing her for the first time. 'What do you want? What are you doing here?'

'I've come to deliver my bill.'

'Oh yes, that's right.' He took the envelope and threw it unopened into his in-tray.

Sam looked at it and sighed.

He walked over to where she was sitting and stood over her as if encouraging her to leave. 'There are still so many different artefacts to check. Some of the replicas are remarkably good ...'

Sam got to her feet. 'Do you think the Sweetmans are involved?'

'I don't understand.'

'All the objects stolen are from the Sweetman donation, aren't they?'

'Yes, but they are also amongst the most unusual and therefore the most valuable. They have been stolen more for their value than their provenance.'

'Do you know Professor Sweetman and Norman?'

'Of course I do. When I first started work here as an assistant curator, Professor Sweetman was in charge of the Pitt Rivers.'

'Was he? Could you tell me what happened to Norman's parents?'

'That was a terrible, terrible tragedy for the boy. Well, not just for him of course ... I'm sure it explains ... well, some of his eccentricities.'

'What do you mean?'

'Well, there was the problem over computer records I believe when he was an undergraduate. He fulfilled a theory of mine that it is the most interesting of undergraduates who get sent down. They are clever enough to get here and then they are clever enough to realise they want nothing to do with the place. Nowadays, of course, the weight of debt hanging over their heads frightens them into conformity and anyway throwing them out would probably be a breach of their human rights.'

'You sound as if you don't like the place.'

'Oxford is Oxford. It has always been deeply conservative with a stultifying resistance to change. Stay here too long and before you realise what is happening all hope can drain away.'

God, he's right, Sam thought, what on earth made me think opening an office here was a good idea?

'I believe Norman works as a film projectionist at the Ultimate Picture Palace. Not an altogether unpleasant profession but hardly very taxing for someone of Norman's intelligence.'

'So what happened to his parents?'

'A head-on collision on a narrow country lane.'

'Was there any evidence of foul play?'

'No, but something went missing. They had one of the best pieces of the Sweetman collection in their possession. It was never found.'

'What do you mean?'

'Exactly what I say. It disappeared from the scene of the accident. Mind you, it's what – about thirty years since it happened? It could be about time for it to surface. Sometimes things are sold into private collections. At a certain point collections can go up for sale and then all kinds of items can come on to the open market. People die and the next generation isn't aware of how the items came into the possession of a relative or they say they found it in Auntie's attic. If they leave it long enough they think they can get away with it. You see the same thing happening sometimes with works of art that disappeared during the Second World War. In well-known cases the provenance can be proved and then a deal is done with the relatives of those who were the original owners. They are basically paid off with a percentage of the sale proceeds.'

'Have you seen anything about this item, then?'

'There was an article in the paper. Maybe just idle speculation.'

Sam thought of the article she had taken from the house in Holland Park. 'Do you mean the shaman's mask they mentioned in *The Times*'s piece on the Christie's sale in New York?'

He looked surprised. 'Yes.'

'So what's so special about this shaman's mask?'

'It's a stunning piece – absolutely unique. If you think about the Tutankhamen exhibits, the most famous piece is?' He held out his hands inviting her reply.

'The golden mask.'

'Exactly. Well, the shaman's mask has that kind of stature in Native American culture.'

'So how did the police explain the fact it went missing from the car?'

'They couldn't, but the car ended up nose-down in a river that was in full spate. There was speculation that it might have been thrown into the river.'

'But no fisherman pulled it out on the end of his line?'

'No, it vanished. Of course at the time there was a lot of nonsense in the papers about how this was a curse. It was the revenge of the tribe. You can imagine the sort of thing.'

Sam could. She could imagine it all too vividly.

'But you didn't think that?'

'I am not superstitious.'

'But you deal with the artefacts of superstition.'

'It hasn't rubbed off.'

'I understand that some artefacts were found at Justin Gittings's flat.'

'Yes, that was rather disturbing.'

'You hadn't given him permission to take them?'

'No, there is no procedure to allow such a thing. Artefacts cannot be removed from the museum unless they are on loan to other museums and there is a strict policy. Now I must ask you to leave. I need to get on.'

'Just one more question. The shaman's mask – which part of the Sweetman donation was it from?'

He shrugged. 'It wasn't part of the Pitt Rivers collection.'

'So what was it doing in the back of the car?'

'I don't think I ever knew.'

The bones of the Tyrannosaurus rex had been cleared away and in the space was a small notice saying that the exhibit had been temporarily withdrawn. That was one way of describing what had happened. Its absence certainly left a large hole. Outside she sat down for a moment on the stone seating in the entrance to the museum and considered her next step. Her aim must still be to find Norman and shake some sense out of him. She remembered the anguished silence that had emanated from him when she'd asked him about his grandfather. It seemed to be the only truthful thing about him. She was convinced he cared for him. She would try and speak to his grandfather and see what she could find out.

CHAPTER EIGHTEEN

This time, instead of running, she took the bus up Headington Hill, a rather more relaxing method of transport. She phoned Phil and told him what Cummings had said about the death of Norman's parents.

'Suppose,' Sam said, 'that this shaman's mask was stolen. Suppose the people who stole it are implicated in the death of Norman's parents. Suppose that this mask has come on to the market and ...'

'It all seems ridiculously far-fetched to me.'

She laughed. 'It does, doesn't it? But it would mean that Norman had a link possibly to the people who murdered his parents.'

'But we don't know that they were murdered.'

Sam crossed her fingers. 'Could you see what you could dig up?'

'Do you know where the accident happened and when?'

'No.'

'Get some of that information together and I'll see what I can do, but I'm not going on some fishing expedition because you've come up with a theory based on no hard facts. Your best bet for finding that information will be the inquest reports in the local papers. Anyway, your theory still doesn't explain the deaths of Justin Gittings or Stephanie unless you're suggesting Norman's involved with those in some way.'

'No, I'm not suggesting that. Maybe he's accidentally stirred up a hornets' nest, maybe he's done it on purpose.'

'That's not too clever is it?'

'I'm going to go and see his grandfather now.'

'Well, maybe you'll have better luck with the old boy than we did.'

'I'll let you know how I get on.'

Sam negotiated her way from reception to lift, to corridor, to correct ward, to correct nurse and introduced herself as a friend of the family. Professor Sweetman was asleep so she pulled up a chair and settled down next to him. He was lying on his back with his mouth open, his snoring reverberating around the room. There was a sickly smell in the room that all the disinfectant in the world could not disguise. The ulcer, Sam thought, the smell of rotting flesh.

She looked at the books on his bedside table. P.G. Wodehouse, a book of Coleridge's poems, G. A. Henty's *Tigers of the Mysore*. P.G. Wodehouse had the most appeal, but if she started reading that she'd end up laughing and she didn't want to wake him up, so she picked up the Henty and opened it at the first chapter, which happened to be titled 'A Lost Father'. They were everywhere. She skipped through the chapters until she found one titled 'Found at Last' and read the reconciliation scene which contained the winning line, 'I am disguised as an old man, but really, father, I am little more than eighteen.' This unfortunately did make her laugh and Professor Sweetman coughed and opened his eyes. They swivelled on to Sam and he frowned and placed his glasses, which lay in his lap, back on his nose.

'I hope you're not the chaplain. Not that I have anything against women priests *per se* but I have been a passionate agnostic all my life and find the presence of members of the cloth a tiresome irritant. They hover around like the angel of death hoping, I suppose, that I will crack in the face of impending death, and I find their opportunism a disgrace.'

'No, no,' Sam said. 'I'm nothing to do with the church. I'm the daughter of Peter Goodman, who used to be head of St Cuthbert's and I'm an acquaintance of Norman's.'

'Peter, yes, of course I know him. Acquaintance? A careful choice of word, I would suggest. Does he owe you money by any chance?'

'Oh, no. Well, for a couple of cans of dog food perhaps but hardly …'

'The reason I ask is that in the past a common characteristic that all Norman's acquaintances have shared at the point that they present themselves to me is that they are owed a substantial amount of money that Norman has inexplicably failed to pay.'

'I see. No, there's no debt.'

'Well, then, you're something of a rarity.'

'I understand the police have interviewed you.'

'And how would you know that exactly?'

Professor Sweetman might be elderly and ill but he wasn't going to make this easy for her. Sam had seen hospitals shrink people in front of her eyes. People assertive and authoritative in everyday life rendered meek and terrified by illness. But this did not seem to have happened to Professor Sweetman. He was not a man who had had the stuffing knocked out of him. The eyes that he fixed on Sam might have been watery, but they were also shrewd and not at all welcoming. She decided to cut to the chase.

'I'm looking for Norman and wondered if you knew where he was?'

He shook his head. 'I told all this to the police. I last saw him two days ago and haven't spoken to him since.'

'I don't believe you,' Sam said.

He smiled a smile of sudden unexpected sweetness. Brown teeth and a black gap peeped from the corner of his mouth. Sam couldn't help but smile back.

'To receive any information from me, you will have to offer me substantially more than you have given me so far.'

'Fair enough. I'm a private investigator based in the Cowley Road. My introduction to Norman was when he asked me to look after a Chihuahua for him. He asked me to have the dog overnight and said that he would pick it up in the morning but he didn't. At the same time, and entirely separate from my dealings with Norman, I had been asked to do some security work at the Pitt Rivers.'

'Who asked you to do that?'

'Cummings.'

'Did he, now.'

'There then followed a series of events.' She paused. 'Thefts from the Pitt Rivers, an attempted dog-napping, a murder at the museum and then the murder in London, in my flat, of the niece of a friend of mine. A murder that the police think was intended for me.'

She paused, wondering if she'd been rash in telling him so much. But she needed to tell him something of what had happened, or why would he co-operate?

'Two murders? The police only told me of one.'

'They may not have known about the other one when they interviewed you.'

'I see.'

'I saw Norman in London three days ago when he gave me the slip.'

'I see.' His hands ran repeatedly over the top fold of his sheet, smoothing it and smoothing it but he didn't say anything else. 'You say Cummings hired you?'

'Yes. To sum up – my life is at risk and I still have the Chihuahua. Well, my stepfather has it. I need to talk to Norman and ask him what the hell is going on.'

'Yes, I see. I see that you would want that.'

'I don't believe that Norman hasn't been in touch with you. From the brief amount of time that I spent with him one thing that came across as absolutely clear was the strength of his feelings for you.'

Professor Sweetman did not reply but he stopped smoothing the sheet.

She continued. 'There is also the fact that it appears that all the artefacts presently known to have been stolen have come from the Sweetman donation.'

'Yes, the police told me about that.'

'So would you be willing to tell me where Norman is or what's going on? If you knew who owned the dog that might help.'

He turned his head to the side and looked at his bedside table. 'Would you mind pouring me a glass of water?' Sam did what he had asked. When she handed the glass to him she saw that a light was flashing above his bed.

'Ah,' Professor Sweetman said, looking over Sam's shoulder. 'Nurse, would you mind escorting this young lady from the room and making sure she never returns. She is here under false pretences. She is no one I know, just a reporter digging for information about the unfortunate events in the Pitt Rivers. I do not want to see her ever again.'

Sam looked at the nurse and the nurse looked at Sam, who then looked at Professor Sweetman. He smiled at her again, a smile of great charm, a smile which defied Sam to take offence. Now she could see where Norman got his from.

'When you talk to Norman,' Sam said. 'Tell him someone's trying to kill me and I'd appreciate having a conversation with him before they succeed.'

She was about to follow the nurse out of the room when Sweetman suddenly said, 'Does Peter like dogs?'

Sam turned round. 'Yes, very much.'

'Does the dog like him?'

'They seem happy together,' Sam said.

He nodded and turned his face away from her.

Sam stopped at the nurse's desk.

'I'm not a reporter,' she said.

The nurse sighed. 'I don't really care. He threw the police out the other day and gave the chaplain a flea in his ear. If he's spent the whole of his life not believing in God I don't see why a leg ulcer is going to make him change his mind. If he doesn't want people in there, it's up to him. He doesn't have to talk to people if he doesn't want to.'

'How's his ulcer?'

'When the consultant looked at it today he was very pleased with the progress. It's one of the worst ones I've seen. Pain can make the mildest of men irascible but Professor Sweetman isn't like that; he's charming to deal with. The tea ladies love him.'

'I'm looking for his grandson.'

'Norman?'

'Yes, has he been about recently?'

'Not on my shifts. He always used to come in the evening. Evenings can seem interminable when you're in hospital. During the day there's much more going on.'

'Could I leave a note for him?'

'He may not come.'

'Oh, I know, it's just on the off-chance.'

Sam took a piece of paper and a pen from her bag and leaning on her thigh scribbled a note. 'I may have a lead on the shaman's mask. Please contact me.' Then she wrote her telephone number. OK, it was a lie but she thought it might flush him out. She folded the piece of paper, wrote Norman's name on it and handed it over to the nurse.

'Thanks a lot,' she said. 'I appreciate it.'

Sam stood waiting for the lift to arrive to take her back down to ground level. It crossed her mind that she had told Professor Sweetman a great deal and he had told her absolutely nothing other than the fact that Norman had a problem with money, something she already knew. She had meant to ask him about the date of the accident but had balked at the idea. His son and daughter-in-law had died as a result of it. He was an old man in hospital and she'd not had the neck to do it. She wondered if he was involved with the thefts in order to fund Norman's increasing financial problems. A snapshot of the cabinets in the house in Harberton Mead came to her. What were those items and how much were they worth? Maybe she should pay the house another visit.

When Peter had been Provost of St Cuthbert's, he'd lived in the Provost's Lodgings, a beautiful copy of an eighteenth-century house which was light and airy and generously proportioned. The same could not be said of the current set of rooms he was occupying. They were small and stuffy and caught the afternoon sun during the hottest part of the day and even now, with all the windows open, it was stifling. He looked out of the window across the quad to where he could see old Crouch bumbling about in his rooms, and wished he was over there in deep shade.

Pip was whining at the door. Peter took the lead from the back of the door, clipped it on to Pip's collar and let himself out on to the cool staircase. As he stepped out into the quad, a wall of heat hit him. A conference was on and small groups of people were dotted around the lawns. He walked round the quad until he reached the stone arch that ran under the chapel tower, slid his key into the lock of an ornate black metal gate and entered the fellows' garden. At first he thought he was in luck, and that the gardens were empty, but then he saw Miles Archer sitting in the shade of the horse-chestnut. He was baring no part of himself to the summer heat, and was attired in a surprisingly stylish panama hat, reading.

For a moment Peter considered turning round and bolting, but it was much cooler here, a slight breeze was ruffling the heads of the roses, and then Miles looked up and raised his hat to him. Now it would be bad manners to leave. He crossed the croquet lawn and sat down next to him.

'Peter,' Miles said.

'Miles,' Peter replied.

'I have just thrashed Neil Pennell at squash.'

Peter smiled. 'Well done.'

'He is trying to reduce his waistline in preparation for filming.'

'I think he's very good. He has a good turn of phrase for television.'

Miles didn't reply. He looked at Pip. 'A new addition to your household?'

Pip had thrown himself on his back, allowing the breeze to ruffle the fur of his stomach, and closed his eyes.

'A temporary lodger. I'm looking after him for Sam.'

'I suspected it might not have been your breed of choice.'

Peter smiled. He liked Miles. He remembered interviewing him for the job. Their choice he'd realised in retrospect had been influenced by the fact that Miles's predecessor had been an exceptionally bad-tempered Scot who had managed to fall out with practically every member of the governing body and all his fellow medievalists in the history faculty. The fellowship had craved a non-bellicose medievalist and Miles had certainly fitted that bill. There had been no doubting his intelligence; he'd received glowing references from his postgraduate supervisor but the very quality that they had craved at the time, a certain mildness of temperament, had also contributed to him not being counted altogether a success.

The problem with Miles was personal confidence and if ever there was a man in need of a good woman it was him. What he needed, Peter thought, was an old-fashioned matchmaker. Jean, who was quite good at that kind of thing, had tried innumerable times to get him together with Mary Astor, the college librarian, but all her attempts had ended in failure.

Peter had himself married late in life and he knew it had come as a shock to his colleagues for whom he was firmly established as a perpetual bachelor. He had assumed much the same himself but greatly to his own surprise he had embraced the companionship of marriage with open arms. Having a partner to discuss the petty irritations of college life, and someone to help in the social activities which were part of college life, had made a great difference. Jean's down-to-earth sensible advice had been invaluable.

'Congratulations are in order, I understand,' Peter said. 'You have your hands on the college wine cellar.'

Miles smiled. 'The cellars are quite extraordinary. I had no idea.'

'I've never been down there.'

'In all your years as Provost?'

'No.'

'Well, we should remedy that. I will take you. Let me know a time that would be convenient. It would be a great pleasure to show you. They're magnificent.'

'Thank you. I'd like that.'

Miles picked up a leather-spined and cornered book from the grass and handed it to Peter. 'Hardwick gave this to me. It's a history of the St Cuthbert's cellars.'

Peter opened it, admiring the beautiful marbling of the first page, and began to leaf through it. There were lists of wines bought, quantities, when they were laid down and when they were drunk. He flicked a few pages on and a name caught his eye. Professor Sweetman.

'I didn't know Charles Sweetman was ever in charge of the wine here.'

'It was before your time, I think. According to Hardwick he was responsible for laying the foundations of the wine supply we have today. I think he's Hardwick's favourite although he'd never admit it.'

Peter handed the book back. 'I understand from Sam you had a run-in with a shrunken head.'

'Yes, neither my jacket nor my nose has fully recovered from the encounter.'

'What happened exactly?'

'I bumped into someone carrying a shrunken head in Holywell.'

'Not an altogether everyday occurrence.'

'No.'

'And you got no clear picture of the person carrying it?'

'Unfortunately it was the same evening I had arranged with Hardwick to be handed the key of the cellar. He was highly effusive in his welcome.'

Peter smiled. 'Ah.'

'So my vision was ...'

'Somewhat compromised?'

'Precisely so and I confess my nose hurt. I was concentrating on my nosebleed, not the man opposite.'

'You've no doubt heard of what's been happening at the Pitt Rivers?'

He nodded. 'Murder, theft ... the destruction of the dinosaur. It crossed my mind that the person I bumped into might well have been involved in all those things.'

'Sam is continuing to work on the case.'

'She has set up an office in the Cowley Road.'

'Yes.'

'Is she coming home?'

Peter frowned. 'I hadn't considered that, my feeling is that it's a temporary measure.'

'I remember her walking through the quad in her school uniform when she was very young. She didn't like to step on the edges of the paving stones.'

'Didn't she?'

'No, she was always very good at baffling the bears. It must have been a strange upbringing for a child.'

'Strange?'

'Unusual, then.'

The two men lapsed into silence. When the silence had extended long enough to become companionable rather than awkward, Miles picked up his book and continued reading and Peter folded his newspaper carefully at the sudoku and unclipped a pen from his shirt pocket. The shadows lengthened. Peter filled in the puzzles and then watched the swifts swooping over the lawn, so low he almost thought he saw one fly through one of the croquet hoops. Pip lay on his back, his soft snores mingling with the shrill cries of the swifts. At least in here they were both quite safe. There was no way the dog could be got at. Sam, however, was not hiding away, that wasn't really her style. She was out there and he hoped she was all right.

Sam sat in the library looking through the microfiche of old copies of *The Oxford Times*. She'd phoned Mrs Eliot and asked her if she could remember the date of the accident and to Sam's surprise she had – apparently it had been the same month Mrs Eliot's own mother died – August 1976. As she was writing it down in her notebook she had come across the date on the piece of paper she'd found in the pool of the house in Holland Park. Four months later. *The Oxford Times* came out once a week on Fridays, unlike *The Oxford Mail* which was daily, and she was hoping that looking through *The Oxford Times* from August–December 1976 would give her the information she wanted.

The library was stuffy and filled with shufflers and mutterers and the mildly evil-smelling. The heat didn't help. Mixed in with these were a scattering of foreign teenagers leafing through their *English Grammars in Use*, while texting their friends.

One of the shufflers, an anxious floral-skirted woman, approached Sam and said loudly. 'Have you got *The Times*? She says it's here but I can't find it.'

Sam shook her head and watched her move on to the next person. Libraries, she thought, were in many ways extensions of the social services; they were places where people could come for company and the papers and, in the winter, places where they could keep warm.

Librarians were saints, Sam thought and luxuriated in the sight of one of the blessed bearing down on a hapless teenage boy who had had the temerity not only to answer his mobile phone but then start a conversation on it.

Sam sighed, took a sip of her bottle of water, and tried to focus on the task in hand. It was boring work and the shufflers, teenagers and texters were no aid to concentration. Also, she found herself becoming distracted by news items completely unrelated to what she was looking for.

A couple of hours later Sam's brain had turned to mush, she'd run out of water and she was considering quitting. She decided she'd do one more paper and then stop, then there on the front page was the item she'd been seeking.

SWEETMAN INQUEST OPENS

The inquest has opened into the deaths of Valerie and Robert Sweetman on 31 August 1976. Robert Sweetman, a classics fellow at St John's College, Oxford, was the son of Charles Sweetman, the Professor of Anthropology at Oxford University. Valerie Sweetman was an English teacher at the Oxford High School. Also in the car was Professor Sweetman's grandson Norman, aged six. Norman Sweetman was the only member of the family to escape unhurt.

The family were travelling back from London where they had been to an exhibition taking place at the British Museum of Native American Indian art. A shaman's mask from the American part of the Sweetman collection had been loaned to this exhibition and was being transported back to Oxford to be put on display in the Pitt Rivers museum. It would have been the first time this exceptionally rare artefact has been reunited with the body of the Sweetman dona-tion since 1914 when the death of Archibald Sweetman divided the artefacts between the American and English sides of the family. The shaman's mask was not recovered from the scene of the accident and the police are treating the disappearance as theft.

The Tsimshian tribe, who have been campaigning for many years for the return of the mask, deny any involvement in the theft but a spokesman said that it was important that the mask was recovered as it was a part of the heritage of the Tsimshian tribe and there was no other item like it in the world.

Sam stopped reading. Norman had been in the car. She remembered what Mrs Eliot had said about Norman holding himself responsible. And the mask had gone missing. Presumably these were the mys-terious circumstances alluded to in the article she'd taken from the house in Holland Park. Had it ever been found or had someone been charged with its theft? She thought about what Cummings had said about items which had been stolen coming back on to the market after a certain length of time. Phil would hopefully be able to get hold of the file on the crash. She could try asking Sweetman, but after last time doubted somehow that she'd get very far. But the pieces were slowly beginning to come together. Then she remembered what Alan had said to her about the man who had attacked her being a policeman or someone with police contacts, and something occurred to her. OK it was a long shot but it might just be worth trying.

Outside the library she phoned Phil.

'I've got dates now. Could you pull an old police file for me?'

She heard him sigh but she knew he'd do it.

'That's an old one,' he said, when she explained which one it was she wanted. 'It'll take a while.'

'Fine, thanks a lot, Phil.'

Then she phoned Alan and updated him.

'The more I dig into this the more I think that the shaman's mask is the key to what's going on here. The article said it was worth a million pounds and that if it's sold with the other items in New York it will increase the value of everything in the sale. That's a big enough incentive to murder. The people in the house in Holland Park had the article giving details about the sale and they had obviously been reading up about the accident and the theft. Maybe they've been hired by the people selling the other stuff in New York to find it, or they see an opportunity to make a lot of money for themselves by finding it and offering it for sale at the same time. Any luck pursuing the ex-policeman track?'

'The team investigating Steph's murder aren't that keen on the idea.'

'How about tracking down the people behind Omega Exports?'

'That's a dead end, I'm afraid. The directors are two solicitors in a scruffy office in Kennington. They're the front. Incidentally Paxton said you could have access to your flat and they've finished with your van. I went and picked it up for you.'

'Thanks.'

Alan cleared his throat. 'Best you get into the flat as quick as possible. It's been so hot.'

Sam didn't say anything. She couldn't ask Alan to help her out with that one.

'Best to get professionals in,' he said. 'I've got a number. They're not cheap but ...'

'Fine.' Sam wrote it down and hung up.

This couldn't be delayed. She phoned the number immediately, explained what had happened and arranged to meet them outside her flat early the following morning to hand over the keys. She closed up her phone and began walking back to the office. A wave of fear washed over her. Tomorrow she had a session with Reg. Ever since she'd left the message on his answerphone there was a piece of her that had been regretting it. Each time she thought about it she heard the voice start up in her head, '*If you tell, you'll die.*' What was that book? *Feel the Fear and* ... momentarily her mind went blank, she couldn't remember the rest of the title. She paused outside the Quod Bar on the High. How about, feel the fear and drink tequila? She entered the bar and ordered herself a margarita. She licked the salt from the rim, drank it very, very slowly and chatted to the American barman. It seemed to do the trick. The fear she felt was numbed slightly. Then she slid off the bar stool and headed for the Cowley Road.

CHAPTER NINETEEN

It was cooler the next day and the doors out on to the patio were closed. Everything else was the same: the table, the jug of water, the box of tissues, Reg. He was searching his desk for something. Sam wondered if therapists had to be conscious of how they looked, if they always looked the same on purpose so as not to alarm their clients. Reg did always look the same; the only change in his appearance was the length of his hair, and this only varied by a few millimetres. She reached for the jug and poured herself some water and drank it. The glass was a heavy-bottomed tumbler with a bubble in the base. She twisted it round and round in her hands. A few months ago she had thrown one exactly like this at the mirror in her parents' bathroom. She had then closed her hand around the jagged remains. She looked at the palm of her hand and the angry red scar in the shape of a half-moon that covered it.

Reg had found what he wanted, the tape recorder, and now came and sat down opposite her. The expression on his face was, as usual, warm and attentive.

'You phoned and said you wanted me to ask you why it was you'd never learned to swim. Shall we start there?'

'Yes.'

'So why was it you never learned to swim?'

And at last Sam told him.

It was only when she had finished that she looked down at the glass she was still holding and saw that she was gripping it so tightly that her knuckles had turned white. Carefully she put it down on the table and opened and closed her hand. Relief flooded through her.

She had told and she hadn't died. Of course she hadn't.

The silence in the room deepened.

'The thing is,' Sam said, 'I've only had these flashbacks since my father came back. At first I was convinced it was him, but now when the flashbacks happen, I don't see his face. In the most recent nightmare I didn't see his face either, but I hear this voice, "If you tell, you'll die" ...'

'But you believe it was your father?'

'Well, why would I get them when he comes back? It doesn't make any sense otherwise.'

Reg cleared his throat and altered his position in his chair. 'There can be all kinds of reasons why we allow memories to surface when they do.'

'But it would be too much of a coincidence for the memories to surface and it not to be him, wouldn't it? Anyway, I didn't think therapists believed in coincidence.'

He smiled. 'We can veer in that direction.'

'So how can I tell if it was him?'

'Memory is a powerful thing. You know who did it but at the moment you're protecting yourself from knowing. But it sounds from the dreams you were talking about that you may well be edging closer to facing the truth.'

'I know I'm frightened of knowing.'

'Tell me about the fear.'

'If it was him, where does it leave us?'

'Say more about that.'

'I mean how can I ... how can we ever have any sort of a relationship?'

'And if it wasn't him?'

Sam looked out of the patio windows and felt something shift. It was a bit like an ear that has been blocked with water suddenly unblocking. Silence again. Reg was horribly relaxed with silence.

'More scary ...' she said eventually.

'Because?'

'Because then there's possibility, then there's hope. There's no excuse and no barrier.'

'No barrier to what?'

'No barrier to loving him.'

'Aha.'

Sam was shaking her head. 'But what I've just said. That's rubbish. He raped my mother and he almost killed my brother. If that's not a barrier, I don't know what is.'

'And if you love him?'

'Sorry?'

'If you love him, what follows from that?'

'Well, I'll care about him. I can't pretend I don't care what happens to him.'

'And if you love him and care about what happens to him?'

Sam shook her head.

Reg continued. 'If there's no barrier to loving him, then what?'

'I'll have to worry about him.'

'Because?'

'He'll be my responsibility.'

'Why?'

'Because he gave me life, because my mother and Mark won't have anything to do with him, because there isn't anyone else, because he came back ...'

Reg raised his eyebrows and nodded encouragingly.

The room felt airless and Sam felt light-headed. 'Could we open the doors into the garden?' she asked.

Reg stood up and opened both sides of the doors.

Sam walked out on to the patio, nudging the green hose that snaked around the begonia-filled pots. She took a deep breath and exhaled slowly.

'I'm not forgiving him,' she said.

'No?' he said.

'No,' she said.

'People are sometimes mistaken about forgiveness,' Reg said. 'They think if they do it they'll let that person off the hook. What they don't see is that they've backed themselves into a corner and cannot see the hook stuck between their own shoulder-blades.'

'What are you talking about?'

Reg smiled. 'I'm going to say a few things.'

'You usually do.'

'Before next time it might be worth thinking about whether anything else happened to you around the time your father re-appeared in your life. Anything else that might have triggered the memories? On the subject of whether you'll ever remember, in our last session you were talking about your best throw and how you felt afterwards, and trying to work it out – why you felt the way you felt.'

Sam nodded.

'At the time you said you let go of having to know what had happened.'

'Yes, I did.'

'Finally, on the issue of forgiveness. Sometimes it helps to have the full picture. You told me that when your father attacked your mother and Mark he was just back from Oman.'

'Yes, that's right.'

'I think I told you when we first started working together that I counsel a lot of ex-services, that I'm ex-services myself, and I special-ise in post-traumatic stress syndrome. If ever you want to get some information about that, I'd be happy to talk to you about it.'

'So you're saying he was justified in what he did because he was ill, and I'll have to forgive him.'

Reg ran his hand lightly over one of his lavender bushes and laughed. 'I think you know perfectly well I'm saying no such thing. Explaining why something has happened is not the same as excusing it.'

Sam looked at her watch but it had stopped. 'What's the time?'

Reg looked at his own watch. 'Quarter of an hour to go.'

'Go on then,' she said. 'Tell me about post-traumatic stress.'

He smiled and gestured for her to go through the door in front of him. She stepped back into the house and he followed her.

When Sam came out of Reg's she felt as if a lot of the things that had made up her internal psychological furniture had been moved around and put in different positions. There seemed to be more room and spaces in unexpected places. She felt light-headed and slightly sick as if she were a balloon that might cut loose at any point and float off into the sky. Therapy was weird stuff.

'Give yourself time,' Reg had said to her, as they parted company on his doorstep. 'Time for things to settle and then we can talk about next steps.'

Next steps had sounded alarming to Sam. Take one step. Hide in a cupboard was more her style. Even as she stood there she was contemplating the luxury of two steps back.

Back in Fulham Sam leaned against the wall opposite the mansion block she lived in and looked up at her bedroom window. Derek and Robbie, the two men she'd hired to clear her room, were on ladders taking down the blinds. The windows were open and she could hear their laughter drifting into the street. Well, it wasn't their tragedy was it? It wasn't their bedroom. A woman rather like the white bouffant she taught in Headington passed Sam carrying a green shopping bag. She glanced at Sam, saw that she was looking at the flat, and hurried past.

Sam thought of Stephanie sprawled across the bed, of the gaping wound on her throat, of the blood sprayed around the room, on the ceiling and across the wooden floors. She thought of the spray of blood over the white paper lampshade.

When she'd handed over the keys to the flat that morning Derek had asked her, 'What about personal items? What about clothes?'

She'd assumed the police would have most of those.

'Everything covered in blood,' she said, 'throw it.'

'Everything?'

'Well, if it can be wiped clean … I just don't want to walk into the room and see any blood,' she said.

'The walls, now we can get it off, but you'll need to repaint.'

'I'll be doing that anyway.'

Then her voice had become shaky and she'd turned away from him.

Now she pushed herself away from the wall and walked round to the front of the block. A van with high, see-through mesh metal sides, open at the top, was parked there. Inside it was her bed, mattress and base and several black plastic bags. Derek came out of the flat carrying an armful of blinds.

'All right, love?' he asked and threw the blinds in the back. 'Another hour and we'll be out of here.'

She opened Edie's letterbox and delivered a low flat whistle through the ferociously thick bristles which guarded it, then stood back and did a Cecil B. DeMille for the spyhole. When the door opened it was on the chain and Edie's face peered through the small gap.

'I've got company,' she hissed and seemed to be about to slam the door. Then Sam heard voices and saw someone else moving beyond Edie in the flat. The door was closed. She was about to turn and leave when she heard the chain come off and a hand on the collar of her shirt dragged her backwards and dumped her unceremoniously on the floor of Edie's hall. She looked up and saw Johnny looking down at her.

'What are you doing here?' she asked, getting to her feet.

Edie was looking down at Sam as if she'd just sucked a rotten egg.

Sam tried again. 'Do you two know each other?'

'Never mind about that,' Edie said.

Mind you, Johnny was Edie's type. She fancied villains. One Christmas she had proudly shown Sam her *Sopranos'* calendar, hung above her bed like an icon. She'd made her look at each month, each one being a different picture of James Gandolfini. It was only when they came to the end of it that Sam realised the calendar was two years old. She suspected Tony Soprano would still be hanging on Edie's wall when she was taken out of there in her coffin.

Frank sauntered out of the kitchen, ignored Sam and wandered over to rub his chops against Johnny's white trainers. Frank was rather like Edie, he thought men were best.

'What happened to Stephanie?' Johnny said.

Sam paused. He looked terrible. Stubble covered his cheeks and a muscle was twitching in his jaw. 'What's Edie told you?'

'Steph was murdered.'

Sam nodded.

'What the fuck happened?'

What should she tell him? What shouldn't she tell him?

'Perhaps we could have some tea,' Sam said, looking at Edie.

'No milk,' Edie said.

That had to be a lie. Edie always had milk. Sam tapped her for it frequently enough to know Edie was a woman who always had stores. It went back to her days working in the black market during the blitz. If she was saying she didn't have any it was a sign she wanted her out of here, and as quickly as possible.

She turned to Johnny. 'I'd rented the flat to her because I'm working in Oxford at the moment. She came back here after Alan's party and was murdered that night.'

'She leave with anyone?'

Sam considered this for a moment. 'No.'

'Yes she did. She was with that coloured bloke who lives across the road,' Edie said.

Sam sighed. 'But he'd known her for years. He had nothing to do with what happened.'

'Isn't it always the last person they were seen with who did it?' Edie continued. 'She was very thick with him. He was in and out at all times.'

'Listen,' Sam said. 'He had nothing to do with it. His mum was awake when he came in and confirmed what he said. The police searched their home. There was nothing to suggest he'd been involved. If he'd killed her there would have been evidence.'

'My mum vouched for me enough times. What else is a mother going to do for her son?' Johnny said.

'You know the police are looking for you,' Sam said. 'You must go and tell them what you were doing that night. Is there someone who can give you an alibi?'

'Why do I need a fucking alibi?'

As he spoke he took a couple of steps towards her and Sam took a rapid couple backwards, standing on Frank's paw in the process and bringing forth a protesting hiss of pain. She bent down to console him but he flounced away from her into the kitchen.

'As far as they are concerned you have a history of violence, you were fighting with Alan that night. You'd visited Stephanie at the pub and she'd sent you away. You must see you have to remove yourself from their list of suspects.'

'They don't care as long as they get a collar. Johnny Knowles, who once hurt a copper, inside for the rest of his life. Yeah that'd suit 'em fine. I was in there. They've probably got my prints.'

'You were in there? When was this?'

'Afternoon. Before Al's party. I came round, we had a chat.'

'Was it you shouting up at the flat?'

'I left my dark glasses. It was after I come out. I was shouting for her to throw them down to me. I'm not handing myself in – they'll stitch me up.'

'I don't understand what you're doing here,' Sam said.

'Me and Edie go way back. Came to see what she knew.'

Edie said something low under her breath, nudged him in the ribs and let loose a filthy cackle.

'You never told me you knew Alan's brother.'

'Who's Alan?'

'He changed your light bulb that time.'

'The poof?'

'Edie,' Sam snapped.

'Keep your hair on, babe. I didn't know he had anything to do with Johnny here. I only ever met him the one time.'

Sam was fed up with standing in the dingy hallway. 'Can we go in the kitchen, Edie? I could do with a glass of water.'

Edie twisted her mouth to one side but led the way into the kitchen, took a glass out of a cupboard and gave Sam some water. The three of them sat down at the pine kitchen table.

Johnny placed his forearms on the table and leaned forwards. 'Edie told me the police thought the killer might have been after you.'

Shit, that was the precise piece of information Sam would have preferred him not to have. She didn't reply.

He continued. 'They arrested anyone yet?'

'I don't know.'

'Someone want you dead?'

She puffed out her cheeks. 'I don't know.'

She didn't want to tell him about the man with the wrecking-ball head. If she did, he'd go looking for him, and things were complicated enough without Johnny Knowles in the mix. She decided to change the subject.

'Are you staying here?'

Edie said something under her breath and he laughed. Sam had never seen Edie in action before. There'd been a fellow tobacco smuggler around for a while, a right lairy sod, who called Sam 'darling' and told filthy jokes. Being round this pair was beginning to make Sam feel like a nun.

'Did you get the delivery of cat food and litter?' Sam asked.

'Yeah, babe, that was fine.'

'Do you think someone was after you?' Johnny said again.

Sam looked into her empty glass. 'Maybe,' she said.

'You know that when you let her the flat?'

'Of course not,' Sam said. 'I rented her the flat as a favour to Alan.'

There was a knock on the door and Edie bustled out of the kitchen into the hall. 'Sam,' she shouted. 'It's the blokes next door.'

Derek was standing on the landing holding her keys. 'Right, love, all done. You want to check it out?'

She nodded and walked across the threshold of her own flat. There was the strong smell of industrial strength disinfectant.

'We've opened all the windows we could. Best to leave them that way until the chemicals have cleared.'

She nodded and paused in the doorway of her bedroom. They'd done a thorough job. The room had been stripped bare, the walls washed down. There was no blood to be seen. She felt someone at her shoulder and Johnny pushed past her.

He stood with his hands in the pockets of his jeans staring down at the area of the floor where her bed had been. She glanced at him. He wasn't the kind of man to get upset, she thought, no, not upset but very, very angry. His eyes came off the floor on to her own, but she didn't want to get into an eyeballing contest with him. For one thing she knew she'd lose; the guilt she felt wasn't going to let her hold his gaze for any length of time. She turned away from him towards Derek and pulled out her wallet.

CHAPTER TWENTY

Sam got the bus to Alan's which involved half an hour sitting in a traffic jam inching along the Fulham Palace Road.

He opened the door, wearing a suit and tie. Sam didn't think she'd ever seen him in one but didn't say anything; the suit and tie were black and didn't invite flippant comment. He looked startled.

'You remember I was coming to pick up the van?' Sam said, as she stepped into his flat.

'No, I – something's come up.' He rubbed his hand across his eyes. 'I'm sorry, Sam. I was about to leave.'

He'd followed her into the living-room. She turned round. 'I just saw Johnny at Edie's.'

'At Edie's?' he picked up his keys from the table and pocketed them. 'I'm sorry, Sam, this isn't a good time. I can't ...' He turned back towards the front door.

'Where are you going?'

'To see Stephanie.'

Sam didn't say anything.

'The police have released her body. She's at the undertaker's.'

'Right,' Sam said. 'Are your family going to be there?'

'No, they've already been. I wanted to go alone.'

He was standing by the front door jiggling the keys up and down in his hand.

'I'll take you,' Sam said.

He nodded briefly and Sam followed him out on to the landing. They waited for the lift. When it came, Alan stood opposite Sam, staring at the floor. The lift began to descend.

As they exited the tower block and walked towards her van, Sam said, 'Where is she?'

'Opposite the Chelsea and Westminster Hospital on the Fulham Road.'

It took Sam a while to find a parking space. She turned off the engine and cleared her throat. 'Would you like me to come in with you?'

He nodded and got out of the van.

A white cloth had been placed across Stephanie's throat to cover the wound but the effect was to make her look like a Victorian lady with a ruff round her neck, not a nineteen-year-old.

Alan looked down at her. Suddenly his hands came up to his throat and he tore off his tie. He shook his head and bundled the tie into his pocket.

'If she could see me in this gear, she'd be pissing herself. She never saw me in a suit in her life. I don't even know why I put it on.'

'Out of respect for the dead,' Sam said. But even as she said it she thought it sounded artificial, like something you thought you ought to say, not like something that had anything to do with what was actually happening.

Alan shook his head. 'Respect for the dead,' he repeated. 'She's not the dead, she's Stephanie and she never gave a toss what I wore. She never did. Poor Steph. Poor, poor Stephanie.' He reached out and placed his hand against the side of her cheek.

Sam moved closer to him, slid her hand into his and looked down at the dead girl. It struck her for the first time that the waxy stretched look of a corpse matched the facial features of the grief-stricken. As if one couldn't look upon death without on some level becoming it. That should be me, she thought. I'm not supposed to be alive. I'm supposed to be lying in that coffin, murdered, and whoever did it is still out there and will probably try again. I shouldn't be thinking this, she thought. I should be thinking about Stephanie and Alan, but I can't. All I can think is that it should have been me.

Her hand tightened inside Alan's.

Afterwards they went to Carluccio's, which was more or less next door, and ordered a bottle of wine, olives, focaccia and Parma ham; the main aim of ordering the food was to disguise the fact that all they wanted to do was drink. Sam matched Alan glass for glass. When the bottle was empty they ordered another. For the first half an hour Alan concentrated on drinking and conversation involved questions from Sam and monosyllabic grunts from him. In the end, Sam gave up on the conversation and did what he was doing, drank and stared into the middle distance. She made a mental list of questions she still hadn't managed to answer.

1. Who killed Gittings and why?
2. Who killed Stephanie?
3. Where is Norman? And what is he doing?
4. What's the big deal about the dog?
5. Have the police picked up wrecking-ball head?
6. Has Phil got hold of the police file on the crash and does it shed any light on what happened to the mask?

Alan suddenly sat upright and spoke. 'What was that you said about Johnny just now?'

'Just now, as in two or three hours ago?'

'Whatever. Where is he?'

'At Edie's.'

'In your block?'

'Yes.'

'What's he doing there?'

'He knows Edie.'

'How?'

'I thought you might know. They looked as if they knew each other ...' She paused. 'Intimately.'

Alan frowned and then a look of amazement cleared his face. 'Your Edie is *that* Edie?'

'What Edie?'

'She was a madam in Hammersmith. She did time for living off immoral earnings. All my brothers used to go there.'

'Oh God,' Sam said. 'Didn't you recognise her?'

'Well, I never went, did I, for obvious reasons, and I only met her once at yours when I replaced a light bulb for her – it was dingy in the hall and when I'd done it she wanted me out of there as quickly as possible.'

'She is like that. She's fantastically suspicious of strangers. I suppose that's why she thought Stephanie was on the game.'

'She what?'

'Well, you know, I told her she wasn't, but ...'

'For fuck's sake, Sam, why did you tell me that?'

'Look, Alan, it doesn't matter what Edie thought, does it? You know she wasn't. Edie was just jumping to conclusions. It was her frame of reference, so to speak.'

He sighed and reached for the bottle.

'Are your brothers behaving themselves?'

'I think I managed to persuade them not to break Floyd's legs but that was about it.'

'Johnny knows Stephanie's killer was looking for me.'

'How did he find that out?'

'Edie heard it from one of the policemen. She's probably had her ear stuck to the crack of her front door for the last four days.'

'How was he?'

Sam grabbed a bit of focaccia and dipped it in oil. 'As you'd expect, a bit wound up. I told him he should go to the police.'

'And what did he say?'

'He said his prints were in the flat because he'd come to see her earlier on the day of your party, that the police would want to frame him with it, that he didn't have an alibi and that there was no fucking way he was going to do that until they caught the actual murderer.'

'He'd been in her flat earlier that day?'

'That's what he said.'

'How come Steph didn't say anything at the party?'

'Maybe she didn't want to bother you. Maybe she would have told you the following morning if she'd still been ... there ... maybe she thought if she saw him it was betraying you ...'

Alan picked up the empty bottle and waved at the waiter.

Alan stood swaying on the pavement outside the restaurant. 'Fucking suit,' he said, looking down at himself. 'Fucking ...' He tore open the front of his shirt.

'Alan ...' Sam began.

But now shoes and socks joined the shirt on the ground. His hands went to the waistband of his trousers.

'Alan, no,' Sam said more firmly.

'Try and fucking stop me,' he said.

She held the palms of both hands face out towards him to indicate she had no intention of doing that and took a step back. He was very drunk, a lot larger than her and she'd taught him self-defence. Instead she picked up his shoes and socks and shirt and waited for his trousers. She put out her hand to wave at a taxi but, not surprisingly, as soon as the driver saw Alan hopping around on one leg trying to get his trousers off, he turned off his light and accelerated past them. There was no way they'd get a cab with him in that state; a bus would be their best bet.

At the bus stop Alan refused to put on any of his clothes, on the bus likewise. They sat together on the top deck at the back, Sam clutching his clothes and shoes.

'Why'd I put on the suit, Sam?' he said quietly. 'Why'd I do that?'

'I don't know,' she said. 'But it doesn't matter. Steph wouldn't have minded, would she? She wouldn't have minded you getting dressed up for her.'

He began to cry then. His head bouncing against the window as the bus turned into Fulham Broadway. Sam threw his jacket round his shoulders and held on to him. This is my fault, she thought, this is all my fault. I should have left well alone. I should never have agreed to have that Chihuahua in the first place. That's what started it all, Norman, that bloody dog and Cruella de Vil, and now Stephanie's dead and my best friend is so distraught he's behaving like King Lear in the storm.

Back at Alan's she got him to bed and then tried to drink as much water as possible to ward off the forthcoming hangover, and threw herself on to the sofa.

She's a small child coming home from school, her thick blue skirt scratchy against her legs, a grey sock loose round her ankle, a satchel almost as big as her bangs against her side. She walks up the steps to St Cuthbert's and begins to make her way along one side of the quadrangle. As she goes, she hops and skips to avoid the cracks between the uneven flagstones. She mustn't step on them or the bears will get her, but then she trips and, before she can help herself, one foot has landed full on a crack. She stops frozen in fright, trying desperately to remove it but it's stuck fast. She's pulling and pulling but there's nothing she can do. Now the ground is moving around her, the stones are slowly being lifted. Masked figures surround her. One stands directly in front of her. He wears combat trousers, soldier's boots and a balaclava. His hands aren't human hands, they're bear's paws, the claws gleam like razor-blades. One of the paws moves to his face to pull the mask away but before he has done that, the other one flashes towards Sam. She can't step back. She feels the claws rake down her face. She hears the words, 'Who are you underneath?' She feels the blood pour down her face.

Her head was hanging off the edge of the sofa when she woke and her whole skull hurt. With infinite care she sat upright and looked at the clock on the front of Alan's video. She'd only been asleep a couple of hours. She hadn't drunk enough water to make her feel human, not nearly enough. She dragged herself into the kitchen got herself some more, drank it and felt sick. Maybe some night air would help. The doors out on to the balcony were open and she stepped outside. What was the message of the dream? If she knew who was behind the mask then she would die. If she allowed herself to remember then she would die. She heard Reg saying, *You could let go of having to know.* Easier said than done, Reg, she thought, pressing her fingers into her temples, so much easier said than done. This was coming out like a splinter.

The following morning after having said goodbye to Alan, Sam was heading back to pick up her van when Phil phoned.

'Where are you?' he asked.

'London, but I'm coming back to Oxford today.'

'We've got some information on the two guys who attempted to snatch the dog.'

'OK.'

'Someone from the Blackbird Leys estate told the local bobby that they'd seen these two guys torching the car. It's the same registration number.'

'Have you picked them up yet?'

'I wanted to talk to you first. If we pick them up then they'll be charged and probably released on bail. They're going to get lawyers and then they won't tell us anything about who put them up to it. I was wondering if you could get Tyler to help you out.'

Sam smiled. 'I see.'

'We'll hold off until tomorrow morning.'

'Thanks Phil. Thanks a lot.'

She finished the call to Phil and phoned Tyler.

'It's Sam. Good holiday?'

'Yeah, OK. How were my girls?'

Sam presumed he meant the pensioners. 'Complaining that you won't teach them to punch.'

She heard his grunt of amusement. 'Not compatible with their osteoporosis is what I tell them.'

'Look, Tyler, I'm coming into Oxford. I should be there in a couple of hours. Could I come and talk to you about something?'

'I'm going shopping but you can get me on my mobile. I should be back by then anyway.'

'Great. I'll phone when I reach the ring road.'

'Is everything all right?'

'Yeah, Tyler, it's fine.'

Again that grunt of amusement and then the phone went dead.

A couple of hours later Sam was getting out of her van outside Tyler's house on the Blackbird Leys estate. This wasn't an area known to most of the students of Oxford, for them picking up a take-away from the Cowley Road would represent a daring excursion into the hinterlands of the city. No, this estate with its box-style terrace housing and numerous high-rise blocks was not an area into which they would accidentally stray. It was only a five-minute bus ride from the centre of town, but it was a world away from the quads and spires of the colleges. In the early nineties it had had its brief moment of infamy when teenage gangs had taken to the streets joy-riding and it had become virtually a no-go area for the police. In the immediate aftermath of that there had been much talk of the social problems arising from a lack of funding for regeneration, but when the fuss had died down no money had been forthcoming, the council preferring to dig up the Cornmarket a thousand times before they'd ever put a penny into the estate. And so the problems of social deprivation remained and so did the teenage terror gangs, the muggers and the class A drug dealers.

Sam looked around her, at the scorched grass, the battered cars and the graffiti-covered bus shelter. Under normal circumstances she would have been worried about leaving her car here but this was directly outside Tyler's front door and different rules applied. In fact, different rules applied to this whole part of the estate. He only acted as a last resort, when the protests to the police and the council had failed once again to come up with a result, when demonstrations outside class A drug dealers had come and gone and the dealer was still there. Only then did Tyler and his friends pay a visit. Tyler had taught judo at the community centre here for the last twenty years. He had a lot of lads he could call on. The end result of the visit was always that the troublemakers moved on. The police knew what happened but turned a blind eye. This had been going on for as long as Sam could remember and over the years this part of the estate had become progressively more popular. She walked up the paved path to his front door and rang the bell.

A few moments later the door opened and Tyler was looking down at her.

'Look what the cat dragged in,' he said, and hugged her so hard all the air left her lungs.

She followed him through his house out into his back garden and sat down under a sun umbrella. He made some tea and joined her. Old age had caught up with Django, Tyler's dog, who lay sprawled out in the shade of a bush. When he saw Sam he didn't move just thumped the grass a couple of times with his tail in welcome.

'So,' he said. 'What's up?'

Sam told him about the attempted dog-napping, about the two men, and about her conversation with Phil.

Tyler smiled and put his cup of tea down on the patio. 'So you'd like me to talk to them before the police pick them up and everything gets too legal?'

'That's about it. Do you know where to find them?'

He nodded.

'Is Jake around?'

He nodded.

'And Zac?'

'Yup.'

'Got any heavyweights in your classes at the moment?'

'A couple.'

'Thanks a lot, Tyler.'

'You decided yet whether you're back for good or not?'

'Until Christmas and then we're going to see.'

He sighed. 'Well, up until Christmas would be better than nothing. I've got a favour in return.'

'Of course,' Sam said. 'Anything.'

He laughed. 'Don't say that before you know what it is.'

'I mean it. You know the indebtedness runs all one way between us.'

He pinched her cheek then picked up the cups. 'Don't talk rubbish, Sammy. There are no debts between friends.'

'So what's the favour?'

'I'll tell you afterwards.'

'When do you want to do it?'

'Night's best. I'll get one of the boys to find out where they drink. We'll get them on the way home.'

'What time shall I come back then?'

'We should know where they are by eleven. I'll phone you.'

Sam was worried about Peter. She'd tried to get hold of him on his mobile without success. This didn't particularly surprise her because he was a man who liked to answer the phone in the traditional manner, while sitting down with a desk in front of him, was always losing his mobiles and had never quite managed to get to grips with the answerphone features of any of them. She had left several messages at the lodge of St Cuthbert's asking him to phone her but she had heard nothing, so, after parking near her office, she walked into town and up the steps to the lodge. A young porter, who Sam didn't know, was there. She explained who she was and asked him if he'd seen Peter around. He gestured behind her and Sam turned round to see Peter walking towards her with Pip and Miles Archer in tow.

'I've been trying to get hold of you,' Sam said. 'I left some messages on your mobile.'

'I'm never quite sure of how to retrieve them.'

'I also left some messages at the lodge.'

'When was this?'

'Last night.'

'They're probably in my pigeon-hole.'

Sam sighed. 'You're all right anyway?'

'Yes,' he glanced down at Pip. 'Both of us are fine. We were just going to visit the college wine cellars with Miles.'

'Would you like to come?' Miles asked.

Sam followed the two men and the dog along the side of the quad to the common room block. Miles took the kind of key which should have opened the gates to Dracula's castle from his pocket and unlocked a door which led down a steep flight of steps. The cellars were massive, stretching out, as far as Sam could work out, underneath the whole length of the hall. The roof was supported by a series of groined arches and a long passage led down one side, off which a whole series of cellars opened. It was the coolest Sam had been in a month.

Miles had started to gabble excitedly. 'You know these are the best cellars in the university,' he said. 'The wonderful thing about them is the evenness of the temperature. Winter or summer, it never varies more than a degree or two from what it ought to be, and that's about fifty to fifty-five degrees. The walls are tremendously thick to support the great weight of the buildings above them. Ah ...' he stopped and stepped into one cellar. 'Here's the port we drink on ordinary nights and this ...' He picked up a bottle and wiped the dust off it as lovingly as if he'd been holding a woman's body. 'This is for special occasions.' He stared entranced at the bottle in his hands. 'You know in the olden days they never drew the corks – they heated a pair of tongs until they were red-hot, placed them round the neck of the bottle and then with one tap the head of the bottle would break off as clean as a whistle.'

Sam caught Peter's eye and a conspiratorial smile passed between them. Miles had moved on from silver tongs into the next cellar.

'You must have a big stock,' Sam said.

'What we have here is enough to last us about fifteen years, I'd say. If the present rate of consumption stays steady.'

Sam's mind boggled at what might constitute steady consumption in an Oxford college. Surely it would be like trying to measure the amount of water passing through Niagara Falls?

As they passed from cellar to cellar, Miles's stream of information continued unabated. 'I'm rather worried about the burgundy and the Bordeaux. There's a lot more of them drunk than there used to be and I do think in the past there has been an over-fondness for buying small parcels of what might be called bargains. Which I personally think is a bit chancy. I'd like us to be a bit more settled with our clarets.'

Sam had never known Miles to be so chatty. If he could just get Mary Astor, the librarian, down here then there might be a chance of getting them together, even more so if she possessed even the faintest interest in wine.

Peter and Sam followed Miles into the next cellar. In this one the bottles were placed on racks with metal frames and some of these could be moved in and out on runners laid on the floor. 'Look,' he said, 'you can pull it back and forth and it runs as smooth as butter.' He demonstrated what he meant. 'I think it was the idea of Professor Sweetman, a long time ago, to install these.'

'Sweetman?' Sam said.

'Yes, he was in charge of the cellars for a considerable period of time. He was responsible for really establishing the college as one of the best in the university. He always said that if a college was known for its wine, it would punch above its weight in the university as a whole because people of influence would flock to it, and with them would come gossip and information and connections, and all those can produce power.'

'There's a lot to be said for that point of view,' Peter said. 'Food and wine do affect a college's reputation.'

'You never told me Professor Sweetman was in charge of the cellars,' Sam said.

Peter looked at her in surprise. 'I only discovered myself the other day. Why? Is it significant in some way?'

'Well, I don't know. It might be.'

Miles had moved on. 'This is the claret I was sampling with Hardwick after which I ran into the shrunken head. We had failed to reach a conclusion as to its readiness for consumption.' He stared lovingly at the label. 'Perhaps you might give me your opinion on the matter?' He waved the bottle at Peter.

Peter looked at his watch. 'It's rather too early for me I'm afraid, Miles, and anyway I'm sure you'll make the right decision in due course.'

Miles bowed slightly. 'Thank you, Peter, for your confidence.'

Again Sam caught Peter's eye and smiled.

Half an hour later, Sam and Peter were back in his rooms with Pip. It was a long time since she'd been here and the rooms were very different to how she remembered them. Peter had not allowed the traditional heavy wooden panelling of the room to restrict what he hung on the walls. His tastes were defiantly modern; not for him the don in his powdered wig with pursed pink lips, and a fat finger sandwiched in some learned tome. Above the fireplace was a Ronald Searle cartoon. In the print a dishevelled cat sat on an ancient bed, his eyes raised to the heavens. Against the bed leaned an ancient bicycle and coffee cups covered the floor. In the corner was an old wind-up record player. The print's title was *Student Dreams*. Sam hadn't seen it before.

'Where did that come from?' she asked.

'A present from some of my research students.'

'It's wonderful.'

'No one does cats like Searle.'

Peter was standing with his back to the fireplace. 'Have the police made any progress with the men who seem intent on harming you?'

Sam shook her head. 'Phil said he'd phone me if they picked up any of them.'

He sighed. 'I'm afraid I have some bad news and some good news.'

'Aha.'

'The good news is that your mother phoned and said that the situation with her aunt had stabilised, but the bad news is that she is coming back this weekend.'

'Oh.'

'I'll have to go back to Park Town and tidy up prior to her arrival.'

'Yes, of course, but can't you get Mrs Parker to come in and do that?'

'She's on holiday.'

'Oh I see.'

'Is it safe for me to go back?'

'Well, no, not really, no more than it was before. Why don't you let me do it?'

Peter smiled. 'Forgive me, Sam, but I fear that your mother's idea of a tidy, clean house and yours may be, shall we say ...'

'Yes, yes you're right, but suppose I make a superhuman effort?'

'Even then I fear it will simply not be enough.'

'Maybe I should take Pip back.'

'I would miss him,' Peter said.

'But what's Mum going to say about him? She doesn't know, does she?'

'No, for some reason that escapes me I have not got round to telling her.'

Sam sighed. 'She'll blame me.'

'Oh, I don't know. I think she's learning not to do that any more.'

'Could you at least wait until tomorrow afternoon?' Sam asked

He looked worried. 'I was thinking of getting a start on it this evening.'

'The thing is we're hoping to find out who hired the two men who tried to snatch Pip.'

'OK, I'll hold off until tomorrow afternoon.'

'Good.'

Peter had walked over to the window and Sam joined him.

'These were the philosopher Jeremy Bentham's rooms as an under-graduate. He came here in 1760. Unfortunately, as you can see, they look down on to a graveyard and he had a fear of ghosts and spiritual visitations.'

'Poor man,' Sam said.

'Apparently the gloominess of the rooms depressed him. When he died he had his corpse embalmed and placed in a sitting position in a wooden cabinet. You can see it at University College London. The head is wax. The real head is kept locked away because it became the subject of too many student pranks.'

For some people, Sam thought, Oxford could be an unmitigated disaster.

CHAPTER TWENTY-ONE

Sam went back to the office and listened to her answerphone messages. One sounded promising. A solicitor whose client was a large insurance firm in Abingdon wanted some claims checked out. Sam spoke to him and said, yes, she would be able to do the work and that she could call on any number of 'operatives', his description, not hers. He said that if he was satisfied with her work on this one there might be a lot of other work he could put her way.

She put down the phone, got up and went and looked out of the window. Helga was down there in the back garden of the tattoo parlour and when she saw Sam she gestured for her to come down and join her.

Sam closed up her office, ran down the stairs to pavement level and pushed her way into the tattoo parlour and walked through to the garden. Helga offered her a beaten-up bright orange bucket-chair and sat down on a faded blue cloth director's chair. She offered Sam her joint, but Sam shook her head.

'They find him yet?' Helga asked.

Sam shook her head again.

'Why'd he want to hurt you?'

'I'm not really sure.'

'He angry boyfriend?'

Sam laughed. 'No.'

'You have boyfriend?'

She thought of Rick. 'Yes ... no ... sort of ...'

'He lives in Oxford?'

'No. He's been away up in Edinburgh.'

'You miss him?'

Sam sighed and then allowed herself to feel an ache in an intimate part of her anatomy. 'Yes,' she said. 'I've missed him very much.'

'I do you a butterfly for free. It will drive him crazy.'

Sam laughed. She had been getting to know what drove him crazy and it certainly wasn't a butterfly tattoo. 'I don't think so, thank you.'

'Why not? It will give you good luck.' She pulled up her loose black trousers and showed Sam a butterfly on her ankle.

'Very nice,' Sam said. 'But not for me.'

'You scared?'

'Absolutely,' Sam said. 'I can't stand needles.'

'I get you stoned. Needles no problem.'

'It's very kind of you, but no thank you.' God, Sam thought, I'm beginning to sound like Joyce Grenfell.

'You go to the dentist, what's the difference?'

'I don't go.'

'What happens when your teeth fall out?'

'Hopefully I'll be dead.'

Helga sucked on her teeth. 'You English ...'

'Do you know anything about shamanism?' Sam asked in a desperate attempt to change the subject, but at that moment a bell rang in the tattoo parlour and Helga got up and walked into the shop.

After a restless couple of hours in the office trying to sort out in her mind the connections in the case, Sam closed up the office and walked over to the cinema. The early evening performance of *The Constant Gardener* had just begun and Helen was standing outside smoking.

'Have you found Norman?' she asked.

Sam shook her head. 'Do you still think he might be sleeping here?'

She nodded. 'It's difficult for a person that large not to leave any trace of himself.'

'Chocolate wrappers still visible?'

She laughed.

'I haven't been able to stake out the place yet. Do you want the keys back?'

She shook her head. 'Why don't you hold on to them?'

'Why are you being so helpful?' Sam asked.

Helen turned, supporting the elbow of the hand holding her cigarette with her other hand. 'You're not used to people doing you favours for no reason.'

Sam smiled. 'I just doubt the no reason.'

She sighed. 'I'm fond of Norman. As long as you don't lend him money, he's a good bloke to work with. He got me this job. Could have given it to any number of students but he gave it to me instead and I haven't got two GCSEs to my name. You know what it's like when you work with people. You spend all that time . . . I was worried about him before he went off. He was so upset about his grandfather. It would be good if you could talk some sense into him.'

'I have not been at all successful in that respect so far.'

She shrugged and threw the end of her cigarette on the ground. 'I wanted someone reliable to keep an eye on him.'

'How can you tell I'm reliable?' Sam asked.

'He adores his dog. He wouldn't have left him with you if he hadn't thought you were reliable.'

'*His* dog?'

'Yes, Pip.'

'The dog's his?'

'Well, his and his grandfather's, didn't he tell you?'

'No,' Sam said slowly. 'He didn't. When he asked me to look after him he spun me a tale about how he was minding him for someone else and that he couldn't now because his grandfather was in hospital.'

She wasn't quite sure how this changed things but knew that it did. The people who had tried to get the dog were trying to get at Norman then, but in order to get him to do what exactly? Maybe just to make sure he kept quiet, but again the question arose, about what? The thefts from the Pitt Rivers? The shaman's mask?

Sam tossed the keys to the cinema in her hand. Helen had squatted with her back against the wall. Sam looked down at the top of her head and wondered if she had a crush on him.

'Norman's got a certain charm, I found.'

Helen looked up and smiled. 'He has, hasn't he? And he never talks down to me. He could do, you know, he's very clever but he doesn't. I like that a lot.'

Sam nodded. She agreed there was a great deal to be said for that.

She got a take-away, went back to the office and waited for Tyler to phone. She thought of all the good intentions she had had for the month of August and how the healthy eating and jogging had all disappeared in this mess of a case. She thought of the things that Reg had said at the end of the last session about what else had been happening around the time her father had come back. Just before that she had discovered the body of Jenny Hughes, a four-year-old child who had been murdered by her father. That was the most obvious thing. Was there anything else? The light was beginning to fade but Sam sat on in the darkness of her office thinking, trying to bring to the front of her consciousness something that she could feel skittering along its edges. It was like turning on the light in a kitchen and hearing something scuttle across the floor. Sam knew there was a cockroach in there somewhere but couldn't see it yet.

The phone woke her. For a moment she couldn't recall where she was and then she saw the open window and the office and remembered. She grabbed her phone. It was Tyler.

'No luck, Sammy. We thought they'd show at a particular pub but there's been no sign of them all night and it doesn't look like they'll turn up now. We're going to try some other places. I'll phone if we catch up with them.'

'OK, thanks, Tyler.'

She closed up her phone, stood up and stretched. Out of her window, she could see the punters pouring out of the cinema. Change of plan, she thought. She waited until she saw Helen come past on her bike and then left the office and stepped out on to the Cowley Road. She let herself into the cinema and locked the door behind her. The smell of sweat and popcorn lingered in the air. For a moment she stood still, waiting for her eyes to adjust. Once she could see the rows of seats, she moved deeper into the cinema and sat down. For a flea-pit it was surprisingly comfortable. She settled herself down and stared at the empty screen. She had initially thought that she'd give it until one o'clock but the seat was comfortable and when she woke and looked at her watch it was an hour later. She heard a noise and realised that something had woken her. A large shadow and a rattle of keys indicated that Norman, or someone she assumed was Norman, had arrived. She got up and walked to the back of the cinema. Someone was moving about in the projection room.

She walked up the short flight of stairs and pushed open the door. It was a very small stuffy room with no window other than the one at the front looking out over the seating.

Norman spun round and stared at her.

'Ah, dear lady,' he said. 'We meet again.'

'Dear lady?' Sam said. 'For God's sake, Norman, what era are you living in? We're not in a Restoration comedy.'

'No.' He swept his hair off his forehead.

Sam closed the door behind her and leaned on it. 'You are now going to tell me exactly what's going on.'

'Ah.'

'You are going to try very hard, Norman, not to lie to me.'

'Oh Lord.'

'And I am going to tell you why you owe me that much. After we had the drink in Notting Hill and you did a runner I went back to Holland Park and paid the house you had come out of a visit. I was discovered and a man tried to kill me. I believe it was because he thought, wrongly, that I had seen inside a laptop in the house. He chased me and that evening the woman who I had let my flat to, the niece of my business partner and best friend, was murdered.'

This time both Norman's hands came to his head.

'I am assuming that because she looked quite similar to me – blonde, short – they were in fact trying to kill me. So I think it's time you told me what's going on, don't you? Because since you deposited Pip with me two people have been murdered and I seem to be the next on the list.'

Norman swallowed. 'I don't know what to say to you.'

'Sorry might be an acceptable but shallow start. I should also add that my stepfather, Peter, has become very attached to Pip in the short period of time he has been looking after him and I'm not sure he will be at all willing to give the dog up.'

Norman took his braces off one shoulder and then the next and sat down. 'I had no idea ... I mean I just wanted you to look after Pip. I needed to know he was somewhere safe and secure. I did not want to have to worry about him as well as everything else. I had no idea that all this mayhem would be let loose, no idea at all.'

'So what's going on?'

'I should perhaps begin at the beginning.'

Sam waited.

'I'm not good with money. I owe my grandfather everything and now I have to be able to ... we have managed while he has one leg because he is able to an extent to look after himself, but if the maggots don't do their job and his remaining leg has to be amputated we will need help ... the house will need to be redesigned ... it will take money to do that and money is what we do not have. This is my fault, the lack of money. I am ... I can't help myself ...'

Sam held up her hand. 'That, Norman, is your first identifiable lie.'

'At this time in my life I seem unable to help myself ...'

'Better,' she said.

'And so you see the background to it all is my problem with money ... or I should say the lack of it ... it is all my fault and I had to do something about it.'

'And what was that exactly?'

'Get it somehow, and a lot of it. My grandfather did not know the extent of the problem and I could not bring myself to tell him.'

'I went to see him in hospital and he seemed well aware of your problems. In fact, he assumed you owed me money.'

'Oh. Well, some time ago I had got into a situation which involved chasing my losses.'

'Presumably you didn't catch them.'

He cleared his throat. 'Let us say that in my case the rabbit evaded the dog and consequently I began to look in other directions for money.'

'Did that direction happen to be the Pitt Rivers?'

'In a manner of speaking it did, yes, indeed involve the Pitt Rivers.'

Norman's eyes had now unaccountably become unable to hold Sam's gaze.

Sam pushed herself away from the door and came and sat down next to him.

'Look,' she said. 'I'm not particularly interested in whatever has been happening at the Pitt Rivers, the thefts etcetera or, to be honest, in Gittings. The police are investigating all that and I dare say they'll find out what's going on. My concern is the murder of Stephanie and my own personal safety and the safety of Pip and whoever is looking after him. Anything you tell me that doesn't relate to that I'm not going to tell the police.'

'My position in that respect is, I would say, somewhat delicate, the one being attached to the other like a Siamese twin, the separation of one most likely leading to the death of the other.'

'What are you talking about, Norman?'

He smiled.

'I assume you know who killed Stephanie and who's trying to kill me? He was in the same house as the woman who you said was an actress you'd been at college with, or was that a pack of lies as well?'

'A very full pack, I'm afraid.'

'Who are they?'

'Contacts of Cummings's.'

'I understand Cummings also has some financial problems.'

'Has he? I couldn't possibly comment on that.'

'Go on then ... these contacts of Cummings's.'

'Yes, I would say that is the best way to describe them.'

'Norman ... you trusted me with your dog ...'

'Ah, you know it's mine.'

'I do.'

'So for God's sake tell me what's been going on. You owe me that.'

'Payment, debt. It never goes away.'

'Well at least this isn't money. You can pay me with information and your dog has been kept quite safe at no cost, which I presume was your intention from the beginning.'

'I miss Pip and when this is over I'll want him back.'

It was the most certain, most true statement he had uttered, Sam thought.

'So, Norman, these contacts of Cummings's. Who are they? And what were you doing in Holland Park?'

This she reckoned would not elicit such a direct reply.

He sighed and scratched his chest, then picked up a bar of chocolate from the table he was leaning on, peeled back the wrapper and offered it to her.

Sam shook her head. She didn't like plain chocolate. Norman broke himself off a double row and snapped four squares into his mouth.

'I was delivering certain items, shall we say.'

'For sale?'

'Indeed.'

'Was one a shrunken head?'

'It might have been.'

'Are you still in contact with the relevant parties?'

'I would say that at this present moment in time we are somewhat estranged.'

'Why? What have you done?'

The directness of the question seemed to catch him slightly off-guard. He smiled a smile rather like the one his grandfather had given Sam before having her thrown out of his room and said, 'They think that I have it in my capacity to deliver an item to them of considerable value. I have not been successful in trying to persuade them that I do not know where the item is and have been unable to confirm that anyone near to me may have it. Because I have not been able to deliver the said item they have become somewhat unreasonable and threatening in their behaviour.'

'Are they responsible for the two murders?'

'I honestly don't know about that. I know nothing about Gittings' murder and I did not know until just now of the death of your friend's niece.'

'Was the item they were interested in a shaman's mask, by any chance?'

Norman frowned and stared hard at Sam, but said nothing. He

cleared his throat and seemed about to say something and then obviously changed his mind.

'I've read the recent article in *The Times* about the sale in New York and the speculation that the mask might come up for sale at the same time. I have also read the reports in *The Oxford Times* at the time of your parents' deaths. They say that the mask went missing at the scene. The item was never found and no one was charged with its theft. It just disappeared into thin air.'

'Why were you reading those reports?'

'Because, Norman, I want to get to the root of what is happening here. People are being murdered and funnily enough I don't want to be the next one.'

He folded his arms.

'Do you know where the mask is?'

Norman shook his head. 'But they are very certain that I ought to.'

'Have you asked your grandfather?'

'I tried.'

'And?'

'He quoted an old friend of his, John Sparrow, who had been Warden of All Souls, "I'm accustomed to my deafness, To my dentures I'm resigned, I can cope with my bifocals, But – oh dear! – I miss my mind."'

Sam laughed. 'When I went and talked to him he seemed alarmingly on the ball.'

'He is. There's nothing wrong with his memory at all.'

'Would there be any point in asking him again?'

'He is a man of great strength of will and his attachment to the items collected by his grandfather is immense. He believed that the original collection should never have been split up on his grandfather's death. He never understood why the mask and other key items of the collection went to the other side of the family. He always hoped that the items would end up in the Pitt Rivers.'

'Was he given to understand that that would be the case?'

'I don't think so, but he hoped.'

'Why are they so eager to get their hands on this item specifically?'

'If you read that article you will know the answer to that particular question.'

'It's that rare?'

He nodded.

'Why don't you go to the police?'

'Your stupidest question so far, if you don't mind me saying so.'

'I don't, but perhaps it's a result of not having the whole picture.'

'The whole picture in my experience is usually a profound disappointment.'

'What do you intend to do now?'

'Keep myself and Pip out of sight and hope that the whole thing goes away.'

'I'm sorry, Norman, but that's the most ridiculous thing you've said so far. You can't keep out of sight for ever. Apart from anything, I presume your grandfather will come out of hospital at some point and then you'll have to go home with him, won't you? And presumably they know where you live?'

'They have already visited with destructive but unproductive results. And anyway there's nothing I can do. I simply don't know where the thing is.'

'I'm surprised they haven't visited your grandfather.'

'The only reason they haven't is that at the moment they don't know where he is.'

'That could easily change.'

'I'm aware of that, but they are not going to kill someone who they think holds the key to what they are looking for.'

'The dog is still at risk, then?'

'Yes. They think if they have the dog I will be forced to find the mask.'

Sam held out both her hands palm upwards and moved them up and down as if they were a pair of old-fashioned scales. 'Dog – one-million-pound mask. That's ridiculous. Norman, I know you're fond of Pip, but even if you knew where the mask was you're hardly going to give up the mask for him, are you?'

He shrugged. 'It's a way of applying pressure, a way of showing they mean business. If they kill the dog … my grandfather …'

Norman stopped and cleared his throat. 'My grandfather is very fond of Pip – he would be devastated by the loss. I have always felt that their lives are in some way inextricably interlinked. With the elderly, pets are ... a lifeline ... I wish I could take him into the hospital because I think it would do him good, help his recovery.'

'Is Pip your grandfather's then?'

'His, mine – the way we live it makes no difference but they are devoted to each other.'

'Well, you've got to take Pip back now. My stepfather has had him for long enough and my mother is coming back home and he won't be able to keep him. We need to arrange a time for him to be handed over. It's all been going on for long enough.'

'But I'm much more vulnerable with the dog. I'll have to go out and walk him. I won't be able to keep undercover so easily. Can't you hold on to him until this all blows over?'

'And how is it going to do that, Norman, exactly?'

He looked downcast. 'Please hold on to him a while longer.'

'Until when?'

'Twenty-four more hours. Give me twenty-four hours to sort all this out.'

'And how are you going to do that?'

'I'll try telling them again that I have no idea where the mask is, that they will have as much to lose as me if they go to the police regarding other matters, and that they must leave me, my grandfather and my Chihuahua alone.'

'Aren't you forgetting something? We suspect one of these people of killing my friend's niece in my flat. He cut her throat. It was a brutal senseless killing. He was trying to kill me.'

Norman stared at her.

'Letting him get away with it isn't part of the deal.'

'But what can I do about it now? I mean I'm frightfully sorry it happened ...'

'Frightfully sorry?'

'Look, I'm aware words are not sufficient at a time like this.'

'Well you can try harder than frightfully sorry. Frightfully sorry is the kind of thing you might say when you accidentally stand on someone's toe in the Tube.'

'What do you want me to do?'

'I want you to arrange a meeting. You must have some way of getting in touch with them. Tell them you have the mask to hand over.'

'But I haven't.'

'Tell them you have. Arrange to meet them. Tell me where the meeting is.'

'There are reasons why I would not like the people involved to be caught by the police.'

'Who said anything about the police?'

'I don't ...'

'I forgot to tell you that Stephanie as well as being the niece of my business partner was also part of a large West London criminal clan. They are not in the habit of allowing members of their family to be murdered and then doing nothing about it. They are not going to let this go. I could always give them your details and you could meet them face to face and explain the situation.'

Norman cleared his throat and blinked a couple of times. 'I would prefer not to be threatened.'

'I would prefer to be a foot taller, but generally speaking it doesn't get me anywhere.'

He stood up. It was a small room and suddenly there was little room for manœuvre. 'We need some air in here,' he said and walked over and opened the door. Sam followed him down the steps and into the auditorium.

Norman gestured at the empty screen. 'Hopes, dreams, fantasies. I never thought my life would turn out this way. I wanted a bigger life. I did not want to be a large man trapped in a small room, eating bars of plain chocolate.'

'What about St Cuthbert's?' Sam said. 'Wouldn't the college consider giving some money towards your grandfather's care?'

He shook his head.

'You could try asking them.'

'His pride won't allow it.'

'Does his pride allow you to plunder the Sweetman collection of the Pitt Rivers for your own personal gain?'

'He knows nothing of what Cummings and I have done. If he did he'd be horrified.'

He moved further to the front of the cinema. 'If there was one film you could see on the screen what would it be?'

'Norman, this isn't getting us anywhere.'

'Humour me.'

'Any film?'

'Yes.'

'Probably *The Third Man*.'

'Ah.' He spoke the word as a long approving sigh. 'A film with a Chihuahua. How fitting.'

'Are you going to do what I asked?' Sam said.

'Do I have much choice?'

'Look, perhaps you can do a deal with the police. Suppose hypothetically you have been involved with the thefts from the Pitt Rivers and that's what you're worried about being revealed to the police. You could go to them. Tell them everything you know, deliver up the perpetrators and do a deal.'

'And escape prison?'

'Well, there's no guarantee of that. I suppose it depends on the extent of the offences, but what are your other options? You can't run out on your grandfather.'

Norman leaned against the wall and looked down at his shoes. 'No, I can't do that. I believe this is what they mean by the proverbial rock and a hard place.'

'Do you have a contact number for them?'

He shook his head. 'They always phoned me.'

'But you knew about the place in Holland Park.'

'Those particular circumstances were unusual.'

'You must have had some way of ...'

'I was not the primary contact. Cummings was.'

'Can't you ask him?'

'We are somewhat estranged at the present time. I have no way of contacting them.'

'But surely ...' Sam's phone rang and they both jumped. She looked at the screen. It was Tyler.

'We've got them.'

'Where are you?'

He gave her the address.

'I'll be there straight away.' She turned to Norman. 'I have to go. We've tracked down the two men who tried to grab Pip. They should be able to put us in contact with who hired them.'

'Why would they choose to do that?'

'In these circumstances choice isn't going to come into it,' Sam said. 'They are in the hands of my old judo teacher and some of his ex-pupils, black belts.'

Norman winced.

'Do you have a mobile?'

He nodded.

'Give me the number.'

He reeled it off and Sam saved it in the phonebook of her own mobile.

He walked with her to the exit.

'Hopefully we'll get contact details from them and then we'll be able to set something up.'

As she was about to step out into the street, Norman's hand landed on her shoulder; it was very warm. 'Thank you for looking after Pip. Thank you for being so ...' He paused, as if searching for the right word. 'Steadfast.' The pressure of his hand increased. 'For not judging me too harshly.'

Sam was in the process of turning round to face him when his lips landed lightly on her own. Oh, he was intending to kiss me on the cheek, she thought, but I was moving so he missed. It was just a mistake, but when she looked at his face she realised it hadn't been and suddenly she couldn't breathe properly. She stepped away from him and stumbled down the kerb.

'Don't disappear, Norman,' she said. 'I'll be in touch as soon as I have the contact details,' and then, thinking what an idiot she sounded, she set off for her van.

CHAPTER TWENTY-TWO

The address Tyler had given her was in the same part of the Blackbird Leys estate as he lived in but this house was boarded up at the front. Sam turned off the engine, got out of the van and, as instructed, walked through a wooden gate swinging open at the side of the house. Zac, one of Tyler's sons, was smoking in the derelict garden.

'Sammy,' he said and hugged her. It was only the Tylers who called her that. They always had, ever since she first turned up at their dad's dojo as an angry seven-year-old, demanding to be called Sam.

'Thanks a lot for this, Zac.'

'Dad said he was getting a favour from you in return.'

'Do you know what it is? He hasn't told me.'

'When this is over.'

He sucked the last bit of life out of his cigarette and ground it under his heel and Sam followed him into the house. The kitchen had been stripped bare – all the doors had been taken off the cupboards and there were gaps with trailing electrics where an oven and washing-machine had been. Zac looked over his shoulder. 'You know what comes next is a bit of play-acting?'

'Sort of,' Sam said.

'A little bit of pain but the threat of a whole lot more. It's usually quicker that way.'

Sam nodded. She knew how it worked.

'Here we are.'

They entered the front room. There was nothing in here but bare boards and a naked light bulb, which illuminated two men strapped into chairs. Duct tape covered their mouths. They were gagged and bug-eyed with terror; both were bruised and bleeding. Tyler, Jake, his other son and a couple of other men turned round as Sam came into the room.

'Two turkeys as requested.'

'Christmas came early,' Sam said.

'You want us to rough 'em up a bit first or do you want to try them with a few questions?' Tyler asked.

'Looks like you already have.'

'Question time, then.'

He leaned forwards and ripped a piece of duct tape off one of the men's faces. He gasped like a fish tossed up on the bank of a river.

'So now this is what's going to happen,' Tyler said. 'Sammy here is going to ask you a few questions and you're going to answer them. If you do that satisfactorily we will let you and your mate go. If you don't, I am going to introduce you to the reality of dis-lo-cation – a finger, a wrist, an elbow, a shoulder. Who knows, but I can guarantee you that I will cause you so much pain that in the end you will end up answering the questions anyway.'

The man stared at Tyler and then at Sam.

'Who hired you to grab the dog?'

'A man came into the pub and put the word around he was look-ing for a couple of blokes to do a job.' The words were tumbling out of him. 'A mate of ours was there and suggested us. He phoned and gave us the address in Park Town and told us what night to go there. We parked up and when you came by, tried to grab the dog.'

'Did you meet him?'

He shook his head. 'We would have arranged to meet if we'd had the dog and then he would have handed over the money.'

'Are you still trying to find the dog?'

'We haven't been able to find any trace of it. The house in Park Town's closed up. The trail went cold.'

'But he still wants the dog?'

The man shrugged.

'Do you have a way of contacting him?'

The man didn't say anything.

Tyler pushed himself away from the wall.

'Yes, yes, the number's in my phone.'

'And where's that?'

Tyler tossed a phone to Sam. 'Frisked him earlier.'

She brought up the phonebook and showing the screen to him scrolled through the numbers.

'That one,' the man said, when she reached 'dog'.

She made a note of the number and handed the phone back to Tyler. There were a few ways she could go with this now and she needed to get clear in her own mind what way would be the best.

'Give me a few minutes,' she said to Tyler, and walked back out into the garden.

What was she going to do? One option was to get the men in the room behind her to phone and say that they had managed to get the dog and arrange a meet-up. She could get the dog from Peter and tell the police. Hopefully they would turn up to get the dog or send someone to take it to them.

The other option was to get Norman to phone them and say that he knew where the shaman's mask was and was prepared to deliver it to them, inform the police and hope they showed up. It was clear in her mind that the person who killed Stephanie had to be found and if that involved Norman being done for theft, so be it. A soft kiss on the lips by a sockless charmer wasn't going to keep him out of prison. Even a tender, soft, kiss ... She shook her head as if trying to clear it of buzzing. Norman was a heavyweight gambler who had lied and lied and lied to her – and in the process put her life at risk. Two people had been murdered. What was she thinking of? Another option was not to tell the police at all but to tell Alan and Johnny et al. Set up the meeting and then see what transpired and only afterwards, when the blood had been wiped from the walls, tell the police.

She sat down on a bit of broken wall that edged the patio, patted her pockets for the packet of cigarettes, lit one and stared at a pile of bricks covered with brambles. The two options seemed to her relatively evenly balanced. There was, however, one thing she had to be certain of, that the man who had attacked her was definitely the one who had killed Stephanie because if he wasn't and she handed him over to the Knowles brothers ...

No, she needed to be certain before she did that. She needed more information. She could always give the number to Norman and get him to phone and set up a meeting on the basis that he had the mask and was willing to hand it over.

She went back into the house and back into the room.

'You got any more use for them, Sammy?'

She shook her head. 'You can let them go.'

'We've got some final discussions to have with them,' Tyler said, 'involving their future habitation. Best if you left.'

'What about the favour?'

'We can talk about that later.'

Sam glanced at the two men, hugged Tyler, and did as she was told.

It was only as she was driving back into Oxford along the Cowley Road that something occurred to her. How had they known that she and Peter would be at the party in north Oxford? How had they known what time they would have been leaving? Who had told them? The most likely candidate was Cummings. Maybe Cummings was not convinced that Norman was telling the truth and was eager to produce the shaman's mask for his contacts. Maybe Cummings thought that if the dog was kidnapped then Norman would move hell and high water to find it. Had Cummings murdered Gittings? She remembered how he had behaved when confronted with the theft of the shrunken head. He had tried to blame Gittings. He had had a feverish, hysterical edge to him, like a person beginning to spiral out of control. But from theft to murder was a big step. Would he really have done that? He had struck her as man for whom reputation was everything. If that was the case then presumably he would do anything to protect it. Maybe working among the strange objects of the Pitt Rivers had addled his brain. A couple of nights had been quite enough for Sam.

As she reached the junction of Parks Road and the Banbury Road, a stream of fairground trailers rolled past her, heading for St Giles. The fair had arrived. On a whim she parked and walked back into town. She'd never seen the fair go up. She leaned against a lamppost in the middle of St Giles and watched the rides take shape around her. She smoked and indulged herself with the fantasy of getting a job at the fair and disappearing out of her life altogether.

'Got a light?'

He was tall and thin with a black fringe, wearing black jeans and a black T-shirt which had Alice Cooper biting the head off a bat. Sam offered him her cigarette and he lit his from the burning tip, nodded his thanks and loped away.

Part of the running away was the fact that she missed the confidence that came with knowing that you were good at something. She'd known she was good at judo, but the PI stuff she'd fallen into by accident. When she'd been offered the business she'd only been working there two years, not long enough to really know what she was doing. If it hadn't been for Alan she'd probably have let the business go when she ran into trouble with the Inland Revenue. She'd been treading water for too long simply because she didn't know what else to do.

She squatted down with her back to the lamppost and waited until they'd finished putting the waltzer through its paces, until it was flashing and spinning in all its glory, and then she set off back to the van.

The following morning she woke early from a highly explicit dream involving Norman and a large amount of candyfloss. It was, to put it mildly, a disturbing way to start the day. She came down into the kitchen to make a cup of tea. No one was up yet and the house was quiet. She took her tea out into the garden and walked amongst the roses and thought of Norman's light kiss on her lips. Perhaps she was imagining things but their lips had felt, *made for each other*. Shit, where the hell had that romantic codswallop come from? She didn't believe in all that stuff and she was absolutely certain that she wasn't attracted to fat people. It was the whole athlete thing. She was used to a certain firmness in her men. Phil had been, Rick was. Norman had done nothing but lie to her, and when he wasn't doing that he had left her annoying Latin quotations and he wore no socks and he owned a Chihuahua, which everyone knew was the most embarrassing dog in the world to own. She could not be attracted to him. In addition, he was a charmer who was used to getting his own way and he had a bad gambling problem and an ill grandfather who had

247

maggots crawling all over his ankle and, if all that wasn't bad enough, Mrs Eliot had suggested that he had been involved in some way in his parents' death. That was something she hadn't asked him in the cinema. What do you remember about the accident? She knew from the reports in the paper he had been there. But then she recalled the heat and weight of his hand on her shoulder, and wondered about his heat and weight in more intimate circumstances, and then she realised she had forgotten to breathe and despaired of herself altogether. She refused to think that she could be attracted to a man who didn't wear socks. He was eccentric at best, louche at worst. She could not be attracted to a fat projectionist called Norman, who had psychotic writing and owned a Chihuahua, could she?

She stared at the dregs of tea left in her cup and threw them at the base of a white rose. She wondered what Reg would have to say about her sudden attraction to Norman at the exact same time that Rick was due back in town. He'd have *something* to say that was for sure.

Luke came out into the garden and joined her. He was wearing striped pyjama bottoms and a white vest.

'You haven't forgotten about St Giles have you?'

'No, I saw them all coming into town last night when I was driving back here.'

'Good. We're meeting at eight o'clock at the Martyrs' Memorial.'

'Fine. I'll be there.'

Sam had sat down at a circular wooden table and was squinting into the sun. 'Do you think that Norman could be capable of murder?'

Luke frowned. 'What kind of a question is that to throw at a man before his first cup of tea has hit his stomach?'

'Well, do you? There's that whole cliché of the gentle giant, isn't there? Do you think that applies to him? What was he like at school?'

'I don't remember him ever being violent, but people change, don't they? It doesn't mean he couldn't be as an adult. I think we could all be if we were put in a corner. Anyway you know all about that better than me.'

'What do you mean?'

'Well, you spent years of your life smashing people into a judo mat.'

'That wasn't violence it was sport.'

Luke laughed. 'Well, a violent sport then.' He put down his mug. 'I'm going for a swim.'

The sun was beginning to break through the poplars at the bottom of the garden.

Rick was due back in Oxford today and here she was having erotic dreams about Norman. She wished he hadn't kissed her like that. If he'd lunged at her and slobbered over her she could have laughed it off and gone on as usual, but the kiss had been tentative at most, his mouth had felt ... Oh, fuck here she was again. Until he had done that she had felt relatively in control, but now she couldn't get him out of her mind. It was a complicating factor. Was she going to be quite so cavalier about him ending up in police custody now? She doubted it. Why the hell had he gone and kissed her? Was he attracted to her or was he simply trying to charm her?

Mrs Eliot joined Sam wearing a red silk dressing-gown and dark glasses.

'Do you think Norman is heterosexual?' Sam asked.

Mrs Eliot laughed. 'I'm not sure those sorts of labels are at all helpful when it comes to Norman.'

'What do you mean?'

'Well, like most charming people he shifts his shape according to the company he keeps. He's a charmer; charmers like to suggest that they are in love with whoever is in front of them, man or woman. It doesn't matter to them. They are expert at making you feel as if you are at the centre of their universe. The important thing is that they know they are loved and they have power over you. It is all in the suggestion. It's all about getting you to fall in love with them. It doesn't really matter who you are.'

Sam groaned. 'So it's all a game, then?'

'It's not to say they don't genuinely feel it at the time. Put it this way. They are promiscuous with their emotional feelers.'

'Any advice?'

'Whatever you do, don't fall in love with him, but if you do, confront him, look into his eyes and then you will see the truth.'

'You've done this before,' Sam said.

'A very long time ago and I wish I'd taken my own advice much faster than I did. It would have saved me a great deal of heartache.'

Sam's mobile rang and she grabbed it off the table. It was Phil. He had the file on the crash and suggested she come down to the station to take a look at it. She arranged a time and ended the call.

'Have you found out anything more about the accident?' Mrs Eliot asked.

'Bits and pieces. I know he was in the car when it happened.'

'You're going to be careful, aren't you, Sam?' Her tone was quite light but her look was serious. 'Norman always worried me, you know.'

'Why?'

'Well, the main reason I suppose was because he didn't seem to know the difference between right and wrong. He seemed to be entirely lacking in any sort of scruples.'

'And what did you think of me when I was a child?'

'Do you want a circumspect answer or a more direct one?'

Sam stood up abruptly and picked up her phone. 'Actually, just forget I ever asked. I don't think I want any answer at all.'

A couple of hours later she sat in a stuffy room in the St Aldate's police station leafing through the crash file. There was an interview with Professor Sweetman and a picture of the shaman's mask. It was the first time Sam had seen it. It was made of wood and painted black. The eyes were narrow almond-shaped slits. The ears were blood-red as was the sash that had been painted across the top of the forehead and the lips. Individual teeth had been carved into the mouth. It looked remote and forbidding. There was also a picture of the car at the scene of the accident. Sam looked at that one for a long time. What had happened to the people in the front seats did not bear thinking about. How on earth had Norman survived? The only other interviews were with the various members of the emergency services who had been at the scene of the accident.

She sighed and closed the file. Suppose the mask hadn't been there. It was only Professor Sweetman who said that it had been in the car. A curator of the exhibition had confirmed that the mask had been removed from there but that wasn't to say that the items had then been transferred to the car. Suppose Professor Sweetman had lied. Suppose the mask had been deposited somewhere else and when the accident happened he had seen an opportunity to hold on to it by claiming it had been stolen. The other option was that a member of the emergency services had stolen it, but Sam thought that was highly unlikely.

Phil came into the room, closed the door and leaned against it.

'There's not much here, is there?' Sam said.

'No.'

'Was there an insurance pay-out?'

He nodded. 'A big one to the American side of the Sweetman family. I've just been told that the prints they lifted from your van match ones found in your flat. We've got a name. Inch McGregor.'

'Inch?'

'Give him an ...'

'Oh, see.'

Phil threw a photo down on the desk. 'Is that him?'

Sam nodded. 'Has he got a police record?'

'Of a sort. Ex-copper.'

'What?'

'Retired.'

Sam thought back to what Alan had said about the background of someone who could have traced her address so quickly if all he had was her van registration number.

'What information do you have about him?'

'Nothing I'm going to tell you, Sam, other than the fact he's a nasty piece of work and you should stay away from him.'

'Phil! He's tried to kill me twice. Three times, if I include what happened to Stephanie. You've got to tell me more than that.'

Phil scratched the stubble on his head. 'Last job he had was in the art and antiquities squad.'

'What's his involvement in all this?'

Someone knocked on the door and Phil poked his head out into the corridor. When he turned round he said, 'I've got to go. Read the file and you'll find out.'

Sam's protests were lost in the noise of the door closing.

She turned back to the file. Looking more carefully now at the names, she quickly came across a police constable McGregor, who had been interviewed because he was the first on the scene. He'd not been on duty but had been passing and called it in. So, he'd been there, but what had happened next? Obviously, he hadn't been the person to take the mask because, if he had, what was he doing all these years later putting pressure on Norman to come up with it? But if he thought Norman had it, or knew where it was, surely that must have been because he suspected Professor Sweetman of having it.

Sam thought of the person who had leaned down towards her when she was covered in the dinosaur bones. It hadn't been McGregor and it hadn't been Norman, the person was taller and altogether more angular. But if it had been Cummings why had he hired Sam in the first place? Surely he ran the risk of her getting in the way. Unless he was trying to make himself appear above board, unless he was trying to divert attention away from himself completely. And who had ransacked his office? Maybe he'd done that himself, to cover his tracks.

She closed up the file and walked out of the police station and up St Aldate's, towards Carfax. Last night she had had concerns about being sure that McGregor was definitely the one who had killed Stephanie. Now from what Phil had said, it was highly likely that he was, so was she going to arrange a meeting that included the Knowles brothers or was she going to set up one that involved the police? She was now walking along the High Street past St Mary's. She passed under the fan-vaulting of the baroque porch and entered the church. A group of tourists was being told about the trials of Cranmer, Latimer and Ridley. Sam had experienced her own trials here, as a small child, sitting through sermons that bored her rigid. She sat down and tried to clear her mind. It didn't take long. She realised that guilt about what had happened had skewed her judgement. She had thought that she had to deliver up justice for Stephanie of a sort that her uncles would recognise but now she thought, it's not my fault and that's not my way. At the back of her mind was also the thought that if McGregor was put in prison the Knowles brothers would find some way to reach him. There were always ways of doing that. She took a deep breath and let it out slowly, then got up and left the church. If the plan was to come off she'd need Norman to set it up and that entailed him being willing to tell the police exactly what he'd been involved with. She phoned him and left a message but as she did it she thought, he's not going to reply, I know he's not.

That afternoon Sam picked up Peter and Pip from St Cuthbert's and went back to Park Town with them. Peter still hadn't told Jean what had been going on, hoping that he'd be able to be back in the house before she returned. But he was going to have to tell her soon because Sam had made it clear that, as things stood, it was too dangerous for them to stay there.

They worked steadily through the house, ending up by early evening in the kitchen. Peter was rubbing invisible smears off the front of the stainless steel fridge and Sam was cleaning the top of the gas-hob.

'Have you told Mum about Pip?' Sam asked.

He smiled and shook his head. 'A surprise for her. And anyway it'll be over soon, won't it, and the dog can go back to its rightful owner.'

'Perhaps you should get one for yourself.'

'I'm not sure your mother would like that, Sam.'

'But if you explained ...'

Peter's eyes were level with the front of the fridge, seeking out more smears.

'We'll see.'

Sam finished with the hob and threw the cloth she'd been using in the bin.

Peter stood back from the fridge. 'What do you think?'

'The cleanest I've ever seen it.'

The beep of a mobile got them both searching for their phones.

Peter frowned at his. 'I think someone's left a message.'

'Give it here,' Sam said.

She accessed the voicemail and handed it back to him to listen to the message.

'I'm going to have to stay here tonight.'

'You can't.'

'That was your mother. She's changed her plans and is coming back tonight.'

'Phone her and tell her to go to St Cuthbert's.'

'She's already set off and she won't turn her phone on again until she gets back here.'

'Try anyway.'

He did but got no reply.

Sam sighed. The two men she'd seen in Blackbird Leys were unlikely to be a threat after further conversations with the Tylers, but that wouldn't stop Cruella de Vil and McGregor from hiring another couple of thugs to try it again.

'Don't open the door to anyone other than Mum.'

'I won't.' Peter looked at his watch. 'You need to be going, don't you? Aren't you meeting people at the fair?'

Sam looked at her watch. 'I think I should cancel it.'

'Isn't Rick going to be there?'

Sam nodded. She'd phoned him and arranged to meet at the Martyr's Memorial.

'Look, if you're that worried you can phone me and make sure I'm all right.'

Sam was torn. She really wanted to see Rick and she'd been looking forward to going to the fair with Luke ever since he suggested it. 'I'll phone Phil and see if he can send anyone round. I'm also going to check that you're securely locked in.'

When she had finished checking the house, Peter followed her into the hall. 'I know I'm wasting my breath, but don't go on anything too dangerous.'

She laughed, kissed him on the cheek and let herself out into Park Town. It was unseasonably warm. The beginning of September had not ushered in cooler weather. The monkey-puzzle hung in the still evening air, a black and spiky edged silhouette against the pale green evening sky. She leaned against the railings and put in a call to Phil to tell him Peter was in the house and asking if there was any chance the police could keep an eye on him. Phil said he'd see what he could do but with the fair in town and gangs of boys coming in from the outlying estates, there would be plenty to keep the police occupied tonight. Peter would have to take his chances. Feeling far from reassured, Sam set off for the fair.

CHAPTER TWENTY-THREE

As Sam walked into town, worry gave way to excitement. The excitement involved seeing Rick, fast rides, loud music and flashing lights. For the moment everything else drifted into the background. She was sixteen again with the fury and glory of raging teenage hormones, and she had a hot date and anything might happen.

As a child, St Giles' Fair had denoted the end of the summer holidays and the start of a new school term and seeing your friends again. One of the things she'd always loved about it was that it was a town event. The university term hadn't started yet, this was about the town claiming Oxford for its own. For two days it was as if a drunken stripper got up on High Table, ripped off her fur-trimmed, sequinned thong and threw it in the face of the most repressed don. The garish camp of the fair contrasted nicely with the grandness and formality of the surrounding colleges.

She'd reached the edge of the fair now and stopped for a moment, taking in the flashing lights, the blaring music and the smell of frying onions. Each year the rides got bigger and faster, flashier and more dangerous; a Dante's *Inferno* of noise and violent movement. She took a deep breath and began to push through the crowd. They'd arranged to meet at the Martyrs' Memorial and that was at the other end.

She had walked the other way earlier in the day when the crowds had been made up of mums and toddlers, grans making sedate progress on the old-fashioned roundabouts and tourists taking photos of the more alarming rides. During the day the rides were much cheaper and longer, but now queues stretched away from Wild Mouse and Big Ben. It was at night that the fair really came into its own. At night you didn't notice the starburst cracks in the glass of the booth you paid at for a ride in the dodgems; at night all you saw were the four rows of red lights flashing on the top, you didn't notice the thickness of the make-up and the bloodshot eyes, just the sequins and feathers.

As usual she was early. The memorial, a popular meeting place, had people sitting on every step so she propped herself against the side of a nearby hot-dog stand and people-watched. It wasn't long before the smell of grease and frying onions became too much for her to withstand. She bought herself a hot dog and bit into it, the mustard and ketchup squirting out of the end on to the ground. God, it tasted good. She'd just wiped her mouth and was checking herself for splats when Rick appeared in front of her.

'Hi,' he said.

So, here he was, warm brown eyes, black T-shirt and baggy black shorts with pockets in the thigh. Sam felt a lurch in her stomach and with it came the hope that he hadn't got back together with his wife.

'Jesus, woman, I've missed you.' He moved to kiss her, but she took a step backwards and stumbled against a generator. He grabbed hold of her arm.

'Sorry,' she said. She pointed at her mouth. 'Onions, ketchup, mustard ...'

'For Heaven's sake I haven't seen you for a month. Do you think I care?' His mouth locked on to hers. She threw her arms round him and kissed him right back.

Sometime later she heard a cough, then a laugh, then she felt a hand on her shoulder; reluctantly she pulled away from Rick to see Luke and a large group of people standing next to them.

'Oh,' she said. 'Sorry, we were getting reacquainted.'

After the introductions had been made, they moved through the fair as a loose group. There was Luke and two couples and their children, young enough to be excited to be out at night with their parents, not so old that they wanted to be there by themselves. They stopped in front of stalls hung about with stuffed toys. Sam won a huge stuffed lion as a reward for getting darts in the right cards. They ate candy floss and burgers and all got into the dodgems and whacked seven bells out of each other, the electricity sparking above their heads. Then they got into the waltzers, Sam and Rick squashed tightly together, while the stern-faced waltzer boys spun the cars so hard the air was forced out of their lungs and any screams were lost in the roar of the fair. Afterwards they watched the same boys balancing on the moving belt with the elegance of bullfighters, all loose-limbed sexy arrogance, and Sam told Rick that the first time she had sex had been with one of these boys and Rick had kissed her so hard her breath was taken away a second time.

As they made their way through the fair some of the group became progressively more daring in the rides they were taking, but Sam had decided that the waltzer was as exciting as it was going to get for her. Rick wanted to try the Wild Mouse but Sam said it looked more like the Very Sick Mouse to her and in the end they compromised on the big wheel.

They got into their seats and brought the metal bar down over their laps, then the wheel moved to take on the next couple. Rick leaned over and kissed her again and she felt as if the air around her had gone hot. She returned the kiss and then feeling the wheel picking up speed, pushed him away. But it wasn't just the wheel that was on the move – it was also Rick's hands. She gasped as they reached the highest point and began to descend and then pushed him away.

'Don't,' she said.

'I've missed you so much. I thought I'd go fucking mad with it. I can't wait to …' He leaned forward and whispered in her ear.

An hour ago she'd been convinced that he'd got back together with his wife and that now he'd be tactfully engineering an amicable split. She'd prepared herself for that. From the top of the big wheel the fair was spread out beneath them. The huge arm of what looked like a giant metallic octopus whirled through the air. It was all madness, she thought, my love life is a catastrophe. It makes as much sense as the cacophony of this fair. Their seat was approaching ground level now and was beginning the trip back up and round.

'Are you all right, Sam? You seem a bit distant.'

She took his hand. 'I didn't think you'd be interested in me any more. So, this is a bit of a shock.'

He frowned. 'Why on earth not?'

'We made no agreements. I thought ... well, to be honest, I thought you'd be back together with Isabel and that you'd dump me as soon as you came back.'

'Are you saying you want us to split up?'

'No, no I'm not saying that. It's just that I suppose I thought we would.'

'Am I going too fast for you, is that it?'

'No, it's fine. I mean, it's nice, really nice ...'

'It's just I'm so pleased to see you, Sam. God, I missed you.'

Sam wrapped her arms round him. Trauma attracts trauma, that's what Reg had said when she'd first told him about Rick. The wheel was going at its maximum speed as Rick and Sam, now locked in each other's arms, or as much as you can be when you have a heavy metal bar across your hips, went over the top again.

When they brought the wheel to a standstill, to let the punters off and the queue on, Rick and Sam were at the very top of the wheel. From here there was a good view down into the quads of St John's College on the east side of St Giles and a great view of the fair as a whole.

Rick was holding her hand. 'Since you mentioned Isabel, there's something I need to tell you.'

Sam slid her hand out of his. 'You did, didn't you?'

'Well, yes, I did.'

'Shit, I knew it.'

'We had no arrangement ...'

'Proof is in the fucking pudding.'

'Come on, Sam, you never indicated you wanted anything committed. Quite the reverse.'

She folded her arms and looked down at the crowds. She felt furious with him but he was right, she hadn't suggested anything. There'd been no agreement.

'Sam?' He put his hand on her arm.

'Look,' she said, 'you're right, but I'm still pissed off with you.'

She looked at him and in a voice dripping with sarcasm said, 'It's a visa thing, you said.'

'Well, it was. I haven't slept with her for years.'

'That doesn't make me feel any better about it,' she shouted.

Down below in the crowd something caught her eye, two men, one very large and the other tall and thin. Standing next to each other they looked like the number ten. The larger one was holding a stick of candy floss but as they got closer to the ground, Sam could see that some kind of argument was taking place because the candy floss was being waved about in what appeared to be a more and more agitated manner. She saw Norman begin to walk away and Cummings grab his arm, but as Norman turned round the candy floss hit Cummings more or less in the face. Norman dropped it and began walking swiftly away from him.

Sam's attention was well and truly wrenched away from Rick and she was now desperate not to lose sight of the pair of them, but it seemed to take an interminable length of time until the wheel returned them to ground level. Once they were on firm ground, she bolted into the crowd in the direction of where she had last seen them, leaving a bemused Rick staring after her.

Peter had spent the evening putting the last touches to the tidying up. When he had changed the sheets, buffed the chrome and wiped away every possible piece of dust, dirt, smear or crumb, he sat in the kitchen with Pip and a glass of Pinot Noir and pondered the likelihood of what Jean would have to say about the Chihuahua. He had noticed in recent days that the dog had started growling at people as if protecting him. He found it rather affecting, but he didn't think Jean would be much taken with the dog if he did it to her. He didn't think that Jean would like the idea of a dog one little bit. Anyway, what was he thinking of? The dog didn't belong to him and when all this was over he'd have to give it back. He sighed and reached for his glass. He had missed Jean but her imminent arrival now made him focus on the various aspects of her absence he had enjoyed. Leaving washing-up overnight, wearing his pyjamas later into the morning than would be the norm, and having complete and absolute control over the remote control. Jean was big on structure and without her the shape of his days had become more malleable, less predictable, and he'd liked that. He sighed. He was only thinking this way because she was on her way home; in the early days of her absence he had been floundering around not knowing what to do with himself. He got up and put on a CD of Bach's Brandenberg Concerto – one of his favourites. He closed his eyes. Soon term would be starting again, there would be an influx of a whole new year of undergraduates. The city would be filled with the buzz and optimism of a new term, of a new academic year and the dog days of August would be well and truly buried. The cycle of renewal would begin all over again. He looked down at Pip snuffling in his sleep and thought of the dog he'd had as a boy, Isotta, chasing after the laces of his plimsolls in the Neapolitan dust. Peter wondered how Sam was doing at the fair and hoped she was taking his advice to keep clear of the more death-defying rides.

Sam was finding out that looking for two men in a busy crowd when you are five foot one was a tricky business. Jumping up and down as if she was on a pogo stick was embarrassing and ineffective, and in the end she resorted to climbing partially up a metal lamppost, holding hanging baskets, in order to see if she could spot where Norman and Cummings had gone. The fair flashed and glittered and roared around her like some jewel-encrusted chameleon, but the two men had vanished. She got down from the lamppost and made her way back to the bottom of the big wheel where Rick was waiting for her.

'Sorry. It's a case I'm working on,' she said. 'I saw a man I need to talk to, but I can't find him now.'

The feeling between them had dissipated. It was as if they were strangers now, not the same people who had been locked in a tight embrace as the big wheel spun them round. They stood looking at each other awkwardly.

'Sorry,' she said again.

'Do you need to be working?' Rick said. 'We can meet later if you like or back at your place.'

She shrugged. 'Just let me make a phone call. If nothing comes of that then I'm all yours.'

She ducked between the dodgems and a burger van and walked under scaffolding wrapped in red-and-white tape, which filled the passageway that ran down the side of the Lamb and Flag. She leaned against the trunk of an enormous horse-chestnut whose vast canopy extended above her into the warm night air. It was much quieter here and at least there was a chance that she might be able to hear and be heard. She phoned Norman and, with one hand clamped to her other ear, waited. The phone rang and rang. If he was still in the fair he might well not hear the call coming in, if, that was, he had the phone on at all. It rang and then as she expected the phone switched to voicemail.

'Norman. Return my call will you. It's Sam.' Then she phoned Peter who told her he was fine and to get on and enjoy herself.

She closed up her phone and stood staring at the side of the pub. Where the hell was all this going? And what had Norman and Cummings been arguing about?

Peter was rinsing his glass out in the sink when the doorbell rang. He looked at the clock on the kitchen wall – eleven o'clock. It was probably Jean, but all the same it was best to be careful. He walked into the hall and said loudly, 'Who is it?'

'Peter.' He heard Jean's voice, tired and exasperated. 'Open the door, will you? I've mislaid my keys.'

He picked up Pip, who was snuffling at the bottom of the front door, and, hoping that the dog was going to behave himself, did exactly that.

Sam was still in the passage at the side of the Lamb and Flag, trying to get her thoughts together. Perhaps Norman had been telling Cummings that he was going to go to the police, perhaps that was why Cummings had been arguing with him so vociferously. If Norman had decided to tell the police what had been going on in the Pitt Rivers and he was involved, then Cummings was going to be looking at jail time and probably quite a lot of it, especially if he was implicated in Gittings's death. Sam couldn't imagine that Norman was involved in the murder. Surely he was too chaotic, too much of a mess to be a murderer. If Norman went to the police and told them about the thefts there would be a lot less at stake for him than Cummings. It flashed through her mind that if Cummings had killed once to stop Gittings from finding out what he was doing, then he might well do it again. Norman could be playing with fire.

She phoned him again. This time she said, 'Norman, I think you could be in danger. Please phone me.'

Then she pushed herself away from the wall and walked back along the passage to join Rick.

Peter opened the front door.

'God,' Jean said, looking at Pip. 'What's that?'

'He's called Pip and it's a long story,' Peter said, leaning forwards and kissing her. 'I'll get the rest of the stuff from the car.'

'Thanks, I'll just put this inside.'

'Good journey?'

'Not terribly.'

Peter put Pip down and walked over to where Jean's car was parked. He opened the boot and took hold of two pieces of hand-luggage and lifted them out, then he slammed the boot shut. Pip was sniffing at the back tyres of the car. I must remember to tell her I've missed her, Peter thought.

'Come on,' he said to Pip, and picked up the bags and began to walk back towards the house.

When Sam rejoined Rick he was talking to Luke and his friends. She took Luke to one side.

'Have you seen Norman tonight?'

He looked surprised. 'Yes, I just passed him. He was heading that way.' He pointed behind them towards the centre of town.

'Shit,' she said, and began to run or rather duck and dive through the crowd in the direction he'd indicated.

She glanced at her watch. He was probably going back to the cinema. It took her a frustratingly long time to clear the crowds but once free of them she made better progress. She jogged along the Broad and past the heads outside the Sheldonian. This part of Oxford was quiet, a world away from the hustle and bustle of the fair. It was as she reached the point where Longwall Street hits the bottom of the High that she saw him, a little bit ahead of her, about to cross Magdalen Bridge.

'Norman,' she shouted, and he stopped and turned round.

Jean unpacked the contents of the cool bag into the fridge and poured herself a glass of wine. A pile of post addressed to her lay on the kitchen table. She sat down and began to open it. She was almost three-quarters of the way through when it occurred to her that Peter seemed to be taking rather a long time to get the bags out of the car. She stood up, massaging the back of her neck, and went to look for him.

'Don't you ever answer your phone?' Sam asked.

'Not always, no.'

'What were you arguing with Cummings about?'

He frowned and didn't reply for a moment. 'I was a bit cack-handed with some candy floss.'

'You were arguing before that.'

'Are you stalking me?'

'I was on the big wheel and saw you walking past.'

Norman leaned on the parapet of the bridge and looked down into the river below. 'Do you know that in 1938 19,200 bicycles crossed Magdalen Bridge in an average day, making it the busiest place for bicycles in the world?'

'Norman,' Sam snapped. 'Get a grip.'

'It's not my forte I'm afraid, not my forte at all.'

'Have you decided what you're going to do?'

'Not altogether.'

He took a couple of steps towards her and rested his hand on her shoulder. Oh Lord, Sam thought, not this again.

'I greatly appreciate all you have done for me. As I said, you really have been most reliable.'

'Have you considered that you may be in danger?'

He frowned again. 'Pip, I think, more than myself. They want something from me and if they hurt me they are unlikely to get it.'

'I mean in danger from Cummings,' Sam said.

He shook his head. 'I don't think so.'

'I think he killed Gittings because he was on to what was happening at the Pitt Rivers. I think he tried to kill me by pushing a dinosaur on top of me.'

'A novel method you'd have to grant, but fortunately unsuccessful.'

'If you were telling him that you were going to the police and that was going to implicate him ...'

'No, no ... you've got it all wrong, that was not the conversation we were having.'

'Then what was it?'

'I was trying to elicit from him if he knew the whereabouts of the shaman's mask.'

'Why would he?'

He shrugged. 'It was a long shot. He worked with my grandfather for many years. He was working with him when the accident happened. I just thought he might have had some idea.'

'Why were you arguing then?'

'It was a frivolous matter.'

His hand was still on her shoulder and he was looking down at her intensely. Fuck it, Sam thought, there is absolutely no doubt that I am attracted to him. No doubt whatsoever. Why was life like that? Months and years went by when you were attracted to absolutely no one and then all of a sudden you had 19,200 of them crossing your bridge at the same time. Well, two at least.

Norman leaned down and kissed her. As his mouth drew away from hers some minutes later, he whispered, 'Are you as in control of yourself as you appear?'

Jean opened the front door and looked across the street at her car. Peter was nowhere to be seen and nor was that horrible little dog he'd been holding. It was late and she didn't want to disturb the neighbours by shouting his name, so it was only when she had walked over to where the car was parked that she saw him, crumpled over the cases in a pool of blood. She assessed his main injury, a nasty blow to the head, made him as comfortable as she could and then called for an ambulance.

*

265

Sam pushed Norman away from her and gasped for air. This was too confusing. She'd just been locked in Rick's arms in the big wheel.

'What are you up to?' she said.

He closed the gap with a step and kissed her on the side of the neck just below her ear. 'I'd have thought,' he said softly, 'that was obvious.'

Sam's stomach lurched.

On the Magdalen College side of the bridge there was a stone ramp that sloped down to the river's edge. It was here that tourists and students could queue for the punts which were tied up under the bridge in rows.

'It's too bright up here.' Norman took hold of Sam's hand and began to lead her off the bridge and down that ramp. Down in the darkness, with the river lapping gently against the base of the bridge, Sam and Norman fell upon each other. Hands tore at clothes, found flesh, touched flesh and the buttons of Norman's shirt ricocheted off the wet stones under their feet and plopped softly into the river …

'Oh,' Sam gasped.

'Is that OK?'

'Oh God, yes,' Sam replied.

This man was sexy, sexier than she'd ever, ever have imagined.

'If you just,' she said. 'Oh, yes…. that's it …'

Made for each other. The words she had thought when he first kissed her came into her mind. Who would have thought that this man could be so surprisingly tender?

At first she didn't register her phone ringing. It seemed to be coming from such a long way away. It couldn't have anything to do with them, could it? It couldn't be in the pocket of her shorts, which were at that moment somewhere round her ankles and in another world altogether. Then she realised it was.

'Norman, I'm sorry but I must …'

'Of course.' Their bodies came apart with a soft squelch of reluctance.

They both laughed.

Sam grabbed her phone and answered it.

'Sam, it's your mother.'

'Is everything all right?'

'Peter's been attacked. He's in the hospital. Can you come? He keeps going on about the dog he had and he won't settle down. He needs to rest but he's very anxious to talk to you. They want him to sleep but he says he won't until he's talked to you.'

'Where are you?'

'The Radcliffe Infirmary.'

'Where's the dog?'

'I've no idea.'

'Can I speak to him?'

'He's not very coherent. I think it best you come.'

Sam closed up the phone and reached for her shorts. Norman was staring at her. 'I'm really sorry, Norman, but they've got Pip. They attacked my stepfather. I have to go to the hospital.'

Norman shook his head and began to order his clothes. 'Could I come with you?' he asked.

'Of course.'

She had started up the ramp and was in front of him. She turned round and placed her hands on either side of his face. 'I'm sorry. That was really ...' She struggled for words.

He smiled. 'It was, wasn't it?'

'Yes, it was,' she said, and kissed him.

CHAPTER TWENTY-FOUR

Sam's mother was waiting for them in the entrance to the hospital. She looked grey with exhaustion but, as usual, elegantly turned out. Sam kissed her and introduced her to Norman. She watched her mother glance up and down at him, taking in his size and the rather inadequate attempt he had made to disguise the fact that most of the buttons were missing from the front of his shirt.

'I'm so sorry about this, Mum.'

'What's been going on? Peter keeps going on about that horrible little dog. Whose dog is it anyway and why's he so worried about it?'

They stood waiting for the lift to arrive. Her mother's arms were folded tightly across her chest.

'The dog's mine,' Norman said. 'And this is all my fault.'

'If that's true then the least you can do is calm my husband down. He's very upset by what's happened and keeps blaming himself.'

The lift came and they got in.

'Is he going to be all right?' Sam asked.

'He's fractured his skull and has concussion. They'll keep him in for a few days for observation. He should be all right as long as there aren't any complications.'

Peter was in a private room, his head swathed in bandages, one eye was black and shiny, the other side of his face red and grazed. When he saw Sam he leaned forwards towards her. 'It's my fault. You said I shouldn't take anything for granted. I was just getting the bags and then the lights went out.'

He looked behind Sam at Norman.

'This is Norman, Professor Sweetman's son,' Sam said. 'Pip is his dog.'

'I'm so sorry,' Peter said. 'Your dog ... I've lost your dog ...'

He closed his eyes for a moment and when he opened them tears were rolling down his cheeks. Norman pushed himself away from the door frame, sat down next to him and took his hand.

'Dear man,' he said. 'My dear, dear man ... you're not to worry about it at all. I'm sure Pip will be delivered up safely in due course. Please don't upset yourself. It's been so kind of you to look after him in the way that you have. It's obvious to me he couldn't have been in more loving hands.' He took a surprisingly clean-looking handkerchief from the inside pocket of his jacket and pressed it into Peter's hands.

Sam, who had never seen Peter cry in her life before, didn't know what to do. Norman, she couldn't help but notice, was handling an emotional situation rather better than her and her mother.

On the way down in the lift Norman was silent. Sam squatted down, head in hands, trying to decide what to do next. Pip had been taken for a purpose. Should she try and use the number extracted by Tyler from the two men in Blackbird Leys or wait until they got in touch? If they did, it would be with Norman and did she trust him to tell her what was going on? Up until recently he hadn't been very good at keeping her in the loop. Another option was to tell the police, but if she did that then they would have to do what the police wanted. What if they called and demanded an immediate meeting? What would they do then?

Norman's gaze moved off his feet on to her. 'What are you thinking?'

The lift had reached the ground floor and opened and Sam stood up and they both got out. 'That we need to talk. You need to tell me everything and then I'll be in a better position to work out what to do next.'

'"Everything" sounds rather alarming.'

'Come on, I'll walk back to the cinema with you. Thank you for being so kind to my stepfather.'

'I had no idea he'd be so upset. I was very touched.'

'A dog was taken away from him when he was a child. The loss of the dog was a symbol of the loss of his childhood. There was more in the mix than just Pip ...'

'Yes, yes, of course I can see quite clearly, and that combined with the shock of the attack ... poor man.'

They walked for a few moments in silence. There were more people around than there would usually be at this time of night because the fair was in town.

'I fear your mother didn't take to me.'

'She was just tired and worried, that's all. Don't take it personally.'

'I won't.'

'Do you think the mask was in the car at the time of the accident?'

'Oh, I know it was.'

'How can you be so certain?'

'I was there with it on the back seat.'

She thought of the picture of the crumpled car she had seen in the police file and considered her next question carefully.

'You told Mrs Eliot when you were a boy that you were responsible for their deaths.'

'Yes, for a long time I thought that was true.'

'Why did you say that?'

'I was melodramatic as a child, attention-seeking. Mrs Eliot, bless her, gave me a great deal of attention.'

'Did you just say it then to get attention?'

'No, no, I genuinely believed it for a long time. The reason I know the mask was there was because ...'

His phone rang and he patted his hands over his body and found it in his jacket pocket.

'Hello? ... Yes, I know that ... no, I don't want you to do that ... I can meet you there ... in an hour ... but ...' He closed the phone and slid it back into his pocket.

'What do they want?'

'To meet in Harberton Mead in an hour.'

'What did they say?'

'They've got Pip. They threatened to kill him unless I can tell them where the mask is.'

'Do you know where it is?'

'No.'

'Did you tell them you did?'

'No.'

'What do you want to do?'

'Get Pip back. Keep out of prison. Make love to you in a horizontal rather than a perpendicular position ... gamble less ...' His hand slid across the top of her shoulders.

'Stop it, Norman, that doesn't help.'

'Are you going to tell the police?'

Sam took his arm. 'No. Come on, we better get going.'

Sam drove and parked in the entrance to Headington Hall. Then they set off along Pullen's Lane. When she'd been here before, it had been swelteringly hot and the trees had provided welcome shade, but now she was shivering and in the dark the lane appeared sinister rather than pretty, the overhanging trees looming over them as they walked. At the junction where Pullen's Lane turned into Jack Straw's Lane they separated, Sam continuing straight ahead and Norman turning left into Harberton Mead. He would go ahead and open up the house and she would take a somewhat more indirect route to the house in case the dog-nappers were already there, waiting for them. The element of surprise, she had decided, was crucial. It was then that her phone rang, breaking the night-time silence and practically giving her a heart attack in the process. She scrabbled for it and answered it.

'Sam?'

She screwed both her eyes shut and brought the hand not holding the phone to her head. It was Rick, drunk. Oh, so very drunk.

'Rick,' she hissed. 'Where are you?'

'Thas whad I'm ringing to ass you, ashly.'

'Who's with you? Is Luke there?'

'Luke ...' she heard him say and the phone went dead for a second.

'So where the fuck are you?' Luke didn't sound so drunk but he did sound pissed off.

'On top of Headington Hill. Where are you?'

'Raoul's. What are you doing there?'

'Long story. Rick sounds completely pissed.'

'Well, he'd been looking forward to a passionate reunion with his girlfriend but then she disappeared on him and he felt upset and several margaritas have glugged down his throat since then. Now he's drunk and upset and has fallen asleep in the arms of a large stuffed lion . . .'

'Look, Luke, something came up. I'll explain it all later. Will you make sure Rick gets back to your place OK?'

She heard him sigh and then the phone went dead. She glanced at her watch and hurried on towards Norman's house. It didn't take her long to reach the path that he had told her about which cut through from Jack Straw's Lane to the top end of his garden. Foliage brushed against her face as she quietly opened the gate that led into the garden and started along the path to the house. Nearby she heard the soft purr of a car's engine driving away.

The ground floor of the house was lit up; he'd got here before her. She leaned against a wooden fence and waited. Night-time noises startled her; a rustle in the hedge above her head and the sudden tearing screech of an owl. She heard her heart thumping in her ears and prayed that she wasn't going to regret her decision to do this alone. She wondered what she was going to do when Norman told them that he did not have the mask, had no idea where it was and . . . now could he have his dog back please; wondered what she was willing to do for him, thought again of Stephanie's bloodied body, crumpled on the bed like a discarded toy and Alan tearing at his tie at the undertaker's.

She, felt as if a switch had been clicked on. She'd always known she was a fighter but this was different, this was something else altogether. It's not my fight, she kept saying to herself, let the police handle it. That's the proper way to behave. But the truth was she'd never had much time for proprieties. She found herself thinking of Reg, wondering what he would say, running through a hypothetical conversation she might have with him. She imagined the expression on his face when she talked to him about Norman, about what she was thinking of doing, and didn't like what she saw, and suddenly she thought, you're being a fool here.

She remained squatting down and absolutely still, and considered the plan they had put together. The main problem was the dog. The best scenario was that they brought the dog with them and then it would be a question of getting hold of him. She didn't think that they would do that. The problem was that Norman did not have the mask to hand over in exchange. She had thought of contacting the police, but suppose they didn't bring the dog, the police arrested them and then they denied all knowledge of Pip. Then the dog would be lost. Norman didn't like that idea one bit and neither did she. She looked at her watch – five minutes to go.

She tried to remember the lay-out of the garden from when she'd been here before and as her eyes got used to the darkness she saw the shape of the wooden hut, the area of the vegetable garden and the lawn running away from the front of the house down towards the road. Quarter of an hour passed, then twenty minutes. Sam was torn. She waited until half an hour beyond the appointed time and then crept round the garden side of the house and through the patio doors that they had agreed Norman would leave open. The room smelled stuffy and dusty and as she crossed the living-room she had to stifle a sneeze. They had agreed that Norman would talk to them in the hall, so she stayed behind the door that led into the hall, listening, but the house was completely silent. She couldn't hear any movement at all. She stood there and waited. Then she did hear something, a groan. She opened the door a couple of inches and peered out. No one was there. Then she heard the groan again; it seemed to have come from the room opposite. Sam walked softly across the hall and pushed open the door.

Norman was sitting on the floor, his head held in his hands, blood dripping from his face down the front of his shirt. Sam flashed back to her blood-stained bedroom then crossed the room and knelt down beside him.

'Are you all right? Did they do this to you?'

Norman was groggily trying to focus on her. He shook his head and flecks of blood flew from his face on to the floor. Sam wet some kitchen towel and started washing the blood away from his face.

'Where's the dog?'

But Norman seemed incapable of answering. The worst of the

damage was a nasty cut over his right eye and bruising on his right cheekbone. She got him to hold another wodge of kitchen towel against the cut, and opened the fridge. She was hoping for a packet of peas or broad beans but the only thing in there was ice in an old-fashioned metal ice-tray. She smashed up the ice with a rolling-pin and put the ice chips in a plastic bag, which she wrapped in a tea-towel before holding it to the damaged side of Norman's face.

'Sorry,' she said. 'I didn't think they were here. They must have left by the time I arrived.'

'Waiting for me,' Norman said.

Sam took the tea-towel away from his face and wiped the cut again. It was actually in his eyebrow but as far as she could make out it seemed to have stopped bleeding so profusely. 'Have you got anything like Elastoplast?' she asked.

'Bathroom. Left, then left at the top of the stairs.'

When she came back down with the plaster, Norman was in the middle of getting to his feet. He winced as he straightened up and clutched his ribs. 'Bastard kicked me.' He took off his jacket, took down his braces and pulled his shirt open. A large livid area on the right-hand side of his body showed where he'd been kicked.

'Do you think they're broken?'

He shook his head. 'Fat pads bone. Not broken just sore.'

'So,' Sam said. 'What happened?'

Norman sat down heavily on a chair and she pulled the ice-pack away from his face and dried it. She got some more kitchen towel, tore it into a shape that covered the eyebrow and then stuck it down with a couple of pieces of plaster.

'Don't go waggling your eyebrows too much,' she said. She picked up the ice-pack from the table and handed it back to him. 'You should keep this against the side of your face. It'll bring down the swelling.'

'I wouldn't have taken you for any sort of nurse,' he said.

'My mother worked in accident and emergency for years. I did a bit of judo which leads to bumps and scrapes. You learn the hard way the best means of treating them.'

'You did a bit of judo.' His eyes crinkled in amusement and one of the bits of plaster came unstuck. 'Interesting way of describing a career that involved being World Champion four times over.'

Sam blushed. She wasn't quite sure why, and then leaned forwards and stuck the plaster back down.

'You didn't think I'd leave Pip with just anyone, did you?'

'Anyway,' Sam said. 'That was a long time ago. Do you want to tell me what happened?'

'They were already here. When I told them I didn't have the mask, they hit me. I told them that I had no idea where it was, that as far as I knew it had gone missing at the time of the accident. The man, you know the one with the hard head, seemed very certain that I should know about it. It's ridiculous because they broke in here themselves weeks ago and went through everything. They didn't find it and they looked pretty hard, so why they think I can conjure it from thin air, I don't know.'

Sam sighed. 'Are you telling me the truth, Norman?'

He smiled and the Elastoplast popped off again. This time he pressed it back on himself. 'I realise that in the past, as far as you are concerned, I have had a somewhat tangential relationship with the truth. But this is not my usual state of affairs, I can assure you.'

'I don't believe you,' Sam said. 'What about the man in the bookies' who was expecting the return of five thousand pounds?'

'Ah, the rabbit got away from that particular dog.' Norman began to stand up but the action made him clutch his ribs.

'Sit down,' Sam ordered.

'There's some Jack Daniels in the cupboard.'

She went over and took the bottle down, found two glasses and poured them both a shot. Norman grasped the glass and downed it. Sam sipped hers, feeling the whisky burn down into her stomach.

'How was it left with them?'

'The man told me to talk to my grandfather or they would. He said when I'd done that and had the mask, I should phone them.'

Sam swilled the remains of her whisky around the glass. 'What do you remember of the accident? Why did you tell Mrs Eliot you were responsible for your parents' deaths?'

Norman reached for the bottle and poured himself another.

'I was in the back of the car. I took the mask out of the box it was

275

in and I put it over my face. I saw my father's face in the mirror and that's the last thing I remember.'

'You think that caused the accident?'

'I know it did.'

'But if you can't remember what happened next how can you be so sure? You could have done that at one part of the journey and the accident could have happened at another.'

'At the inquest they said that they could discover no reason why the accident happened. There was nothing on the road to indicate that there was a reason for my father to have lost control of the car in the way that he did. They put it down to driver error, an error I know was caused by my putting on that mask and frightening my father to death, killing both him and my mother.'

'But you can't know that for a fact, Norman.'

'Look, Sam, I've lived with the knowledge of that all my life. I know it. That's not to say I can't see that I was a child then, that I did not know what I was doing, that it was an accident and any number of other things to let me off the hook, but however much of that I come up with, the bottom line is that I did something that caused an accident that killed both my parents. The last thing I remember is the expression on my father's face. The road was quite deserted and I remember a car coming up behind us and its headlights lighting up the inside of our car. My father looked in the driver's mirror and saw me in the mask. The expression on his face will stay with me for the rest of my life. I know what happened, Sam, and there's no point in pretending otherwise.'

Sam noticed that he had dropped all the affectation from his speech and wondered if that meant he was telling her the truth. She felt chilled. She'd been right to be frightened by the witch in the bottle, the shrunken heads. Sacred objects were not to be messed with. The mask had used a child to destructive ends and in such an innocent way. Hold a mask up to your face and ... you meddled with these things at your peril.

'So the mask was definitely in the car at the time of the accident.'

'Yes.'

'Are you going to ask your grandfather about it?'

'It's very difficult for us to talk about the accident. We've had a kind of tacit understanding about that. It's too late to start now. It'd be a bit like breaking a taboo.'

'But you have to, Norman.'

'I can't.'

'So what are you going to do?'

'Come on, I'll show you.'

He heaved himself to his feet and Sam followed him through the hall and out through the living-room on to the patio. The light from the house lit up the garden and she followed Norman across the lawn to the large wooden hut. Before Sam had thought it was some sort of garden shed but as they got closer she could see that it was much more solid than that and there was what looked like some sort of generator attached to it. Norman unlocked a padlock, which was holding a metal bar in place across the door, and entered. He turned on a light and Sam followed him into the hut. To the left there was a long wooden work-surface covered with a selection of tools, bits of plastic, wood, and a wig of long black hair. To the right was a work-station and a computer; a variety of different books were piled up against the wall. Sam picked one up, a glossy hardback titled *Masks, the Art of Expression*, and leafed through it. Norman was searching through some papers next to the computer.

'Here,' he said. 'Have a look at this.'

Sam was staring at the black wig. 'What exactly do you get up to in here, Norman?'

'This and that. Look.'

He handed her a piece of paper. It was a photo of the shaman's mask. Seeing it again, Sam thought it was the face of something that would eat you alive and spit out your bones.

'I saw this in the police file. It reminds me of some of the gargoyles on the side of New College.'

Norman nodded. He was over in the far corner of the hut now, leaning down into a large cardboard box. Sam's attention moved off him. Attached to the wall next to the computer were a series of photos, including shrunken heads; on the table were three-dimensional drawings with measurements drawn on them. Sam stared at them, frowning. What did he do here exactly?

'Norman, what ...?'

A noise brought her attention away from the drawings to where Norman was standing. Black almond slits had replaced his eyes; the lips were blood-red and the teeth sharp. He stepped towards her. A wave of absolute terror seized Sam from her toes to the top of her head. The last time he'd had that over his face two people had been killed and not just any people, two people he was very close to. Maybe Mrs Eliot was right about him. She stood paralysed, staring at him.

He took the mask away from his face and looked at her. 'Are you all right?'

Sam released a breath she didn't even realise she'd been holding. 'For fuck's sake, Norman, how on earth can you do that after what happened, even as a joke.'

'Sorry.'

He handed her the mask and reluctantly she took it, turning it round and round in her hands. She felt uncomfortable; it was a sacred object, not hers but someone's. It just didn't feel right to be holding it.

'Is it the mask?'

He shook his head. 'To coin a phrase from our youth, it's one I made earlier.'

'You *made* it?'

'Yes, I blame *Blue Peter*. I was always interested in making things and then I realised that something that had always been a bit of a hobby could actually be put to financial use.'

Sam pointed at the wig. 'For the shrunken heads?'

He nodded.

'Have you got a supply of fakes?'

'You can buy them on the internet for quite a reasonable sum. But the ones I bought needed a bit more hair. The important thing was that they were good enough not to attract undue attention, that they would look OK in the cabinets. Cummings, of course, was complicit.'

'When did this all start?'

'It was an accident really. I had done some models for Luke's father. You know he has the archaeological site out towards Chedworth.

278

Well, he had decided to set up a small museum there and charge people for access to the site and he wanted me to make models of some of the things that he had discovered. Luke knew about my model-making from when we were at school together and that's what made him suggest me. Cummings visited the museum and then he heard from my grandfather, I think, about my financial problems and decided to put a proposition to me.'

'And your grandfather never knew what you were doing?'

He shook his head. 'My grandfather doesn't have access to this hut because he is wheelchair-bound. It was easy enough to hide it from him.'

'So you made this replica from pictures?'

'Yes, and detailed descriptions in my grandfather's papers.'

Sam looked at the mask which she had placed on the work-top and then held the photo of it next to it. 'It's good,' she said.

'Good enough to get Pip back?'

'I don't know. Why didn't you just hand it over to them now?'

'It's not quite finished. You see these markings here?' He pointed at the upper lip of the mask on the photo. 'I need to put those on and there are a few other touches. Also, they didn't bring the dog with them. I don't trust them to do anything once they have the mask in their hands.'

Sam ran her finger lightly down the length of the nose and shuddered. 'Didn't it freak you out a little bit creating something ...' she paused '... something that has such strong resonances for you from the past?'

Norman rubbed the end of his nose and looked away from her. 'It had to be done.' He picked up the mask and held it so it was level with his own face. 'In some cultures masks are viewed as having so much power that they are never worn, only carried at ceremonies.'

Sam shuddered. 'It seems to me to be a face of implacable cruelty.'

For a moment they were both silent.

Then she continued. 'What do you think happened to the real one?'

He shrugged his shoulders. 'I don't suppose we'll ever know that.'

She decided to try again. 'Your grandfather must know something.'

'I've already told you why I can't talk to him about it.'

'Aren't you curious to know?'

'It's obvious, isn't it? Someone at the scene of the accident helped themselves. Accident scenes are chaotic and messy and people are rushing to save the victims. It must be the easiest thing in the world to swipe things. Then it was sold on and now it's in the hands of private collectors. It happens all the time. Or it was swept away in the river. Or it was destroyed in the accident.'

'Or,' Sam said, 'your grandfather took it and then pretended it had been stolen. The man who tried to kill me, McGregor, was a policeman at the scene of the accident. If he didn't take the mask, which presumably he didn't because otherwise he wouldn't be coming after you for it, he must think or know that your grandfather was involved in some way.'

'I disagree. Someone saw the article in the paper about the sale in New York and decided to do a little digging about. Collectors are obsessive and will pay astronomical sums. They've got a buyer. Someone's asked them to find it and it's brought them to him and then to us. They're on a fishing expedition to see what they can come up with.'

He was bending down now, rummaging in the corner of the hut. When he straightened up, he was holding a wooden box in his hands which he placed on the work-surface next to Sam. It was filled with straw. He took the mask and cleared a space for it in the box and covered it in the straw.

'The box is original to the collection. If what it comes in looks authentic, they're more likely to go with it.'

'Won't they suspect it's a replica if they know that's what you've been doing with Cummings?'

'They don't. They don't know anything about the replicas. As far as they were concerned I was merely the delivery boy of the original items. It was only when they realised that I was Sweetman's grandson that they showed any interest in me whatsoever.'

'And in Pip?'

'Yes.'

'Why did you lie about Pip the first time we spoke?'

'I didn't know if I could trust you.'

Norman locked the hut and they walked back across the lawn to the house. The pale green of dawn was lifting the darkness of the night sky. In the kitchen, Norman placed the box on the table and threw open the fridge.

'Bacon sandwich?'

Sam wasn't altogether sure how her stomach would feel about that but nodded a yes, and as the bacon began to fry was glad that she had. When the food was ready they took it out on to the veranda and watched the sun coming up through the fir trees to their right.

'Being brought up in Oxford equips one for nothing that is any use in later life,' Norman said, wiping his mouth with a large linen napkin. 'I have found it to be the worst possible start.'

Sam laughed. 'Why do you say that?'

'Well, you were brought up in St Cuthbert's. You must know what I mean. You end up with an entirely misguided set of values because you are surrounded by people for whom the life of the mind is of the greatest importance. This helps one in no way to meet the realities of the world.'

'Which are?'

'Mortgages, houses, starting a family, putting food on the table, proper jobs.'

'The two are not completely incompatible, Norman.'

'Look at us – we are not a good advertisement for the offspring of Oxford.'

'Speak for yourself.'

'But when I leave and go, for example, to London I feel that it is, if you'll pardon the expression, "Life, Jim, but not as we know it", don't you?'

'No I don't. I couldn't wait to leave.'

'Yes, but here you are back again. Oxford has reclaimed you as its own.'

'No it hasn't.'

Norman shook the napkin he had draped across his knee. 'The silken thread that ties you to your past has exerted its pull.'

'That's not the case for me.'

'And yet here you are. I have come to the reluctant conclusion this the city suits me, it is what I am and I have relinquished all hope of escape.'

'You may feel differently after your grandfather ... I mean when ...'

Norman smiled. 'After and when – precisely so. I might, it's true, but I doubt it. I was born in this house. Look.' He gestured at the garden. 'Why would I want to leave it?'

'Because it was time to move on?'

'But move on to what, to whom, to where? I don't believe in moving on purely for its own sake. I never have.' He paused and rubbed his face. 'Maybe I don't feel I have anywhere else to go.'

The sun was breaking through the firs in front of them.

Norman stood up, turned round and pointed to a window above them. 'I was born in that room there. The first noise I remember from my childhood is the wood-pigeons calling from the trees behind the house. I know how this garden looks under a foot of snow in the winter and when it's been burnt to a frazzle like this summer. I await the arrival of the martins in the spring and know how the cabbage whites fly over the nettle beds in the late-summer evenings. I fell face down in that bed of nettles when I was four years old and have never forgotten it. Tell me, why would I leave here now? Why would I do that?'

Sam shrugged. 'Horses for courses.'

'Why is it that people always think you have to leave in order to grow up? Simply leaving isn't a sign of adulthood. In fact, leaving can be a sign of teenage rebellion.' He stretched his legs out in front of him. 'You know what Philip Pullman said about Oxford? That to live in this city of birds and shadows is like being the offspring of a ghost and a hooligan.'

Sam smiled. 'Why does that sound so horribly, horribly accurate?'

'Which bit of it?'

'The birds, the shadows, the ghosts, the hooligans.'

He laughed. 'The thing is I rejoice in that parentage. Raised by the ghosts and the hooligans, I'm not fit for anywhere else.'

The wood-pigeons had started their lulling cooing. Norman

looked at his watch. 'Right on time,' he said. 'That sound gives me feelings of the strongest and deepest contentment. We have a picture of my mother out here when she was pregnant with me. I imagine I must have heard them when I was in the womb.'

He closed his eyes, his face transfigured with happiness.

It's like a spider's web that has caught him, Sam thought. He's a great juicy fly, trapped in his own past, too frightened to move on. And then she felt a stab of envy for his sense of belonging and his sense of rootedness, and underneath the envy she felt something she didn't want to feel at all, something that felt horribly like grief.

CHAPTER TWENTY-FIVE

Sam left Norman listening to the wood-pigeons and drove back into town. It was a stunning September morning with the slight nip in the air that augured cooler weather but the sun was still hot on the side of Sam's face as she enjoyed the helter-skelter rush of the van down the hill. She parked outside her parents' house and phoned Alan to update him on what had happened. They agreed that he would come down immediately.

She let herself into Park Town with some trepidation. Her mother was sitting at the kitchen table drinking a cup of tea. She looked exhausted. Sam sat down next to her.

'How's Peter?'

'He had a good night. They'll probably let him come home at the end of the day.'

'I'm so sorry, Mum.'

'It's all right, Sam, he explained. He said it wasn't your fault and he's enjoyed having the dog. It's been good for him.'

'I think so too,' Sam agreed. 'Was it difficult with Aunt Rose?'

'It was sad.' She paused. 'She didn't want to leave her home. Who would? But if you haven't got the money ... I'm going to go for a swim later. I'll feel better after that.'

Sam nodded and then was surprised to hear herself ask, 'Can you remember who taught me to swim?'

Her mother frowned. 'Do you swim? I thought you were allergic to the chlorine.'

'I am, but I have a memory of being taught when I was quite little. I wondered who it was.'

Her mother had got up to fill the kettle and was standing with her back to her.

Sam cleared her throat. 'I remember wearing a swimming costume with strawberries on it.'

Her mother turned round and smiled. 'Oh yes, I remember that. You know, I think Max might have.'

'Sorry?'

'Your godfather, Max. I think he might have tried. When your grandfather died, we left you with him and his girlfriend when we went to the funeral. We took Mark but decided you were too young to go. When we came back I remember him saying he'd taken you swimming and I thought I'd try and build on that and take you myself, but the first time I took you, you began screaming and had breathing difficulties.'

'You're sure it was Max?'

'Yes. Why?'

'Where was Dad?'

'It was his father's funeral. We were both at the funeral.'

She stared at her mother.

'Are you all right, Sam?'

'Yes, yes, I'm fine.'

'As far as you know Dad never taught me to swim?'

'I never left you alone with your father, Sam. His behaviour didn't lead me to think he could be trusted with a small child. It wasn't something I would ever have done. When he was back on leave he was much too volatile. And anyway we'd disagreed over him teaching Mark. He threw him in the deep end. I wouldn't have allowed him to do that to you.'

'But you trusted Max?'

'Yes, I did. I always trusted Max.'

Sam lay on the bed staring at the ceiling. She felt as if she was back on the waltzer, spinning, dizzy, sick. She picked up her phone and rang Reg. She had to speak to him. The answerphone greeted her.

'Reg ... it's Sam ... are you ...'

He picked up the phone. 'Sam?'

'Can I speak to you?'

'Yes, what's happened?'

'Why would I think it was my father who abused me when it wasn't?'

'What's made you think that?'

'I talked to my mother. She said she'd never have left me with Dad because she didn't trust him. I was left with my godfather, Max. I saw Max for the first time in years shortly before I met up with my father. That could have triggered the flashbacks. But why would I think it was my father?'

'Why do you think?'

'To protect myself. To give me a good reason to keep him at bay. But why do I have to hate him?'

'What does the hate do?'

'Creates distance.'

'And why do you need the distance?'

Sam felt her hands tingling.

'I'm starting to blank out,' she said.

'Take some breaths, Sam. Deep, slow breaths.'

She did as she was told.

Then Reg said, 'What do you need to protect yourself against?'

'Losing him. Losing him all over again.' She brought her hands up to her cheeks and realised they were wet.

'Because what happened when you lost him before?'

Sam didn't say anything.

'What happened, Sam?'

'You know what happened. You spoke to Mark, didn't you?' She was shouting at him. 'Why are you asking me what you already know?'

'What did you do when you thought he was dead?'

Sam's hand went instinctively to the scar on her neck. Suddenly the phrase 'the accumulation of silent things' came into her mind. Feeling sick, she said, 'I tried to kill myself.'

'Yes,' Reg said.

Sam felt completely disorientated now. 'Is this making sense, Reg?'

'What do you think? Is it making sense to you?'

She had that feeling again of water clearing out of her ear. She sighed. 'Yes,' she said. 'It all makes sense.'

'How are you feeling?' he asked.

'Sad,' she said, and began to sob.

The mask hangs suspended in darkness. Behind it shadows move back and forth. Sam reaches to touch it, but each time it moves away from her. The shadows are passing it between them with invisible hands. She stops trying to grab it and steps back looking at the almond slits of eyes, thinks she can see the gleam of a white pupil behind there, thinks there's someone human behind the implacable façade, is frightened to know, turns to go. But now the mask is in front of her again. Whichever way she turns, she can't get past it. She's panicking now and runs at it with her hands out covering her face as if running through a forest and protecting her face from the branches. She's thrown to the ground, as if she's run at a brick wall. The mask is near her. This is her chance. She scrambles towards it and gently picks it up and this reveals the figure beneath it. Gradually it dawns on her that the figure she is looking at is herself and she is dead.

She woke to the ring of her mobile. It was Norman.

'Something downright peculiar has just happened.'

Sam sat up on the side of the bed and tried to shake the dream from her. 'Peculiar in what way?'

'Hardwick just phoned from St Cuthbert's. He said he'd told my grandfather before he went into hospital that he was going to have to move the crate he was keeping stored in the wine cellar. Apparently it has been there from the time he was in charge of the cellars. Miles Archer is now in charge and is undergoing a bit of a spring-clean. He wants to build some more racks and has asked that the crate be moved. From what I could work out my grandfather has been slipping Hardwick some money every year to store it there.'

'Did you know anything about this?'

'No, my grandfather never mentioned it to me. I'm going to go and have a look and see what's there. Will you meet me?'

Sam scrubbed at her eyes in a vain attempt to open them. 'What do you think it is?'

'It's something he didn't want me to see.'

'You think it's the mask, don't you?'

'Yes, I do.'

'I'll meet you outside the lodge in half an hour.'

The conversation she'd had with her mother and then with Reg and the revelations that had followed sat in the base of her throat like a marble. She coughed and swallowed but it made no difference.

Sam was waiting for Norman to turn up. There were still quite a few dons at St Cuthbert's who had been there when Sam was a child. The young ones then were now the senior fellows, broader in the midriff and more confident in manner, established members of the college. After one too many conversations along the lines of how are you and what are you doing now, Sam moved away from the lodge and out on to the steps that led up into the college. Standing on the flagstones outside the lodge her dream had returned to her, the cracks opening up under her feet and the masked figure, with bear's claws, tearing off her face. Masks allowed you to do all kinds of things that you would never do with the cold light of day touching your skin. Masks hid you from view. She wished for one now.

At that moment Norman appeared at the bottom of the steps. As they walked along the side of the quadrangle towards the cellar, Sam found herself shuffling and hopping over the paving stones. Norman glanced sideways at her.

'Are you doing what I think you're doing?'

She blushed. She'd been trying to do it without being noticed, obviously that hadn't worked. 'I don't know. What do you think I'm doing?'

'Jumping the cracks.'

'Maybe. It's an old habit. I used to do it as a child and then when I was doing judo I'd do it to speed up my footwork.'

'I thought it was a sign of obsessive compulsive disorder.'

She laughed. 'Sounds about right.'

They found Hardwick, a tall, thin lugubrious man, in the buttery and followed him down into the cellar.

'So, Mr Archer is throwing himself at things with enthusiasm is he?' Sam said.

'In my experience, miss, there is a tendency for much talk of innovation and new beginnings and after a while they revert to the old ways of doing things for the simple reason that they've always worked rather well in the past and they continue to do so.'

They were at the bottom of the stairs now and the change in temperature made Sam shiver. They followed Hardwick along the corridor off which the various cellars ran to the very end one.

'What's kept in here?' Norman asked.

'Port, sir.'

Hardwick stepped forwards and pulled the rack holding the bottles to one side. Behind it and up against the base of one of the massive arched pillars was a recess in which sat a small crate.

'How long has it been here?' Norman asked.

'A good long time, sir. I used to ask Professor Sweetman about it from time to time, but he always seemed happier that it remain here than to have it moved to your home.'

He leaned down and picked it up and handed it to Norman, who moved it up and down in his hands assessing its weight. 'Did he ever tell you what was in it?'

'No, sir, and I didn't feel it was my place to enquire.'

'Could you give us a moment, Hardwick?'

'Of course, sir,' and he melted away from them, back along the corridor towards the stairs.

Norman placed the box on a narrow wooden table that ran along one side of the corridor and took a Swiss army knife out of his pocket. He levered opened the box and reached inside and lifted out the contents. The shaman's mask looked back at them. Even though Sam had been expecting it, she took an involuntary step backwards. The phrase 'sacred object' shot into her mind. Looking at it now, she had no doubt that that's was what it was, a sacred object with all the sense of fear and awe that inspired. The one Norman had made didn't come anywhere close to the power of this thing.

Norman must have felt something of the same because he didn't hold it in his hands for long. He quickly placed it on the table and tucked his hands under his armpits as if they'd been burnt. There was no way that Sam could ever imagine him holding this up to his face.

He swallowed. 'I was expecting it, but I wasn't expecting it to be so ...'

'Terrifying?'

'Yes.'

They both stared at it in silence. The light in the cellar was dim and suddenly the lights flickered, making both of them jump. Sam knew one thing with absolute certainty – she did not want to be stuck in a cellar in the dark with this thing much longer.

'Let's go,' she said.

Norman was leaning into the bag he'd brought with him. He took out the replica and placed it in the wooden box and then gingerly placed the original in his bag.

'What exactly are you planning, Norman?'

'If I bring them down here it's going to make it all much more authentic, isn't it? I'll tell them I spoke to my grandfather and he told me it was here. I'll say I've only got the key for a short period of time. I'll get them to come here and ...'

'What about the police?'

'Well, I was hoping to avoid ...'

'That man killed my friend's niece. It's not part of my agenda to let him get away with it.'

'The trouble is ...'

'I know what the trouble is, Norman, but what I'm saying is that this is non-negotiable. What I suggest is the following. We go to the police and you tell them everything.'

He winced and ran his hand through his hair.

'Do you really think that is such a good idea?'

'Look, what you're saying is that you are willing to hand over to them a murderer and do a deal on the thefts.'

'Mmm ... and you think they'll go for it?'

'They'd be fools not to consider it ... anyway what were you thinking of doing?'

'Handing over the mask and hoping that all the rest goes away.'

'And when they find out it isn't the original?'

'If I can concoct a good enough story around the discovery of the mask I think they'll go a long way with it. They are going to want to believe that it's true.'

They were walking along the passage now with the cellars running off to their left. As they came out into the daylight of the quad Norman said, 'I wonder if I might ask a favour of you?'

Sam was staring down at her feet, both of which were on the cracks of the paving stones. She moved them and said, 'Why do I have the feeling I'm not going to like what is about to come out of your mouth?'

'Would you look after this for me for a while?' He waved the plastic bag containing the shaman's mask.

'Norman, give me a break! Isn't it enough that you dumped Pip on me? I didn't do a very good job of keeping him safe, did I? Now a shaman's mask.'

'Only until all this is sorted out.'

She shook her head. 'Give it here.' She put the bag containing the mask in her rucksack and slung it over her shoulder, tried not to imagine that it was burning a hole between her shoulder blades. It had been hidden down in the cellar for many years. She had an image of the darkness muffling its powers. It mustn't see the light of day, she thought. If it does, anything might happen. And then she dismissed everything she had just thought as superstitious nonsense. It has no power other than the meaning I attach to it. That was the truth of the matter. Remove the meaning – remove the power. What she couldn't quite work out was why she was investing it with so much.

Hardwick appeared at their side.

Norman put his hand on his arm. 'Hardwick, I wonder if I might ask you one final favour. For reasons that I do not want to go into, it would be helpful to me if we could leave the box where it is for a short while longer and if you might allow me to have the key to the cellars until tomorrow. It would be useful for me to be able to bring certain people down there and discover this crate *in situ*.'

Hardwick considered this proposition for some time. An expression of contemplative sorrow suffused his features.

'Did my grandfather reward you for allowing him to store this here over all these years?'

His face brightened. 'Indeed he did.'

'Perhaps I might offer you the same remuneration for your indulgence in this matter.'

Hardwick smiled. 'In that case it should be no problem, sir. No problem at all.'

Norman patted his chest in a futile money-searching gesture and then turned to Sam. 'Would you mind doing the honours? I'm afraid I find myself momentarily strapped for cash.'

Sam took her wallet out of her rucksack. 'How much?'

She could see Hardwick judging what he might get away with. 'Fifty-five pounds.'

The five was a nice touch, Sam thought, as she gave him the money.

Hardwick handed over the key, and, fifty-five pounds happier than when he started out, drifted back towards the cellar steps.

They were out in the High Street when Sam's phone went. It was Alan. He was at the Headington roundabout and would be at the office in five minutes or so. Sam said that she and Norman would meet him there.

Norman had taken the squishy executive chair, Sam was sitting on the other chair and Alan was leaning against the wall by the window, which looked out of the back of the building. They had gone over their plan several times but they had reached a crucial sticking point. Alan and Sam were at loggerheads and neither was giving any indication of being the one who was going to budge.

Norman sighed, walked over to the fridge, threw it open and gazed mournfully into its gleaming white emptiness.

'It doesn't make any sense,' Alan repeated for about the fourth time. 'You said yourself you only just got away from him the first time. He almost killed you. Why do you think you're going to come off any better this time?'

'To be forewarned is to be pre-armed.'

'Even you would admit that there are circumstances where size does matter. You are five foot one and McGregor is six foot tall and, from what you said, about six foot wide, most of it being solid muscle.'

'Either we do it my way or this doesn't happen at all,' Sam said. 'This part of the plan is non-negotiable.'

'I'm going out to get some beer,' Norman said.

'Fine,' Sam said.

He patted his pockets. 'I'm a bit …'

She looked at him. 'You already owe me fifty-five pounds. Alan, give him some money.'

'Why?'

'Expenses.'

Alan dug in his pocket and came out with ten pounds. Norman looked at it despondently, but confronted with Alan's stare, pocketed it and left the room.

Alan walked over and sat on the edge of the desk. 'The real reason you're being so stubborn about this is because you think I'm going to kill him, don't you?'

Sam folded her arms. 'Yes.'

'I can't pretend it hasn't crossed my mind.'

'I thought it best that you weren't put in the position of finding out what you might do.'

'We can't be sure what they'll do.'

'Norman's going to tell them how it's going to work. It's that or nothing.'

'They may not go for it.'

'We'll see.'

'You really think you're going to be able to handle him?'

She smiled. 'I do.' She patted her pockets and came up with the pepper spray. 'This would stop a charging grizzly in its tracks.'

'Well, don't make it easy for him.'

'I won't.'

By the time Norman had returned they were in agreement. Now there remained two calls to make, one to set it up, another to the police.

Sam and Norman waited outside St Cuthbert's. It was five to nine and beginning to get dark. She shivered, not so much from the cold, because it was a warm balmy night, but from anticipation. It was how she'd felt before a championship fight, before she stepped out on to the mat.

The expression on Norman's face suddenly changed and his gaze moved from Sam's face to above her left shoulder. 'He's here,' he said.

Sam turned round and saw McGregor standing directly behind her.

In silence they climbed the steps to the college and turned right towards the cellar. Sam had cleared the way earlier with the lodge, spinning some story about a visiting wine expert who was advising Miles Archer on future wine purchases. They reached the door of the cellar and Norman led the way down the steps followed by Sam. She felt McGregor at her back in the same way she'd felt the shaman's mask, a tickle between the shoulder-blades. Maybe more than a tickle, maybe more like a sharp jab. They entered the last cellar and Norman pulled forwards the rack of wine and picked up the box and handed it to him. McGregor pulled off the lid and took out the mask, took a picture of the mask from his pocket, compared the two and then placed the box in a nylon holdall and zipped it up.

'So,' he said. 'The old boy had it after all.'

'Make the call,' Norman said.

McGregor took out a mobile and stabbed a number. 'I've got the mask,' he said. He passed the phone to Sam and Alan came on the line. 'Pip's here. He was where they said he'd be.'

Sam closed up the phone, handed it back to McGregor and they left the cellar. Outside in the quadrangle it was dark now and a gibbous moon was rising above the green dome of the chapel. They were about to leave the college, when the loud blare of a walkie-talkie tore into the silence. Norman and Sam exchanged glances and in the same instance McGregor was off, tearing across the lawns towards the passageway that led under the chapel tower. Sam swore and set off after him. She knew exactly where he would go; there was only one way out of the back of this college. From the back quad he was forced to turn left and go along the narrow passageway that led to the fellows' car park. Sam almost caught him as he climbed over the top of a black metal gate but then he was away from her and she had the gate to climb. Her shirt got caught on one of the spikes and disentangling herself from the metal held her up. When she finally got into the car park, for a moment she couldn't see where he was, then she saw him silhouetted against the minarets of All Souls on top of a high wall that separated St Cuthbert's from the gardens of the warden of New College.

She jumped on the bonnet and then the roof of one of the cars and leapt on to the top of one of the garages. From here she reached up and pulled herself on to the high wall on which McGregor was poised. He jumped and disappeared from view and Sam moved cautiously across the top of the wall to where he had been standing. The smell of dislodged wallflowers hung in the night air. Soon she was where he'd been standing, looking down into the street below. She jumped, landed safely and stood listening for a moment; then she heard footsteps running off to the left along New College Lane. She set off after him, past the entrance to New College, past the house were Haley had discovered his comet. As she ran under Hertford Bridge she saw him turning right into the Broad. He's heading for the fair, she thought, he thinks he'll be able to lose me there. That's what I'd do. All the running she'd been doing over the summer was standing her in good stead, she was steadily gaining on him but she had not caught up with him before he disappeared into the body of the fair. Now there was the hustle and bustle of the crowds to cope with, groups of people strolling and looking around at the stalls and rides and the queues stretching away from the most popular rides. Halfway into the fair next to Wild Mouse she lost him. She jumped up on a lamppost to look around her, but a 360-degree scan of the crowds delivered up no sighting. She jumped down on to the ground and phoned Alan.

'Tell the police he's in the fair. I've lost him by the Wild Mouse ride. They need to put as many people into here as they can.'

But she knew it was likely to be a hopeless task. You couldn't seal up the fair. There were too many roads that ran off St Giles.

She began walking through the fair, first north and then back round towards the Martyrs' Memorial, but wherever she looked, in the dodgems and the waltzers, in the crowds round the stalls and the queues for the hot-dog stands, there was no sign of him. She was standing on the steps of the Martyrs' Memorial looking around her when she glanced off to her left and saw the figure of a large bald man walking swiftly along Beaumont Street, past the Oxford Playhouse. She phoned Phil and told him what she'd seen and then, despite his request that she leave well alone, followed him. He turned left into Gloucester Green and Sam keeping a discreet distance behind him, tracked him as he crossed the car park and went under the arch that led to the coach station.

Then he was directly in front of her, coming back through the arch towards her. She stopped stock-still and for a second so did he, but obviously what was behind him was more worrying than the sight of Sam. He ran straight at her, handing her off and heading back across the car park and past the cinema towards the centre of town. Sam picked herself up and hared after him but the blue flashing light in George Street announced the presence of the police so he was forced to stop and turn again to face her.

This time Sam was ready for him. As he ran at her she stepped to one side and punched him full in the face. It was a good punch as well because she felt the force of it run down her arm through her body and into her feet. It was good enough to stop him dead in his tracks with a smashed nose, pouring blood, and it was a good enough punch to hold him up sufficiently for the police to have time to get him on the ground and put the cuffs on him. It was also a good enough punch to have Sam hopping around in agony shaking her hand and staring at an obviously broken thumb.

CHAPTER TWENTY-SIX

In her office two days later Sam stared down at her newly plastered hand and stuck one of her mother's knitting needles as far up the cast as she could in a vain attempt to scratch an itch on one of her knuckles. Alan, who was sitting opposite her, shook his head.

'Why didn't you use the pepper spray? You should have known better than to punch him. God knows you've taught enough people not to do that and you just had to look at the man to see it would be like punching granite.'

'I wanted to hit him,' Sam said.

Alan was holding a contract from the solicitors who had phoned Sam about the insurance company. 'Well, I think we sign this, don't you? It looks promising.'

Sam nodded. 'Looks like there might be quite a bit of work in it.'

He pointed at the box on Sam's desk which contained the shaman's mask. 'Do the police know about that?'

She shook her head. 'We only told them about the replica.'

'What are you going to do with that?'

'When Norman's grandfather's out of hospital I'll give it back to him.'

'And Norman?'

'The police are still holding him. Phil says they'll probably let him out on bail, pending his trial for theft.'

'What about Cummings?'

'The police found him hanging from the upper balconies of the Pitt Rivers when they came to arrest him. They were going to charge him with the murder of Gittings. They'd put a bit of pressure on his wife and she admitted the alibi she'd given was false. The blood on the dinosaur's tooth matched his so it places him at the museum that night. McGregor said that he'd got photos of Cummings at an international conference in London a few years ago doing what he shouldn't and he'd threatened to send them to his wife if Cummings didn't keep coming up with the goods. Maybe he started out doing it to clear his debts and then found they wouldn't allow him to stop. It doesn't surprise me he killed himself. Someone like Cummings could never tolerate being unmasked in that way.'

'What about Pip?'

They both looked to where the little dog was curled up in a basket in the corner of the office.

'That requires some negotiation between Peter, Mum and myself. At the moment Peter's not in a fit state to look after him so I get to take care of him.'

'Shall we get some coffee?' Alan suggested.

They left the office and walked the short distance to the Tick Tock Café. They both had double espressos with milk on the side. It was the best way to get a caffeine fix here. One of the waitresses came over and made a fuss of Pip.

'September is my favourite month,' Sam said. 'There's all this hope and possibility in the air. In September I feel I could be anybody or do anything I want. It feels transformative.'

Alan frowned. 'That's just about the most optimistic thing I've ever heard you say.'

'Well, don't you feel it?'

He looked away from her and she felt immediately remorseful. How was he going to be feeling optimistic after what had happened to Stephanie?

She touched his arm. 'I'm sorry, Alan.'

Their espressos arrived and their cakes. Sam tore off the top of a chocolate muffin and tucked in.

'Is Rick still in town?'

'Mmm.'

'Have you made up with him?'

'Sort of. I don't feel that guilty about what happened, if that's what you mean. He did go and sleep with his wife while he was in Edinburgh, just like I thought.'

'Where will it all end if men start sleeping with their wives?'

'Shut up, Alan, you're beginning to sound like Oscar Wilde. What I mean is I don't feel I have anything to explain to him. He slept with his wife. I had sex with Norman.'

'Was it tit-for-tat sex?'

Sam gave him a look and drank some coffee. 'I'm not sure, Norman does have a certain ... it's difficult to put your finger on what it is exactly.'

'Superficial charm is what you're looking for I think.'

She laughed. 'Do you think so? I don't find him that superficial. He sent me a note via Phil.'

She took a piece of paper out of her pocket and handed it to Alan. He stared at the mad scrawled writing for a moment. 'Anyone with handwriting like this deserves to be locked up. What does it mean?'

Sam shrugged. 'I've no idea. It's in Latin.'

'Tell me, Sam, have you allowed yourself to be seduced by a Latin-quoting fat man?'

She squished the last of her muffin crumbs together and put them in her mouth. 'Yes, I think I might have.'

'Well then, hopefully they'll keep him in prison long enough for you to come to your senses.'

They paid and left.

Sam walked with Alan to where his car was parked and kissed him on the cheek. 'I'll be back in London next week.'

When she came back to the office Tyler was waiting for her. She hugged him and he followed her upstairs.

'So, what's the favour?' Sam said.

'You remember Karen Lewis?'

'Yes, the kid I gave my *judogi* to?'

He nodded. 'Well, she's eleven years old and the Olympics are in 2012.'

'She'll be too young.'

'I don't think so.'

'She's *that* good?'

'I've told you before she reminds me of you.'

'Poor kid.'

He smiled. 'In a good way. Anyway we've got funding for her.'

'So she is that good?'

'Yes, but she's got family problems.'

'Who hasn't?'

'Single mother with an iffy taste in boyfriends, two younger brothers, one of whom's disabled.'

'So what's the favour?'

'I want you to act as her mentor.'

'Men-tor.' Sam said the word slowly.

'Yes. That's the favour, Sam, to mentor her.'

She picked a dictionary off the window-sill and looked up the word.

'Mentor,' she read out. 'A wise or trusted adviser or guide.'

'Sounds about right.'

'Come on Tyler,' she burst out. 'I'm not wise and I can't be trusted.'

Tyler gave her a look. She remembered that look. It was the look he'd given her when she was coming out with excuses for not having turned up for training or not having done the exercises he'd given her. It took her back to being seven years old when she'd broken her toe on his tree trunk-like shins. It was his 'you are talking utter bullshit' look.

'It's six years, Tyler. I can't guarantee I'll be in Oxford ...'

'You don't have to be. London's not far away. Yes or no? It's a simple enough choice.'

She opened her mouth. 'I'm frightened.'

'I know you are.'

'Of letting her down.'

'Well, don't.'

Everything was always simple with Tyler. If he said he'd do something, he generally did it. His word was his bond. That's just how he was.

'I don't know ...'

'I know you don't. Just say yes and the rest will follow.'

So she did.

That evening she phoned St Cuthbert's and asked to speak to Miles Archer. He was a medievalist, he must be able to translate Latin.

'Could you translate this,' she said when he came on the line. '"*Quos amor verus tenuit, tenebit.*"'

'Ah – it's Seneca. "Those whom true love has held, it will go on holding."'

'Thank you.' She was about to put down the phone when something crossed her mind. 'I bumped into Mary Astor the other day and I mentioned to her our visit down into the cellars. She seemed very interested and said she'd never seen them.'

There was silence on the end of the phone.

'Anyway, I thought I'd mention it.'

Miles cleared his throat. 'Yes, thank you. Well, that's food for thought.'

Sam put down the phone and smiled. God knows how long the mask had been down in that cellar. Masks were about transformation. Everything could be hidden behind a mask. Perhaps some of its transformative powers might work on the vexed problem of Miles Archer and his love for Mary Astor, perhaps his enthusiasm for the wines of St Cuthbert's and his newly acquired position would break through his natural shyness and romance would bloom among the port and claret, amidst the Sauternes and Bordeaux. She hoped so.

She walked over to the window and looked out. Helga was smoking outside the back of her shop and ferret-face was having a cup of tea with his feet up. The cardboard cut-out of Michael Owen was still leaning against the wall giving the betting for the 2006 World Cup. She walked over to the fridge, took out a beer and cracked the lid. Pip opened an eye and then settled back to sleep. She pushed her chair over to the window and put her feet up on the window-sill. She sat sipping her beer and waiting for the stars to come out. Every now and again she turned and looked at the box containing the shaman's mask, sitting in the darkness on her desk. In a month the city would be filled with a new generation of undergraduates. The ebb of August and September would give way to the flow of a new term. People who lived in Oxford felt it in their blood, the energy and electricity of newcomers pumping life into this most ancient of universities.

To her surprise Sam felt it now and welcomed it, whatever it might bring. She drank from the bottle and closed her eyes, enjoying the evening breeze on her face. Perhaps she had come home after all.